GW01236645

BOUND TO THE BOUNTY HUNTER

THE BOUND SERIES

HAYSON MANNING

Previously published 2016

Published by Innes Field LLC

Cover design: Regina Wamba of ReginaWamba.com

Proofreading: Pat Anderson, Sherry Willingham, Amy Hart Proofreading, Jen Katemi Proofreading.

PRAESIDIO

Praesidio–Protect

Ex boarding school brothers bound by a life-shattering event and a vow to protect the vulnerable.

ONE

"*Don't* do it, Nick. I swear I will *kill* you if you do."

Sophie Callaghan begged Nicholas Newman not to walk away from the love of his life, again.

A salt and vinegar chip wavered halfway between Sophie's mouth and the Pringles can that lay on her lap.

After a long, lingering look, Nick closed the door with a soft click. *No...*

Wistfulness settled on her shoulders like soft snow.

The notes of "Nadia's Theme" and the closing credits of *The Young and the Restless* sealed the chip's fate, which was followed by the rest of the contents of the tube.

She searched for any last crumbs. "Imagine living like a Newman or an Abbot, Pongo. No overdue bills, no finding quarters for the laundry, and never dining on two-minute noodles in Genoa City. How good would that be?"

Pongo lay sprawled on his back, stubby legs in the air, opened one eye, then went back to sleep.

I'm having way too many conversations with my dog.

Sophie sighed and collapsed back onto her awesome yellow

Goodwill couch. She ignored the growing stack of bills on the counter and hugged Pongo's warm, squishy body.

"One day we'll get you a nice Mrs. Pongo and adopt Pongettes from the shelter and have a little family. Wouldn't that be nice?"

Pongo, who looked like he was made from different dog parts stuck together, wagged his stumpy tail, and answered in his own unique style. She swooped sideways in a practiced move as Pongo's contribution to global warming hit the room in a string of ripped popping sounds.

"Whoa, that was ripe even for you." She fanned the air. "The sooner I get you back on your insanely expensive, indoor-outdoor, salt-reduced, perfect-coat, fart-reducing dog food, the better."

She leaned in and kissed his forehead, then stood and retrieved the empty tube of chips and the bowl of cornflakes she'd eaten for dinner from the coffee table. Two flakes clung to the side of the bowl like prisoners scaling the walls.

A few more dinners like this, and I'll have to down an orange so I don't get scurvy.

She eyed the empty fruit bowl.

Yeah, like I can afford fruit.

"Time to go to work, Pong."

She ruffled her dog's head, walked to her bedroom, and changed into her work clothes of dark jeans, flat boots, and a black sweater, then wrestled her unruly mass of mahogany brown hair into a prisoner ponytail.

She glanced in the mirror and looked away with a shrug. From an early age, her father had told her daily it was better to go through life *natural*, like her, instead of having unwanted attention, which is why no one noticed her when she snapped his or her picture. Being a good PI meant she could blend into the background, and blend she did. She could wear Waldo's jersey in a sea of gray and people wouldn't remember her. She'd always been the too-tall, too-plain girl that boys didn't notice, which she now owned, but occasionally a remark snuck past the goalie and scored a direct hit.

She snatched her keys from the counter where she'd thrown them earlier.

If all went according to plan tonight, she'd be recording a man named Babic so she could get info on his boss, Alexander Petrov, and try to figure out why her late father had secret journals; one filled with pages of names of people he'd swindled along with amounts and the towns where they lived. The other journal had shown an obsession with Petrov—a Lithuanian billionaire shipping magnate.

Which made no sense.

Her father had been a traveling preacher for the people... or so she'd believed.

For six years since her father died, she'd been chipping away at the journals, trying to understand how the man who'd rocked her to sleep when she woke from nightmares, the man she'd adored, had deceived her.

If a girl couldn't trust her daddy, whom could she trust?

No one.

The thought hurt like a pressed bruise. She pushed past it, set the six alarms, then headed out the door. Another Friday night sitting alone in a sex club recording her target's conversation while slaves whipped him.

Fan-friggin-tastic.

FORTY MINUTES LATER, Sophie slid into a booth at Hostage. Whips, chains, and medieval racks had found a home in the artsy Colorado town of Yaw Yaw. The club became an instant hit when it opened six months ago. Nestled behind galleries, crystal shops, and yoga studios, the thriving sex club was packed as usual.

She stared at a woman sitting on a stool to her left. Her dress was hoisted above her hips, her back arched, a blond head buried between her thighs. A pink wristband dangled from the blond's wrist, which meant she was a slave... and hungry.

Her cheeks hot, Sophie turned away and intently studied the information chart on the table advising the color-coding of the wristbands, until her eyes burned.

Green meant you were here as an observer. If you wore red, you were a dom. If your wristband came in orange, you liked to be spanked. If being a slave was your thing, then pink was your color. Gold if you were submissive, and if purple dangled from your wrist, then you were up for *anything*.

Sophie shifted uncomfortably in her seat. She'd been taught that body contact between a man and a woman was for reproduction only. Anything else was the equivalent of eating kittens' souls and chanting in tongues.

The scent of sex, expensive perfume and high-end whiskey soaked the air.

She glanced around the club. The furniture, the floor, and the ceiling were painted a matte black. Only the long, rectangular, acrylic tables in the booths, teeming with tropical fish of every highlighter color, broke through the murky darkness.

Groups of people or couples occupied satin-curtained booths or clustered around the bar.

Or *not*.

A woman was bent over a fish tank table, being hammered home by a Greek god of a man. Another man stroked himself, his gaze locked on Zeus.

Sophie stared at the swirl of fish, the tips of her ears flaming.

Poor Nemo, I bet he wants to be out of here as much as I do.

She turned her head and took a sip of the lemony sweetness of margarita. Admission alone was putting a sizeable dent in her dwindling bank balance. Thank God she was starting a new job tonight because she was barely scraping by. Between paying back her father's sins, getting her car fixed—again—and cooking for her elderly neighbors, this was two-minute noodle week, again.

On that happy note, she scanned the club. If Babic followed the same pattern as the last two weeks, he'd soon be settling in the corner with a pair of twin busty Barbies with boobs so perfectly round and symmetrical they could be used as flotation devices. Barbie number one would straddle his lap, Barbie number two straddling *her* lap.

Playtime without Ken or the Malibu camper.

She stood, smoothed her hands down her jeans, and walked the club's perimeter in the shadows. She usually smelled him before she saw him. The man bathed in scent so strong that Killer Hornets collapsed when he walked past.

Got him.

Blond buzz cut, botox forehead, veneered teeth so white they glowed in purple light.

Babic.

While Babic watched the Barbies make out, she sidled up to his table pretending to be fascinated by the threesome and pressed a tiny microphone against the underside of the smooth wood. She'd collect it when playtime finished.

She walked back to her booth, sat on the smooth leather seat, and picked up her drink. A man who could be Babic's twin slipped into his booth. A heated conversation followed, judging by the wild hand gestures from the other man. Babic rapid-fired back while positioning Barbie's head in his lap.

Babic the multitasker.

The margarita turned sour in her mouth.

She kept watching Babic, ignoring nausea and Barbie's bobbing head. After agonizingly long minutes, the other man slid out of the booth.

Babic's soulless eyes pinned Sophie. His lazy gaze dropped to the gold band on her wrist, then rose back to her face. The air in Sophie's lungs froze. She let out a breath when his eyes shut. His head hit the back of the leather booth when Barbie picked up the pace.

She glanced around the club, desperate for something else to look at, and jolted when a man's smoky eyes locked on hers.

No way.

No freaking way.

With shaking hands, she set her glass down.

As usual, he looked like he'd stepped off a Harley: scuffed boots, aged denim hugging muscled legs, mirrored aviator glasses perching on messy black hair. Powerful arms crossed under his wide chest. The man cranked out enough testosterone to fuel the NFL. A woman stopped beside him, her mouth open, *'yes, please'* written on her face.

Sophie rolled her eyes before she ripped her gaze away and ignored her galloping heart.

Damn it.

Harlan Franco, Colorado's busiest bounty hunter.

And a total ass.

She'd heard the rumors he had a listing with Groupon where he delivered pleasure to armies of panting women. She drew in a long, shaky breath before releasing it slowly.

Eighteen months ago in a hotel bar where they'd been trailing the same jumper, she'd fallen into Harlan's arms, literally, like the clichéd chick in a Hallmark movie. Her breasts had mashed against his hard chest. She'd caught one whiff of him and much to her dismay, her body had flooded with hormones of the reproducing kind. She'd seen herself reflected in his sunglasses, flushed, her bottom lip snagged between her teeth, as if he'd delivered on his Groupon promise.

Harlan had booked a room, and they were devouring each other, stopping only to remove clothes. He'd wanted her as much as she wanted him, or so she'd thought. His tongue dominating her mouth, his hands on her aching, swollen breasts. She'd melted against him like chocolate. Harlan had steered them into the bathroom and instead of having mind-blowing shower sex, he'd grinned, kissed her hard on the mouth, walked out of the bathroom, and wedged a chair under the door.

The embarrassment of standing in her underwear with a kind security guard who'd told her Harlan had flicked him fifty to wait for twenty minutes before letting Sophie out had wounded her. She'd stared at the security guard blankly until the Harlan fog had cleared and stinging reality bit deep. What was it about Harlan Franco that scrambled her self-control? No other man affected her like Harlan did which was painfully embarrassing. But the humiliating kicker that stole her breath was that Harlan had faked his attraction to her, all to bring in a skip.

Lesson well and truly learned.

Since then, she'd seen him a few times, always with a breathless blond attached to his arm. He never acknowledged her presence.

Turns out she'd been the delusional one. Hurt, humiliated, and furious with herself, she'd retaliated by taking Lopez from under his nose.

She picked up her drink, licking salt from the cool rim, her eyes scanning the room before locking onto Harlan's. Nothing moved on his face. As usual, she was as attractive to him as a blocked drain.

Sophie raised her eyebrows, saluted him with her drink, and turned away.

A woman glided past her holding a platter of frozen fruit. Sophie stared at a banana.

I wonder what they do...

Her cheeks heated.

Oh, right.

She stood, turned to gather her bag, and move to another part of the club, but Harlan materialized at her side. Her breasts brushed against his solid arm, and her body shivered.

His fingers clamped around hers without invitation, surprisingly gentle but with authority.

Lightning traveled through her bones.

Well, this is plain embarrassing.

"What are you doing here, Sophie?"

There was no need for him to know she was here working.

"I'm searching for a big, bad dom." She flashed her gold wristband, a joke reminder to herself that she would never let herself be dominated by a man again.

She'd had three alpha-male, powerful, demanding lovers, and

three humiliating times she'd turned into their expectation of who they wanted her to be. She didn't understand why she let it happen, but it would *never* happen again.

He'd been scanning the crowd over her shoulder, but at her words, his eyes locked on hers. "Are you alone?"

"I am." She adjusted the strap on her bag.

She was her own best friend.

The techno beat from the packed dance floor sent vibrations up her spine, then changed to a low, sexy Latin American dance. She didn't have to turn around to imagine what was happening on the dance floor.

His Chris Pine blues roamed from her head to her boots in a lazy, insolent way that fused her molars.

You can drop the act—we both know you're not interested in me and back at ya.

As much as it pained her to admit it, the man was delicious. Long, dark lashes framed sinful sapphire eyes that on any other man would be pretty, but you wouldn't call this man pretty. Naturally tanned skin stretched over high-cut cheekbones that could probably cut paper and diamonds. Straight white teeth. Lips made for pleasuring. It appeared he shaved when he wanted, and he hadn't wanted to for a while. She'd tucked nicely under his chin at five eight in flat boots.

Unfortunately, she knew he tasted like a tall glass of sin and deceit.

He walked into any room like he owned it. Heads turned, both male and female, *especially female*, and Harlan looked like he didn't know or care.

"Got to say I did *not* appreciate you stealing Lopez," he said after a beat. "I'd been trailing him for weeks. That man was mine."

She stared at him, stunned. So he was going to ignore the elephant in the room that he'd left her dressed only in underwear after pretending he was attracted to her, just to get a jumper?

Her mouth dropped open, but she slammed it shut.

Fine by me. I'd rather forget that terrible afternoon existed.

But she couldn't forget, because at unintentional times it reared up, and that horrible feeling of thinking she'd been invited to a party, only to turn up and find out she'd been the only one *not* invited and what was she doing there, still burned.

"I didn't steal him from you. The man was mine. I flirted with him, and he followed like a horny teen thinking he was about to get *lucky.*"

Harlan looked about as happy as if he were attending a knitting convention. His stance was wide, face unreadable. She cocked her head. "I hear the medieval rack has an opening. You should take it, might loosen you up."

His warm chuckle rolled across her skin. His blue eyes sparkled, and for one long moment, she forgot to breathe. Luckily, her lungs obeyed biology, and she hauled in a breath.

He leaned in close, his heat hitting her like a summer storm. "Show me how you got Lopez to follow you, and I'll tell you why I'm here."

She blinked. "Are you here working?" She deflected and took another sip of her drink, and her brain cranked up a gear. If he was here working a case, she could nab his jumper and pay back another name in her father's journal.

Tempting.

Very tempting.

Her gaze slid around the high-end club. Babic pounded into Barbie number two while Barbie number one whipped his butt. Angry red welts crisscrossed his skin.

Sophie stared, perplexed. *How can he be so comfortable naked in a room full of people, having sex while getting flogged?*

Someone bumped into her from behind. She pitched forward. Harlan's arm curled around her waist. Her fingers clutched impossibly hard biceps, and her body heated to the point she could toast her breakfast cinnamon rolls on bases one and two.

Why does my body turn into a hormonal mess when he's around?

He released her as if she were diseased.

Yet again, the sting of humiliation slithered across her skin. She pulled the band holding her hair tighter.

If he were here following a jumper, she'd get the reward *and* the satisfaction of beating Harlan. Oh yeah, she'd *so* take his jumper.

"I'll show you how I got Lopez to follow me, and *then* I'll be finding Mr. Big Bad Dom for the night, so let's get this show on the road. I'll need a new margarita with a cherry."

By a miracle of intervention, a black-suited server materialized. Before she could pass the server money, Harlan lay bills on the tray, murmured something in his ear and, in record time, the man appeared with a frosty glass.

She tried to hand Harlan a twenty.

He ignored it.

Her head snapped back. "I don't take drinks from strangers, and I always pay my own way."

"We're not strangers, Sophie."

They entered a stare-off. Blue clashed with brown. When her eyes started smarting, she pressed the bill into his hand.

"Yeah, we're strangers," she replied. "And for the record, you'll never know me."

He blinked, his eyes narrowed, but he took the twenty.

She breathed deep and ran through the routine in her mind.

The last time she'd attempted this she'd waited in the dark pool hall until Harlan had headed to the bathroom, then she'd sidled up to Jermaine Lopez—nursing a beer at eight in the morning, the breakfast of champions—and had produced her one and only party trick. The man followed her, his tongue practically hanging out. She'd had him cuffed and in her car when Harlan's expletive-fueled rant had hit her ears.

The smooth cherry was cool against her lips. She took her time nibbling the sweet flesh from the stem.

Without looking up, she could feel Harlan's stare. The room melted away.

"Hold out your hand," she murmured.

He held his steady palm between them.

She closed her eyes, bending the stem a few times with her tongue, softening it. She opened her eyes and looked up at him.

It looked like he was fighting a yawn.

She pushed down on the stem with the tip of her tongue until it formed a U. She crossed one stem over the other, using the back of her front teeth to keep the stem stable. A drop of sweat slid between her breasts. His eyes flared but stayed locked on her mouth.

Now came the tricky part.

She used her front teeth to hold the X while she maneuvered the stem, her tongue performing Olympic-style gymnastics. Leaning forward, she dropped the knot into his palm, resisting the urge to grin.

His intense burning gaze blistered her skin.

"So, where's Mr. or Mrs. Jumper you're tailing?" She gazed around the club. "Is that him?" She pointed to a group of men flexing whips at the flogging station. Her eyes were drawn to movement to her left. "Wait. Is that her?" She pointed to a woman on a sex swing, her legs open, heading toward a man ready to receive.

Harlan leaned in closer, his mouth brushing her ear. "Tell me, Sophie, where's the wire?"

She kept her face set and met his gaze. "Why would I be wearing a wire? I told you, I'm here for a big strong man to tell me what to do." She took a slug of her drink. "I *love* being a good girl." She forced the liquid down her throat and somehow managed not to choke on the words.

His eyes and nostrils flared.

She couldn't make out a band on his wrist. "No pink band tonight?"

He chuckled unexpectedly, his eyes sparkling. "I'm not a slave."

She stared at him for a second, mesmerized, before she kicked herself. "Shame, I think it might suit you. You never know, you might enjoy getting flogged into submission." She shrugged tight shoulders. "So where's the jumper?"

His hand curled around her biceps. "So there's no wire in your thong? Maybe it's in a lacy black bra. I wouldn't mind finding it with my tongue."

"What?" She struggled to keep her face neutral while her bones dissolved.

"Do I have to strip-search you? Make sure it isn't *hidden*?"

She blinked, her mouth flooding.

This so isn't happening again.

"I told you the only reason I'm here is to find a man who understands my *needs*." Her mouth became drier with every word. This man, his words, scrambled her. "See you around, Harlan."

He gripped her hand, and she froze.

Harlan raised his other arm, the cuff on his leather jacket sliding down to reveal a red band.

Oh no. Oh, hell no.

"I'm a big, bad dom." His velvet voice slid across her skin. "Let's talk about your needs."

Her stomach curled into a little ball and played dead.

Think, Sophie, think.

She'd have to play along. If she backed away from him, he'd figure out she most definitely was not a submissive, and she was here for an entirely different reason. No one knew the truth about her father. That fun fact would go to the grave with her.

The ass thinks I'll fall for him a second time only to be locked in a backroom here?

Oh yeah, she'd totally play along. Maybe it was time for *him* to get locked in a bathroom.

He leaned in and whispered. "I'm going to sign my name on your body with my tongue. I *will* have my mouth on you before I fuck you until you come so hard and so many times you'll have to learn to walk again."

She opened her mouth, hoping something would emerge from her mush of brain and land witty and smart on her tongue.

Nothing.

It would appear her brain had taken a cruise to Guatemala.

She pulled back when Harlan traced a finger from her hip to her shoulder. Even through denim and thick cotton, his fingers left a trail of fire.

She clenched her hands, trying and failing to stop her body's disastrous reaction. Smoldering blue eyes captured hers. "You will be on your knees, calling my name when I take you."

"In your wet dreams." The words came out strong and sure. Well, at least in her mind they did.

His lips brushed her ear. "You smell like sin and tonight I'm a sinner." He pushed against her and the hard length of him pressed against her thigh.

"Stop it," she whispered.

"I like what you did with that cherry. I've had a taste of your mouth, and I plan on finding out what else your talented mouth can do."

He pushed farther in to her thigh, and she bit back an ill-concealed moan.

He stared down at her, his eyes blazing as if she belonged to him. "Are you ready?" he asked, his knuckles tracing across her jaw, igniting nerve endings and scattering goosebumps from her jaw to her hip.

"For what?" She kept her voice even when her body ached with need.

"For what I'm about to do to you."

His words detached bone from muscle.

And it was killing her.

The part of her brain that wasn't on the Guatemala cruise dumped a bucket of ice water over her head. "No."

Harlan turned, one insolent eyebrow cocked.

"My needs don't need discussing, and especially not with you," she said.

A smile that could turn a nun transformed his face. "Oh, we *will* talk about your needs."

Her heartbeat ramped up to *just won Olympic gold.* "No, we will *not.*"

He crushed the distance between them and kissed her. Hard, hot, and powerful, and her body responded instantly, *again.* His tongue touched hers, and she moaned into his mouth. His breathing fractured.

He broke the kiss but kept her an inch from his mouth. "Tell me what I'm going to do to you, Sophie." His voice was low and strained, his eyes molten.

She shook her head, clinging to the barest thread of control.

A sound like a submarine's ping came from somewhere. In a haze, she watched him frown, grab his phone from his jeans pocket, and swipe his finger across the screen. He turned.

"Don't move. I've got to take this." He then jogged toward the back of the club to a private room—the only place you could use your cell.

She took a shuddering breath.

Her hand covered her mouth.

What is wrong with me?

She cringed.

He's playing me just like in the hotel room, and I'm letting him.

With her head down, she willed her racing heart to steady. She made her way to Babic's table, where a new Barbie was bouncing on his lap. Sophie forced a fascinated smile while her trembling hand skimmed the underside of the table. She plucked out the device, leaving most of the clay behind.

Babic paused, his gaze roaming over her face. "You want to be next?"

TWO

Harlan Franco jogged to where he'd left Sophie and turned a tight circle.

No dark hair. There was no curvy, warm body. No cuffs required.

Fuck.

He pulled his hand through his hair.

A group to his left was working on building a pyramid, naked.

He scanned the crowd a second time.

No Sophie.

He'd been on the phone way longer than he'd intended, but he didn't miss calls. Especially this call.

Talking to your client while the asset you're supposedly guarding has been looking at you with come-fuck-me-now eyes *should* have deflated his cock in a second.

What had started as a game had quickly spiraled out of control. Again. Tough as sailors' balls, Sophie Callaghan was as hard as they came. He'd been intrigued when she'd flashed her sub bracelet because nothing about her hinted at submission. Part of him, the cock part, wanted to spell out how she'd be soft and compliant under him. The gray matter in his head told him he was on a job.

Cock won.

Go figure.

He'd been playing with her tonight, trying to work out why she was here. His job was to learn everything about Sophie and report back to his client, which was why he'd trailed her to Hostage tonight. That game had taken a dangerous turn when she'd looked up at him with want swimming in her big brown eyes, the scent of her slamming into him.

His mouth *still* throbbed from her kiss. Her moan had soaked into his blood. Her body melting into his had nearly brought him to his knees.

He closed his eyes.

Number one rule of being on a guard and intel extraction:

Be detached.

Rule number two:

Be professional at all times.

Rule number three:

Don't fuck the asset.

Frustration and disappointment in himself slithered through his gut like a bad burrito.

When Sophie had fallen into him at a bar eighteen months ago, his body had reacted like it had tonight, like it had found its mate. Dressed in her uniform of jeans, no makeup, hair back, hiding every feminine trait. With nothing on his mind except telling her to back away from his clients, he'd booked a room to have a private conversation, but her scent, her hair, her everything had wiped logic from his brain. They were going at each other like horny teens until he'd found just enough strength to pull back, when he'd heard the ping from his phone, alerting him that the jumper they were tailing was on the move.

He scratched the back of his neck. Shame flooded him.

Not my finest hour, leaving her locked in a hotel bathroom.

Was this payback for that night? Leaving him with blue balls and walking away?

He deserved it.

Tonight, like that other twisted night, he couldn't rip his eyes away from her; his dick had sprung to attention like a teen who'd discovered *Porn Hub* and lotion.

Everything about her was the opposite of what he wanted in a woman. Small and blond? Nope. She'd have to be about five foot eight or taller. Legs that went on for freaking ever. Her olive skin stretched over angular cheekbones, full lips, almond-shaped dark brown eyes framed by thick inky lashes. Gym-toned and disciplined? Hell no. Sophie came with mouth-watering curves. Her butt filled her jeans in all the right places. He wanted her legs wrapped around his hips twice while she gave in to him totally. A submissive who wanted only a physical relationship? His walking, living dream was not Sophie.

Apart from the physical attraction, which he could control, Sophie Callaghan had always been a giant pain in his ass, which was going to make guarding his newest assignment *interesting*. She had attitude, a smart mouth that intrigued and pissed him off all in one sentence.

His phone pinged with an incoming message from Zeb, his second in command, and boarding school friend for life, stationed by the front door: Babic was on the move, as was Sophie.

He stilled. Is that why she'd left?

A blond woman broke away from a group and walked to him, flashing her gold wristband. He shook his head and headed to where a waitress cleaned Babic's table, still littered with whips.

Babic liked his pain delivered hard.

He slipped the waitress a sizeable tip and sat in the booth. He pulled on disposable gloves, and made a slow and methodical search of the top of the table.

Nothing.

Probing the underside, he paused over something clinging to the smooth surface, then carefully detached it. Modeling clay. He turned it over in his hand. Crude, but effective.

Shit.

Sophie was here tailing Babic who works for Petrov, and I'm on retainer to Petrov and here tailing Sophie.

Even saying that sentence hurt his brain.

He walked into an empty room at the back of the club. A cream comforter covered an enormous bed. Leather, chains, and hard-plastic ties dangled from the padded black headboard. Shelves were lined with sex toys of every description. He sent a text to his 2IC and waited.

"What up?" Zeb Carmichael sauntered in, nodding. "Pain and Gain room, brother, I approve."

The pounding of the music dulled to a throb when Zeb closed the door.

"We could have a problem."

"A chat about the birds and bees?" Zeb indicated the toy cabinet, grinning.

He held out his hand and dropped the clay into Zeb's palm. "I think Sophie left this under Babic's table."

Wide eyes hit him. "I saw her at Babic's table for a beat before she shot out the door. Babic left a few minutes after her with a couple of blonds. She's here following him? What's the deal?"

Harlan sucked air through his teeth. "I didn't know Babic would be here tonight, but I think *she* did, and I'm interested in why she's trailing him and what went down with him and his meet."

Zeb's penetrating gaze hit him. "Any reason to be concerned?"

"Not that I know of." But Harlan had seen Babic's startled face. It had been fleeting, but it had been there. Babic had spotted Harlan and been surprised by his presence.

There were too many scenarios playing out in Harlan's head. None of them came with a happily ever after. If Petrov was right, and he and Sophie shared a connection and any of Petrov's rivals and restless business associates found out, Sophie could be used in ways that chilled Harlan's marrow.

Zeb blew out a long breath, which pulled Harlan back into the room. "If she and Petrov are related, why doesn't Petrov take a meet? Clear it all up. Why all this cloak-and-dagger shit?"

Harlan shrugged, trying to loosen the tension in his shoulders. "Petrov lost his daughter, Seraphina, twenty-three years ago. His wife was at a religious retreat in Southern California, when the kid was snatched—the child had been around two. The girl wasn't his biological daughter, but he loved her; still does. His wife killed herself two years later, blaming Petrov's business for the child going missing. That's when he went legit. Now, he wants to leave his empire to his daughter, but he wants to be sure. There've been times over the years he was sure he'd found her, only to find out he'd been played." Harlan pushed his hands deep into his pockets. "He's had a likeness of her drawn every year. Babic saw her and thought there was enough of a similarity to mention it. Petrov wants us to watch her and report back. Make sure she's the real deal before he gets any closer, which is where I come in."

Zeb's shrewd blue eyes took in the room and came back to rest on Harlan. "So this is a bodyguard and intel job, right?"

"Yep, and the reason we're guarding her is on a need-to-know basis. At the moment we're the only ones who have the intel." He cracked his neck. "I'll be reporting back to Petrov until he's ready to make his move either way."

Zeb crossed his arms, his gaze penetrating. "You want me to take this? Give up your need to control every case, brother?"

Harlan hired the best people around, but his name was on the door, and he had to have his finger on the pulse at all times. "Next time."

Zeb stared at him hard. "Looks like you lost focus tonight. If there's anything between you and Sophie it has to end now. You know the rules." Zeb stared him down. "I'm telling you this because you're my brother, and we made a blood oath with our circle. We will always be there for each other, tell each other the truth, and protect the vulnerable."

Harlan closed his eyes as Zeb went on. "And we know what happens if we lose focus."

Yeah, he did.

"Yeah. That night," Zeb said.

That night.

That night flashed into Harlan's head on a grenade.

He and the boarding school circle jammed into one cell, waiting for the call that would either send them back to school or expulsion.

"I wouldn't change anything we did tonight," Harlan said. Licks of rage still fired his blood.

Zeb Carmichael grunted beside him. "Agreed. Though the execution could've been better."

"What about your place on the team?" Harlan threw Zeb a look knowing that being the starter QB meant a shitload to him. The first black QB at the school.

"Don't give a shit. This is far more important." Rage shone in his arctic blue eyes.

"Will this affect your scholarship?" A pair of black eyes belonging to Jason Johnson pinned Harlan, who knew he'd be running the statistics in his head.

Harlan's head went back. "Pretty sure taking the fall for setting that fire might be the end of academia for me."

"It's fucked, that's what it is," Zan Gillard said, pacing in the small space, his voice anguished. "I had no idea... I had no fucking idea, and I should have." His easy, charming smile was missing.

"We've got you, brother," Jason said at the same time as Harlan.

It would suck for Harlan to go back to California, but if they'd saved that kid's life, he'd take it. Jason had noticed the smoke, Harlan the flames and without thought they'd run in and hauled the kid's butt out of there, and it had shocked the shit out of them when desperate eyes stared at them, appalled and heartbreaking, his face melting.

And it wasn't just any kid.

A boy they should have been looking out for, especially this boy who didn't want to be treated differently, but he was. Badly. The bullying, the taunts, the whispered threats had been going on behind their backs and they hadn't noticed. And they fucking should have. In a desperate, insane act to fit in, he'd nearly killed himself. All for a fucking dare.

That night, a pact was born along with the band of the brotherhood. Harlan, Jason, Zeb, Zan, Brayden, Israel, and Gabriel had sworn in blood. Harlan had inked Praesidio above his heart. The others had it inked in different places, didn't matter where. Meant the same thing.

Protect.

"You thinking what I'm thinking?" Somber denim-colored eyes held his.

Harlan rubbed the back of his neck. Something about Sophie Callaghan with her eyes swimming in hurt and lust pulled at him. Her vulnerability kicked him in the guts.

"You think Sophie's vulnerable." Zeb widened his stance. "She needs our protection." Statements, not questions.

He nodded once. "Can you speed up the report on everything there is to know about Sophie Callaghan? I'll stay close and work my angle."

"On it." Zeb headed out the door, where he stopped and turned. "You got this?"

A slow, steady pounding started at the back of Harlan's skull, in time to his sluggish heartbeat. "Yeah, I got this."

The door closed with a click.

Tonight he'd lost control, and he *never* lost control.

He'd kept people at a distance his whole life. After his mom's death and a quick detour to an aunt who'd decided she couldn't cope with a grieving, angry seven-year-old, he'd been delivered into the system.

He'd learned how to survive fast.

Until a teacher took an interest in him and sent his marks to

Stamford Brook Boarding School for boys who accepted him on a full scholarship. Aged eight with nothing but pride, attitude and knowing this was his way out of a shit life, he'd found his pack. Admittedly, it hadn't been a brilliant start. He and Jason Johnson had tried to beat the shit out of each other, both lost, bruised and angry. Both had lost their parents, and they'd formed an unlikely alliance. When he'd started his business Franco Security, he'd pledged:

Never let your guard down.

Always stay detached.

Never lose control.

Lessons he lived by.

Tonight, he'd come close to losing everything he stood for, and he couldn't. There was too much at stake. Not just his reputation, which he lived for, but to protect Sophie. Keep her safe and he could only do that from a distance because he lost the ability to think when her scent invaded his lungs. Their tongues dueled when he forgot his Social Security number. He'd come close to losing control tonight when her depthless eyes pulled him in. He wanted to drown in them.

Steel straightened his spine.

Little head was firmly in his pants and big head was back in the game.

———

SOPHIE PULLED her car keys from her bag as she walked, her fingers slipping on the cool metal.

Damn.

Her hands still trembled, along with the rest of her body. She wasn't going to analyze whether it was because of how close she'd come to losing her sanity along with her underwear.

And part of me liked it.

She increased her pace.

Shoot me now.

Groups of people spilled from bars, laughing from the high of alcohol and what the night promised. Homeless people picked through bins. A man in a bathrobe walked a ferret.

The timer on her phone pinged, alerting her that her shift started in twenty minutes. She unlocked the car door and slumped in the driver's seat. She forced long breaths until she wasn't breathing like she'd run a marathon, and her hands weren't shaking like she'd seen a ghost and not the friendly variety. She sent a prayer upward and turned the key. Thankfully, her car chattered reluctantly into life. She plugged the address into Google Maps, then pulled into traffic, noting a vehicle three cars back that had done the same. With one eye on the road and the other on the rearview mirror, she deviated from the route.

Sophie changed lanes, and her shadow mirrored her move. Cold sweat slithered across her body. At the next set of lights, gripping the wheel, she sent a silent prayer to her ailing car and when the light changed, gunned the accelerator, made a sharp left, and apologized with a wave to the line of traffic.

While she drove, she ran scenarios in her scrambling mind.

Was Babic onto her? Had he noted her interest in him at the club over the past weeks? If Babic's men were following her and they found the recording in her bag, she had no idea what they'd do.

But she had a fairly good idea.

The map on her phone showed a park ahead. She pulled into a side street and navigated her way to the entrance. She killed the car engine and lights.

She grabbed the recorder from her bag and jogged the circumference of the park. Lilac scented the tepid night air. The moon played chase, dipping in and out of silvery clouds.

Streetlights hung shadows across the park but gave her enough light to navigate. She discounted the play equipment—small hands could find the expensive electronics gear and if swallowed would cause harm.

A band rotunda rose out of the night, silent and empty as it loomed over the playground like the captain of a ship, guarding its charges.

Perfect.

With peeling paint and a general air of neglect, it mustn't be high on the council's maintenance list.

She swung her head to the left, then right, holding still.

A flash of light in her peripheral vision snapped her head left. She dropped into a crouch. Another sweep of light carved through the darkness. Dog walker or someone looking for her. Either way, she wasn't hanging around to find out.

With her calves cramping, she crouch-walked up the stairs of the rotunda. She counted the number of spindles and, still crouching in order to keep under the height of the railing, made her way across from the entrance.

I hope I have enough clay.

She pressed the recorder against the bottom of the hand railing—the thick wood cut with ornamental designs—and prayed there was enough clay to hold it in place until she could come back tomorrow.

Her thighs now joined her protesting calves. She retraced her steps.

Another sweep of light to her right pierced the inky night.

Damn.

Scurrying to her car as the wandering beam approached the rotunda, she thumped the check engine light.

I swear the next time I can afford to get you fixed, I will.

She flew out of the parking lot, narrowly missing a sedan entering.

Her mouth dried, and fear pressed against her pounding heart when the car did a quick U-turn and exited the lot.

THREE

Sophie pulled on the hem of the barely-thicker-than-dental-floss black skirt of her new uniform. The faded wood and carpet at Pipe's had soaked up beer, whiskey, and Marlboro cigarettes, giving the room a smoky scent that blended with the smell of leather and sweat.

In a whirlwind, she'd signed forms, received a plastic super-market bag containing a uniform, and been directed toward a cubicle curtained off with a sheet covered in smiling purple dinosaurs.

Vintage Barney at a biker bar. Who knew?

She bent an inch to the left and the dental floss hiked up.

Awesome.

Yep, she'd flash a room filled with bikers in her sensibly priced underwear.

To top off her night, she'd be starting work with damp underwear thanks to Harlan. Humiliation prickled her face.

He's not into me. He's playing me and I totally fell for it again.

Sophie tugged on her hem. "Are you sure about the skirt? There isn't another size?"

"Very sure." The gorgeous brunette who'd hired her, Gemma,

looked up from strapping a black stiletto shoe to her foot, the heel so high and thin it could be a weapon. Warm, startling golden eyes danced in her heart-shaped face. She had a body that every woman craved: petite, curvy, with a generous serving of natural boobs.

Sophie tugged on the hem again to no avail. A black tank top five sizes too small with the word "Pipe's" spelled out in diamantes pulled tight across her B cups.

"You might want to get a pushup bra." Gemma surveyed her with a critical eye. "Get those puppies on display. You'll bring in more tips."

Sophie pulled at the strap of her comes-in-a-multipack bra. Her small puppies were staying right where they were. There was far too much of her already on display.

"Dudes are going to blow their loads when they see you in stilettos. Be sexy, flirty, and unavailable."

A cold weight settled in her chest and expanded outward. She had to walk around a crowded bar full of men and feel the full weight of their smirks and laughter at her attempt at being sexy or flirty.

A stupid prickle of tears burned her lids.

I can't do this.

She needed this job. Her car would not be thumped into submission forever, and she couldn't afford to keep taking it to mechanics who promised they'd fixed it, only to have them scratching their heads when she returned. Every Thursday she cooked for her neighbors, Sally and Titus Carroll, and since it was the best meal they got all week, she cooked up a storm, with enough leftovers for two to three days of lunches and dinners. Sadly, her invoices sat at the bottom of her clients' "to be paid" pile, gathering dust.

You can do this, Buttercup.

She choked back a bitter laugh at the name her father used to call her. It still seeped into her thoughts at unexpected moments when she needed strength—his sweet, happy Buttercup.

She pushed him out of her head.

I need this job.

She blinked the tears away.

Tonight, hopefully, she'd pay the overdue gas bill, *and* Ona Evans from Wichita, Kansas would receive a crisp hundred-dollar bill in a card with a bogus return address signed with the name Josiah O'Connor and the word "Sorry" scrawled across it. Another name scratched from her father's journal.

Gemma squeezed her shoulder. "Hey, what's up? If you're worried about the guys, don't be. This may be a biker bar and yeah, some of them are badass, but if one of them lays a hand on you, Pipe will remove his balls and deep fry them. I hired you because I know you'll be able to take shit from a guy and send it back twofold."

She gnawed her lip, staring at Gemma's shoes. Another dilemma. She'd never mastered the trainer heels that progressed to gliding in killer stilettos. She'd attempted to wear high shoes once. She and her drink had face-planted into her date's lap, not bringing him the happy ending he'd hoped for.

Sophie waved her hand. "I... um... can't do the sexy thing."

"You are sooooo sexy. Seriously. The boots are hot. With your long legs, you rock it." Gemma cocked her head to one side. "Are you sure about the whole no makeup and hair up thing?" Sophie frowned and thought back to her interview last week. She'd stood in a long line of hopeful applicants at ten in the morning. The on-call position suited her perfectly. She'd arrived with her CV wondering if she'd read the ad wrong. The women were dressed in clothes that showed leg to their butt or cleavage spilling out of tops they must have stolen from their tween sisters, hair either keratin-straight or in big, bouncy curls down their backs, fuck-me heels strapped to their feet, and with enough makeup and cologne to start their own beauty supply warehouse. When Sophie had joined the line, a few had smirked at her, then turned back to their pack. She'd been less than thrilled to overhear about one woman's now-hairless vagina and deeply unhappy to hear about the procedure to achieve lifelong baldness.

The slamming of a door had brought her head up. Gemma had walked in, stopped, and scanned the room. Her eyes had locked on

Sophie. She'd smiled, made a beeline to her, and announced to the room that the position had been filled. Gemma had taken her to a tidy office and explained the job. She didn't glance at Sophie's carefully typed CV. Turned out the primary qualification was a server who wouldn't take shit or want to bang the clientele, would turn up on time, do her job, and go home.

Ticked boxes all around.

Gemma continued, "Your hair is amazing. So thick and wavy. And you've got killer bee-stung lips."

Sophie touched her still-tingling, normally completely average lips. Harlan Franco's mouth had made them swollen and sensitive and for some weird reason, red.

"I've got an eye shadow that would make your eyes pop. Want me to go get it? Give me fifteen minutes with my flat iron on your hair."

"No," Sophie barked.

Gemma flinched. That came out sharper than intended. Being homeschooled, the whole girlfriend thing was lost to her. She'd never had a best friend, a sleepover, or done the girly things girls apparently did.

Sophie went to reach out a hand, leaving it quavering in no-man's-land.

"Sorry, this is all new to me. Thanks for the offer and for your help."

Gemma stared at her for a long second. She pulled her phone from her bag, checked the time, and shot Sophie a quick smile. "No problem. I'm training you tonight. It's pretty easy. Stick with me and you'll be good." Sophie stowed her phone and bag in a locker, her mind in a washing machine spin.

She tugged on the hem of her skirt one more time, squared her shoulders, and followed Gemma out into the packed bar. Five huge flat-screen TVs hung from the ceiling showing cage fighting, drag racing, or what could be the Miss Hot Boobs USA pageant. To her left sat a long row of pool tables at which denim-clad men and women stood in groups. The chink of ceramic balls could be heard above three girls' singing.

"Unskinny Bop," indeed.

Gemma stood beside a man ripped straight out of every girl's California surfer wet dream. Cali Surfer towered above Sophie's five-foot-eight frame. His dirty-blond hair flopped on his forehead. Muscular body outlined under a black T-shirt and low-slung faded denim. Sparkly, navy-blue eyes, strong chin, a slightly off-center nose, a dusting of dark stubble on his cheeks. She bet it got him laid, often. He oozed sex appeal and charm and had an easy air about him, but her sixth sense told her that if he were pushed underneath his playful puppy exterior, a pissed-off pit bull would emerge.

Gemma threw her arm around his waist. "Sophie, this is Cope. He tends bar while working his way through every available woman in Colorado. The man is a walking petri dish. If I didn't love his whorey ass so much, I'd report him to the CDC."

Warm blue eyes focused on her. "Sophie, nice to meet you. If you have any problem with any guy here, hold up your hand and I'll be over. The girls aren't to be touched. They might test a new girl, but don't take their shit." He pulled Gemma tight to his side. "Don't believe a word she says. I'm Catholic schooled. If I ever touched my impressively-sized penis other than to attend to bathroom duties, there is the high possibility I'd go blind. The only work I could find would be as a eunuch where I'd work in a sheik's harem, surrounded by beautiful naked women giving each other facials."

Sophie couldn't help but smile. His warmth and charm were infectious.

Gemma elbowed him in the ribs and rolled her eyes.

Cope held up his hands in surrender.

Gemma laughed, shook her head then tugged on Sophie's arm.

An hour into her shift, Sophie found her rhythm. She and Gemma had allocated sections. She'd write customers' orders, which didn't change much from beer or spirits, and take their money. Cope or Dave, another bartender she'd only briefly met, would hand over the drinks, she'd serve the orders, return their change, calculating it in her head then move to the next table. Rinse and repeat.

Not being a gym junkie or a yoga guru, exercise to Sophie was running after perps or lifting the lid of Pringles tubes. Her biceps and triceps had been stretched beyond their limits. The burn in her muscles had turned into a long-standing ache, which had morphed into a quivering numbness. She'd kept her back ramrod straight so as not to flash the bar her underwear. Her shoulders had sent out protest notices an hour ago and would be a no-show tomorrow.

Her tank top had taken a hit when she'd spilled beer on herself after one of the scariest men she'd ever seen materialized in her path. Massive, with hams for arms, dump trucks for legs, and a plaited gray beard that landed at the button of threadbare jeans that looked like he'd been born in. Tattoos snaked up his neck and possibly spelled out something on his bald head. She wasn't about to get a stepladder and find out.

Man Mountain didn't say a word. His eyes dropped to her boobs, her boots, then back to her face. He'd crossed his arms across his mountain range of a chest and stared at her.

She tapped her foot and arched a brow at Mr. Probably Whacks People for a Living.

After a standoff lasting forever, he'd smiled, revealing three teeth, told her to call him Boris, and welcomed her to Pipe's.

On her way back to the bar, a man blocked her path.

Is this a tag-team test or something?

"Sweetheart, I'm Mick, and baby, you'll want my dick. You want to take a ride with me after your shift? Have my Harley throb between your legs, then have *me* throbbing between your legs." He grabbed her hips, pressing his hips against hers, and gyrated.

Beer, onions, and "I'm allergic to deodorant" wafted over Sophie.

She moved back out of his reach and arched a brow. "Touch me again, and I'll snap off that dick of yours, turn it into an itty-bitty sandwich, and serve it back to you with a single fry."

His eyes narrowed, and he took a step toward her.

She held her ground.

"You're not woman enough for me, anyway." His eyes wandered over her.

Sophie the PI shot forward. "Baby, we both know you're not man enough for me."

His eyes hardened. "I expect you've got a dick there under your skirt."

"Yep, and it's bigger than yours."

He loomed over her, a vicious look on his face. He raised his hand to slap her. She jumped left, caught his arm, scissor-kicked his legs. He dropped to the ground with a heavy grunt. Sophie landed on his back and grabbed his wrists.

A hand landed gently on her shoulder.

"I've got this, Soph."

With her heart hammering, she looked up at Cope, whose narrowed gaze was directed at Mick. He held out a hand which she grasped and stood, her legs shaking. Cope hauled Mick to his feet.

Mick's flinty eyes narrowed, his face heart-attack red. "You'll regret that, bitch."

She smiled down at him. "Don't choke on your dick sandwich."

Applause and laughter rippled across the bar. She smoothed a hand across her hair, gave a tight smile, and walked back toward Gemma. She caught the eye of a few patrons. One man saluted her. Boris openly grinned at her, and a biker chick gave her a thumbs-up.

"Look at you, girlfriend." Gemma grinned at her.

Sophie took an order for a round of Wild Turkey when the door flew open and a gorgeous, tall, blond woman walked in wearing designer shoes so high Sophie wondered if she had to alert air traffic control when she put them on. A floor-length silver sheath hugged every part of her perfect, curvy body. She wove through the bikers, greeting some, smacking others playfully on the shoulder, and headed toward the bar.

"I think Cinderella got lost coming home from the ball," Sophie said to Gemma, who passed her holding a tray filled with glasses of Coors.

"That's Annie, my bestie. Her date mustn't have gone well." Gemma's lips thinned. "None of her dates go well. Let me get this tray, then come meet her."

Sophie opened her mouth to protest but shut it at Gemma's questioning look.

Five minutes later, she stood next to Gemma. Annie sat at the bar, two empty shot glasses in front of her. Cope filled a third. Seemed Annie's idea of having hot and horny sex in the back of a limo while it cruised around town hadn't been met with a positive reaction. Her thick honey-colored hair curled down her back, almond-shaped eyes the color of emeralds, sun-kissed skin, sparkly pink lips, and a body that could grace covers of magazines, and she'd been turned down?

"I don't understand," Sophie blurted out. "He turned *you* down? Is there something wrong with the universe?"

Shrewd eyes appraised her. "He wanted a relationship. I want fun." A manicured hand with blood-red nails waved. "He'll fake that he only wants fun, but then he'll get clingy and possessive. Neither rocks my boat."

Gemma shook her head and made introductions.

Annie smiled, her questioning gaze landing on Sophie's boots.

Sophie crossed her arms across her chest and stepped back. "I... um... don't do heels."

Annie stared at her until Sophie squirmed.

"There's a shoe shop out by me that does fabulous shoes in all size heels. My motto is a girl can never have enough shoes. The next time I'm going, want to swing by with me?"

Sophie opened her mouth, her lips forming the word "no."

Annie held up her hand. "Not that I'm saying the boots don't rock, because they totally do. Just saying there's a special pair of shoes out there for everyone." She held up her shot glass, twirled it, then flipped the amber contents into her mouth without her eyes watering. "Mother's milk."

"I'm not paying you to stand around." A man who looked like he'd been living under a bridge walked to the bar, shrugging off a leather jacket. Faded jeans and scuffed biker boots. Piercing blue eyes locked on Sophie, then narrowed. "Who's this?"

"Keep your hair on." Gemma rolled her eyes. "We're taking a two-minute break, and this is your new server who, incidentally, the patrons of your fine establishment love."

Eyebrows hit the biker's hairline, and scary eyes turned to Gemma, who didn't seem to pick up on the arctic glare directed her way.

"No it isn't. I told you to hire someone men will want in their station and who'll come back because she's in their station. That ain't her."

Her life summed up. Too tall, too plain.

She flinched at the barb.

Gemma's hands landed on her hips.

"She's good, Pipe. She didn't take Boris's shit, stared him down, and tapped her foot until he smiled. She had Mick on the ground when he went to slap her after she told him she'd cut off his dick and serve it to him in a sandwich with a fry. She's quick and does her job well. I'm fairly certain she isn't out for a quick fuck with a biker."

Sophie's eyes widened.

"I'm tired of working shifts on my own because you hire girls who are only here to get a glory fuck by a biker before they walk up the aisle in their WASP dress and marry their missionary position boyfriend." Gemma poked Pipe in the chest. "She's better than good."

Her heart threw in a double beat. "Thanks," she murmured to Gemma, who reached over to squeeze her hand.

"Besides, I think the boot thing is hot. I'm guessing half the guys tonight will go home and jack off thinking of her mile-long legs wrapped around their hips."

Sophie pulled on the hem of her skirt, her cheeks burning.

"No stilettos, no job," Pipe barked. He turned to Cope. "No one touches the girls. Mick's banned."

Sophie pressed her lips together. Not like there was an HR department. Lodging an official complaint about sexism in the workplace would fall on deaf ears. She could either inform him it was sexist to make women wear ridiculously high shoes and he must be breaking some UN Women's Rights legislation, or tell him to stick his job, get changed, and never come back.

She mentally calculated the tips she'd received so far. She'd already paid the overdue gas bill *and* Ona Evans. Next up, she'd be paying the electricity. She liked electricity. Electricity cleaned clothes, granted her access to *The Young and the Restless*, and provided hot water. If this kept up, Andrea Veliscek from South Florida would receive two hundred dollars.

Another name paid back.

Gemma moved into Pipe's space, hands on her hips again.

"If she goes, I go."

Pipe stared at Gemma for half a second before his icy glance cut to Sophie.

"You're only here because of her. Give me a reason to get rid of you, and you're gone."

AT THREE A.M. when she started swaying with fatigue, the bar emptied. Sophie hauled herself around, each step feeling like she'd dunked her boots in another layer of cement. Finally, Dave, the other bartender, closed the door. The four of them delivered empty glasses to the kitchen area, stacked empty bottles in the keg room. Gemma had tossed her a cloth, and they'd sprayed the tables in artificial lemon and wiped them down. Much to her horror, Pipe insisted on walking her to her car, leaving Cope to escort Gemma to her Prius.

After insisting she was fine five times, Pipe ignored her and walked by her side.

Well, this isn't awkward.

"For the time you're working at the bar, if you need a place, for whatever reason, you can come here," Pipe said, looking straight ahead.

If they weren't the only two in the parking lot, she'd have thought he was talking to someone else. He didn't turn his head to address her, instead aimed for the only car left in the lot. She'd parked under a light with what looked like drunk moths slamming into the glass.

"Right," she said. Having as little as possible to do with the man seemed the best way to keep her job.

As for turning up here?

As much chance of that as being flogged naked by Babic in a room full of nuns.

"I mean it." He stood beside her door.

"Um, thanks." She hoisted her bag higher on her shoulder.

She unlocked the car and willed him to walk away.

Pipe hadn't said a word when the car took five turnovers to fire or when she tapped the check engine light until it shifted from a steady glow to a flicker. Disapproval oozed from the man. He'd stood under the fading neon until she turned the corner, the tension leaking from her shoulders.

On the way home, she checked her rearview mirror. The plan of detouring to the park was nixed when a sedan came out of a side street and sat on her tail a few cars back.

Is it me being paranoid or am I being followed?

She shouldn't chance it. If there was something on that recording, she couldn't risk losing what Babic had said. In a few hours she'd go back to collect it, taking public transport, changing her route if she was being followed, or she'd join *Paranoids Anonymous.*

She made it through her front door as Pongo lumbered through the dog door. She lavished praise on her dog and gave him a treat. After she washed her face and brushed her teeth, she slapped on supermarket moisturizer. She kicked her uniform to the floor, changing into PJ's she'd grabbed from under her pillow, then crawled into bed, whispering her prayers as she went.

SOPHIE'S PHONE danced out her favorite ringtone, and Pongo's face flashed on the screen announcing an incoming call, pulling her from a coma-like sleep.

She groaned. The soft light of dawn filled her room with pale tangerine streaks and watery shadows. Birds were up and doing their rounds, judging by their joyful songs.

Why can't they sing the blues for once?

Pongo pushed open her door, looking like he'd starve to death if food didn't arrive in his bowl. She went to stretch her shoulders and groaned. Seems they weren't turning up today. It wasn't just her shoulders. Every muscle in her body ached.

"Hello," she answered in a rusty voice.

"This is Franco. We need to meet. How long would it take you to get here?"

"I'm not meeting you. Go away." She ended the call and flopped back on the bed.

Her sluggish brain jogged into life. Did he know about the recording? Had *he* followed her last night?

Crap.

Fully awake, she threw back the covers and stumbled to the bathroom where she had a shower, a quick shampoo, and an even quicker condition. She slapped on her favorite raspberry-scented body butter, brushed her teeth, then pulled her wet hair into a band.

Her home phone roared to life.

She ignored it for ten rings but, worried it might be Titus—the only reason she had a landline—who could be in trouble, she picked up the receiver, keeping silent.

"Did you hang up on me?" Harlan's clipped voice made her smile.

"New experience, I gather."

"How long would it take you to get here? Or I'll come to you."

She clutched the cordless phone while dashing around the room, pulling on her boots. "It's illegal to get an unlisted number. I could have you charged and arrested."

His voice purred. "The strangest thing, I found your number on a piece of paper you left for me last night at Hostage."

Her blood started a slow boil. "I swear to God, if you were standing in this room I'd squeeze the life out of you, and no jury would convict me."

Amusement softened his sexy voice. "You're into dirty talking this early in the morning? Interesting."

She pulled on her jacket and grabbed her keys, calculating how long it would take to make it to the park, grab the recording, make it back home, and hide it in her safe. There was no way he'd be coming here. This small, barely two-bedroom house was her sanctuary. Her first home.

The last thing she wanted to do was serve him coffee out of a Goodwill cup. Have him smirk at her snow globe collection. He only knew Sophie the PI. He didn't know Sophie Callaghan, and he never would.

"I can be there in two hours. I have an appointment this morning," she lied, having no intention of going anywhere near Harlan Franco ever again.

"I know what you have."

She opened her mouth to protest but his words, wrapped in stone, stopped her.

"And if you're not here in two hours, I'll find you."

"I don't know what you're talking about." Amazingly, she sounded crisp and formal.

"You have something I'm *going* to have." His voice, like molasses, flowed through her.

She squirmed at the shiver of remembrance of when he'd kissed her.

Scrap that. Harlan didn't kiss. He devoured. Demanded.

Owned.

She shook her head.

Nope, he played with her. He was a big tabby cat, and she was the little mouse.

Well, this little mouse was done with his games.

FOUR

The I-36 passed in a blur of flat land, brown grasses whispering in a dying wind. The ground was so parched that, if Sophie lowered her window, she was sure she'd hear the earth groan.

She checked in the rearview mirror at the black Silverado sitting two cars back. She'd pushed her brave car to its limits and tried to ditch the pickup, but a strange whine and unfamiliar shudder had made her pull back. She'd thrown in unexpected turns, and a few times she thought she'd lost it only to have it reappear.

Once again, she ran through the meeting with Harlan in her head.

Sophie would walk into the office.

She'd be professional.

She'd be polite.

They'd clear up the misunderstanding of whatever he thought she had.

She concentrated on last night and how he'd played her, and she blew out a breath with a giant whoosh.

She could imagine the conversation.

Sophie Callaghan? Yeah, I know her. Tell her you're going to fuck her hard, and she's all yours. Easy.

Heat pounded her face in a fresh wave.

Be polite. Be professional. She'd briefly considered nixing the meeting but hadn't been able to shake the tail and retrieve the equipment. She was anxious to find out if the recording would give her any intel on Babic's boss, Petrov.

After her meeting with Franco, she had to get some shopping done, then get home, change, and head to a strip club. Another of her clients was suspicious that her one-and-only disappeared every Monday, supposedly working late in retail. Last week, while dressed as the world's lamest runner, Sophie had trailed him to the door of the club. Tonight, appropriately attired, she'd follow him inside and film him, then hand her client the evidence.

Once again she'd deliver heartache along with an invoice.

A little rock lodged in her throat that *maybe* somewhere there was her one-and-only who'd want to jiggle great grandbabies on his knee. Whose face would light up when her ninety-year-old self waddled into a room.

She made a mental note to check in with the client of the potential cheater in a few days and see how she was going.

She'd checked her phone this morning. Still nothing on the jumper who frequented Javier's gym. Weeks earlier, Javier had told her to go have sex with herself when she'd asked him to contact her if the man appeared, but after laying out her case, he'd told her if the prick showed he'd call her.

At least one potential client had moved to actual. A straightforward case of a daughter searching for her lost mother.

She jolted when the map app on her phone kicked into life as she hit downtown Denver. By a miracle, Sophie found parking and squinted up at the standard office complex.

She allowed herself a single smile.

She'd always enjoyed the kindness of the people of Colorado when she and her father had passed through. One year a woman in a local church had found out it was Sophie's birthday and had made her first birthday cake—strawberry shortcake with vanilla frosting. It was the reason she'd moved here after her father's death. A small gesture had left a lasting impression on her.

The whir of a high-end coffee maker mixed with the scent of freshly ground coffee halted her momentarily. A business executive in a crisp suit walked out of a nearby café holding a cup in one hand and his phone in the other like a conductor having a public conversation. A wave of shimmering heat rolled up the pavement. Sweat gathered at the back of her neck due to the humidity and what awaited her.

She pushed the edge of her red T-shirt into the waistband of aged jeans, the shirt that made her upbeat whatever the circumstances. She pulled on the tie holding her hair in a high ponytail at the back of her head and walked inside the building. After consulting the business directory, she took the elevator to the fourth floor and stood outside a solid, polished pine door with FRANCO SECURITY engraved in plain black ink.

Body, this is your brain. There will be no tingles, no tightening, no flushing, no drooling. Definitely no drooling. Hormones will stay in the box labeled "monthly". Brain is in charge at all times.

Be polite. Be professional.

She knocked, squared her shoulders, then opened the door.

Be polite. Be professional...

Her mouth dried.

Harlan wore his uniform of choice. Tight black T-shirt, worn Levi's that hugged in all the right places, and scuffed boots. Stubble darkened his jaw. Dark silky hair still messy. Aviator glasses perched on his head. He held a phone to his ear, leaning one hip against his desk.

Damn.

Her brain sent urgent messages to her body to shut down *now*. She breathed deep and gazed around, getting her stupid body under control, concentrating on the office. No Broncos coffee mug on the smooth wood. No rogue stapler. No paper clips spilling out of the top of a container, threatening revolt. She craned her neck. Even the trash can lacked garbage. The man took "neat" to a whole new level. She moved to admire the artwork, her boots heavy on the polished wooden floor. Two nudes in charcoal adorned the walls. Beautiful. She knew the artist. Local guy. One day she hoped she could afford a small sketch of his work.

"Sophie."

She turned.

Harlan pushed his phone into his back pocket, moved from the desk, then planted his legs wide.

His gaze dropped to her chest.

"What are you wearing?"

She frowned at his tone and looked down at the red *K* and *C* interlocking against the white arrowhead. "The best team in the NFL's shirt. Go Chiefs."

"I should shoot you for wearing that in here." He shook his head. "A Kansas City fan."

The blood drained from her face.

One of the fiercest rivalries in the NFL. The most hated team in the league. Harlan had to be...

Well, of course he is.

"An Oakland Raiders fan? Oh God, I'm so sorry. You know there's rehab for that, right?" She cocked her head. "Why are you an Oakland fan? Isn't that illegal in Denver?"

"I'm not from Colorado. What about you and Kansas City?"

She shrugged, not even knowing herself. Her father hadn't followed the NFL, but somewhere along their travels she'd seen a Kansas City Chiefs flag, and something had clicked in her head. A heart-shaped memory of a strong, warm arm around her waist, the scent of deep-fried chicken, and weirdly, beets. A flash of red and white. A feeling of belonging. For years she tried to figure it out, but the more she delved into her subconscious, the more the memory floated out of reach.

"Well, hello? Because Kansas City is the best team in the *universe*. Have you seen our quarterback?"

His eyebrows hit his forehead.

Her eyes feasted on his muscled forearms as he crossed them over his chest. She tightened her ponytail, eager to be on her way. "As much as I want to chat about why your team sucks, I have a lot to do today, so let's get this done."

"Where's the recorder, Sophie?"

She blinked and her body jerked slightly.

Damn.

He'd noticed.

His eyes widened, then narrowed.

His gaze roamed over her body, like she was a bowl of ice-cream he was about to lick dry.

Nope. Not happening.

"I have no idea what you're talking about." She was pleased that she sounded calm and efficient, hoping she hid the firestorm going down in her body.

He put his hands into his jeans pockets, pushing down the denim and showing tanned skin.

He shrugged one sexy, muscled shoulder that she wanted to bite.

Hard.

He moved close, too close, and the scent of soap and him drilled through her, flooding her body with hot, desperate, inescapable need which she was doing her best to ignore. Okay, so it had been a while since she'd bumped uglies but getting hot and heavy with Harlan Franco who had no interest in her apart from getting her between the sheets for a ten-minute tumble?

I'd rather wear a meat bikini and let loose amongst starving lions.

"You left behind a sizeable amount of clay at Babic's table." His laser-beam eyes pinned her.

She stilled, and with every fiber in her body, blocked him.

Just.

"You'll never find it," she whispered.

His gaze swept down her frame and stopped at her traitorous rock-hard nipples.

"Oh, I'll find it. I *bet* you I'll find it." His dark, gravelly voice swept through her like syrup.

She forced a lazy chuckle. "I take your bet and *I* will win, because I'll retrieve it, and you'll never know."

A lazy smile that would melt icecaps stuttered her breath. "You won't, but I want something when I win."

From the look in his eyes he was running through scenarios of what he wanted, and none of them were G-rated.

She tackled the hormones running rampant in her body. Hormones that demanded she be naked and plastered against his long, hard body and start reproducing *now*. She froze when he unexpectedly pulled free the band holding her hair in a ponytail and buried his face in her hair.

"Raspberries," he murmured. "I fucking love raspberries."

He touched his tongue to the side of her neck, so fleetingly she wondered if she'd imagined it, but her body didn't. It responded by flushing from head to toe.

Damn.

His dark, weighty gaze dropped to her mouth. The intensity of it stole her breath.

His total focus centered on her. Her lips parted, and she forgot how to breathe. Didn't know her name or what state they were currently standing in.

I want to feel you swell in my mouth, stare up at you, and hear you tell me I'm yours.

I want to be slammed against a wall and wrap my legs around your hips while you pound into me.

I want to run my tongue over every part of your body and hear you moan my name.

His eyebrows rose and his gaze that had been molten was now scorching. "I wish I could get inside your head. I like the look on your face."

Self-preservation kicked in and, by a miracle, her brain ran into church and started chanting Hail Mary in Latin.

She had to get out of here, *now*.

On trembling legs, she walked to the door, stopping with her hand on the knob. She glanced back to find his gaze locked on her butt.

With distance, and without his scent filling her head with all kinds of lusty images, she studied him, curious why he'd been at Hostage. Was it the same reason as her? Did he have something on Babic?

"What were you doing at Hostage last night?"

He folded his arms across his wide chest again. "I was there looking for a sub."

She blinked. "So that really is your thing? Small, blond, and submissive?"

He nodded once.

A small stabbing feeling of hurt caught her by surprise.

Evidence he'd been playing her.

Again.

"I'm hard-wired for control. The women I'm with *want* to be dominated. Demand it. They do what I say when I say."

Her eyes widened, and she took a step back.

Wow. The essence of the man right there.

No white picket fence in his future. No putting together a bike at three a.m. on Christmas Eve. No bouncing grandbabies on his knee.

"But, you'd know the rules of being a sub, wouldn't you, Sophie?" His sapphire stare had her tilting her chin.

She shook her head. "Giving up who I am and disappearing to fit what a person wants me to be? I can't do that," she said quietly.

"When I win the bet. You and me, Sophie. One night." His velvet voice skimmed across her skin. "One *long* night where we play the rules my way."

SOPHIE'S HEAD SHOT BACK. Color flooded her cheeks, and her dark, smoky eyes narrowed.

"Oh, hell no. You won't win the bet, so there will be no rules being played your way."

Harlan had been semi-hard all morning thinking of her, but after she'd walked through the door, her fruity scent trailing her, his cock could be snapped off and used as a weapon.

To beat himself to death.

Her nipples were still hard through the cotton of her T-shirt. He'd heard the small gasp when he'd touched his tongue to her neck. The need to taste her skin was overwhelming. He'd wanted to mark her, show every man she walked past that she was off-limits.

The bet was an inspired moment. Without realizing it, she'd played into his hands. When she clocked his security detail she'd be assuming he was trailing her for the bet and not the actual reason that she was under surveillance.

Perfect.

And one night when this assignment was over?

Fuck yeah.

She tilted her head to one side, assessing.

"For curiosity's sake, what if one of your small, blond subs wants more?"

"I don't do more."

And he didn't. He never had. He liked his partners. They set mutual rules. They ticked each other's boxes on expectations. They wanted sex only. If he saw a woman more than once and caught the softness in her eye, he let her down gently and walked away. He wasn't a prick who'd use a woman who had feelings he didn't reciprocate. He controlled the situation as he did everything in his life.

Control freak? Ask his boarding school friends and they'd agree.

A man who did not delegate? Much to Zeb's endless frustration.

A man who lived by his own set-in-stone rules.

Be detached.

Be professional at all times.

Don't fuck the asset.

He strode to where she stood. His hand wrapped around her forearm. At the physical connection, his body jolted. Hers did a full body shiver of the good kind. Her raspberry scent mixed with her filled his lungs. He'd wanted to hold his breath longer, keep the flavor of her inside him. At this rate he'd walk past a fruit stand and get hard. Even wearing *that* T-shirt, which should make him blind, he couldn't rip his eyes away.

His gaze dropped to her nails digging into her palms.

You're sitting on my face. My fingers are holding you prisoner while I fuck you with my tongue. You're going to beg me to fuck you with my tongue, then my cock. I'll be using toys, because, baby, I like them and I think you will too.

"No." Her voice strained with need.

I want to taste you. Feel you spasm around my tongue. Have you beg for more.

"I didn't say anything." His voice was fracturing by the very second.

"You didn't have to," she whispered.

He sucked air through his teeth.

She pulled herself away, her skin flushed, her forehead damp.

Her mind may say no, but her body was begging for him. Her chest heaved, face flushed.

She tried to pull away, and he held her hair for a beat longer then released her.

"When I win the bet, you won't come within two miles of me."

He chuckled.

"That wasn't a joke," she said over her shoulder, then walked out the door, his eyes drawn to the curve of her hip, the way her butt filled her jeans and her slightly unsteady step.

He smiled.

When this case was over, Sophie Callaghan would be his for one long night. Oh, how she'd be his. *Until then...* It would be a challenge to convert her to his way of thinking, and he enjoyed a challenge.

Scrap that. He loved a challenge, and Sophie was a puzzle he craved to unwrap.

He walked to the window. Sophie strutted her sweet butt to a car that looked like Henry Ford had assembled himself. She eventually merged into the traffic. A brown nondescript sedan with one of his men at the wheel followed her.

He grinned.

Perfect.

He stood lost in thought, mostly about Sophie and their night together. His cock twitched painfully against denim at the image of her cuffed, panting, and looking up at him.

Yep, he'd definitely be winning the bet.

His back pocket vibrated. He smiled and swiped his finger across the screen just as Zeb Carmichael sauntered into the room who lifted his chin at Harlan.

"Hey, man, heard it took you three hours to watch *Sixty Minutes*?" He grinned at the phone and switched it to speaker.

"Gotta say, shit happens and you're living proof," Jason Johnson barked.

"You still yelling into mailboxes to send a voicemail?" Harlan's grin widened.

"Figured out how to program your VCR?" Jason's amused chuckle fills the room.

A comfortable silence stretched between Los Angeles and Colorado.

They'd been in each other's faces for years. Jason was a financial genius while Harlan had recorded 4.92 in the forty yard dash.

"Hey. Need a favor," Jason asked.

"You don't have to ask for a favor, man. Just say what you need."

Although they didn't see each other that often being in different states, he and Jason were tight, as were all the boys. Well, he and Holden butted heads and had tried to rip each other's heads off. They were bound by the brotherhood—a vow they'd uphold until their last dying breath, but underneath they were similar. Harlan would go to war for him.

"Need all the info on Asia Brown and her sister Jamaica who is in the wind. Whatever you've got, I'd appreciate it."

Harlan's eyebrows rose. The only person Jason was committed to was his grandmother, and even that was tenuous. Both he and Jason were orphans—Jason technically even though his father was still on the earth. Between Harlan and Jason, they'd had no family visits at holidays; instead they tagged along with the Gillard brothers. Harlan didn't have anyone to return to. Jason had never returned to his childhood home after a tragedy he rarely spoke about.

"Personal or business?" Harlan hedged.

There was a moment's pause before Jason blew out a long breath. "Personal. As much as you can find."

Now that intrigued him.

"I'll let you know." He smiled at the phone. "Send me through what you have."

"Appreciate it."

Harlan tucked the phone into his back pocket.

"Jason his usual charming self?" Zeb chuckled. "I think he's smiled twice in his life and once was when he figured out the dark, broody type was catnip with the girls."

"The man can cast a death-eating shadow over the happiest place on earth," Harlan countered. "Love the brother."

Zeb clapped him on the back. "Yeah."

A food truck pulled into the lot in a park across the street. The email Harlan had read earlier surfaced in his brain. Today they'd be serving tomato soup and either a chicken club sandwich or pastrami on rye along with a hot drink or bottled water plus a toiletries pack.

"You still playing white knight?" Zeb now stood beside him.

"Still paying back, brother. Life's shitty when you're homeless, but it's fucked when you're homeless, starving, and want clean teeth."

Zeb squeezed his shoulder.

Zeb would never know, coming from one of the richest real estate families on the East Coast, but Harlan remembered freezing nights wrapped in newspaper huddled under a freeway overpass.

Zeb cleared his throat.

Harlan turned.

Zeb poured his massive frame into a chair, his face serious. "We have a problem. A big fucking problem."

Every muscle in Harlan's body locked.

Zeb passed him a sheet of paper. An autopsy picture of a middle-aged white dude — O'Connor. Harlan skimmed his vital stats. Six foot, blue eyes, no distinguishing marks. "Your girl, Sophie Callaghan, doesn't add up. There's a birth certificate issued in the state of Montana, twenty-three years ago when she was two. Mother is listed as a Jane Callaghan, and I can find no evidence of her birth or death. Father listed as Josiah O'Connor. There's a notation that the certificate was issued without hospital proof of birth. O'Connor signed an affidavit that Sophie was born in Montana, in a field with no witnesses. O'Connor died six years back. I had to dig hard to get his story out of the woodwork. Turns out he was a con-artist preacher who, with his direct connection to God, could heal cancer, bring rain, grow crops and find love... for a price." Zeb looked pained. "Sorry, brother."

A pit opened up in the bottom of Harlan's stomach, and his internal organs tried to squeeze out his ass. When he was eight, his mom had sold everything for a healing prayer from a preacher when the doctors gave her no hope. All his mom wanted was to stay on the planet longer to care for her only child while cancer ravaged her body. When the prayer didn't arrive and the preacher disappeared, his mother had died, broken.

He hated the preacher who'd stolen his mom's hope and her dignity. He wanted to find the man his whole life and snap every bone in his body, then hack out his heart and feed it to vultures.

At least it wasn't O'Connor. Wrong ethnicity.

"A small token of consolation. O'Connor liked girls and blow."

Zeb shook his head. "A man of fucking God. Took a beating after trying to get out of paying for both. Brain hemorrhage."

Harlan stilled.

Fuck.

Fuck.

"Leaving Sophie exposed." He stood, then paced, clenching and unclenching his hands, adrenaline spiking through his body. "What kind of sick father does that to his daughter? Jesus." Different scenarios played out in his head, all ending badly. "Imagine if any of O'Connor's victims wanted revenge and found Sophie alone and vulnerable."

Wait.

Could *still* find Sophie.

He stilled.

Harlan had brought in sick, depraved, and flat-out desperate people who'd do anything for money or revenge. If any of them had found Sophie, could *still* find Sophie, she could slip from this earth in a heartbeat.

"Brother, there's more."

Harlan braced, breathed heavily, and nodded.

"I got to her house before she left to come here, took over from Arabella. Someone else is on her. There was a guy parked on her street with a telescopic lens, under the guise of reading water meters. I lifted this envelope from the passenger seat."

"Arabella didn't notice him?" A steel band clamped around the inside of his head and tightened. He'd have to deal with that snippet of news later.

Zeb shook his head, his face pained. He placed photos of Sophie on the desk. Harlan's heart went to hang out with his feet. He forced in a slow breath, staring at a montage of photos. Sophie hauling on the lead of a hog of a dog. One of her in running clothes, taken last Monday. One, date-stamped last night, showed Sophie wearing a long trench coat walking out of Pipe's with Pipe.

"Whoever this crew is watching Sophie, they're serious. This fucker had high-end camera equipment. Professional. I ran the plates. They don't match the registration. The car was listed as stolen last week in South Dakota. I'll confirm if the car changes daily. This type of operation takes money. A *lot* of money."

"Yep," Harlan ground out.

"Brother, Sophie Callaghan came into this world aged two. No confirmed birth that fits her age with her parents in fifty states. Someone out there is paying large to keep her under high-end surveillance. Someone with a lot of bank, someone—"

Cold sweat gathered on Harlan's forehead. He stopped pacing and faced Zeb, who looked grim. "Someone who knows of her possible connection to Petrov and who'll use her as collateral or someone out for revenge for her father."

Zeb's unflinching icy blue stare met his. "That's what I'm thinking."

Harlan nodded, trying to digest the information that sat like a lump of concrete in his stomach.

"Protect the vulnerable," Harlan blew out on a breath, ice coating his skin. Their mantra born from that one soul-sucking night in boarding school when they *didn't* protect the vulnerable.

"Ab-so-fucking-lutely. Sophie Callaghan is one vulnerable target right now. You know what that means," Zeb blew out a breath. "I'll keep digging, but I don't have a good feeling." Zeb headed toward the door, his phone in his hand, punching out a text. The door closed with a click.

Harlan knew exactly what it meant.

The ink on his ribcage seemed to throb. *Praesidio*—protect.

A lot of people had been unhappy when Petrov went straight. The man was a business genius. Everything he touched turned to gold. If he took an interest in an abandoned diamond mine, it would start spitting out diamonds bigger than fists. The man had run guns in and out of countries without a single shipment ever being stopped. He now used those traffic lanes for legitimate purposes.

If someone wanted to get Petrov to open up the profitable transport routes, using Sophie may get them to change his mind. Worse still was the scenario that a rogue player or players wanted Sophie for revenge for her father's cons.

Harlan had run a financial check. Sophie had under one hundred dollars in her savings account and scraped by on her checking. Anyone looking for revenge thinking she was sitting on a nest egg would be cornered when they realized she had nothing. Maybe they'd play with her before they killed her. Maybe not.

The foul mood that had been kicking around his head morphed into a starving ten-foot troll breathing fire and swinging an axe. Whether she liked it or not, and he was guessing not, Sophie would move in with him.

From tonight, she was under his protection.

FIVE

"Coming, Titus."

After a mouthful of noodles, Sophie placed the plate and fork into the sink.

Pongo lifted his head and opened one eye before laying his sorry head back down—tired from waking up.

She smiled at her dog before heading toward the door. "I swear if 'Bark in the Park' has a *Useless Guard Dog* competition this year, I'm entering you." She laughed when her dog responded with a thump of his tail, and a quick, explosive fart filled the room.

She knew, if push came to shove, Pongo would lick any intruder to death, then gas them with his lethal cocktail, and she loved every inch of his trusting, fart-filled soul.

When a second heavier knock echoed around the room, she hurried her pace. "I'm here."

The Carroll's must have seen her shoot down the driveway an hour earlier. She'd spent longer in Denver than she'd expected. After leaving Harlan's office, she'd headed for a cappuccino and a slab of banana bread dripping in butter. Tequila would have calmed her nerves faster, but busting out the top shelf wasn't a daytime option.

It had outright disturbed her how badly she'd wanted Harlan. If the man had touched her neck with his tongue one more time...

They both knew he had no interest in her apart from a quick fuck where he'd call all the shots.

Her fingers skimmed the crescent-shaped welts on her palm, where she'd dug for control.

But thoughts of Harlan and his sinful body had to take a backseat, because she had more pressing matters: getting her equipment from the park, listening to Babic's conversation. Then her demand when she won the bet—Harlan leaving her alone.

Getting to the park unnoticed might not be so easy. Harlan's people moved fast. A brown sedan had tailed her after she left the office.

After tonight's surveillance job, she'd lead Harlan's people on a chase around the streets of Denver before she'd collect the microphone and secure it in the safe.

A win-win situation.

Sophie unlocked and opened her front door, expecting to see Titus's sparkling brown eyes, leaning on his walking stick, a smile on his face, a fuzzy felt hat on his head. Instead, she gazed into intense dark blue eyes. Harlan's ripped body filled her doorframe. A black T-shirt hugged every washboard on his rock-hard stomach; faded blue denim had been replaced with aged black molded over long, long, muscular thighs. His full lips were pressed into a tight line.

As usual, he looked about as pleased to see her as catching his grandma naked.

"What are you doing here?" Blood thicker than molasses finally made its way to her brain. She stood on tiptoes staring past him to see a state of the art black Range Rover parked behind her hatchback where the words "Clean Me" were written on her passenger side window. The sinking sun cast a halo around his head, highlighting strands of dark mahogany. He couldn't look more like a Greek god chiseled from granite if he tried.

He scanned over her shoulder. "How long would it take you to pack a bag?" He gently turned her sideways and walked inside.

Pongo, sensing an extra food source, lumbered off the couch. A series of popping sounds accompanied him.

She sucked in a breath at Harlan's grin.

"Did your dog fart?"

Perplexed, she shut the door and followed him in.

"Yeah," she said, distracted. "I'm guessing it's why he was left on the side of the road with 'unwanted' written on a note attached to his collar. If he's in a joyous mood, he can clear a room in less than ten seconds. It's his gift to the world."

Harlan stood in the middle of the room, hands on his hips, executing a slow circle. Her couch housed a selection of throws, an empty tube of Pringles, and three of her dog's chew toys.

Dark brows hit his messy hairline when he took in the usual disaster of her living room.

Her hands went to her hips.

Seriously?

After a childhood of moving from state to state with no warning, sometimes in the middle of the night, not having to mold her life and her possessions to fit into one bag was freedom. Leaving a bowl in the sink meant she was coming back. A messy throw on the back of her couch meant she'd be snuggled up watching her soaps later. A set of drawers meant she had a home.

She folded her arms across her chest. "Why are you here, and why would I need to pack a bag?" Her brain finally shook off the shock that Harlan was standing in her living room. "Are you here because of the bet? Because if you are, you can turn around and strut your cute butt out the door."

Pongo had made a thorough inspection of their visitor's pockets. Although he hadn't found food, he gazed up at Harlan like he'd found a new best friend. His stump of a tail beat against the wooden floor.

"Cute butt?" Harlan's blue eyes twinkled. "Men don't have cute butts. Babes have cute butts."

Exasperated that he stood here, and annoyed that he exasperated her, she threw up her hands. "God, you're right. Women never think *cute butt*. They *always* think, *now that's a well-proportioned set of gluteus maximus muscles.*"

Harlan grinned before his face stilled, his laser stare focused on her. "Without going into details, you're being followed. Someone is taking photos of you with a telescopic lens. At your house, walking your dog. Walking out of Pipe's Bar."

She mentally rolled her eyes. Did he think she'd been beamed down to the planet and she couldn't see this was all a ruse to win the bet?

"Where're the photos?" Her hands landed on her hips.

"In my office safe. I had you under surveillance when you came to my office. My colleague clocked the guy taking photos of you."

"So you admit you had me followed. Stalkery much?" She leaned forward until their breaths clashed. "Seriously. You need to go. The only reason you're still breathing is I hate orange jumpsuits."

His eyes sparkled, and that panty-melting grin transformed his face.

"We need to move. I'll find out who it is. Since you're staying with me, no one will get close to you."

She stepped backward. "I'd no more pack a bag and jump into your machine of a car than I would enter myself in a Miss Venezuela bikini pageant."

The humor died in his eyes. "This is serious shit, Sophie. You need to listen to me and do what I say."

Wow. Just wow.

Harlan folded impressive arms across his chest, widened his stance, and stared at her. She shook her head in disbelief. Where was the man from last night and this morning in his office who'd looked at her like he wanted to devour her?

He'd morphed into I-will-control-the-situation-and-you-at-all-costs, and here he stood in her living room doing what he did best.

Demanding. Ordering. Controlling.

This Harlan Franco she knew. This man she took bail jumpers from. The man currently looking at her as if she were a stain on his favorite shirt.

She took a deep breath and held his gaze. Time to dish up some facts so he'd be on his merry way.

"FYI, I've got a great security system." And she did. It had cost a fortune. She'd beefed up security after a cheating husband had followed her back here. Her hands landed on her hips. "My neighbor Titus is the self-appointed neighborhood watch captain. He writes down every car that comes into the street, and if that car hangs around he has a detailed description and the boys in blue on speed dial."

His eyes narrowed. "You rely on your neighbor?"

She blew out a breath. "Are you listening to me? No, I don't rely on my neighbor. I *know* this neighborhood. I know the people who live here, their vehicles, and when they change vehicles. I would know if someone was following me."

Harlan gazed around the room, as if inspecting her security system, his eyes resting on the antique cabinet that housed her treasured snow globes. All ninety-four of them and counting.

Her favorite, the one that had started her collection, sat proudly at the front. Dorothy wearing her trademark ruby slippers with the date her father gave it to her engraved on the bottom:

S. *You are my night and day. 7 May.*

The globe calmed her. Made her feel safe.

She had carried on the tradition of engraving the date she purchased a new globe until she'd received her father's personal effects and the world she'd thought she belonged to exploded, leaving her lonelier than she thought possible and distraught at her father's deception.

"I don't have much time." His impatient voice could have world dictators scrambling to pack a bag.

A tentative knock sounded at the door.

She checked her watch that ran ten minutes late, no matter how many times she changed the battery. A sweet sixteen birthday gift from her father she couldn't part with. "Turns out neither do I. You need to leave. *Now.*"

His eyes heated and lazily dragged down her body as if she were naked. "Not a big fan of the insubordination, but nothing a good spanking won't fix." He reached out and tucked a length of hair behind her ear.

Poof, there it was, that instant hit when he touched her. Her blood thickened, her heart rate kicked up several gears, and exquisite pleasure built between her legs.

When Harlan was near her, why did she want to climb him like a cat? As for being spanked?

Never.

She didn't know how he did it but, by a feat of physics, Harlan got to the door before her and peered through the peephole.

She tried to push him, but moving Jupiter would be easier.

Close. He was too close. His scent battered her defenses. Standing next to the man, her brain shut down, but her body trembled in embarrassing anticipation.

Why, why, *why* did she want him more than breathing?

Surprise flared in his eyes.

One hand landed beside her head. "You want me?"

She shook her head. She hated him, hated herself, hated everything about this.

"Hell no," she said, sounding thankfully formal. "As for being spanked? Maybe it's you who needs a flogging."

Electricity crackled between them. She lifted her chin and refused to get lost in the depths of his deep blues or acknowledge the mesmerizing gold flecks in his eyes. She held his stare.

"Miss Sophie, are you all right? There's a tank of a car parked in the driveway. I've written down the license." The concerned voice of her neighbor filtered through the heavy wood.

She turned and opened the door, ignoring the wall of man next to her.

"Hey, Titus." Her neighbor's dark eyes widened as he took in Harlan, who'd crossed his arms and stood guarding the door as if Viking robbers were about to break in. She elbowed Harlan out of the way. "I've got your pickled onions."

"I didn't know you had a *man*." Titus's smile lit up his face. At five-foot-two, he tilted his head back. "Well, I am pleased." Titus thrust out one hand, leaning on his trusty cane with the other, his eyes trained on Harlan, who grinned and shook her neighbor's hand, introducing himself.

Sophie's heart threw in a mini-beat. Titus would hurry down their shared driveway, his cane on 'rapid stomp'. He'd tell his wife, Sally, who'd forget in two minutes, so he'd repeat himself, hoping something would stick. All the while he'd be planning her "big day".

"I don't have a man, Titus, but if I did, it wouldn't be this man." She squeezed Titus's shoulder. "I'll get your pickled onions, and I'll see you on Thursday as usual." She paused, knowing Titus relied on her more than he cared to admit. "You know I've got a huge leg of lamb in the freezer I'll never get through. I'll roast it up and bring it over."

The only thing hanging out in her freezer was an expired Lean Cuisine and two frozen fishcakes that had escaped the box ages ago and lay like golden eyes staring at her.

She loved her neighbors and often ate oatmeal for breakfast, lunch, and dinner on a slow workweek so she could help them out. Like her, they had no family. Titus had caught Sophie watering his garden at midnight after she had come back from a job and noticed the normally beautiful flowers looked thirsty. She'd turned down Titus's requests for dinner until she'd run out of excuses. She'd joined them and they'd sat down to watery canned tomato soup, toast, and four potato chips laid in a row on the toast. Now, every Thursday night she loaded up her groaning credit card at the supermarket and inflicted her cooking skills on them.

"Well now. Since you have a man in your life, you should be on dates, cooking for him. Getting wooed." Titus's brown eyes twinkled.

A bark of unexpected laughter broke free from deep in her chest, breaking the tension. "Ah, Harlan doesn't woo, Titus, he commands his army of small, blond 'yes-women'." She checked her watch. "And I'm commanding him to leave." She ignored Harlan, walked to her cluttered kitchen table and hoisted the jar of Olde English pickled onions. She held the jar out to her neighbor, whose eyes lit up at the size.

"I know you said a small one, but these were on sale," she lied. Heat radiated from her face. She turned to Harlan whose eyes were trained on her. He stared at her like she was a code and he'd been given the letters, S, E, and X.

"I'll see myself out." Titus grinned. "I'll see you Thursday and bring your young man. He might want to catch the fishing channel with me after dinner."

"I'll be there," Harlan said.

Sophie turned and glared at him.

"He won't, Titus, but *I'll* see you Thursday, if not before, and don't forget Fly-fishing Phil cheats." She leaned forward and hugged her neighbor, inhaling his pine aftershave.

Titus lifted his cane and shuffled out the door.

She turned to Harlan. "Now, I have a job tonight, and you need to leave." She walked to her bedroom, closed the door, and jumped at the sound of the front door slamming. Unable to resist, she opened her door to see her living room and house Harlan-free. Only his spicy male scent lingered. Without thinking, she breathed deeply, and her girly bits danced into life, again.

"Wow, that was easy," she said to Pongo, who opened one eye. "Suspiciously."

The clock on her bedside table drew her eye.

Crap. I've got to get a move on.

She swapped her polo for a slinky black top. She wore her newish black jeans, the ones that kind of flattered her ass if she squinted and it was a dark night. Black boots on her feet. If she didn't eat so many Pringles her ass wouldn't be so round, nor her hips, but giving up the Salt and Vinegar chips? Never going to happen.

She added a touch of gloss to her lips, then grabbed her bag, set the alarm, and locked the front door. Scanning the area, she found no cars out of place.

Sophie sang along with the awesomeness that was Beyonce and headed toward the aptly named strip joint Beavers and Buttheads. She checked in her rearview mirror countless times, but only a gray sedan stuck with her until she threw in an unexpected left turn. She let out her breath. Harlan's words still sat in her brain. If he *was* telling the truth and someone was following her, tomorrow she'd launch her own investigation.

HARLAN STOOD at the rear of the packed club, eyes on Sophie. She was good. Exceptionally good. She'd clocked him the minute he walked in. She'd raised an eyebrow, then shot him a glacial look. He nursed a warm beer, scanned the bar again, looking for any threats.

Nothing.

His gaze slid back to Sophie, who sat on a stool away from the front of the action. Jeans cupped her bitable ass and clung to her long legs, a shirt pulled across her mouth-watering breasts. He itched to pull the tie from her hair. He loved her hair down around her face in a mass of shiny, dark, shimmering curls. His dick sent him an "I'm here and functioning" message.

If he closed his eyes, he could imagine a hot running montage of Sophie naked, in various positions looking up at him, her body straining... for him, her eyes begging... for him.

Damn.

Getting a boner in a strip club was never a good idea. Girls would offer lap dances when he only wanted one girl on his lap.

His phone buzzed with an incoming text.

JASON: *Any news?*

Harlan tapped out a reply. *Working on it, brother. Not like you to be impatient.*

If he were a female, he would have thrown in a laughing emoji.

JASON. *Got a plan that needs executing and I need the info ASAP.*

Interesting. Jason was a committed workaholic. That he needed the info on his personal assistant and her sister was interesting.

HARLAN: *Working on it.*

And for the hell of it threw in a smiling heart-eyed emoji.

Little bubbles appeared.

JASON: *You emoji'd me? Assuming you've contracted Ebola and are on your deathbed or you've been abducted by alien pirates who are currently probing you, and you're sucking down your last breath. Let me know where to send a case of Johnny Walker Blue.*

Harlan laughed out loud at the middle finger up that appeared on his screen.

The brother was one grumpy, broody mother, and he loved him.

Another sip of overpriced beer slid down Harlan's throat. He'd confirmed with Petrov that his client wasn't running a double-team on Sophie—something Harlan had encountered before. Playing two teams against each other only stripped resources, wasted time, and pissed everyone off.

He'd tightened the circle around Sophie. If Sophie spotted a detail, she'd think he was trying to find the recording because of their bet. He didn't care if she complained. If he didn't have eyes on her, one of his team would, twenty-four-seven.

He gazed around. He hated this strip joint. Filled with trust fund college students and an owner who preferred profit over pretty much everything, including under-agers with their older brothers' IDs. The place was so packed it had to be breaking a fire code violation. Stale beer and pretty-boy aftershave tainted the air. The sooner Sophie finished the better, so they could breathe clean air.

To his left, a bunch of guys in their late teens or early twenties were having a "drink as much shit tequila as you can" session. Above the techno base beat that made his teeth throb, their catcalls and whistles got louder as they downed more shots they didn't know were watered down. A topless girl on a swing swiped on her phone.

Even if he weren't being paid to guard Sophie, something about her pulled at him. Like some fucked-up magnet that both repelled and drew him at the same time. He couldn't explain it, and he couldn't stop it.

The woman of the hour turned and looked at him, rubbing a spot on the back of her neck as if she knew he had been staring at her.

Sophie stood and played her mark—a man enjoying a lap dance at the back of the club. She circled him, her handbag on her shoulder. Pausing, her hand moved up the strap, taking a photo. The man with his head thrown back and eyes closed, getting his happy ending, oblivious to everyone except the bored-looking woman grinding on his lap. Sophie headed toward the exit.

Thank fuck.

In Harlan's peripheral vision, two men dressed in Armani suits, sunglasses covering their faces, moved toward Sophie, hands moving to the insides of their jackets.

Shit.

They weren't here for the show.

Harlan's blood turned to slush.

Fuck.

He threw bodies aside, ignoring protests. His hand slid to the Glock in the holster at the back of his jeans. If the suits got to her before he did, they'd be a serious problem. It would be messy. There'd be gunfire, and the probability of someone with a hole in them leaking blood ran high.

Not in the game plan.

Sophie stopped by the group of dickheads wearing college

jerseys. She then threw her arms around two jocks' shoulders and pulled them in to her body, moving sideways into a crowd of drunk teens who'd stood to applaud two of their friends who looked like they were getting a longed-for, but largely mythical, threesome. If one of the boys so much as laid a finger on her, he'd dislocate his shoulder.

He tossed one of the college students aside, ignoring his startled grunts, and grabbed Sophie's wrist, curling her into his side and guiding her toward the stage.

Sophie pried at his hand on her waist. Anger vibrated in her voice. "I've seen the threat, and I was positioning to get to the side exit."

She'd been using the college boys for cover. Brilliant strategy.

"Harlan. Stop." Sophie pulled on his arm.

He strode past the stage where two girls worked one pole. He threw open a door marked EMPLOYEES ONLY, and jogged past a group of women applying lip gloss and adjusting costumes.

He hit the back entrance, pushed open the door, and chugged cool air. Without letting go of Sophie's hand, he scanned the area. All clear. He ignored Sophie trying to peel his fingers from around hers.

Getting the asset safe—his only priority.

"This is ridiculous. Stop. Right. Now. I can take care of myself."

Sophie absolutely could look after herself under normal circumstances, but this was a whole bigger ballgame.

Harlan tightened his grip on Sophie's hand. "We've got to get to safety."

An earsplitting scream ground him to a halt. Sophie stood, glaring at him, her mouth open and a sound that could launch a zombie invasion piercing the night air.

When the scream gathered in intensity, he picked her up. She landed with an oomph on his shoulder, which silenced her for about half a second.

He bent low and ran, her fists beating against his back.

He increased his pace, his muscles screaming.

"What the hell are you doing?" she said in a voice that would crack ice. "I'm a grown woman and a private detective, for Christ's sake."

With his free hand, he pulled his phone from his back pocket and barked the word, "office."

"Arabella. I need a car picked up." He gave the address, the make and model of her car. "Call me when the car's in the driveway." He pushed the phone into his back pocket.

He opened the passenger door and, ignoring her startled protest, he deposited her on the seat, reached in, then buckled her in.

They both needed to be far, far away.

And he needed to be on his game. He hadn't noticed the suits entering the building; he'd been staring at Sophie's creamy neck, her thick, luscious hair, her pouty lips he had major plans for. He was nothing more than a pussy-whipped teen.

An *unprofessional,* pussy-whipped teen.

By the time he'd opened the driver's side and jumped in, the back door to the club opened, and the men jogged out. He gripped the steering wheel and threw the car into drive, keeping his headlights off until they cleared the lot.

"Stop the car."

Her fury slapped him. He didn't glance at her, but headed toward her house, monitoring the rearview mirror.

He gripped the steering wheel tighter, replaying the past few minutes in his mind. Granted, she was good at her job. Yep, she'd clocked the trained militia, but those men played at a different level. He'd trained with the likes of them. Intelligent, professional—they'd snap a neck, slice a liver, or sever a spine in a single move without a backward glance. All the things he'd been trained to do. They were well paid and didn't leave until the job was done, under any circumstances.

Fuck.

Fuck.

Was this the same crew at her place this morning?

His muscles twitched. If he could get out and drop, he'd do fifty without breaking a sweat.

He'd turned up at her house today hoping she'd move in with him where he could keep her safe. After leaving her place to let her calm down, he'd left one of his people around the corner and driven to his house to pack a bag.

He glanced over at her, then back to the road. Red cheeks underscored her pale face. Her eyes narrowed. He also noticed the tremble in her fingers.

Her hand landed on his arm. "Stop the car."

"No."

He gripped the wheel until his knuckles throbbed, his eyes focused on the road, running how this would play out. He'd find out if Sophie was who Petrov thought she might be. Winning the bet, because he was a man who didn't like to lose at anything, and having Sophie for one night after this had played out, would be the icing on the cake. Until the job was done, Sophie would be plastered to his side.

His head swiveled to take in her clenched jaw. "From now on, you have a house guest."

SIX

The next day Harlan stood at the back of a gym—gym might be pushing it. More like a disused warehouse. A hand-painted sign propped on the pavement let him know that Javier's Gym was open for business. Sweat tumbled freely down Harlan's back. Industrial fans moved stale air around the room.

He'd hung around gyms like this, desperate to get away from life for a while and wanting to stack on muscle. Nothing sucked more than being a small kid starting school on a full scholarship to one of the most prestigious schools in the country. Having about a buck and a quarter in his pocket, a barbershop haircut and Goodwill clothes he did not fit in at Stamford Brook School for Boys. Thank fuck he'd found the other boarder misfits who'd absorbed him into their fold.

Sophie had pulled on gloves after putting on headgear while chatting to a man who looked like he crushed rocks for a living. She tilted back her head in laughter. Her chocolate eyes sparkled, and her teeth flashed. Rock Crusher grinned.

Harlan forced his muscles loose and took in his surroundings. He'd read the rules when he walked in. If you were here to lift, then you were asked to throw in what you could. If you were here for the ring, then you threw in ten if you had your own gloves and fifteen if you didn't.

His fingers probed a painful crick in his neck. His idea of moving in hadn't gone down well. Sophie had sprinted from his car before it had come to a full halt. She'd secured the door to her house and set the alarms, then refused to answer her phone. Instead of creating an unholy scene and waking the neighborhood, he'd spent an uncomfortable night in his car's front seat. During the night, a blanket had arrived on the hood of his car.

After a quick shower, a protein shake, and an update from Zeb, he'd relieved his comms man colleague Israel, at midday and picked up Sophie's tail. He hired only the best, and all the boarding school boarders excelled in their field. Zeb, surveillance. Israel, comms. He'd contracted Holden Abbot occasionally, who could chameleon his look at breakneck speed. A man no one remembered unless he wanted them to—an impressive skill.

Harlan had been surprised when Sophie turned her car into this gym where there were no rules and no limits, and you took your punishment with a smile. He was coming to the fast and uncomfortable conclusion that a lot of what Sophie did would be a surprise. He'd learned the fastest way to piss her off was to tell her what to do. Those big brown eyes narrowed, her tanned skin flushed, and she looked like she'd send him off to the afterlife without a hearty goodbye.

He could jump in the ring and dispatch any man who entered, and he'd rip the face off any man who'd harm Sophie. He'd *love* to join the group of men lifting weights in one corner, alternatively shouting encouragement or the word "pussy" in equal measure followed by laughter. He'd missed his exercise this morning and, on top of last night's events, he was wired.

Sophie broke away from Rock Crusher and walked toward him. Tight black shorts highlighted her insanely long legs and the flare of her hips. A black wife-beater hugged her frame. Hair scraped back. Feet bare. Her beautiful brown eyes trained on him. A man could get lost in those eyes.

Before he could shut it down, he caught a whiff of her unique raspberry scent, and his body jerked. He dug his hands into his pockets trying to hide the evidence. At this rate he'd have to put in an insurance claim for blue balls.

"What are you doing here?" he asked.

She smiled. "I need to relieve some *tension*. Care to join me in the ring?"

Oh, the possibilities of joining her in the ring, for a wrestle where she'd be underneath him, wriggling. But hitting women? Hell no.

"I don't fight women."

Picking up female bail jumpers, he'd been bitten, scratched, and nearly lost his balls dozens of times, but he couldn't hit a female. Some in his profession did, but he had a moral code that all his staff adhered to, and hitting women wasn't tolerated.

She leaned in, and his body pulsed in response. "Honey, you wouldn't get that close."

He couldn't help the grin stretching across his face.

He shouldn't love how her attitude made his entire body smile, but that flicker in her eye, that tilt of the chin, and her confident smile was one tempting package that needed to be tamed.

By him.

Sophie turned and walked to the now empty ring.

Shit.

A couple of these guys looked like they could take on an eight hundred pound pissed-off frustrated bull and win. They came for a serious workout. Male, female, or wolverine. They didn't care—once you stepped into the ring, you left your name, age, sex, and occupation at the door.

He pushed off the wall, but as if sensing the movement, she turned and arched a brow. He pretended to slouch back against the rough concrete, but every muscle was coiled to launch if anyone hurt her.

After twenty minutes, a man a couple of inches shorter than Sophie, but who clearly worked out, entered. Sophie walked toward him.

Harlan pushed off the wall and walked to the ring. He couldn't hear their conversation, but the man shrugged a shoulder and thrust out his hand, which Sophie shook.

At Harlan's growl, a few men shot him curious glances, but he ignored them. The metallic scent of blood mixed with sweat and liniment filled his sinuses. He walked to where the honor fridge sat, threw four dollars on the top, then took two bottles of water, his eyes never leaving Sophie. His gut did a full clench when Sophie stepped between the ropes and into the ring. The man she'd been talking to joined her.

The rules were simple. Three rounds lasting one minute each. If you went down and stayed down longer than ten seconds, you lost.

Sophie hit what looked like a light switch on the wall. A sharp buzz followed.

The man, who had enough attitude to fill a maximum-security jail, swaggered toward Sophie. His gaze crawled across her body, then landed on her chest. He licked his lips and adjusted his junk. A sleazy grin stretched across his ferret-looking face. He and Sophie circled each other. Sophie kept her hands up, her eyes never leaving her opponent. The man pretended to fall. Sophie went to reach for him to break his fall. He reared back, a gloved hand sweeping across her face. One second she was upright and the next she was down, having been felled by a leg sweep, the Ferret hitting her with sharp jabs across her face.

For what seemed like an ice age, Sophie didn't react. Harlan fought to pull in shattering breaths.

Fuck.

Harlan gripped the mat, hands bunched, about to swing into the ring, when Sophie's legs wrapped around the fighter's neck and squeezed. He tried to pull back, but she held him in a vise grip.

The buzzer sounded.

Both stood and went to their respective corners.

Harlan stalked to Sophie's corner and went to hand her a bottle of water.

"No, but thank you," she panted.

He opened his mouth, but she held up a hand.

Before he could say a word, the buzzer sounded, starting round two. Sophie pranced into the center of the ring where she and Ferret squared off, circling each other, neither making a significant move, exchanging blows against the other's gloves a few times. Sophie lunged left, but the man had anticipated her, and she stumbled back when a jab had her rocking back on her heels. She said something to him. Surprise flittered across his face.

The buzzer sounded. The Ferret started walking to his corner, stopped, and looked at Sophie over his shoulder. She smiled at him, the smile not moving past her lips.

The buzzer sounded for the third and final round.

This time Sophie wasn't taken by surprise. The buzzer had barely sounded when she darted forward, knocking the startled man off his feet with a left hook Harlan felt from outside the ring.

She followed the fighter down and sat on his chest, dipping and swaying away from his legs, trying to get her head in a grip.

His normal heart rate of seventy felt close to one seventy. His dick ached and something weird was happening in his chest, which swelled with pride.

Christ, I'm turned on watching her.

One of the men who'd been lifting weights came to stand next to Harlan, crunching a massive hand weight.

"Fuck that's hot."

Harlan turned his head. The man stared at Sophie, his mouth open.

"I wouldn't mind taking a beating from her."

He stared at the man, who caught his vibe and turned away, grinning. Ferret still kept lashing out, hate twisting his features.

Sophie wasn't letting him go. She seemed to gain strength.

"How does it feel to be powerless and have someone hitting you?" She grunted. "Feel good?"

The group of lifters had abandoned their weights and now stood in groups around the ring.

"You expected your-about-to-be-ex to drop the restraining order?" Sophie held him by the throat, ducking and weaving from the blows connecting with soft tissue. "She got smart. She's gone. The next time you'll see her is when she testifies against you."

Harlan stared in surprise and grinned. He circled to where Sophie had maneuvered the man into a corner.

"A jumper?"

"Yep," she grunted, flipping him onto his chest and pulling his arms behind him. "Princess here likes to beat on his wife in front of his kids. I talked to his wife who got smart, got a restraining order, which he broke. His about to be *ex*-wife told me he sometimes turns up here for a session, so here I am."

"Bitch got what she deserved. So will you," the Ferret spat.

"Oh, sweetheart, are you threating me? Because Sweetie, you're getting roasted by a girl."

Harlan pulled a bunch of cable ties from his pocket and held the plastic restraints out to her. She shook her head then using her teeth, she ripped at the Velcro on her gloves, pulling her hands free one at a time, keeping the pressure on his neck, then pulled ties from inside her T-shirt. He guessed her bra.

Lucky cable ties.

She grabbed a long cable tie and in a swift move had the thin but strong tie in place, pulling until it locked tight.

The man's face went crimson, hatred in his eyes.

She hauled the jumper to his feet, her chest heaving, sweat layering her forehead, muscles in her shoulders flexing under smooth skin, and her eyes sparkling.

Hot.

Scrap that.

Volcanically hot.

He shook his head. "You're a schoolboy's wet dream."

Harlan followed Sophie and the man out of the gym. He waited until Sophie had the jumper buckled up in her car. She stood and moved to the driver's side door.

The scent of raspberries and sweat was way more intoxicating than Jack Daniels.

And far more deadly.

Frustration, sexual and otherwise, clawed at his insides. The sexual he could take care of later, in the shower, a picture of Sophie tied and begging him playing in his mind. The frustration of guarding her when she wouldn't do a thing he said...

"Are you planning on sleeping in my driveway again tonight?" she asked, her head tilted to one side, a mischievous smile pulling at her puffy lips.

"Every night," he barked.

She frowned. "Every night?"

"Every single night," he shot back.

She studied him until her jumper started banging on the roof of her car.

"Why do you care?" she asked quietly.

He couldn't tell her he was guarding her, working her, keeping her safe. Nor could he tell her that the thought of anyone laying a hand on her could turn him into a felon. Instead, he spun her a patchwork of truth.

"You're not getting hurt or worse when I can do something about it." He leaned in, and because he was a stupid fucker, he scented her neck.

Her body jolted, and she stilled.

"I *will* win the bet. You *will* be mine for one night," he said, touching his tongue to the side of her neck, licking a drop of sweat.

He'd sit in her driveway every night thinking of when he'd run his tongue along every curve on her body.

Anger rolled off her and slammed into him.

"We were going to have a *night* until you played me and left me locked in my underwear in a hotel bathroom," she hissed, frustration, hurt, and despair rippling across her face. "I had to wait until a security guard came and let me out." She shuddered. "I was in my underwear. Did you even know who he was? What could have happened?"

Shame and guilt splintered him.

Yeah, he'd been the biggest cock on the planet.

He rubbed the back of his neck. "Not my finest moment. I'm sorry. In my defense, I confirmed he was gay. After I processed the jumper, I went back to make sure he'd let you out."

He'd been called out. Lionel, the attendant, had called him a dick, given him a lecture about leaving a woman in her underwear locked in a bathroom with tears in her eyes, and returned his money. He'd stomached the lecture, ate a shame sandwich, and chugged back a gallon of jerk.

She got straight into his face. "Let's stop this bullshit act you've got going of pretending to like me, pretending to care. We both know this is an act, so just stop." Her eyes dropped to his dick, digging painfully through denim, and her cheeks stained pink. "I mean your big head. Listen up. There will never be one night."

An act? She thinks walking around with a boner every time I'm near her is an act?

"What do you mean pretending to like you? I'm hard every time I'm around you. It's hard to be around you, Sophie, because *I'm* hard around you."

And I care.

"Just stop." She swatted at her eyes.

Shit.

Tears rarely affected him, but Sophie's tears made him want to pull her into his arms and stroke the back of her head until all the shitty hurt he'd inflicted would be gone.

For the fifteen hundredth time, he mentally decked himself with a right hook, dug his own grave and set himself on fire.

If he could turn back time to that night, he would, and it would have a way better ending. One where he wouldn't be the dickhead who'd left her humiliated. Instead, he'd give up the jumper and have her curled around his body.

"I hurt you, Sophie, and I'm sorry. It was a dick move, but I wanted you that night as much as you wanted me."

"Our time has passed," she countered, standing proud, blinking back tears. "Different rules this time. The game has changed, so when I win the bet, you'll leave me alone."

Nope.

She stared at him.

He stared back.

Sophie, being Sophie, startled him again.

"Since there will be nothing between us, you can stay in my spare room until one of us finds out who the militia is." At his surprise, she continued. "I'm only doing this because it will keep Titus up all night writing down different license numbers, and I won't have that."

She turned and got into the driver's seat. After repeatedly thumping the dashboard, her car spluttered to life.

Harlan jumped into his SUV and followed her, keeping his distance one lane over and three cars back. A black Jeep pulled in three cars behind Sophie in her lane and stuck close. Not one of his cars.

Harlan gripped the wheel. Tinted windows concealed the occupants. Sophie took a sharp left ahead. He breathed easy when the Jeep went straight past. He forced himself into gaps and took the turn at the last minute. Two minutes later, the Jeep tucked in behind Sophie again.

Harlan cursed under his breath and maneuvered behind the vehicle. Another Jeep pulled into position beside him to his left. Same tinted windows. Another Jeep pulled in beside him, to his right.

The hairs on the back of his neck lifted.

Cornered.

The bet was now a memory.

Keeping her alive and finding out who wanted her were the only things on his mind.

SEVEN

Around seven in the morning, Sophie padded into the kitchen, poured a coffee, and stared at her immaculate countertop. She gripped the counter and willed her aorta not to explode.

As soon as she put down a spoon or a fork, Harlan washed it and put it away. Her idea of bringing home a bucket of KFC with all the sides and sharing the deliciousness that was deep-fried chicken coated in secret herbs and spices had taken on a new meaning when Harlan removed the skin and chowed down on naked drumsticks and glasses of water while she kicked back with box wine. He'd then tidied with the prowess of a seventies sitcom mom. No leaving the plates in the sink until the morning on his shift.

At the supermarket he'd raised his eyebrows when she'd loaded up on Pringles, frozen meals for one, and had rummaged through the marked-down produce, meat, and bakery items. They'd had a stand-up fight at the checkout when he'd tried to pay for her groceries until she threatened to make a scene.

The experience of living with Harlan was as much fun as Ebola.

And then there was the kicker that walloped her heart like a pissed-off pony. Two days ago, he'd looked at her like he wanted to devour her. At Javier's Gym she'd seen a flash of admiration in Harlan's eyes when she'd had Williams in a chokehold. He even seemed genuinely sorry for being the jerk of the century. He'd looked at her with hunger and tenderness.

Now he looked at her as if she were diseased.

And it burned.

Like a deep, blistering scar.

The Jeeps scared the shit out of her—she wasn't afraid to admit it. Outmaneuvered in her little hatchback, she had no move to make. She had no idea what Harlan's play would have been if two of the trio hadn't peeled off, and she didn't understand why they had. Some sort of pissing competition? Letting one another know of their presence but not ready to make a move? She'd started her own investigation, but whoever was following her had a lot of money and resources, two things she didn't have. That didn't mean she'd be sitting around doing nothing.

An idea had wiggled into her brain and wouldn't leave.

Could this be payback for one of her father's cons?

Her fingers made circles on her temples.

Good old Dad.

The memory of the bony, parched hand of a farmer's wife in the throes of the death rattle, the smell of grief and disinfectant in the room. Sophie had bit the inside of her mouth to stop from gagging. The anguished man pleading that the prayer would work, and his wife wouldn't die of cancer, leaving him a widower with six children.

She closed her eyes as shame flooded her.

The horror that she hadn't figured it out earlier made her feel equal parts idiot, gullible, and humiliated. The hopelessness and rage that he'd used her, used vulnerable people for a quick buck burned her soul.

And there was another kicker. She'd adored her dad. He'd call her his princess—his reason for living and she'd bathe in his glow. She'd genuinely believed they were helping people, but they were fleecing them of their last quarters and dimes.

After he'd died, when she could finally look at his journals without sobbing, the horror of his deception sliced through her and kept slicing. She'd started cross-referencing the names in the journal to the places they'd visited. She'd bought a stack of cards and written "Sorry," and returned the amount he'd stolen, printing the name Josiah O'Connor.

It wouldn't be enough. It would *never* be enough, but she'd never stop trying to pay it all back.

Pongo squeezed his body through the dog door. She dropped to her knees and hugged his warm, wiggling body. His tail whipped the air like an out-of-control windshield wiper.

"Morning, baby boy."

She smiled when he burrowed deeper into her neck and gently whined.

"You know how much I love you, right?"

She stood and stretched aching muscles, sore from taking the jumper at Javier's gym. An army of knots had camped out on her spine and was holding it prisoner. She groaned, tensed, and turned to find Harlan staring at her.

The man must be part stealth.

Straight from the shower, his fingers stopped combing through damp hair. She wasn't even going to think of him naked in the shower, with droplets of water running down his torso, lathering his body in soapy circles.

She swallowed.

His gaze locked on the pink tank top covered in sleeping baby sloths with zzzz's in cartoon circles above their heads. His gaze clung to her torso, then dropped to matching pajama shorts.

He'd come dressed for the day. Denim stretched across his powerful thighs. A white T-shirt had replaced the seemingly endless stream of black shirts he usually wore. She'd wondered if Harlan had a factory somewhere that pumped out tight-fitting T-shirts that hugged every muscle—the fit so perfect and identical. Aviator sunglasses perched on his head, scuffed boots on his feet.

Normally, she dressed before exiting her bedroom, but after a restless sleep she needed caffeine flowing through her veins. There'd been no sound from her spare bedroom, so she'd assumed Harlan either slept or was doing workouts with a bar thingy that he'd hung from the ensuite doorframe.

She lifted her red and yellow polka-dotted Chiefs mug, and pain sliced through her shoulder.

"You doing all right?"

She stared up at him, not comprehending.

"Your shoulder. Your jumper landed a few good ones."

Because her brain wasn't yet soaked in the marvelousness of caffeine, she stood staring at him with all the intelligence of a sponge.

He walked the short distance between them.

"Let me."

She winced when his gentle fingers probed at a tender spot on her shoulder.

Yep, the knots were in for the long haul.

"I think it's better living life as a knot." She went to move away, but his enormous paw stilled on her shoulder.

"If you don't get them out now, they will turn into boulders." His fingers probed deeper into the protesting muscle. "Relax," he commanded.

"I'm okay with boulders." She wriggled to get away from his warm touch.

He swept her hair from her back over one shoulder, creating a wave of goose bumps that broke over her body.

She held her body as stiff as she could.

Tension swept into the room on a wave.

"You handled yourself well against your jumper."

She nodded.

His fingers were delicate yet powerful.

The paradox of the man equaled calculating Pi.

Rough, then unexpectedly gentle. Controlling, but protective.

"There were other men at the gym you could have taken."

Air trapped in her breastbone.

Were they talking in some kind of code? In a roundabout way was he referencing himself?

"Your legs wrapped around your jumper's neck. That hook to his jaw. Your arms strained to breaking point. Hot... apparently."

Apparently.

"Anyone stand out?" she asked, her breath now lodged hard in her throat.

His fingers flexed on her neck. "Nope."

No hesitation there.

She winced, partly from the comment and from his fingers that had dug out that knotted muscle into smoothness.

"Didn't mean to hurt you." He brushed his hand across her back, sweeping her hair from her shoulder.

"You can't hurt me."

Tension thickened until breathing became a challenge. His eyes, hotter than coal, pinned her. Like he wanted to devour her, right here and now. And just as quickly, he looked like he had mistaken her for a week-old burrito left in the sun. She let out a long breath.

This man wound her tighter and tighter until she thought she'd physically explode. No other man had made her feel this way. Admittedly, she could count her previous lovers on one hand, okay on three fingers. Until Harlan had bulldozed himself into her life, she'd decided one day she'd find a nice man, they'd have a nice marriage, have nice sex, maybe a couple of nice kids, and they'd grow old together, nicely.

Anger at herself for her inability to block him twisted inside her and morphed into frustration and fear that one of her father's victims was out for revenge.

She picked up her coffee cup, took a last gulp, and placed it back on the counter.

His mouth tightened, and his jaw clenched. He reached out to pick up her mug.

"Don't touch it!"

His hand froze mid-air.

Annoyance fizzed inside like a shaken can of soda. "I like my counter with a cup on it. I know when I come back home tonight, it's going to be waiting for me to rinse it out."

He drew in a breath and held it before he blew it out in a long exhale.

She put her hands on her hips. "I know I probably have food past its expiration date. I don't want everything sorted into the weird color-coded, height thing you've done. I know there are yogurt containers waiting to explode and withered carrots. I like magazines open to random pages. The remote under a cushion." She leaned in to him, ignoring the scent of soap, spicy deodorant, and man. "My house. My rules. What I don't like is having you here straightening things up. I like messy, it makes it a home. I like a home. I don't like a house."

Impatience washed across his face. "A house needs order."

"A home needs the stamp of the person living there."

The sun hit the cabinet in the corner, throwing prisms of rainbow on the polished wooden floor. "Take that cabinet." She tilted her head. "I could have gone to Ikea and nearly committed suicide putting it together. It would have been less work than renting a U-Haul and driving to Goodwill, then sanding through a million layers of paint to the beautiful wood beneath."

He blinked at her as if she now spoke in tongues.

"It gives the room a personal touch. Makes it a home. So do dishes in the sink. I didn't have that growing up, and I like having it now."

Dark brows drew together, his eyes appraising. "Where did you grow up?"

She blinked at the change in conversation.

"What?"

"Where did you grow up?"

"Everywhere. You?"

He scanned her. "Any place you stayed longer than usual?"

"Seriously?" She dragged a cloth across the spotless counter.

"And stop buying pine disinfectant. That's Titus's scent, and you're ruining it." She knew she sounded illogical, but she wouldn't explain how Titus's scent left her feeling warm and loved, but the harsh smell of disinfectant made her think of cramped bedrooms filled with grieving relatives and her father praying for a dying person to live.

He stared at her, waiting.

She blew out a breath. "I'm not unfamiliar with interrogation techniques, Harlan. If you want to ask me a question, ask me, but don't do it under the guise of *wanting* to know anything about me."

"I know you."

She stilled, her breath trying to burrow back into her lungs.

Did he know about her father and what he'd done?

"You tighten your ponytail when you're nervous. You rub the back of your neck when you're tired. You go through life hiding. You keep people at arm's length. There's PI Sophie who's got balls and there's Sophie Callaghan who guards her heart—the woman who'd give her last cent if someone needed it."

Sophie sucked in a breath.

A loud audible breath.

He advanced, his eyes soft.

"I'm guessing you can count on one hand the number of men in your life. You don't want to be attracted to me, but you are. And you *hate* being told what to do."

I don't know what to do with this.

She pressed her lips together to stop the bubble of emotion slipping up her throat and sliding out of her mouth into the room.

She turned her head and stared at her snow globe collection.

This complicated man confused her. One minute looking like he'd rather be chowing down on slugs, the next as if he'd glimpsed her soul.

"What are we doing here, Harlan?" A tiny tremble filtered through her voice.

Damn.

"Keeping you safe."

She pressed on the knot in her chest and kept to the facts. "Those men haven't been seen for two days," she said, emotional, tired, and wanting to be far, far away.

"Because I'm living here. They won't, knowing I'm here." He rubbed his hand across his chin, looking thoughtful before he headed to the fridge, opened the door, and popped the lid on one of his protein shakes. The scent of artificial banana filled the room.

"What do you mean you grew up everywhere?"

"I don't want to talk about my childhood," she said, the need for space gaining strength. "What about you, Harlan? Your parents. What made you want to be a bounty hunter? In what country did you do your training? Who was your best friend growing up? What's your favorite TV show?"

He took a long gulp and paused, wiping his mouth with the back of his hand. "This isn't about me."

They entered a stare-off.

God, the man was as stubborn as Pongo giving back a stolen treat.

"I give you something. You give me something."

She waited until he gave one sharp nod.

She stared at her couch with a *Soaps* magazine open to *Y and R* spoilers and concentrated on Victor Newman's face. "My father died. Before he did, we traveled a lot and traveled light. I was home-schooled, and we never had personal items. I have one photo of us taken on a beach when I was around seven."

Her peachy life in a nutshell.

Silence stretched between them.

"I gave, now it's your turn. What about your mom? What made you want to be a bounty hunter? What's your favorite color, TV show, and your star sign?"

He stared at her a beat before answering. "I've wanted to be a bounty hunter since I was a kid. Bringing in the bad guys. I wanted my own business. Never knew my father. I don't have a favorite color. I watch the news, sports, and *Deadliest Catch* if it's on and I'm around, and I have no idea what star sign I am."

"When's your birthday?" At his confused look, she blew out a breath. "So I can tell you your star sign so you can read the correct one in the morning."

His eyes sparkled, and his mouth twitched. "November sixth."

"Now you can read your Scorpio horoscope before flicking to sports and getting in an instant foul mood that the Raiders were voted suckiest NFL team *ever*. Again."

His eyes sparkled brighter.

Damn.

"I will have you, Sophie. For one night, you'll be mine and do exactly as I say."

She crossed her arms over her chest. "I believe we've had this conversation. As for losing myself to fit who you want me to be? Never."

The first time she'd lost herself to a powerful man, she hadn't realized it until he'd tossed her aside because she'd become *boring*.

The loss of dignity still shamed her.

The second time, she'd somehow slipped into what her lover expected, sliding deeper into him, until he walked away.

The third time, she'd realized what was happening, but she'd been so caught up in him, so caught up in the possibility of the relationship, she'd let him dictate. She'd fallen hard. He'd ended the relationship when she wouldn't give up her profession. Without a backward glance, he'd walked away, ripping out her heart and throwing it to the wolves.

After a long night of soul-searching, Two-Buck Chuck, and tears, she'd come to the cold conclusion that, in reaching for a connection, she'd been afraid that the too-tall, too-plain woman wouldn't be enough, so she changed to who they thought she should be.

"Being dominated isn't like that."

She stared at up him. "It *is* like that."

His eyes roamed over her face, then dropped to her chest, lingering on her breasts, which hardened under his hungry gaze.

"Do you wear that to bed every night?"

She looked down at her pajamas.

Hello. Sleepy sloths I love you...

"What?"

"Did you wear that last night?" His voice sounded strained.

"Yes."

"Did you sleep well?" He edged closer.

Oxygen was being sucked from the room.

She clamped her arms across her chest, trying to hide tight, aching nipples.

"It took me a while... but I got there," she murmured. "You?"

"Straight out." He stared at the coffee machine as if it were art.

"Right." She stepped back and turned away.

"I've got a full load today. I'm meeting a potential partner at my office. I'll meet you at Titus's."

The blood dropped from her head to her feet in a long roller coaster swoop.

"Small, blond submissive partner?" Her throat tightened with each word.

He shrugged.

It shouldn't bother her, but it stung.

She tried to steer the conversation away from complicated feelings swarming in her head. "You never said what happened to your mom."

He stared at her a long time before answering. "Died when I was seven. Had her heart broken and her money stolen by a con-man preacher who promised to cure the cancer eating her."

The hatred on his face left her with no doubt what he'd do if he came across the preacher again.

Oh my God.

A sickening thought forced bile up her throat.

"Sophie?"

Harlan's voice came from another era.

"I just remembered an appointment." She pushed her trembling hands to her hair. "I've got to go."

She had an appointment. With her toilet. She barely made it to the bathroom in time.

After emptying her stomach of its contents, she stood at the sink, her body in a full tremble.

"Damn you," she whispered. "Why couldn't you have been a regular dad?" She wiped her hand across her face.

"Sophie, I'm going. Are you okay?" Harlan spoke from outside the door, concern in his voice.

"I'm fine," she managed, sounding relatively normal.

She cleaned herself up and brushed her teeth. She opened the bathroom door to an empty house.

She knew when Harlan had left. His presence filled the tiny space when he was there. She changed into her workday uniform, then stepped into her walk-in closet. On the top shelf, behind boxes and paperwork, she pulled on a sliver of wood built into the wall which slid out, taking the side of the wall with it. She spun the dials on the safe until the door clicked, then took out her father's journal. She forced herself to read each line, her hands trembling, looking for the name Franco.

Nothing.

But some entries showed only initials. Pages and pages of initials.

She slid the journal back into the safe and carefully reconstructed the scene. She made it back to the kitchen and drank a tall glass of water.

Her phone vibrated on the counter where she'd left it last night.

She grabbed it and headed toward the door, swiping the screen, ignoring the quiver in her fingers. The first of three texts was from Gemma.

GEMMA: *Hey Gal Pal, can you work the 10 to 4 tonight? Candy's grandmother has died for the fifth time. Don't worry about Pipe, he's a big teddy bear underneath.*

"Yeah, the Chucky of teddy bears," she murmured at the screen.

The second text was from her client, Beth. She'd emailed the information she had on her missing mother, and she was looking forward to working with her.

The last text was from Annie.

ANNIE: *Girlfriend, Gem and I are having a snack and wine-fueled evening tomorrow night where we will be talking male appendages, and all things girly. Bring wine, snacks, and your insanely long legs. Here's my address.*

Sophie worried the inside of her cheek with her teeth. Her budget wouldn't stretch to expensive snacks and wine after she'd cooked tonight's dinner *and* sent fifty dollars to Jenny Mannering from Winter Haven, Florida. But that wasn't totally it. She envied Gemma and Annie their easy friendship and the way they talked about themselves and their pasts. She knew she was guarded and tried hard to be breezy, but her father had taught her to deflect personal questions until it became second nature.

Heat surged into her face, thinking about a conversation on vibrators where she couldn't contribute a single snippet.

She couldn't exactly tell them the truth.

There's a hot bounty hunter named Harlan living under my roof, the man used to look at me like I'm his favorite snack and he's a death row inmate. Now he looks at me like I'm some half-eaten burrito he found on a bus and he's starving, and it's my fault.

Another interesting snippet. My father was a two-bit con artist preacher. Fun fact. Harlan's mom lost everything to a con-artist preacher.

Her fingers slid across the glass.

SOPHIE: *Sorry, I'm busy tomorrow night, but I'd love to come another night.*

A little white lie hurt no one.

Harlan would despise her if he found out. Flat-out hate her. The raw emotion on his face didn't look like it had diminished in the years since his mom had died.

A queasy sensation burrowed into her stomach lining.

With Harlan elsewhere, she'd have to ditch the hot Viking who often tailed her. If she played her cards right and her car cooperated, she could get to the park and retrieve her equipment. Then she could get rid of Harlan before he got it firmly in his head that she'd be his for one night, then tossed aside like a candy wrapper.

Never happening.

SOPHIE SAT IN TRAFFIC, one foot on the accelerator, the other on the brake, her car protesting with a bone-shaking rattle. She sent a prayer upward to any mechanics in heaven, hanging around, discussing crankshafts.

The Viking had left his shift twenty minutes ago and the hot Black dude had pulled in behind her.

Miss Sub sashayed into her head. She'd arrive at Harlan's office in a crisp white business suit, a leather bag swinging from her gym-honed shoulders. Slender and petite, her straight, long blond hair would be in a high ponytail, bouncing against her toned shoulders. Six-inch heels on her feet. Large sunglasses shading her big blue eyes.

A UPS van stopped unexpectedly beside her. A harassed, brown-clothed driver dove out the door clutching a box, and ran into a building.

Sophie didn't delay. Her foot left the brake, and her protesting car shot forward. She found a gap in the traffic and waved her thanks to the cars behind her. She took a left, another left, and ducked into an underground parking lot. She drove down three floors and parked between two cars in the long-term parking section and listened for a screech of tires.

Nothing.

She checked her phone.

Damn.

She had a burning, irrational need to catch a glimpse of Harlan's latest, but she'd need to hurry if she was going to retrieve her equipment and get dinner prepared in time. Titus stuck to a schedule that became stricter as Sally deteriorated. Thrown off routine, Sally became agitated and distressed, which seemed to make her condition worse.

Sophie pulled a hoodie from the backseat of her car and buried her face into the side of the fabric. She exited through a gray door and blinked back sunlight. She kept her head down and wound through streets toward Harlan's office. Her hunch had paid off. His black Range Rover was parked on the street.

She walked to a park across from the building, where a large food truck was setting up. The scent of baked chicken, ham, and mashed potatoes and gravy had her stomach rumbling.

A man adjusted a blackboard showing a menu with the choice of a ham or chicken and mash and gravy and mixed vegetables followed by fruit and custard. A hairdresser would be on hand for anyone wanting a trim, which seemed odd for a food truck.

She briefly wondered about how the interview with Miss Sub was going. Would she be on her knees, head bowed, waiting for his command? Would she be on his desk, her skirt pulled over her hips, gasping when he rammed home?

Sophie dug her hands deeper into the hoodie.

Women with floaty dresses and spiky summer sandals that would have Annie sighing drifted past in a pack of fresh scent. Mothers hummed with efficient strides, dragging their protesting children toward stores with the bribe of a fast food lunch, keeping the gripes to scowls.

Sophie swiped her finger across the screen of her phone and read an incoming text.

Nice maneuver. Give me your address before Harlan has my balls.

Sophie's fingers flew across the screen.

Sophie: *Keep your balls. Harlan doesn't need to know. I'm on a case.*

She stood as Harlan stepped out of his building and started toward the park with determined strides, no blond attached to his arm. A group of admiring women poofed their hair; two turned on their heels, dazzling smiles on their faces.

Harlan didn't glance their way.

Crap.

Had he finished his *meeting* with the small sub? Is that why he was all loose-limbed and with a smile on his face, because he'd eaten?

Ugh.

She turned her face farther into her sweatshirt, trying to rid herself of the image that flashed into her mind of Harlan with his head between a woman's legs.

As stupid as it was, she wanted to throw something at him. A small truck would do.

Harlan headed toward the food truck, a large canvas bag in his hand.

A panty-dropping grin transformed his face.

Probably got panties stuffed into his pockets.

She managed not to choke.

Harlan slapped the menu guy on the shoulder and was rewarded with a back-clapping man hug.

People started arriving. They stood patiently in line waiting their turn.

Sophie stared at the line of people taking their plate of food with thanks. No money was exchanging hands. This was a soup kitchen. She looked closer. A soup kitchen Harlan was, at the very least, familiar with, judging by the way people shook his hand and thanked him. Sophie's heart hitched.

Harlan helped an elderly man, shuffling forward, his back bent with arthritis, his feet visible through his shoes. The man looked like he might have been good friends with Moses.

"Clarence, you'll lose your feet in those shoes. I know you said you didn't need them, but I found an old pair at the back of my wardrobe. Size eight."

The old man looked down at Harlan's feet, then down at his.

"You ain't taking a size eight, Mr. Harlan. Yous has to be at least a ten, maybe eleven."

Harlan shrugged. "They've been there for a while."

The man looked up at Harlan, his face a roadmap of age. "I don't want no handouts. I'm getting on my feet any day now."

Harlan's eyes softened. "I know you are. I want your feet to make it."

The man took the canvas bag from Harlan, a shoebox sticking out the top.

Harlan nodded. "You've got my number, right?"

The old man nodded.

"You need anything, anytime. Call me."

The old man nodded. "I'll do that, Mr. Harlan. I'll do that."

He smiled. "You getting a trim, Clarence?"

The old man ran his hand across his head. "I think I will take a trim. Make sure I'm looking my best for when Miss Devine calls."

Harlan squeezed his shoulder.

"If you could have a word to young DeMilo." Clarence gestured with his head to where a young boy who looked no older than twelve shuffled his feet and looked longingly toward the van. "His mom's on a bender. My guess is he's feeding his sister before feeding himself. He's skin and bone."

"Leave it with me."

"You're a good man, Mr. Harlan." The man looked down at the bag, then wiped his hand across his eyes.

Harlan clapped him on the back. "Don't let anyone know, Clarence, it'll blow my cred."

Harlan's head jerked, then swiveled left, then right, scanning. He eventually turned away.

Sophie stood, her heart hammering in her chest, and walked away, head bowed. At the edge of the park, she turned to see Harlan sitting next to DeMilo, the boy inhaling a plate of food.

"Wow," she breathed out with a wobbly sigh. She pressed the

image of Harlan on a new, fresh memory where she wrapped it in delicate parchment and placed it on a shelf in her heart.

She walked toward the underground garage, taking a different route. Alert and vigilant but deep in thought. Something she couldn't quite define pierced her deeply, making her insides unsteady.

She'd researched Harlan. He'd been a highly regarded and successful bounty hunter before opening Franco Security as a one-man band. According to the company bio on the web, the company had grown to fifteen highly skilled operatives trained in personal and business security, espionage, and bounty hunting. Harlan had trained extensively with operatives overseas, but nothing personal about where he'd grown up. No siblings. No photos.

He'd said there was Sophie the PI and another Sophie, and in a way he was right. But there was way more to Harlan Franco than *he* let on. Her fingers drummed on the steering wheel.

Talk about the whole pot-kettle thing, but I wouldn't mind finding out about this side of Harlan.

"The man has more layers than a pickled onion," she murmured.

If the equipment stayed a little longer at the playground, it wouldn't be hurting anyone. She could extend the bet while she explored *this* side of Harlan that she wanted to know.

Purely for professional reasons.

After exiting the garage, she'd taken care of the shopping for dinner, sticking to the busiest stores she could find. As far as she could tell, there'd been no tails.

She'd taken the freeway home, arriving to find Harlan's Range Rover in her driveway. The smoldering Black dude, the hot Viking, and the man of the hour stood in a group, not hugging, but looking like they wanted to rip apart something. As she pulled in behind Harlan, three pairs of pissed-off eyes swung in her direction.

Guess the person they want to rip apart is me.

EIGHT

Sophie plastered on a perfected sunny smile that made her cheeks ache and exited the car.

"Howdy folks." Key in hand, she walked to her front door.

At the scowl on Harlan's face, she unwrapped the memory of the man at the soup kitchen and let it envelop her, before she carefully stored it away and took a satisfying breath.

"Why the hell did you ditch Zeb?"

"Oh, is that the hottie's name?" She turned and shot Zeb a sunny smile. "Nice to finally meet you."

Zeb grinned.

Harlan practically threw open her front door before she'd turned the handle.

"Why'd you ditch Zeb?" His voice could shred steel. He punched in her security code with extra venom.

"Because..." She lifted her chin.

"Because?" A cold glint transformed his eyes to cyborg blue.

"Because you can't keep ordering me around and expecting me to do what you want." Sophie swept past him into her kitchen, heaving plastic shopping bags onto the neat-as-a-pin counter. "I wasn't tailed.

I checked. I don't need you in my life twenty-four-seven. I am a trained private detective. I'm not a client."

She eyed the sparkly sink that could double as a mirror. Towels were folded on the countertop ready to be distributed into respective drawers. Mail sat in tidy stacks sorted by content.

Sophie sighed and flicked the top utility bill onto the counter.

A tick worried his left eye.

"Where'd you go?"

"Out and about." She leaned against the fridge door, a magnet in the shape of a dog digging into her back. "Where were you?"

"In the office. Working lunch."

"Really? You didn't leave your office. Just worked through?"

Nothing moved on his face.

"Yep."

I wonder if he had a meeting at all.

He advanced until their breaths clashed.

"You can't ditch the detail. This is about—"

She pushed up higher on her feet until they were impossibly close, her temperature rising.

"Fuck, Sophie, you've got to listen to me." Harlan swept his hand through his messy hair, making it messier and sexier. "I'm out this afternoon. *Please* don't ditch the detail."

"Is it Thor?"

Confused eyes cut to hers. "Thor?"

"Yeah, Thor. The hot, blond Viking he-man."

He rubbed his chin. "I assume you're talking about Israel?"

"I don't know his name, but don't send him."

"Why?"

"He's distracting," she lied.

He stood there a moment, looking like he wanted to hog-tie her.

"I'm out. I'll see you tonight," he said.

After Harlan closed the door behind him, Sophie prepared the lamb and vegetables for tonight, then set the timer on the oven. When she walked back into the kitchen, rosemary, garlic, and her secret herb ingredient, sage, would fill the room, and the roast would fall off the bone.

"Time to get to work, Pong. I need the distraction and the money."

Pongo waddled along beside her to her desk. She opened a manila folder and reread her case notes, looking for something she'd missed.

Suzie West, also known as "Slow-Screw Suzie," had hit the jackpot when she'd met her husband-to-be while working as a lap dancer in Vegas. A VP for a large accounting firm, Jim West had fallen hard for Suzie and treated his new wife like a queen.

Beth had been born a year after leaving Vegas, and Suzie had packed a bag and walked out on her husband and daughter six months later. In a note, later verified as authentic, she'd asked to be left alone. Jim, Beth's heartbroken father, tried to do his best for his daughter, but he became a shell of a man who passed when Beth turned eighteen. Now twenty-five, Beth was searching for her mother.

So far, no one by the name of Suzie West née Jones with a matching birth date had been registered as dead in the state of Colorado. She'd sent out requests with the woman's birth date to other states. Results were trickling in, none of them a hit so far. She was still contacting Suzie's known friends and family. So far, nothing. This wasn't going to be a straightforward case, and Sophie's gut feeling told her she might not be delivering the good news her client hoped for.

———

SOPHIE STOOD IN A LARGE, warm, messy room. Books, some upside down, were crammed into a bookcase. Magazines crowded a table. A multitude of framed photos dotting the walls showed a couple with their arms entwined, laughing.

Sunlight poured through the window and captured what looked

like an art project of stained glass, sending spears of green, orange, and pink colliding in a waterfall of color down the opposite white wall. Sophie's socked feet scrunched on the faded beige carpet.

Love and memories filled the room. She could almost taste the joy of Christmas Day, the dried-out turkey on Thanksgiving, and the laughter that gravy would fix it all. The sadness that Beth didn't have a mother around to share the joy of her first child. The room was wrapped in the fabric of family.

Something pulled at Sophie's heart. A twinge that if things had been different, if her father's cons had been found out sooner, they would have stayed in one place, and she could have had a little slice of this pie.

Don't let anyone in, Buttercup.

Her father's words floated unwanted into her head, and she pushed them straight out.

Beth walked into the room, wiping her hands down leggings. "I thought she'd never go down. I've been up since four trying to figure out why she won't stop crying." She smiled uneasily. "I think if you can survive leaky boobs, evacuated body fluids, and not go insane, it must get easier, right?"

Sophie stared at Beth, having no words. The whole female dynamic was still lost on her. Beth stood in front of her, her dark eyes smiling, hair ratty in a messy bun, T-shirt over black leggings, purple crescents under her eyes. She looked back into the room she'd walked from. The lines melted from her eyes.

"She's the reason I wanted to find out what happened to my mom. Now that my daughter's in my life, I feel like there's this box in my past that isn't checked off, and I get fixated on it." She hugged her torso.

"I know," Sophie said, a wry smile touching her lips.

Beth's head tilted to the side, observing Sophie. "Yeah, I think you do."

A clock somewhere in the house counted down time.

Beth waved her to sit.

Sophie sank onto a buttery, worn couch.

Beth starting folding laundry, her face wistful. "It wasn't the big picture stuff I missed, I don't think. It was the little things. Mother and daughter day at school. Poor Dad, he sat at the back, red faced, trying to fit in. I envied girls having a mom around to tell them that putting Vaseline on your face to make it sparkly, which you'd read in a magazine, probably didn't mean half an inch worth. Or the fun fact it's water-resistant. Not what you're going after on a first date."

"Handing your father a note from your PE teacher that you need a bra?" Sophie pressed her hands to her cheeks. "My father looked like he'd rather have a close-up and personal with Satan than try and pick out a bra." She smiled. "Luckily, a woman in Macys spotted me. The next thing I knew, I'd been ushered into a cubicle. She helped me pick out a selection. She patted my shoulder, hugged me. She smelled of rose petals."

Beth's face melted. "Yeah, it's the little things. Like your mom knowing what brand of pad and tampon to get without having to write specific instructions for your dad, which is torture no teen should have to go through."

"Or knowing not to flush five tampons when you can't figure out that stupid 'how to insert them' diagram, then tell your father you'd blocked the toilet."

Beth laughed. "Or what everyone else is wearing in school. The cool shoes or the specific brand of jeans. By the time I got them the trend had shifted and yet again I rocked the has-been look."

Sophie smiled, lost in a watercolor memory. "Or having something girly on your birthday. Something pretty for your hair or a strawberry lip gloss instead of a practical book on growing herbs." Sophie grinned. "Call me the Cilantro Queen. I can grow that sucker anywhere."

Beth put her hand over her mouth, her eyes dancing. She walked to an iPad and stroked her finger across the glass, showing a beaming older couple holding a baby swaddled in a blue blanket.

"My husband was raised by his grandparents, who aren't around anymore. His parents have been in and out of rehab for years and have no interest in getting clean. My dad's gone... that's why I'm doing this. If anything happened to me, I want Hannah to have a family tree. Some roots."

Sophie nodded, and when Beth didn't continue, she carefully prodded. "But there's more, isn't there?"

Sophie startled at the raw emotion that twisted Beth's features before she ironed them flat.

"If she's still alive, I want to know why." Beth paused, her voice quivering.

An uncomfortable knot tightened in Sophie's chest. Her fingers went to rub the ache away.

Beth cocked her head. "You think you'll have this one day?"

Sophie automatically shook her head and pressed a manufactured smile onto her face.

That would mean letting someone in and allowing him to see the real me.

Beth stared out the window. "I couldn't imagine not having Hannah in my life. I could never up and leave her. I know this sounds weird, but I often wondered if my mom left because of me. It's kind of haunted me. My dad never got over my mom leaving. He always said he hit the Vegas jackpot when Suzie came into his life." She pushed a long strand of dark hair behind her ear. "He never moved on. I kind of always thought it was my fault."

Beth stretched. Her daughter wailed, and on cue, a stain formed on her shirt. She hurried from the room and returned with her daughter, whose mouth turned toward her mom's chest.

"Boobs are a go." Beth settled in a rocking chair and started feeding her daughter, rocking back and forth, humming quietly. A small fist rested on her mother's breast as if in triumph. Dark eyes held her mother's, her face almost fierce until her little features softened as her belly filled.

Beth looked at Sophie and smiled. and she realized with a start she'd been staring.

"I've got a bit to go on." Sophie gathered up the files, her face hot, and placed the papers in a folder.

Beth sang softly to her daughter.

Both mother and daughter looked entranced.

Wistfulness and longing filtered through her in a warm wash.

Did my mom sing Hush Little Baby to me?

She shrugged off the loneliness that swirled around her like a mist.

"I'll be in contact in the next few days and let you know what I find." Sophie hoisted her bag higher on her shoulder.

Beth looked up. Hannah's chubby fingers wrapped around her mother's thumb. "I know you need a retainer up front. I've saved two hundred dollars, which is in my purse. It's on the kitchen counter if you could bring it over."

Two hundred would stock her freezer with some legs of lamb, Titus's favorite expensive stinky cheese, and Sally's favorite triple-churned, salted caramel ice cream and pay back another person from her father's list. Sophie eyed the stack of bills on the counter that rivaled her own and the nearly empty box of generic-brand diapers sitting under a changing table.

"Don't worry about the retainer, I'm good," she lied. "I'll send you the bill later."

Beth closed her eyes, and when she opened them, they glistened. "Thank you," she whispered.

Sophie cleared her throat. "I'll do everything in my power to find out what happened to your mom."

"I know, and thank you."

HARLAN WIPED HIS PLATE CLEAN.

Sophie could *cook*.

The lamb had been tender, the potatoes with crispy skins and fluffy innards. Carrots that didn't make him want to barf as they usually did. Buttery corn sweeter than he'd ever tasted. Earlier he'd quietly gone through Titus's cupboards and noted the empty shelves. Groceries would be delivered tomorrow.

The four of them sat at a small table which fitted them snugly. Sophie's warm thigh pressed against his. A thick white tablecloth with square creases covered aged wood. A framed black-and-white photo of teenaged Titus and Sally, their cheeks pressed together, laughing at something off-camera, dominated the wall. A polished mahogany cabinet that held the same china as on the table sat underneath the photo.

With a smile and a twinkle in his eye, Titus turned out to be a master interrogator. He'd hire the bastard tomorrow. Harlan had deflected questions about his youth and his parents. He'd then tried to steer the conversation to neutral topics, to no avail.

Sally, who called Harlan by the name of Pat, was convinced he was her long-lost cousin who'd come for a visit but had neglected to bring his sister Sherry. Sally had pressed her powdery cheek to his, reminiscing about the time they'd visited Yosemite and he'd eaten a whole container of Cool Whip. The next minute, she'd shrunk from him, tears in her silver eyes. Titus had excused himself and guided her out of the room, a nod in Harlan's direction. Getting old blew, but getting older and not having a clue who you were sucked.

Sophie excused herself to clean the dishes and headed into the kitchen. Harlan checked his watch. In another forty minutes Sophie would head to Pipe's, leaving him to search her place. Then he had a Zoom with Petrov, followed by a surveillance job with Arabella. He had depressingly little in the way of facts to tell Petrov, except that Sophie *was* being followed, and he genuinely felt in his gut that they meant to do her harm. Zeb still ran angles on her father. All they had was a small string of people scattered around the country who'd come forward after the prayer for cash failed. They'd stayed on the move and the law couldn't touch O'Connor—who didn't promise rain, cures, or finding true love. O'Connor took donations rather than charge for his services—even if they had caught up to them. Prayer was what it was, the power of hope.

Sophie's terrible singing cut through his thoughts.

How she'd grown up to be the warm, thoughtful, and kind woman when she was raised by a fucker like O'Connor intrigued him. No, it flat-out fucking amazed him.

Sure, Sophie kept her guard up—with her upbringing it wasn't surprising—but he'd made inroads with her, gained an inch of ground, and he wasn't giving it back. He wanted to know Sophie, the real Sophie, with a vulnerability about her he wanted to protect. Not the one who walked out of her door in the morning with balls bigger than Atlanta.

Titus tapped him on the shoulder.

"What are your intentions with Sophie?"

Harlan bit back a grin. Titus had to be closing in on his nineties. His face was a roadmap, worn but proud. Tonight he stood puffed up like a dad on prom night, releasing his virgin daughter to the quarterback with a pocket stuffed with condoms.

"There's stuff going down with her. I'm keeping her safe until the threat has been dealt with."

Titus tapped him on the chest. "She comes across as hard, but she's not. Don't break her. If you don't want her, leave her for a man who does. A man who will cherish every breath she takes."

Harlan's hands formed into involuntary fists.

Titus chuckled. "I'm guessing you don't like the thought of Sophie with another man."

"About as much as I liked living in a group home in Compton," he muttered.

The idea of another man looking at her all sleepy and soft in the morning, his hand in hers, his tongue in her mouth.

I'll snap the fucker's head off.

Titus said in a quiet voice, "If you had someone like Sophie in your life, you'd be thanking the stars every day. Like I do. She's a wonderful woman. You'll be a fool to let her go." Titus patted

Harlan's hand. He'd had the "touch her and you die," speech and now they were back to being friends.

Sophie walked into the room, wiping her hands down her standard uniform of jeans and polo. She sat across from him and started humming along to a scratched Sinatra record on an ancient turntable. Her eyes sparkled.

"Did you know, Miss Sophie, that Harlan grew up in Compton?"

"Where?" she said in a verse of 'Fly me to the Moon'. She took a sip of wine. Her tongue snaked out and licked a drop at the corner of her mouth.

"*Compton*," Titus said, as if this would mean something.

A soft light from a lamp highlighted chocolate and caramel strands in her hair. "Is it nice?"

Harlan bit back a fake laugh. He'd gone from a small town outside of the Catskills, to his aunt's place in LA when his mom died, then to a group home in Compton where you either grew up fast or you didn't grow up at all. He got smart, had a great homeroom teacher, Mrs. Veliscek, who sat with him after school, helping him improve his grades and who'd applied to Stamford Brook College on a full scholarship for the underprivileged.

"It's a neighborhood that makes or breaks you." He paused. "Was there a place in Cali you liked?"

She shrugged. "I've never been. My father had a thing about California. He never said why."

Whoa.

He kept his face neutral while his mind pounced on the fact O'Connor had never been to California.

"What do you mean, a neighborhood that breaks you?" Her large dark eyes were trained on him. Assessing eyes he could drown in.

"Gangs, drugs. Your skin color dictated which side you ran. Either you joined the flow of salmon to the slaughter or you got out. I got out."

Titus excused himself and said he'd be back in a minute.

Harlan looked up to find Sophie studying him.

"Who is Miss Devine to Clarence?" she asked in a quiet voice.

A cold boulder dropped heavily in his stomach. Only the brotherhood brothers knew about his soup kitchen and it was deeply personal and important to him it stayed that way.

He'd done a complete scan of the park and hadn't clocked her.

She was good. Exceptionally good.

"It's personal."

She held his gaze and nodded.

"Miss Devine died ten years ago," he said finally. "When she died, Clarence couldn't go back to the house they'd shared for forty-six years. He's drifted ever since. In his mind, Miss Devine is going to come back, and he's going to be ready."

"That's heartbreaking and beautiful," she said more to herself than to him, some sort of emotion moving across her beautiful face.

The real soft-centered Sophie stared at him.

Gorgeous.

He held his breath, wanting to hold the moment for as long as he could.

"How do you figure that?"

"That he so loved Miss Devine that he can't move on is heartbreaking. That he found his soul mate is beautiful," she said, her dark brown eyes misty.

"Do you want that?" he asked quietly, hearing his heartbeat in his head.

She shrugged.

He stood, something unpleasant stabbing him in the gut.

"Are you about ready to go?"

Titus shuffled in and hugged Sophie, his eyes on Harlan. "Keep her safe."

"That's the plan."

Titus released Sophie and the old man's hands grasped his, the bones barely covered by his skin. "Could use some company when the fishing channel's running. I'll crack some of the good stuff."

Harlan nodded without committing.

Harlan held Sophie back at the front door, ignoring her sharp intake of breath, and scanned the area. Satisfied, he grabbed her hand, shielding her with his body, and he tucked her into his side, ignoring her scent, her curves, how well she fit under his chin. Women usually reached his shoulder wearing heels. Having Sophie tucked completely into him, plastered to him, felt good.

Really good.

Too good.

She moved forward. His fingers flexed to deactivate the alarm, but wanting to avoid a ten-minute fight out in the open, he relented.

Sophie threw her purse on the dining table along with her keys. With deliberate slowness, he hooked her keys on the key rack he'd screwed into her wall.

Harlan counted to twenty when Sophie stiffened beside him, unhooked the keys, and threw them in a fruit bowl next to a dying lemon and a liver-spotted banana.

His blood pressure spiked, but he said nothing. He walked to his makeshift bedroom and sat on the rainbow quilt. He pulled his phone from his pocket. No update from Zeb, but he sent his 2IC a questioning text about Sophie being at the soup kitchen.

Harlan headed to the empty living room, hit the remote, and started channel-surfing. Pongo landed by his side and then crawled on his lap. He'd given up arguing. He'd move the dog out of his lap, but it would make no difference. If history played out, the dog would sidle back up. If he moved him again he'd be rewarded by a fart that could be used as a nerve agent.

Sophie walked into the room adjusting an earring. His mouth watered at her long legs in sheer black stockings. She had on a jacket that came to her knees. The flat boots on her feet somehow made her hotter. Her hair pulled back. No makeup. Stunning.

The thought of the patrons at Pipe's gawking at her fused his back molars. He knew Pipe wouldn't let a hand land on her. He'd seen Sophie in action and knew she could handle herself.

His cock strained against thick denim. There should be a hole burrowed into his jeans by now. He should put in a claim for blue balls on his insurance. Every time Sophie walked into the room, his brain dropped into a coma, leaving his cock in charge, and that only had a one-way thought pattern.

She looked at his arm flung around her dog's neck, and her face softened.

Damn, it would be nice to have her look at him that way more often.

At the knock on the door, he went to stand, but Sophie moved to the door, checked the peephole, and then opened the door with a sigh.

"Hey Zeb," she said when his 2IC walked into the room. "This isn't necessary." She looked like she wanted to rip off Harlan's head and shrink-wrap it.

Zeb squeezed her shoulder and walked toward him. "Looking domestic there, Harlan. Is that *Happy Days*?" A smile lit his face. "Gotta say man, it suits."

"Fuck off." Harlan shot off the couch, Pongo in his arms. He resettled the dog back on the couch with a pat to his head.

He didn't do cozy, but fuck it felt kind of good kicking back with her dog, knowing Sophie was safe.

Sophie and Zeb walked out the door. Sophie without a backward glance in his direction. Zeb shot him a grin. The door closed with a click.

Two hours later, he'd searched every part of her small house.

Nothing.

An hour after that, he sat in his office in Denver after a short, static-filled phone call with Petrov, who was in Lithuania checking up on a problem with a shipping route.

Petrov had told Harlan that he wanted him to check in with Babic, as communication was going to be difficult. If an emergency came up, Babic had ways of contacting him. Ways Petrov wasn't willing to share. Harlan had expressed concern, but Petrov was insistent and reminded him firmly that as the client he issued the instructions. The call ended, and Harlan sat staring at the wall, unable to shake the feeling that something was off, but he couldn't figure out what it was.

Harlan's phone pinged.

Tonight he and Arabella were playing a couple who'd be sitting in a darkened booth in a bar filming a man.

He closed his eyes, and Sophie drifted into his head. Her sparkly smile. Her hand on her hip, eyes shooting daggers in his direction. In the morning, all sleepy, soft, and cute.

Jesus, it had happened again. Sophie had wandered into his thoughts, plonked her sweet butt down, and smiled at him.

He had to get his game on and get her out of his head.

There was too much riding on tonight to let anything or anyone get in the way of his work, including one luscious, tempting, and giant pain in his ass, Sophie Callaghan.

NINE

"I may have died and gone to heaven."

Sophie turned at Annie's whisper.

Zeb lounged against the entrance to the bar. He gave Sophie a slight chin raise, his eyebrows hitting his hairline when his gaze slid down the length of her. She blushed and pulled on her skirt. Zeb's gaze drifted around the room before locking on Annie.

"He's with me." Sophie turned to Annie, rolling her shoulders, a ripple of knots moving with them. Where were Harlan's fingers when she needed them? She grabbed her tray.

Scrap that.

"So... that long lick of chocolate over there is your man?"

"No." She turned to Annie, beer sloshing over the sides of a couple of glasses. "I don't have a man."

Annie's head swung between her and Zeb.

"He's my ride," she clarified, her face getting hotter. "But he's... ah... half an hour early."

"Something wrong with your car?" Gemma arrived at her side and rapid-fired off her orders to Cope. "I can give you a lift. You're not that much out of my way."

She smiled at Gemma. It was a forty-minute round trip out of her way. The engine needed more persuasion to start lately, but it relented, eventually. "Thanks, I've got it covered."

He's here because there were dudes trailing me, and I have a badass bounty hunter whose only concern for me is that I'll get whacked, and he'll feel guilty if he did nothing about it.

Annie's narrowed gaze zoned in on Sophie, who squirmed under the intensity. "Wait. Holy hotness over there is your ride, but he's not your man?"

Gemma's golden eyes got wider, and she opened her mouth. Her gaze slid to Zeb. She'd rather make a voodoo doll of herself and stick pins in tender places than explain her situation.

She'd phoned Titus earlier to check in on him and Sally. All he'd talked about was how wonderful Harlan was and did she think he'd come over and maybe catch a game with him. Her heart went out to him. Titus would be so disappointed when this was over, and Harlan stopped showing up.

At Annie's skeptical look, she turned away and headed back into the bar.

The pool table area had been busy until midnight, but now only a few tables were active.

"Hey, Sophie."

She jumped when her name was said in a soft purr.

"Hey, Dug."

Dug leaned against a pool table, a warm smile on his face, intense dark eyes trained on her. Tonight, he didn't have a mostly naked girl draped over him. Over six-foot, with dark brown messy hair, a killer smile, and heart-stopping eyes. Tall, ripped, with a body made for sin, the man oozed sex.

From the moment he stepped into the bar until he left, whenever she turned around, his eyes would be on her.

Supposedly, Dug had earned the nickname when he'd sat back while two girls fought over him, the winner digging a hole and burying the other woman up to her neck. Considering he came dressed in layers of girls, Sophie figured there must be holes all around Denver.

"What are you up to after your shift?" Dug lounged at the pool table, one muscled thigh resting against the pocked wood.

"I'm going home."

"Want to get breakfast?"

"Thanks, but I think I'll go home and face-plant on my bed."

A panty-melting smile that rendered her mute for a second spread across his face. "I could help you with that." His dark eyes sparkled.

She turned her head, embarrassed. Why did this man scramble her? Why did he render her as intelligent as a wet sock?

Zeb materialized next to her.

"Okay?" he asked, his light-blue eyes scanning her. He jolted when they trained on Dug. Surprise flitted across his face before it was gone.

Dug straightened off the table, chest out, and the two men stepped toward each other.

"A word," Zeb said cryptically before walking away. Dug followed and a low-toned discussion occurred—obviously heated by the hands on hips of both men.

Well, that's weird.

Dug arrived back at her side. A scowl the size of Scandinavia marred his forehead.

"Do you two know each other?" Her head swung between Zeb and Dug.

"A case of mistaken identity, that's all." Dug's warm eyes hit hers, but his body was tense.

She studied him again for a beat. No matter how many times she talked to him, she couldn't get a reading on the man. Couldn't figure out his angle. He seemed interested, but there was a guarded edginess to him.

Unbalanced and with nerves fighting some kind of never-ending duel in her stomach, she headed to the next table. She smiled, tapped her pencil on her tray, took their order, and headed toward the bar.

"Don't think I didn't see what went down over there," Annie said when Sophie dumped her tray down with a smack.

Annie's Chanel perfume mixed with the scent of whiskey, beer, and faded cigarettes of the bar, now as familiar to Sophie as her raspberry cocoa butter moisturizer.

"You had two men having a pissing match over you." Annie swiveled her denim butt in her chair, crossing her impossibly long longs, her head swinging between Zeb and Dug, eyes narrow. "I know who I'd choose."

Annie tapped a red lacquered nail on the bar, a frown marring her smooth forehead, her eyes on Zeb. "Why does that man not notice me?"

"His name's Zeb." Sophie stacked her tray with shot glasses brimming with Wild Turkey.

Pipe walked out of his office.

"Great," Sophie said under her breath.

Annie squeezed her shoulder.

Pipe looked around the bar, his head jerking when his eyes landed on Zeb and stayed there, his gaze narrowing. "What's Carmichael doing here?"

Sophie stepped forward, swallowing. "He's my ride." Surprise and something else moved in Pipe's eyes. She turned and headed to the bar to give Cope her order. Last call had been issued, and the bar slowly emptied.

She dragged a hand across her eyes, wishing the hands on the clock would hit twelve and four. She looked up to find Pipe scanning her. She tucked her head and went to move away.

"Bring your car in early tomorrow and I'll have a look at it."

She opened her mouth, but he cut her off.

"I want you here on time. Can't do that if your car won't start. You'll be fired."

Really.

Did Pipe think praying for a miracle from Jesus that her car would start was how she wanted to live?

Her hands landed on her hips and, being emotionally and physically exhausted along with being worried about paying back her dad's debt and paying her bills, tears burned the back of her throat. "For your information, I've taken it to five different mechanics who've all promised they fixed it. *Five*. Right now I can't afford to get it not-fixed for the sixth time, and I can't afford another car." She sucked back the tears. There was no way she'd cry in front of Pipe. He'd probably fire her for crying. Along with the money, she enjoyed the company of Gemma, Annie, Cope and the people.

He stared at her, eyebrows raised. "Bring it in tomorrow morning."

Was the man not listening?

"I can't afford it."

He glanced at her feet, then back at her face. "Get some stilettos. Consider this your one and only warning, and bring the car in."

Without another word, he turned and walked away.

"I think he's warming to you." Gemma winked.

"Yeah, it's positively cozy in our neck of the woods." She looked at her shoes, then at Gemma. Some kind of crazy hysteria, fatigue, and a bit of fear fizzed her blood. "Did you know that tomorrow Pipe and I are going shopping for vacuum cleaners, then we'll have tea and eat tiny sandwiches and cupcakes?"

Gemma threw back her head and laughed.

"I knew there was more to you than what you give out."

Sophie stilled, unsure of what to say.

"Girlfriends, I'm rescheduling margarita and appendage discussion night." Annie twisted her long blond hair into a rope and threw it over her shoulder, her eyes locked on Sophie. "And you're coming."

Sophie opened her mouth to say no, but the questioning look on Annie's face stilled her.

"Tomorrow night. 'Tits-Out Terri' is working. I don't care if fifteen hundred bikes turn up tomorrow night. I've worked nine days straight, and I'm done." Gemma slid her tray onto the bar. "I'll bring the tequila, margarita mix, devils on horseback, and we'll discuss 'Hello Handsome,' who only needs four AAs to have me shouting to my savior."

"Jesus, Gemma," Cope said, his cheeks pink. "I'm going to have to think of washing my grandma's smalls trying to get to sleep tonight."

"Oh, please. You've had more women than I've had beer spilled on me." Gemma swatted his shoulder.

Sophie stared at the heat and something else that blazed in his eyes before he turned away from Gemma.

"So we're settled, my place tomorrow night." Annie's narrowed gaze fell on Sophie. "No excuses."

Sophie wondered if she could catch a fictitious but possibly fatal twenty-four-hour virus between now and tomorrow night.

"I mean it."

Sophie pulled her ponytail tight. "Let me check my calendar and I'll text you tomorrow, okay?" She tried to calm her voice as it came out of her mouth, but winced at her rushed words.

Annie stepped back, regarding her. "You only get so many shots at a sideshow alley game. You know what I'm saying?"

No.

But she got Annie's body language. She could only blow them off before she'd be whistling in the wind. She wanted this, wanted the warmth of friendship, but opening up would leave her vulnerable, and that scared the crap out of her.

"I get what you're saying," she whispered.

"All righty, then bring your man troubles, your shoe troubles, we'll discuss male appendages, and we'll get answers."

Out of the corner of her eye, Zeb approached.

Annie turned her head. "Bring him. He's a long lick of Dairy Milk, and I love me some Cadbury."

"Are you about ready?" Zeb stood in front of her, his crystal-blue eyes flashing in his mocha face.

"We close in twenty. I'll be ready in forty-five."

Annie patted the seat next to her. Zeb shook his head, regret in his eyes.

The electricity bill, think of the electricity bill, or imagine the face of Ona Evans from Erwin, Tennessee when she receives her fifteen dollars back.

An hour later, Sophie unlocked her front door, her muscles wilting with fatigue.

Zeb walked in front of her, throwing on lights. He disappeared into her room, flicked on the light, and walked back into the living room.

"Thanks, Zeb. I'm sure there's a flock of pissed women out there who'd wrestle me to the ground since I've deprived them of you."

A smile warmed his eyes. "I like where I'm at, girl."

She toed off her boots, curious. "Is there a Mrs. Holy Hotness waiting for you at home? Hordes of panting women you need to service? Are you listed on Groupon?"

A full smile hit his face. His light blue eyes sparkled, pearly whites that would make an orthodontist weep in admiration.

Sophie stared.

Holy crap, that is one beautiful, testosterone-fueled man.

"No woman waiting for me. No women in need of service. I don't know what Groupon is, so no."

She smiled at him. "Good to know."

Pongo sprawled on the couch. She walked to where he lay. He lifted his head, his tail thumped twice, and three pops sounded. She moved in and hugged him, holding her breath.

"Jesus. Did your dog just—"

Zeb moved back as if he'd taken a javelin to the chest.

"Yep. That's Pongo. He can reliably empty a room. It's his gift to the world."

"Good night, baby boy." She buried her face in his neck and wrapped her arms around his sausage body. "Love you."

She stood. Her head snapped when she hit a barrier of perfume.

Oh, no. Oh, hell no.

Harlan had dialed up Submissive Blonds R Us and brought her here?

Her head swung to the closed door of her spare bedroom. She gripped the back of the couch to keep upright. She closed her eyes, her nails biting into her palms.

She didn't give a shit what he did at Casa Franco, but slapping her in her house after playing that he was interested when she knew he wasn't?

No.

Hell no.

Part of her wanted to march into her spare room and demand that he and his sub get out, but another part didn't want to see the woman's head thrown back in ecstasy, her body slick, Harlan totally concentrated on her.

Why does it hurt? It shouldn't hurt. This is me doing this to me.

She flinched, processed, and folded the hurt over and over, then buried it deep in her soul.

"Sophie?" Zeb's voice came from a distant galaxy.

She waved her hand. "Good night, Zeb."

Zeb closed the front door with a click and wouldn't leave until she'd locked it. Set the alarm and turned the deadbolts. Two minutes later, a throaty car roared to life.

She leaned against her front door, mashed her lips downward to stop the emotion building. Her head turned at the spare room door opening.

No way. No freaking way am I going to be confronted by him and his woman in my home.

She walked with purpose to her room and closed the door. She threw her clothes into a pile in the corner, pulled on her PJs, washed her face, brushed her teeth, slapped on Olay, and avoided her reflection in the mirror.

She grabbed her phone, wiped her eyes against the back of her palm, and sent out a text to Gemma and Annie.

Sophie: *I'm in for the girl's night. I'm shopping for appendages, Pringles, and French onion dip.*

She quickly said her prayers hoping God would be cool with a shortened version tonight. She crawled into bed, left her phone charging on the bedside table, and stared out into the inky night.

Tomorrow I'm getting the recorder back and this is done.

TEN

Sophie downed coffee and forced a piece of toast into her protesting stomach. She'd planned on an hour's sleep before she hit the park, but Karma wasn't playing in her sandpit today. Her alarm had failed, or she'd slept through it. The usual sound of Pongo head-butting her door then landing on her bed with all the finesse of a shipping container being dropped off a cliff hadn't happened. Her body had betrayed her by slipping into a coma until sunlight hit her face, and she'd woken with a start.

Ten o'clock had rolled by, and her early start to the day was in the gutter.

The door to Harlan's room was closed.

Wait.

The door to *her* spare bedroom was closed.

She'd not wanted to hear the front door clicking, the sparkly laughter of a sated woman after Harlan had delivered on his Groupon promise.

She choked on her coffee.

Submissives R Us probably purchased a multipack, and they're getting through each voucher one position at a time.

Her stomach twisted into a complicated knot.

God, why do I feel like this?

"Because there's something wrong with me," she said to the plate.

And it pisses me off, and I don't know why I'm pissed off.

She grabbed her jacket and shrugged it on.

The door to her spare room opened.

"Hey."

She swiped her phone and keys off the spotless counter and without a backward glance headed out the door.

Harlan's string of curse words followed her.

She jumped into her car, which started after a couple of thumps. She shot down the driveway with a screech of tires, heading to the park. Her foot hit the accelerator when Harlan's beast of an SUV came into her rearview mirror. She gripped the steering wheel. "Come on, baby girl, please don't let me down."

She threw in a sharp left, the map on her phone calculating the fastest route. A black Jeep slotted three cars behind her.

I've used up my Karma quota today.

Twenty minutes later Sophie roared into the lot, threw her car into park, turned off the ignition, and laid her head against the steering wheel. Her damp hands gripped the wheel, her knuckles white, her heart playing pinball against her ribs.

She'd driven like a teenager on a joyride. In a last ditch effort to lose Harlan and the Jeep, she'd sent a prayer upward to anyone listening, made a tight turn, and headed the wrong way down a one-way street, her emergency lights blinking. She'd hogged a lane and by a miracle had emerged at the end of the street bombarded with one finger salutes, but intact.

Sophie turned her head, and her mouth dropped open.

On the bandstand, elderly couples dipped and swayed to oldies music. The women wore vintage party dresses, all with matching white orthotic shoes. The men wore shiny suits, their black shoes gleamed, pressed white handkerchiefs in breast pockets. A jazz quartet played in the corner.

Sophie exited her car and made her way to the bandstand. A small sign announced that the Happening Hits of the Heyday was in full swing and anyone could join in.

The sun beat down on her neck, the thick cotton of her polo plastered to her body.

She stopped at the steps to the bandstand. An ancient man sat guarding a neat stack of dollar bills.

"Do you want to join in?" The man smiled at Sophie showing veneers so white she was momentarily blinded.

"Thank you." She pulled her wallet from her back pocket and handed him a twenty-dollar bill.

The man's eyes widened. "That's too much, my dear."

A memory surged into her head. She'd been young. She and her father had stopped at a small town in the Midwest. Farm folk with little to give paying for her father's prayers to bring rain and good fortune. She remembered the grandfathers and their families flocking to the man who could save them and their farms.

People like the man in front of her.

"No, it's not." She pushed the words past the lump in her throat and squinted at the wooden post where she'd hidden her equipment. Nothing looked out of place, but it was too hard to tell from where she stood.

"You may have to wait a lickety-split minute until one of our younger gents comes free." At Sophie's bewildered look, he continued. "You need a partner. I'd offer, but my hip's been acting up, and I'm saving myself for the limbo. Got my eye on Gladys." He winked, and Sophie couldn't help but grin.

"That's okay, I don't mind—"

"She's taken."

Sophie stiffened at Harlan's growled words.

No, she is not.

Her blood pulsed through her veins, and her heart kicked it up an extra two notches.

Harlan grabbed a fifty from his wallet and passed it to the man, who looked like he might cry with appreciation. His hand moved to the small of her back, gently propelling her up the stairs.

She dug in her heels.

Even through the thick cotton of her polo and the denim of her jeans, his heat, his touch, seared her.

"You nearly got yourself killed," he said, anger vibrating in his voice. He grabbed her hand.

"So did you." She tried to pull her hand away. She wouldn't tell him how many times she'd wanted to bust into her spare room and murder him.

"What are you doing here, and why did you ditch me?" His warm breath danced on her cheek, flooding her blood with sparkles.

"I've come for the dancing and I ditched you because I wanted to."

He dug his hand through his hair, making it all messy and sexy in an *I've had sex all night long* kind of way, which pissed her off even more.

"Let me go," she said, anger and something she didn't want to define bubbling in her chest.

"Jesus, won't you ever listen to me or do what I say?"

"Well, let's see." She cocked her head to one side and pretended to consider his question. "No."

"I'm doing this to protect you."

"You are *not*," she shot back. "You're doing this for that stupid bet and your Everest-sized ego, thinking you can have me for one night. Delusional much?"

She flashed a manufactured smile at an elderly woman who'd stopped dancing to greet them.

"Next up is the Virginia reel. Join in, my dears."

She ignored Harlan and tried to concentrate on counting the number of posts opposite her, which was nearly impossible due to the moving bodies.

She moved away, but Harlan's fingers pressed into her hip.

Her overactive memory planted a vision of Harlan and a petite blond at the front of her mind.

She broke free from him and joined a line of dancers facing their partners.

"I don't know what you're doing here, but I'm doing the Virginia reel," she said over her shoulder. She followed the line of women and walked four steps toward her invisible partner. "After that there's the 'Come near my house again and you'll be missing your balls'." She stepped backward four steps. "I have to say that last one is my favorite, it's a real jaunty tune."

Her jaw clenched when he moved to stand opposite her, but she somehow managed a full-wattage smile in his direction.

She hated that she felt jealous that he'd brought a woman home to her house. *Her* house. Her sanctuary.

She concentrated on the dance moves of the line of women. Moving toward Harlan and slipping away at the last minute. He stood impersonating a lamp post.

"I don't know what's pissed you off."

"Where were you last night?" she said.

"Working."

She nodded.

Working with Miss Dior.

"I don't want you at my house, Harlan. You need to leave. Today."

His eyes widened, then narrowed. He opened his mouth to speak, but she cut him off.

She held up her hand. "There's nothing to say, so don't." She took two steps forward.

A pair of dancers shuffled down the middle of the line leaving Sophie closer to the pillar she searched for.

Awesome. At this rate, I should be at the front of the line in two weeks.

Before she let her bad mood settle over her like a persistent, rainy cloud, she smiled at the woman standing beside her, who'd shuffled down the line of people. Her powdered cheeks were pink, her fore-head damp, her green eyes sparkled like polished emeralds.

"He gets better every year, my Ron," she said to Sophie behind her hand. "I don't tell him, though. I like to keep him on his toes."

Sophie laughed.

The tempo of the music changed to a slow waltz.

She looked around for a single gent whom she could shuffle around the bandstand toward the post where her equipment was.

"Hey, what do you think you're—?"

She got no further. Harlan's hands were on her hips, dragging her until she was plastered against the long, hard length of him. She placed her hands between them to push him away, settling on his hard pecs. She turned her head to hide the heat pounding into her cheeks.

"What are you doing?" she whispered.

"I don't know what you're doing, but I'm waltzing."

Before she had time to react, he pulled the tie, releasing her hair. He leaned in and buried his face in it.

"Gets me every time," he said.

"Stop doing that. You—"

"What *exactly* are you doing here?" he asked. "Doesn't seem your scene," he said, leading her again across the creaking wooden floor like a professional.

She moved left and tried to pull him in the same direction.

"Been on my bucket list for a while," she said through gritted teeth when he wouldn't budge. "Next week is knitting coats for cats."

She went to move left again, but he went to move right.

"You have to let me lead," he said, his breath tickling her ear.

She stood on her toes, her lips brushing his earlobe and thought for a moment she heard him growl. "No, I don't."

"Yeah, you do."

His hands tightened on her waist, and with gentle force he moved her in the direction he wanted her to go.

"What are you doing?" she demanded.

"We're waltzing." His fingers pressed deeper.

One hand splayed across the bottom of her spine, his arm wrapped around her shoulders, pulling her in tight.

Hip to hip, chest to chest, his unique scent of soap, sweat, and man filled her.

Everyone else melted away.

His pulse was steady and slow against her fingertips. His head rested lightly on the top of hers. They moved in time to the slow beat.

"Letting me take control wasn't too bad." A smile teased his kissable lips.

The mood broke like a parent walking in on teenagers making out. She stiffened and pulled back.

His eyes flashed. "Oh, hell no. You all soft against me? I'm not giving that up." He pulled her against him and touched his lips to her neck.

She fought the heat that traveled down the column of her neck, then exploded throughout her body.

And failed.

The music turned into a sultry tango.

Her head whipped left.

A tango.

A sexy tango when you weren't sexy, with a man who radiated sex appeal and whose tank was topped up?

No.

She tried to fight her way out of his hold, but he tightened his grip.

All the insecurities of growing up as the too-tall, too-plain girl, growing into the too-tall, too-plain woman, clawed at her insides.

"Let me go," she whispered.

"What's wrong? I thought you were here for the dancing." His fingers flexed around hers.

With effort, she spun out of Harlan's arms and into the surprised face of an old man who beamed down at her.

Irish moss aftershave along with the scent of faded roses filled her head as couples moved around them, their faces either smiling or set with steely determination.

"Now this is more like it," he said, his arthritic fingers lacing with hers, her cheek pressed to his, and she laughed out loud when he marched her across the floor.

The man twirled her into open space.

She landed on a hard chest, hands gently gripping her hips.

Before she could protest, Harlan marched her forward, hip-to-hip, zigzagging around the smiling faces of the older dancers.

"Going to twirl you now."

"Don't, please," she said, desperate.

He twirled her as if she weighed a hundred pounds, which she did *not*. Her feet tangled, her stomach lurched, training kicked in, and she twisted her body so her shoulder would break her fall. The bandstand floor loomed.

Powerful arms scooped her up and plastered her against a hard chest.

"I wouldn't let anything happen to you." He swept her hair off her face in a gentle gesture, one hand now cradling her head, one hand splayed at the base of her spine.

Sweat streaked down her forehead, her polo stuck to her body. Harlan looked as if he were delivering a lecture on climate change to icebergs. No sweat on his brow. No damp shirt for him.

"You're hot," he murmured.

"I know. Let me go and I promise not to shake all over you like a Labrador after a bath."

He chuckled. "No, I mean you're hot. Panting and flushed face with your chest pressed against mine. Hot."

He pressed in to her, and his attraction was apparent. Long, thick, and her mouth watered.

"Oh."

"Yeah, oh."

He dragged her hips closer to his, nestling his hand lower on the waistband of her jeans until his hand slipped underneath the denim. His fingers seared her flesh.

When she licked her lips, his eyes blazed, leaving her in no doubt of what he wanted, which made little sense. One minute she thought he wanted her and the next he was barking orders at her. The man was more confusing than a *Survivor* puzzle.

Sophie needed a distraction. The last two functioning cells in her brain banded together and devised a plan before she melted into him, lost herself, only to find she was locked in a bathroom in her underwear, his laughter trailing her.

The music changed, breaking their connection. She managed to unplaster herself from Harlan's long, hard body, one part harder than the rest.

Time to get back on track and the reason I'm here.

Panting and with her head in a spin, she moved to the railing housing the equipment and leaned against it. She waved her hand at Harlan. "I'm sitting this one out, but make Maude's day." She gestured with her head toward a fit-looking woman, a paper label on her checked dress announcing her name. Harlan shook his head and stood next to Sophie.

Sophie's heart thumped into her throat. Her fingers curled around the smooth wood. The bet was about to have a winner.

Her.

No more Harlan in her house on the pretense of being here for the bet. No more Harlan screwing with her mind and her body.

No more Harlan, period.

Swallowing became a chore. Her hand probed the wood while she kept her head forward, her eyes on the dancers, a plastic smile curling her lips.

The tiny lump of modeling clay where she'd left it.

She let out a heartfelt sigh.

Slow and steady.

She worked at keeping her breathing even, her body seemingly relaxed.

A bubble of clay started to loosen and slip through her fingers.

Yes.

Harlan's hand encased hers.

No.

"This is mine," she said, anguish underscoring the words.

She'd fought for this. It wasn't just the bet; it was trying to figure out if her entire life had been a lie.

He looked down at her, his face thoughtful, not releasing his control on her fingers.

"We'll listen to it together."

Whoa.

This wasn't the Harlan Franco she knew. The Harlan Franco who did *not* compromise, *especially* with her.

"What's the catch? You've never given me a break. *Ever.*"

His jaw worked. "I think we can call this a draw."

Her mouth dropped open. "But you don't compromise."

He dug his hand through his hair, his face thoughtful and troubled. "For you that's all I seem to do."

Confused, she stared at him, her mouth open. She clamped her mouth shut when Harlan guided her through clapping couples doing the Hokey Pokey.

In a daze, she walked to his Range Rover, then slipped into the passenger seat and hugged her knees to her chest.

He connected the recorder to his car stereo. Static filled the car, then Babic's voice started commanding his slaves at Hostage. The beat of the music didn't drown out the slurping sounds.

She stared in fascination at the dashboard, her face hot.

Oh God, please let this be over soon.

She snuck a glance at Harlan, who looked like he'd eaten a toad.

Sophie squirmed in her seat as the recording progressed and more commands, grunts, and groans of pleasure filled the enclosed space of the car.

"What is that woman doing here?" A voice she didn't recognize, the man who sat down at Babic's table. The sound of skin on skin halted momentarily, then started up again. A gagging sound and Babic's voice.

"Relax," Babic replied. "I have already told Petrov about her. Everything is going according to plan."

A murmur of protest from a Barbie was followed by a barked command for her to sit and stay.

Babic, forever the charmer.

Sophie stared out the window worrying her bottom lip.

What woman were they talking about?

She'd only been there on Friday nights; there were probably a whole range of people turning up at his table during the week.

Babic's voice, stronger and filled with bone-freezing venom, reeled her mind back to the conversation.

"Sophie Callaghan will get what she deserves."

ELEVEN

Sophie's head snapped back and her blood froze in her veins, Babic's words echoing in her head.

Sophie Callaghan will get what she deserves.

Winded, she couldn't pull a breath.

Babic knew about her father's cons?

Is this why her father had a detailed journal on Petrov and his movements, because her father had conned the man?

"Sophie?"

Cold sweat coated her body. She couldn't look at Harlan. She could only concentrate on one thing at a time.

It fit. Her father had conned Petrov, who was now out for revenge, which is why her father had kept the journal.

She stared out at a group of children hanging upside down on monkey bars, their faces stained red with laughter. She'd vowed to pay back every last person. True, she hadn't expected this level of debt, but one buck or ten thousand, she owed.

"Look at me." Harlan's warm hand cupped her jaw. His touch, his gentle voice, could dissolve her and leave her exposed and more alone than she'd ever been.

And she'd been alone all of her life.

I can't do this.

She turned in her seat, one hand on the door. "I have to go." She sprinted to her car, which, sensing her mood, started on the first try.

She drove around Denver, concentrating on driving, letting her mind wander. If her father had conned Petrov, she was screwed. She didn't have the money it took to pay back a man like Petrov. Besides, robbing banks wasn't in her future.

The ping of an incoming text distracted her. She pulled over and read the reminder from Annie, who'd texted her address again. There were four texts from Harlan and two missed calls.

She rubbed the throb in her temple.

For the first time in her life, she'd found a home. Leaving Titus and Sally? Starting her profession again in another state? Knocking on doors day after day, handing out flyers, hoping someone would take one. Taking low-paying jobs, sitting in dirty bars and strip joints photographing cheating partners.

She couldn't think about this now. She needed a distraction to do normal stuff, like shopping. She drove home and parked in her driveway next to one of Harlan's cars.

She walked to the passenger side window of the SUV, which opened on her approach.

"Hey, Thor. I've got a few things to do and I'm heading out. I'm giving you a heads-up. I've got a girls' night out and I'll be hitting Safeway, a liquor shop, a pharmacy, and a sex shop that sells male appendages." Thor blinked and rubbed his hand across his chin, scowling when she said "appendages". "I'm not sure how long I'll be shopping for male appendages, having never shopped for male appendages before."

She held back the flush that heated her chest. Just saying the words, she expected something heavy to drop on her head, possibly in the form of a bible.

"Jesus, Sophie, stop saying the word 'appendages'. You know I've got my orders. I have to stay with you at all times."

She leaned in to the window. "I'd check your phone. All bets are off between your boss and me, who isn't *my* boss." She smiled. "If you feel the need to shop for male appendages, please come along. What do you think—vibrating or not? Rabbit or dual action? Seven, nine or twelve inches?"

She'd spent way too many hours checking them out online. She'd made the sign of the cross and backed away with smarting eyes at twelve inches of silicon.

"Christ, you're going to fucking kill me." He stared at her, brows drawn together over eyes that looked black, but were a deep, inky blue. His dark-blond hair was messy.

"I realize stepping into a sex shop for 'man power' might give your street cred a bit of a hit, but looking like you do, I think you'll survive."

The suffocation of always being followed, coupled with nerves about the night ahead and the knowledge that she might have a debt she couldn't pay left her jumpy, freaked out, and pissed that Harlan still had men trailing her.

Keep it together, Buttercup.

She bit down the hysterical bubble of laughter that her father would wander into her head right at this moment when she was thinking of vibrators.

After a stop in the kitchen for a quick Diet Coke, she took a moment to scratch Pongo's stomach—his second favorite thing in the world behind food. Knowing there'd be no time for soul-soothing TV later, she'd already Googled the spoiler alerts on the drama surrounding the good folk of Genoa City.

Normality achieved, Sophie walked to her car. She considered whether she should have brought the car in like Pipe said, as the engine debated whether it felt like starting. Finally, she pulled into traffic. Thor trailed her two cars back.

"Damn it," she said under her breath.

She threw in a tight left turn and heard a squeal of brakes behind her. At the next intersection, when the light turned green, she threw on her indicator and swerved right, apologizing to the bus she cut off.

Freedom. No Harlan, no tail, just herself.

At an unfamiliar Safeway, she picked up Pringles, sour cream, and French onion soup for a dip. She added carrots and celery sticks in case anyone was eating healthy. She couldn't afford expensive snacks, so she picked her favorite ones and hoped they would be okay. She grabbed a bottle of Chardonnay and a merlot, hoping that covered all bases.

On the way to her next stop, in her rearview mirror, she noted that a brown sedan had sat three cars behind her for a while. She took the next left, ignoring her phone telling her to turn around when possible. Instead, Sophie gripped the wheel tighter, her gaze flicking from the car to the road ahead. She took a right, pulled over, and pretended to go through her handbag, her eyes on the car that sailed past. She pulled back into the traffic, noting a dark pickup that turned out of a side street she'd passed and sat behind her, one lane to her left.

She pulled into a parking lot a block from the sex shop, one hand on her bag with the Taser, another gripping her phone. She had a clear view if the pickup went left or right. When the pickup turned left and disappeared from view, she let out a long breath and parked the car.

She walked into Spanky's not knowing what to expect, but standing in front of a wall of vibrators, her face flaming, she did her best to summon an 'I have so many I can't decide' expression, until she imagined Harlan's mouth in soft places, and a river of warmth headed between her legs. She tried to picture Thor's blue eyes, blond hair, and panty-melting smile, but Harlan materialized in her mind and slayed Thor.

"Can I help you?" Sophie stuffed a vibrating silver bullet back on the shelf and ran her hands across her hair.

A woman about her age wearing jeans and a T-shirt covered in skulls walked to her.

"She doesn't need any help." Harlan moved into her line of sight, eyes flashing.

She stared at the floor and willed it to open and swallow her whole, but her pleas went unanswered.

"What are you doing here?" she asked.

She went back to studying the description of the silver bullet.

His hand landed on her shoulder. "I'm here because you're out in the open and unprotected."

"What are you doing here?" His eyebrows rose, then pulled in when he took in the shelves.

"Research. I'm going to discuss my favorite vibrator, which I can't do if I've..." She could toast bread on her burning cheeks. "So, this afternoon I'm going to be doing some *research*." She ignored the splintered breath beside her. She was having a hard time breathing when Harlan sucked all the oxygen from the room and replaced it with testosterone.

She put the silver bullet into her basket and added a "lick me ten times" vibrator.

"You'll be doing that with me," his deep rumbly voice vibrated through her and she clenched her thighs together.

His hand branded her through her jacket, her self-control dissolving into a puddle at his feet. "Please take your hand off me or I'll Taser you." Her voice was breathy, high and needy.

Damn.

His lips twitched, and his eyes sparkled. "Don't make me laugh, babe, because I'm kind of pissed and that's funny."

"Bet's off, Harlan. Our arrangement is done. You can take small, blond, and submissive back to your place." She grabbed lube from the shelf before heading for the register. "I'm going to take care of myself." She eyed the basket.

Heat flared in his darkening eyes before he frowned. "What are you talking about?"

"Want to tell me about the job you were *working* last night?" She hated the stab of jealousy she heard in her own voice.

"If he's bothering you, I can call the police." The shop assistant arrived to stand beside her. Sophie silently thanked her for her "girls looking out for girls" solidarity.

"Thank you, but that won't be necessary." She handed the girl the basket with a smile, ignoring Harlan. "Which would you recommend?" she asked the shop assistant. "Out of these two."

The woman's gaze shifted between the two. "I'm on my own at the moment, and the bullet is working for me."

"Well, I'm on my own at the moment, so that will do it for me." She swiped her card, then punched in her PIN.

Sophie walked out of the shop and threw her purchase onto the passenger seat. Without a backward glance at Harlan, she jumped into the driver's seat and headed home, not bothering to check her rearview mirror.

She pulled into her driveway where Titus stood, his hand raised in greeting. She grabbed her stuff and went to meet him. Harlan pulled his Range Rover in behind hers.

"Hey Titus, what have you got here?" she said, eyeing a brown box in his hands.

"This came for you, about half an hour after you left. A man on a loud motorbike that had the word 'Master' painted in flames left the box. Said his name was Mick. Could have used a shower and some mouthwash, quite frankly."

Mick's face flashed into Sophie's mind. After she'd had him on the ground, she could feel the hatred that had risen through his body on a stench. She knew that he would have hit her. He'd been banned from the bar, so maybe it was his way of apologizing. She'd tell Pipe, and he'd be back in his favorite place in the world. She reached to take the box, but before she could, Harlan grabbed it from her.

She opened her mouth, then closed it.

Wait. How would Mick know where I live?

Harlan turned the box over in his hands. Using the knife on his key ring, he slit through the brown paper, flicked open a lid, and pulled a snow globe from the box.

"It's gorgeous," she breathed, momentarily lost in its beauty. She took the dome from him and shook it. "It's an over-water bungalow in Tahiti. Look, instead of snow it's little fish." She read Bora Bora on the metal strip, then tipped the heavy dome.

A smile started in her stomach, expanded until it spread across her face. A warm feeling settled in her bones. She became lost in a memory. "My father gave me my first snow globe. Dorothy and her ruby slippers."

She blinked.

How had that snippet floated out of her mouth?

She turned the globe over, the cool Lucite warmed by her hands. She righted the globe, and the glittery fish settled on the bottom in a carpet of tinsel.

"This is high-end stuff in the world of snow globes."

The question of how Mick would know she collected snow globes raced around her head like a Chihuahua on speed. Had he crept around her house and seen her collection through a window? Had he found her address at Pipe's somehow? Had he followed her?

Blood trudged through her veins like slush. She'd have a quiet word with Cope about how Mick could have her address—the bar being their only connection. She took a slight comfort that if Mick had followed her here, Harlan or one of his crew would have seen him.

"You look lost in thought. Want to share?" Harlan's voice pulled her out of her head. She gave him a tight smile. There was no way she was discussing her internal thoughts with Mr. Control Freak; she'd be handcuffed to the man twenty-four-seven. She squirmed when one part of her anatomy thought that was a fabulous idea.

"I'll get one of the boys to check it out." He pulled his phone out of his pocket.

Something about the snow globe flashed a memory she couldn't catch. A fragment lost in a sea of images. She closed her eyes trying to capture it, but it disappeared. An unsettling feeling of walking into cobwebs crept across her skin.

Titus's hand landed on her shoulder.

She shrugged off the unsettled feeling and quick-smiled at her neighbor. "Is everything okay with you and Sally? Do you have enough bread? I've picked up a spare loaf at Safeway, that fruit and cinnamon swirl that Sally loves. I'll bring it over."

Titus's head swung between her and Harlan. "Please tell me you two young things are off on a date tonight. That would make an old man's day."

"I *am* going on a date tonight, but it isn't with Harlan." She leaned forward, kissed Titus on his leathery cheek, inhaling his pine aftershave, and semi-relaxed. "Besides, Harlan doesn't date or woo women. He commands." Stepping to the door, she punched in the alarm code, unlocked the door, and walked in.

She'd no sooner thrown her Spanky's bag on the couch than Harlan stood in front of her.

"How do you know Babic?"

Her hands on her hips. "I thought I told you to leave."

Harlan's eyes flashed, but he said nothing.

She took a deep breath. "I don't know Babic. At all. He's probably got me mixed up with someone else."

A girl could hope.

LATER THAT EVENING, she pulled up outside a stylish condo and checked the text. Harlan's throaty demon of a car came to a stop behind hers.

Yep, right address.

She kept the motor running.

Annie's words floated through her brain. *You only get so many shots at a sideshow alley game.*

Vultures were swooping in her stomach.

Could she do this?

Sweat rolled down her back. She wiped clammy hands down her

jeans. She could make her excuses and slip out the door, or take a chance.

"WOW," Gemma said thirty minutes later.

Annie topped Sophie's cocktail glass. "That's some life story you've got there."

"So, to clarify." Gemma held up her glass, which Annie refilled. "Your father—I note that you never call him 'Daddy', a preacher, died being obsessed with Alexander Petrov. You met Harlan at Hostage where you melted into Mr. Tall, Dark and—"

"Control Freak," Sophie added.

Sophie held up her hand, surprised Gemma had noticed she didn't refer to her father as her dad. That had stopped when she'd found out the truth about him.

"I think you've both got a bit of that going on, but let me continue, where you wowed Harlan with your party trick, which you need to teach me," said Annie.

Gemma held up her hand. "Hang on. Bad dudes as in mercenaries tried to take you at a strip joint, and Harlan moved into your home after you made a bet about equipment where he claimed he's going to have you for one night." Gemma stared at a spot on the wall, her brow crinkled. "He's pointed out he doesn't do relationships and likes small, blond and submissive women. You're working at Pipe's because you're helping your neighbor." Gemma's eyes twinkled. "Oh, I can add to your story. Dug has been asking when you'll next be on shift. Me thinks he has it baaaad. He's cute."

Sophie said nothing, feeling the eyes of Annie assessing her.

So she'd left out a few details.

"That pretty much covers it." Sophie popped another devil on horseback into her mouth, ignoring the Dug comment. "These are fantastic," she said, squirming under Annie's relentless stare.

"Prunes wrapped in bacon... who knew?" Gemma grinned at her.

"That's everything?" Annie asked, looking skeptical.

"Yep." She stared back at Annie who, after a long beat, nodded.

"Get Harlan out of your life and move on." Annie sipped her drink. "He's not the one for you, Soph."

Before Sophie could answer, Gemma held up her hand.

"I disagree." Gemma crunched down on Pringles. "Sure he's got issues, but don't we all?" She stared pointedly at Annie. "Give him time."

"Forever the eternal optimist," Annie said under her breath.

"Forever the pessimist." Gemma shot her a sunny smile.

Annie laughed.

The love and friendship between the two women wrapped around Sophie like a warm sweater on a cloudy day.

"I'm thinking we need a girls' night out. A proper girls' night out. At Hostage," Annie said. "Where we get all dressed up and wear *wristbands*."

"Wristbands," Gemma breathed. She leaned forward, her golden eyes bright. "Come to my place first."

The answer "no" on Sophie's lips, Annie unexpectedly squeezed her hand.

"I won't go unless you do."

"Which means I must go on my own," Gemma said, picking up her glass. "And take my chances."

Damn.

Gemma would never survive Hostage on her own.

Her head swung between the two. Annie's lips twitched, and Gemma flat-out smiled at her.

"If I give you an address can you pick me up?"

Gemma nodded.

Annie stared at her and nodded once. "Next week we're going through your finances. I'm a financial whiz," Annie said.

"She is," Gemma said, breaking the tension. "Never play her in Monopoly."

"No, that's all right." Sophie tightened the band of her ponytail.

If Annie was a financial whiz, she'd have to explain the withdrawals of money, and that would mean explaining her father and his fleecing-the-needy scheme, something she'd only talk about in the afterlife to her father in a loud, painful conversation.

"Thursday's my night off, so this works." A gleam came into Gemma's eye when she scanned Sophie's face. "There's something I've been dying to do."

HARLAN WALKED into Babic's office, not feeling over friendly about the text message he'd received summoning him. Still, good to kill two birds with one stone, so to speak, and get this done.

Babic was on his mobile, rapidly barking in a language Harlan didn't understand. He'd glanced at Harlan when he knocked and walked into his office. Harlan's jaw clenched at the dismissive look on Babic's face. Harlan sat across from Babic and took in the office, looking for a glimpse into the man. An enormous desk dominated the room in an open-air warehouse. The sound of huge rigs backing in accompanied by the sharp beeps and the whir of forklifts and male voices scrambled the air. Petrov ran trucking operations using Colorado as his hub. This was the first in a group of warehouses that lined the street. Petrov's distinctive logo of a dark blue cursive *P* painted on large sliding doors.

A map of the world covered one side of the wall in Babic's office. Different colored pins stabbed countries. Gray generic filing cabinets hugged a wall. A picture of Babic and Petrov with their arms flung across each other's shoulders, standing in front of a massive cargo ship, sat in a solid silver frame on the desk. Babic had stopped speaking, but Harlan kept looking around the room.

Harlan hadn't been shocked at Babic's words. Babic was the one who had told Petrov about Sophie. From what he'd observed in meetings, the man had all the warmth of a cyborg. He also hadn't been unduly concerned by Babic's tone—it was how the man spoke. But it had freaked Sophie out. She'd jolted as if she'd been stabbed deep in the gut. Her face had paled, and she'd visibly trembled before locking down her reaction and fleeing like a herd of religious folk were trying to convert her.

Interesting.

Still, what had Babic meant when he said she'd get what she deserved? Time to find out.

He stared hard at the man across from him. Nothing moved on Babic's face. His eyes, a light blue, were striking against his pale skin. He always dressed well; today was an expensive handmade Italian suit.

"You will bring me every file you have on Sophie Callaghan and if she is Seraphina or not," Babic barked at him.

Interesting development. Babic was in charge while Petrov was out of communication range, but he'd never been instructed by Petrov to hand over all the case files. Harlan shifted in his chair, buying time, trying to figure out Babic's angle.

The man at the club who liked to have the shit whipped out of him until he bled was a complete contrast to the man who sat across from him. Babic was feared and respected as Petrov's right-hand man. If you fucked with either of them, Babic would deal with you personally.

"Petrov has instructed me to only pass files to him."

It was well known that Petrov was grooming Babic to take over his operations when he eventually retired and went to live on his island in Fiji or sail the globe on a super yacht. Judging by the photo, the two men were tight. Harlan had no reason to question the man's loyalty.

Babic leaned back in his chair. "It is I who am in charge when he is not here, and I want to review the files."

No one knew about the exact relationship between the two. Something had happened in Lithuania to Babic's parents and Petrov had stepped in and taken an interest in the boy. Petrov had paid for Babic's education. He'd started out in Eastern European countries, but had proven himself a valuable asset, so Petrov had promoted him to the USA. There'd been a lot of speculation over the years, but no proof. It was rumored he was Petrov's secret son, an illegitimate child of a member of his wife's family.

Babic leaned forward, his fingers steepled, a smile on his face that didn't meet his eyes. "I think it is time we move this forward. You are living at her place, are you not? Is it hard living with her?"

Harlan leaned back, keeping his posture intentionally loose.

If they were referring to his dick as the "it" then yeah, he spent most of the time with balls so blue they were practically violet.

Harlan grinned, testing the man. "Yeah, *it* gets real hard."

Something flashed across Babic's face and the fine hairs raised on the back of Harlan's neck.

"Are you married?" Harlan asked, fishing. "Got a long-term girl or guy?" Harlan held up his hand in mock surrender. "Love is love."

"There is a woman…"

The man was so emotionless it wouldn't surprise Harlan to crank open his head and find a bunch of microchips and circuitry instead of flesh and blood.

Sophie Callaghan will get what she deserves. The line flashed through Harlan's brain. "Do you have anything on Sophie that can push this case through?"

Babic shrugged a shoulder casually, but a small tic vibrated under his left eye. "No, I know nothing about Sophie Callaghan."

Harlan nodded once, then stood.

"Your case notes." Babic also stood, his hands behind his back.

Harlan looked at him hard. "If Petrov gives the all clear, the file will be delivered, but until then, I take my instructions from Petrov only."

Babic's top lip curled slightly. He then nodded once, picked up his phone, swiped his finger across the glass and turned his back, dismissing Harlan, who noted the slight tremor in Babic's hand.

Harlan walked out into a gray, blustery day. The wind held a hint of a storm. The street vibrated in a low hum as trucks rolled into the compound. There was something about Babic that Harlan couldn't put his finger on. Harlan sat in his car trying to pinpoint what it was, but could find nothing concrete. He started the car and headed back to Sophie's.

———

"I THINK I've had too much margarita," Sophie said. She'd blushed and giggled at the description of Gemma's 'Hello Handsome', and how her elderly neighbor thought she had a cat she greeted at night. Sophie admitted she hadn't had time or the confidence to try out the bullet, but would. Annie started singing something about 'sisters doing it for themselves', before collapsing in laughter.

Sophie stood, and the room moved with her. "I should get an Uber," she said, reaching for her bag and missing.

"Stay the night," Annie said. "Both of you. There's a spare room and I can make up a bed on the couch."

"I've got to do the books for Pipe first thing. Family first," Gemma said.

"He's family?" Sophie choked.

Gemma grinned. "Yeah. He hates me calling him Uncle Marcus at work."

After digesting that information, her brain sluggishly remembered Annie's question. "I can't either. I'd hate to think of poor old Thor standing out there all night. He probably has a lovely Viking girlfriend named Heidi tucked away. I'd hate to deprive her of him."

"I'll call an Uber." Annie reached into her bag for her phone.

Ten minutes later, Sophie walked outside with Annie and Gemma, waved at Thor, and stumbled to a Nissan Maxima and said hello to Daphne, ignoring Thor's string of swear words. Back at her house, she stumbled to her front door.

"Where'd I put the keys?" She blinked at the beam of neon white that flooded the front door when she approached. "Oh, here they are." She grabbed her key ring and tried to insert a key into the lock.

The door opened as she leaned forward. She stumbled, falling into a solid chest.

Sophie grabbed a fistful of T-shirt. "I'm going to miss how you smell."

Blue eyes flashed. "You caught an Uber? Jesus, Sophie, I should put you over my knee." Harlan slung an arm across her shoulder and pulled her into her house. "You're drunk."

She ignored his statement about putting her over his knee, because she kind of wanted that, but not to be spanked. "No, I'm not. I'm margarita'd. First time." She tried to focus. "Why are you still here?"

"I'll get you a glass of water." Harlan's amused voice infiltrated the margarita crowding her brain.

"I think I'll go to bed." She leaned her cheek against his chest. Warm, hard and soft, it ticked all the boxes. "Here's good."

The next minute he cradled her to his chest. She felt the floor move, then she was lying on something soft.

"No." She clawed her way out of the bed, her knees hitting the floor.

"What are you doing?"

"Prayers. I can't go to bed without saying my prayers. I'll say one for you."

She clasped her hands, dropped her head, and said her prayers, ending with hoping Harlan found peace.

"Thanks for praying for my immortal soul and all, but I'm good with where I am." Harlan's amused voice permeated her haze.

She frowned.

"I think only the Dalai Lama and the Pope have that sewn up. The rest of us struggle."

He paused before answering, "You don't have peace?"

She shook her head.

Not until every single person had been paid back, which now included Alexander Petrov.

She sank into the mattress and closed her eyes, halfway to dreamland. Her boots were pulled off, then her socks. When a hand reached for her jeans zipper, she batted it away.

"No." She forced her eyes open to find Harlan staring down at her.

"You can't sleep in jeans."

"Oh, it's you. That's okay. I'm not a woman to you." She lifted her butt slightly, giving him access to her jeans.

She thought she witnessed a white-lipped mouth, but keeping her eyes open had become an industrial problem. Even stranger, she thought she heard her boots being thrown against the wall.

———

HARLAN SAT on the bed in Sophie's spare room. Petrov had called and was now in a better spot for communication—just—although the line was prone to be filled with static at random times. He gave Petrov a quick update with minimal facts over an unsecured line. A detailed written report would follow, encrypted and sent electronically. He didn't mention the meeting with Babic, preferring to do that in person. In the meantime, his people had been turning over every rock looking for Mick, but, so far, they had nothing.

He threw his phone on the bed and rubbed at the throbbing spot on the back of his neck that was getting harder to erase. After pulling off his clothes, he dropped onto the bed.

Tomorrow night he'd be meeting Diaz at Hostage with Arabella. The timing wasn't ideal, but too much rode on a positive outcome to postpone the meet. Diaz wanted out of a drug syndicate and, in return for safe passage for him and his family, he would deliver the key players in the cartel. If anyone caught a whiff that the man wanted out with a clean ticket, he and his family would be landfill.

Exhausted but wired, Harlan let his mind wander. And it went straight to its favorite subject. Sophie's creamy thighs filled his vision, along with the white boy-cut underwear that hugged her soft stomach. He'd never known white cotton underwear to be so fucking hot.

He'd always craved a *CrossFit* toned body—hard abs, lean muscles—until Sophie with her curves and her attitude came into his life.

Oh yeah, when this assignment was over, he'd be having her for one long night. His mind flicked between a hotel with a Jacuzzi and twenty-four-hour room service or a secluded cabin in the woods with Sophie naked on a rug in front of a fire.

Fuck it. They'd have both.

An image of Sophie's hair fanned across his stomach landed in his mind.

Yeah.

Sophie sitting on his face, his name tumbling from her mouth, her sweet juices on his tongue.

Yeah.

Sophie on all fours, silk scarves securing her to the bedposts.

Hell, yeah.

His hand dropped under the waistband of his boxers to his twitching cock, and he started stroking.

A low, deep, terror-filled moan filled the air.

Adrenaline fired throughout his body.

Sophie.

He threw back the covers, grabbed his phone and the gun from the bedside table, and crept to his door. He opened the door, gun drawn, twisting left and right. Cold sweat cloaked his body. With no obvious threat, he worked his way down the corridor toward Sophie's room. Another moan assaulted his ears.

Fuck.

A wet nose butting against his ankle, along with a string of farts, announced Pongo on the scene. He rested his hand on the dog's head for a beat, then opened Sophie's door. He slid in and silently closed the door; the Ruger trained on the bed.

A full moon splashed silver into the room. Sophie thrashed in the bed, fighting an invisible demon.

"Sophie."

Nothing.

He advanced, setting the safety on the gun, and placed it on the bedside table. He then caught Sophie's right wrist. Her body came off the bed, her foot connected with his thigh. He grunted, absorbing the pain. He leaned forward and took a hook to the head, followed by a blinding pain in his temple.

"Sophie."

"Daddy." She thrashed on the bed. A moan like that of a wounded animal chilled his blood.

He kneeled by the bed, gripping her hands. "Sophie, wake up."

"Daddy," she moaned, tears streaming down her pale face, her mouth open, hands punching, narrowly missing the wall, legs and feet kicking out.

Instinct kicked in. He slid into her bed and pulled her into his arms, her back to his chest. She stiffened, her body locking straight, then she fought him.

"You're safe."

He grunted when her heel caught his shin.

He burrowed his face into her hair, swallowing a snarl. "You're safe."

The tension bled from her body.

He wrapped his arms around her, nestled his face in her hair, and breathed deeply. Shit, she felt good in his arms. He kissed the back of her head and stared into the darkness.

A WEAK DAWN light brushed the curtains. Harlan stirred, pulling Sophie's thick hair off his chest. Sometime in the night, she'd lost the hair band, and her hair lay like a blanket. She lay on her side, her head on his shoulder, her arm slung around his stomach.

Ah, the reason he'd woken up.

Sophie had straddled his thigh. Her nipples pushed through her bra, hard against his chest, her breath coming in short pants. Her eyes closed, her face flushed.

A dream into which he wished he could insert himself.

She whimpered, arched her hips, and angled herself higher on his thigh.

He nuzzled her hair and licked her neck. "Do it. Rub harder, baby. Make yourself come. That's my cock between your legs."

She moaned deep and low.

His cock begged to replace his moisture-slicked thigh, straining against his stomach. If she didn't come soon, he'd blow, scenting her.

"Tip over the edge. I'm jacking off watching you."

His hand found his dick, and he started stroking. He ignored the deep pinch in his balls. Her spine arched, and she clamped around his leg, her body in a long spasm, before she went limp. He arched into his hand, past the point of sanity, and pumped his load on her stomach, then rubbed it into her creamy skin.

Her body relaxed. Sleepy eyes opened. She stretched, pushing her chest against his, and wiggled.

Realization hit her hazy chocolate eyes, which widened.

"Oh no, no, no. That did not happen." She blinked rapidly, her face reddening, her voice thick. She ducked her head and winced. "Please tell me that did not happen." She paused. "I'm sorry for assaulting your leg. All that talk about vibrators must have triggered an erotic dream."

Vibrators? Watching Sophie getting herself off? Fuck, he'd buy the entire stock of Spanky's.

She stilled, red creeping up her chest.

"I have to stop talking."

He propped himself on his elbow. Sophie in the morning with her guard down. He drank her in.

"I know how you feel about me and all, so I apologize for fooling around on your leg." Her hand waved around her head.

She had no fucking idea that thoughts of her body, her mouth, her breasts pushed against his chest, infiltrated his brain at random seconds of every minute.

"You can use my leg anytime." He pushed her riot of hair behind her ear.

"Why are you in my bed?" She moved backward until she hit the edge of the bed and scrambled out. Her hands on her hips, her guard well and truly up.

Her white cotton underwear accentuated the curve of her hip. Her breasts in a plain white bra. Two articles of clothing stood between him and paradise.

He propped himself on an elbow. "Nightmare. Something was dragging your soul out of you. I couldn't wake you up and, to save you from breaking a hand against the wall, I held you until whatever you were fighting had gone."

Yeah, keep telling yourself that's all it was and why you didn't leave when she settled.

Because he knew. She felt perfect in his arms, and for the first time in a long time he slept deep and still.

She slumped on the fluffy flower-covered comforter. "I remember," she said in a quiet voice, staring at nothing. "I couldn't breathe. My head was being held down, then a hand pushed against my mouth. Someone kept whispering it would be all right. I had my Dorothy snow globe in my hand." She looked puzzled. "I didn't remember that before."

Instantly alert, he came up to a sitting position. "Is that a dream or a memory?"

"I don't know." She opened her mouth then clamped it closed. Shutters moved across her face.

"What?"

Her eyes narrowed. "Why are you here? The bet is over."

The spot on the back of his neck ached.

"I'm not moving out until we've got a handle on the militia who want you."

"Why do you care?" she said in a quiet voice.

Surprised, her words threw him.

"Got my night with you to plan," he answered, but it wasn't the truth and he knew it. The hunk of muscle in his chest thawed around her. For the first time in a long time, he wanted to feel, be pushed, challenged, and it was all down to one woman.

There was no way he'd tell her he was being paid an insane amount of money by Petrov, he'd still be protecting her. It gnawed at him that he couldn't tell her the real reason he was here.

She blinked, and her mouth tightened. "There is no night. We listened to the recording together. The bet is done, so you're going to stay away from me. Quid pro quo."

"So, when you won the bet, your prize was for me to stay away from you?" The words burned his throat, and a spasm shot through his heart.

"Yes," she answered in an instant.

Not going to happen.

"There's going to be a night, Sophie," he said softly.

She studied him.

"Don't you get it? I won't be used for one night then thrown away like a candy wrapper," she said in a quiet voice.

He stood and ignored the ache at the back of his skull.

As if suddenly noticing she stood in her underwear, she snatched the comforter from the bed and wrapped it around her body.

"Um, could you leave so I can get dressed?"

He chuckled at her late show of modesty.

"Is that..." Her eyes widened when she glanced down at her stomach.

"I told you, you were hot; I jacked off while you got off."

Her mouth dropped open. "Why didn't you wake me? I would have stopped."

"And risk you waking up and being all embarrassed and not giving me the satisfaction of watching you come? Fuck no."

Her face pinked. "Right. I've got a lot to do today before I kick back with Devon Hamilton and Nick Newman tonight. We've got a marathon scheduled."

He stilled, ignoring the burning in his gut. "You've got two men coming here tonight and you've got a marathon scheduled?"

"Yeah. I hope Sharon makes an appearance. I've got a soft spot for her. She's had it tough." She looked thoughtful. "I'll need Pringles. Lots of Pringles."

He blinked, not getting why she looked all dreamy.

She shuffled toward her bathroom with the comforter still wrapped around her body.

At his growl, she turned and rolled her eyes.

"It's *The Young and the Restless* night."

He folded his arms. "I don't know what that means."

"Only the best show on TV."

He shook his head, bewildered. "I don't know what it is, but I'm guessing it's your shit TV."

Her eyes narrowed. "Say that again and you lose what's between your legs." Her gaze dropped to where his hand curled into a fist. "Are you okay? You're looking a tad tense."

"Not as tense as ten minutes ago. After our night, I'm going to be so loose I'll teach yoga."

Laughter shot out of her. It sounded great. Deep and throaty, it reverberated around his body. He wanted to hear that every day and be the one to make her laugh. He walked back to the spare room. A sonar ping heralded an incoming text. He swiped his finger across the screen, still smiling.

The smile slid off his face when he read the text from Zeb. A brown box addressed to Franco Security had arrived. Typed address. Generic label. No markings. No return address. He tapped on the image of the contents of the box until it filled the screen.

Fuck.

No Eiffel Tower. No pyramids of Giza. No cute scene.

A doe and her baby lay dead on an emerald hill.

A knife mark slashed through the thick Lucite snow globe. The words written in dark red turned his blood to ice.

Back off. She is mine.

TWELVE

"Listen here, Fang. I've got a can of dog food or a Taser. Take your pick."

The mammoth-sized dog, who looked like it had eaten its owner, all the neighborhood children, and wanted to floss its teeth with Sophie, growled at her. She dumped the can of dog food on the ground, set her Taser to stun, and backed away.

Twenty minutes earlier, she'd left the living room in shadows, angling the blinds so it looked like she lay sprawled on her couch with a blanket hanging half on the floor next to a pair of boots. "Nadia's Theme" played in the background. She'd DVR'd her favorite soap, which now played in all its mega drama.

The enormous dog sniffed, and Alpo's Chop House won out. Fang devoured the food, giving her time to climb the neighbor's fence, hook her leg over the top, and land with a soft grunt on the other side. She made it through another fourteen backyards and four other dogs—three friendly, one not. A ginger cat had opened one eye, appraised her, then ignored her. She pushed down the baseball cap, which shielded her face should anyone glance out their window the moment she scaled their fence. She'd mapped out the maze soon after moving into her house. It had taken months of observation and a few near misses and dead ends, but she'd finally determined a path that was all but undetectable. After she vaulted the last fence, she pulled out her phone and sent a text to Gemma, then jogged across the road to a children's playground and waited in the shadows.

A car pulled into the lot and flashed its lights twice.

Sophie groaned, then sprinted to the car and jumped in.

"This is fun. Like we're operatives on a mission."

Sophie pulled off the cap and pulled the band on her hair tight. "If you call cutting through fourteen backyards past a dog that could rip the heart out of Satan and eat it as an appetizer 'fun'."

Half an hour later, she sat on Gemma's couch, eating more devils on horseback.

Delicious.

She looked up to find both Gemma and Annie advancing on her. A flat iron dangled from Gemma's hand. Annie held a bag filled with enough cosmetics to stock CVS and Walgreens.

"We've had a girl conference without you. Sorry," Annie said, looking not at all sorry. "I know your look is hot, but we want to play dress-up tonight. Change you up a beat."

Is this what girlfriends did?

"I... ah... don't know." Sophie stumbled, not having a clue what to do.

"Do you trust us?" Annie asked, catching Sophie off guard.

"Yes," she replied without hesitation.

She did.

Working as a private detective, she'd been deceived by the sweetest, most innocent types, who'd screw their grandmother for a dime. She'd grown to trust her instincts and had only been wrong a handful of times. Her father's voice loomed in her head, which she pushed out.

Annie and Gemma were good people.

"Okay." She pulled on her ponytail. "But nothing too drastic."

"You can't go back on what we do."

Nerves detonated in her stomach.

Sophie blinked up at Annie.

Wait.

"Trust us, okay?" Gemma stepped forward and squeezed Sophie's hand.

Hot prickles crept up her neck.

"Okay," she said, twisting her hands.

Annie grinned, and Gemma whooped.

An hour later, Sophie stood in front of the mirror, frozen. "Who are you?"

Her hair hung in a thick, silky wave over one shoulder. Annie had worked some kind of voodoo magic and had transformed her face. Dark, smoky eyes stared back at her. Ruby lips sparkled. Skin glowed. Long turquoise earrings hung like chandeliers from her ears.

Gemma walked into her family room holding a scrap of material. "You'll look sensational in this."

"I can't wear that." Sophie backed away. "That's not a dress."

"I know it's short, but with your legs? Wowzah." Gemma threw the dress at her. "My room's through there. Try it on. Oh, wait."

Gemma handed her a box. Nestled in tissue paper sat a black lace thong.

"I hope I got your size right." Gemma gnawed her lip.

"I don't understand," Sophie said

"It's for the dress we chose for you tonight. You can't wear a bra, and you have to wear a thong or go commando." Annie cocked an eyebrow.

An unexpected lump formed in Sophie's throat.

Her first gift from a girlfriend. Over the years she'd dreamed of gift exchanges with friends and what they'd be, but sexy underwear wasn't on the list.

"Thanks," she whispered, the lump getting bigger.

Gemma smiled, her eyes glassy. "Go."

Sophie shut the door of Gemma's room and pulled on the black, sparkly jersey fabric shot with turquoise, which clung to every part of her. A thin silver strap over her left shoulder attached the dress to her body. Her legs, excluding two inches at the top, were completely on display. She tugged the hem of the dress, but it was pointless. She didn't need to turn around to know that a slit in the back of the dress dropped all the way to the base of her spine.

This is worse than the uniform at Pipe's.

She walked out of Gemma's room, her arms across her braless chest. "I think this classifies as indecent. I'll be arrested if I step outside."

"Gotta say, you in that dress, I'm thinking of jumping camps." Annie whistled. "You're hot."

"I'm not hot." Sophie wrapped her arms tighter around her body.

"Babe, you're smoking hot." Gemma grinned. "I've got the perfect boots for you, and you are totally gorgeous." Gemma walked out of the room and came back swinging a pair of boots.

"Check us out," Gemma said after she and Annie had changed. "We're like badass Charlie's Angels."

Annie stood in a blood-red pair of skintight PVC pants; a black lace-up bodice hugged her chest, her breasts spilling over the top. An oversized silver crucifix nestled in her cleavage, red stilettos on her feet. Her long blond hair was a riot of ringlets.

A black, tight-fitting sheath hugged Gemma's curves. It fell to the floor and appeared almost demure until she moved and the slit on either side of the dress parted to above her hipbone. Her hair was keratin-smooth, face artificially pale, her tawny eyes smoky, lips stained crimson.

"Say 'Hello Handsome'." Gemma angled her phone for a selfie. Standing between her friends, high-end scent clinging to her, Sophie smiled, the feeling of belonging and friendship sweeping through her like a warm summer wave.

———

AN HOUR later they found a booth at Hostage. Sophie turned to her friends and pointed to the chart on the table. "Okay, girls. A green wristband means you're an observer. No one can touch you, but he or she can ask you to join in. Red means they're a dom, orange is spanking, whips, etcetera. Pink shows they're a slave, gold's submissive. If they're wearing a purple band... anything goes." She indicated with her head. "There are rooms at the back if you want to join in."

"I think I'll stay here," Gemma said, her eyes wide.

"Dear God," Annie whispered, her jaw hanging loose.

A beautiful Black woman wearing a silky white thong walked past, her mile-long legs encased in red, thigh-high boots. She led a man in skintight black latex, the top half of his face covered by a leather hood. A metal bit between his teeth, his wristband pink. The scent of talc trailed him.

Guess she found her My Little Pony.

A woman wearing a silk dress with matching jade heels approached their booth, her brown eyes zeroed in on Gemma. She flashed a gold wristband.

"What do I do?" Gemma shifted back in her seat. "She's beautiful, but I'm into dudes."

"Hold up your wristband," Sophie said out the side of her mouth.

Gemma flashed her green wristband.

The woman shrugged and turned away.

Sophie sipped on her margarita, let her gaze drift around the club, and caught a messy head of dark hair.

Wait.

She blinked, her gaze slid back.

Oh, no. Oh hell no.

Pain exploded in her chest, making it hard to breathe. The liquid that had been sliding down her throat now threatened to reverse course. "Oh my God," she choked, unable to rip her gaze away from a booth in the corner.

"Is that—?" Gemma asked, moving closer.

"Yes," Sophie managed, her throat thick, hearing and hating the ache in her voice.

In the corner sat Harlan, his arm around a gorgeous blond who sat snuggled into his side like he was a heat source and she needed thawing. A beautiful smile lit his face.

Nausea swirled in Sophie's stomach, and with a shaking hand she wiped her eyes.

God, I am such a fool.

Only this morning he said he'd been planning their one night. The look on his face when she'd opened her eyes after coming on his leg had stolen her breath. She knew that coming on her stomach he was telling her she was his. Hunger and ownership swimming in his baby blues—it had scared and excited her.

And just when she thought he wasn't playing her, and she started to bank her insecurities, because maybe, just maybe, they could have something together. Yet again her world imploded, detonated by a Harlan grenade.

"I need another drink." she said, and grabbed her bag. "I'm getting this round. Margaritas?"

Gemma nodded, her face pale.

Annie stared at Harlan like she wanted to knife him in the heart with her shoe.

"THIS IS SO UNCOMFORTABLE. Couldn't Zeb have been my date for the evening? And I hate that I have to be a blond."

Arabella sat beside Harlan with her head bowed, her hands neatly in her lap, in a floor-length, dark-blue dress that he guessed she hated, since she'd been pulling on the material all night.

Harlan tilted his head and murmured. "Almost done. We've got to hang for a few more minutes, then we can leave." He brushed a knuckle down her cheek. "Something about you and Carmichael I need to know?"

Arabella shrugged one shoulder. "I prefer to be out in the field with Zeb."

Surprised, Harlan raised an eyebrow. Quiet and shy, it was rare for Arabella to speak her mind.

"What I mean is," Arabella said, angling her head up to him, "Zeb's an excellent teacher."

"And I'm not?"

"Um, no. Tonight you'll run everything your way, but Zeb lets me take the reins for a bit and listens to my ideas. That never happens with you."

Small stab to the gut.

"A lot is riding on tonight," he countered, not liking the tightness in his chest at her words.

"There's high-stakes on every job. Maybe other's ideas are worth listening to."

Bigger stab to the gut.

"We'll talk about it later," he said, not liking the growl in his voice. Arabella's words had cut closer to the bone than he'd admit.

"Yeah, I've heard those words before, so I'm sure we won't."

He blinked down at her in surprise.

She shrugged a shoulder and continued to keep her head bowed.

Words to chew over later.

There was no debate that Arabella was a genius in front of a computer, a total nerd who could hack a feed or infiltrate state-of-the-art security systems. If she couldn't hack a system, then nobody could. She wanted to work in the field and was fluent in several languages but lacked the physical presence needed for a surveillance job, which is why Harlan was here and not fighting with Sophie.

Maybe he should have delegated this to Zeb.

That statement pulsed in his head like a throbbing sore. He struggled to keep his leg from bouncing. Nervous energy zinged around his body with no outlet, but he had to work the job. Another ten minutes of this torture, then he'd head to the bathroom and Diaz would drop the chip into his hand. Diaz had just walked into the club with his boss and an entourage.

He leaned down to speak low in Arabella's ear. "Time to make your move."

"Right," Arabella murmured, keeping her face blank. "FYI, in my head I am currently on my tropical island after I've won the Powerball this week." She hitched her dress and went to straddle him but overcompensated and, before he could grab her, she slid across his lap onto the floor.

Diaz's boss turned and stared at Harlan. Surprise, then something cold, flickered across the man's face. Diaz trailed his boss, his face tight.

A pit opened up in Harlan's stomach. "Fuck," he hissed under his breath.

"Oh God, I'm so sorry." Arabella stumbled upright, tugging on her dress, her face crimson. "I thought it was like getting on a horse."

Pressure built in Harlan's head. He couldn't run this on his own. If he'd been made and Diaz was suspected, Diaz and his family would be fertilizer.

Harlan jogged outside, pulling his phone from his jacket. He swiped his finger across the second name in his contacts.

"Zeb. I'm at Hostage. The meet with Diaz is screwed. Can you take over? The code word is satellite. He'll know to drop the chip."

Zeb confirmed he'd be there in five.

Harlan pulled his hand through his hair, the ache in his stomach intensifying. He slid his hand across the phone and jogged back into the club to a pale Arabella.

His head turned in slow motion at a familiar scent.

A stunning brunette marched across the floor, oblivious to the stares of every male and some females she passed. Tall, with a dress that clung to jaw-dropping curves, her dark straight hair tumbled down her back. The dress ended a couple of inches below her curvy butt, leaving a slice of creamy skin exposed. Flat black thigh-hugging boots encased her long, long legs.

Wait.

Something about the sway of her hip. If he didn't know better, he'd swear it was Sophie.

Jesus. Now I'm seeing her everywhere.

Her dark eyes slid to where Harlan stood.

He knew that challenging stare. *Fuck.*

A cold knot formed in Harlan's stomach and grew, pushing against his internal organs until he could barely breathe. Sophie stood before him, unprotected.

Today's snow globe delivery confirmed that someone wanted her unguarded and for Harlan to back off. He juggled too many balls, and the pressure to catch them all was intensifying.

He'd decided not to tell Sophie about the mutilated snow globe delivery. He didn't know how she'd react. He could control the situation, but controlling Sophie was another matter, as was painfully obvious at the moment.

He stalked toward her.

Sophie cocked her head, one hand on her hip.

If she tried to run off, he'd cuff her.

When he curled his fingers around hers, her beautiful dark eyes flashed.

"We're leaving," he growled.

"I'm not leaving," Sophie said. "I'm here for a girls' night out, so you can back off."

Christ, even with Zeb on the way, he did not need to be making a scene and drawing more attention to himself. He leaned in to Sophie. "You want to tell me why you're here with no security?" he murmured in her ear.

Sophie shivered.

There it was. The instant DNA connection that had slammed into him. The connection he fought *every* fucking day.

Harlan pulled Sophie to the back of the club. She protested loudly. He stopped and turned to her.

"I have no problem picking you up and carrying you over my

shoulder kicking and screaming. It won't raise an eyebrow in here." It wouldn't, and while he'd prefer not to attract too much attention, she didn't know that.

Her eyes flashed, and her mouth tightened.

They passed the table where her friends sat. A stunning brunette gave them a thumbs-up. A beautiful blond sent him a death stare.

He spied a green light above one of the rooms at the back of the club. He threw open the door, pulled her inside, and locked it behind them.

He held up his hand to silence her when she opened her mouth, barely holding it together. "What the hell are you doing here without Israel? What the fuck are you wearing? Every guy here wants his dick in you." He ignored her sharp intake of breath. "Ditching the security detail. You. Here. Unprotected. Fuck me, Sophie. What the fuck are you doing?"

Pulsing anger spilled out of her and slammed into him. Her voice could snap ice. "For your info, I was heading to the bar to get a round of margaritas for the girls."

He ducked, grabbed her waist, threw her over his shoulder, then dropped her on the bed.

"What the hell are you doing?" She gasped and twisted on the bed, scrambling to the side.

"I'm doing what I should have done when I first met you." He inhaled raspberries, his dick agreeing that particular fruit was awesome.

She rolled off the bed and faced him; the chain holding her dress had slipped off her shoulder, giving him an eyeful of delicious breast. Her chest heaved, eyes snapping. He had no doubt that if she could, she'd remove his limbs and enjoy doing so.

She was the most beautiful, mesmerizing, bewitching, pain-in-the-ass woman he'd ever met.

And he'd never wanted a woman more.

"I can't win physically, so, what is it your 'yes master' girls do? Do

I lie there and let you do what you want?" Her lips parted, her eyes trained on his mouth. "Because that's not what I need."

"I know exactly what you need," he ground out.

"You've got a woman out there waiting for you," she said through clenched teeth. Heat rolled off her body in thick, delicious waves.

"I'm here working."

"Is that what you call it?" She shrugged a shoulder. "Working a case, working a woman. Interesting."

He stared down into her flashing eyes. "I've been working a case for a year. There's no way I could shift the date of the meet. I thought you were safe. You should have been home watching shit TV."

Her eyes narrowed. "What about last night?"

"What about it?" It was a struggle to keep the exasperation out of his voice and not trace his fingers along the curve of her waist.

"You brought a woman into my home. Dior number whatever clogged the air for *hours*." She blinked and turned her head, but not before he caught the glimmer of tears. Anger, frustration, or something else, he didn't know.

"I *did not* bring a woman to your house. I would never disrespect you. I was working with Arabella." He pressed in close, his hard cock digging in to her stomach. "Fuck, Sophie, don't you get it? All I can think about is *you*." His voice was hoarse.

Her eyes widened, and she blinked.

Sophie, being Sophie, surprised him. She arched up and touched her mouth to his, her sweet lips barely brushing his.

He didn't give her a chance to retreat. His mouth slammed down on hers with a growl.

When his tongue touched hers, a shudder moved the length of his body, then down the length of hers.

"Fuck, but I want you," he breathed. "Get your dress off."

For once she complied and shimmied out of the dress.

Her face flushed. She stared up at him.

He drank her in. Rock-hard nipples that begged for his tongue; soft stomach; the flair of her hips. He trailed a finger from her ear to her hip, smiling when goose bumps rose across her skin. His gaze drifted down. A black, sexy thong that he wanted to remove with his teeth separated her from being naked.

Not for long.

He drew the scrap of thong down her thighs and flicked it to the corner, then ripped his T-shirt from his body.

"You're the most beautiful woman on the planet, and I'm going to fuck you until my name falls from your lips." He leaned forward and pulled her nipple hard into his mouth, his tongue trailing over hot flesh. "I'm going to fuck you so well that if you ever fuck another man, it's only my face you'll see, my body you'll feel, wishing it was my cock inside you."

She moaned.

He lifted his head and stared at her flushed face. Her bottom lip snagged.

"I want to hear you whimper when you come. I want your mouth on me. I'll fuck you with my tongue, you'll ride my leg, then I'm going to bend you over and take you from behind. I won't do anything you don't want me to do, or you're uncomfortable with, but I've gotta say, we've got one night, and I want to do it all."

"So do I. Starting with you inside me, now," she panted. Her voice, like gravel, shot straight through to his aching cock that twitched for release.

Insubordination.

Oh, she'd pay for that.

He yanked open a bedside drawer and pulled out a condom.

"Can I?" Her voice fractured.

He paused for a second.

The thought of her hands on him, peeling the rubber over him, had his balls twitching and could have him blowing on the spot, but he wanted her hands on him, caressing him, touching him. Without a word, he handed her the condom.

With deliberate slowness, he undid his belt and pulled down his zipper, his cock finally free.

"Oh," she breathed.

She ripped open the packet; her fingers moved down his shaft, rolling the rubber to the base. He shuddered, barely holding it together.

"Need to be inside you, baby." He gently grabbed her shoulders but, with surprising strength, she flipped him down on his back and straddled him.

She wiggled herself into position and lowered herself an inch at a time, as if testing her limits. He slid into her incredibly tight, wet heat, his hands on her hips, guiding her.

Her eyes were barely open, her mouth in a barely formed "oh", her wild hair everywhere.

He growled, about to make her his.

He closed his eyes, his fingers digging into her hips, searching for control.

Being inside Sophie was way better than he'd imagined. And he'd imagined it a lot.

If he wasn't careful, he'd come in two seconds, and he planned on making this as much about her as it was about them.

"Don't stop," he growled, and the tiny smile morphed into a grin but melted from her face when his thumb worked her clit. Her dark eyes grew hazy. He angled his hips off the bed and hit higher. Her eyes widened, and her breathing quickened. Sweat beaded her forehead. He thrust high again. She whimpered, her core coiling.

His stomach muscles quivered when her hands landed on his abdomen. Her body strained upward then stiffened, her face red, before she convulsed around him, her body shaking. He thrust out his orgasm, coming seconds later.

She collapsed, the side of her face landed on his chest, her hair a smooth blanket around them.

With both hands at her waist, he sat up, breaking their connection, pulled off the condom, and kissed her shoulder, then flipped her back onto the bed.

"Hook your knees over my shoulders... I'm hungry."

She blinked up at him, her eyes widening, then growing dark. Soon her calves were resting on his back.

He stared down at her beautiful body.

The scent of her musk and raspberries made him dizzy. He reached forward, his tongue finding her clit, then circling her hot flesh.

"You make me dizzy." She moaned and pushed herself against his mouth.

He thrust his tongue into her sweetness, alternating fucking her with his tongue and flicking her clit, feeling her build, her muscles tightening.

"You taste better than I imagined." He kissed her thighs and smiled at her moan of protest. Without warning, he sucked her clit hard into his mouth. Her body bucked off the bed, her thighs a vise around his head.

"Are you going to do what I say?" he asked.

Her orgasm shook her body. He dragged his mouth up her body, kissed her, then grabbed a condom from the drawer and sheathed himself.

"No." Her eyes were unfocused, her body still pulsing.

He grinned. He'd never admit it, but her challenging him had his dick throbbing for her, and his heart throwing in an extra fifty beats.

He thrust into her.

Her legs wrapped around his hips, her arms around his neck. She raised her hips to meet his, her heels digging in to his back. A silent current coursed between them. He felt it and knew she felt it, too.

He pulled out, grabbed her hips, and flipped her over. She widened her legs to accommodate him. Her butt tilted, and in one thrust he entered her.

"Jesus," she moaned.

The lines of who was in control blurred after he'd taken her from behind. She straddled his face. After she'd come, she licked her way down his body, and smiled when she took him deep into her throat.

Her lips locked around him, which took him to the brink and tipped him over.

They wrung each other dry, and he knew he wasn't anywhere near finished.

He hadn't even made it to the toy cupboard. Sometime later, she curled beside him, her head on his shoulder, her arm slung around his waist. He leaned down and kissed her forehead, tucking blankets around her and pulling her tight into him, knowing full well that one night with Sophie wouldn't be enough.

THE SOUND of laughter infiltrated Sophie's exhausted brain. She opened her eyes. Milky light from the bathroom tinged the room. Her head lay on Harlan's shoulder, her legs entwined with his. Her arm was around his waist. A thin sheet covered them, the blankets long gone. Not that it mattered—the heat their bodies generated could power Colorado and neighboring New Mexico, Utah, and Kansas.

Night's over, Cinderella.

A horrible sinking feeling settled in her stomach.

She untangled her legs from his and held her breath.

Nothing.

She stilled, stared at Harlan, and her heart did a weird hitch. Dark hair flopped on his forehead, his lips parted, his face soft in sleep.

One night; now we're done.

Unexpected tears filled her eyes. She moved to the edge of the bed and her feet hit the ground. Two strong, warm hands grabbed her hips and, before she could stop him, she lay plastered against his warm bulk.

"Where are you going?" he asked, his voice gravelly.

"Home," she said, holding her body still, hating the kick of emotion in her voice.

He kissed her neck, his lips soft against her skin.

"I'll take you."

Too many hot, sticky emotions twisted her heart.

Distance. She needed distance.

She ducked her head, avoiding him. "It's okay, I'll catch a cab or call an Uber or Lyft."

"Sophie, I'll take you home." The sleepy voice was now gone.

She figured there was no point standing outside waiting for a cab. She'd be picked up for indecent exposure before one arrived. Harlan would do his he-man stunt while they had a stand-up fight, which she didn't have the energy for.

She nodded, got out of bed, found the scrap of material that masqueraded as a dress, and pulled it on. After a couple of minutes, she abandoned the search for the thong, grabbed her boots, and sat on the bed.

Denim slid up his legs. The sound of a zipper. Heavy boots were pulled onto his feet. The scent of sex and him slurred her brain.

She'd had her fill. He'd had his fill, and now they were done.

As it had to be.

Pressure built behind her eyelids.

She walked to the door, her lips pressed together, holding back the emotion. His jacket landed on her shoulders. He grabbed her hand and tucked her in to his side.

Exhausted, physically she felt as smooth as a roll of silk. But mentally she clawed the walls. All she wanted to do was go home, curl into a ball in her bed, and forget. As if she could ever erase the night.

A night where she'd let go and lived with Harlan. One delicious night where she'd woken curled into his body and the words "safe and wanted" had drifted across her mind.

Out of the passenger window of Harlan's car, Sophie absently watched two homeless men picking through bins, a black Chihuahua dog following them. The city came to life. A street-sweeper truck rumbled by. A couple of people stood blowing into their hands at a bus stop, their heads turned left in anticipation. She stared, turning her head at a man in a bathrobe. Wait, was that the same person she'd seen days ago walking the ferret?

The car pulled into her driveway.

She twisted in her seat. His eyes moved to where her dress had ridden up, offering him a serving of thigh. In most states, the dress wouldn't pass as clothing.

Out of the corner of her eye, she caught Titus's blinds lifting.

"Right. Well, um, thanks for everything." Heat crept up her cheeks. How to say, *thanks for the most amazing night of my life?* Was there a Hallmark card that covered this scenario?

"Later."

He stared straight ahead.

Right.

There were those stupid over-tired tears again.

She exited the car and made it to her door without flashing the world. She unlocked her door, deactivated the alarm, stepped inside, and leaned against the door, giving her heart time to slow down.

Shower. I need a shower, and lots and lots of Pringles.

She couldn't process what had gone down with Harlan without a full load of sleep and some distance. Part of her, and they were the physical parts, were still throwing streamers and popping celebratory champagne corks. Part of her wanted to go to a quiet corner, curl up, and watch *The Young and the Restless* until she'd had her fill of drama and love.

I have no one to blame but myself. I pressed my mouth against his.

Her fingers drifted over her tingling lips.

He'd fucked her out of his system and was now they were done.

Her heart twisted in a painful mass.

Pongo stared at her from his mountain of pillows, looking tired from sleeping all night.

"Hey, baby boy."

She paused in front of her snow globe collection; a bubble of overwhelming loneliness pushed aside her heart and slid up her throat.

"Damn it." She wiped her eyes, shed the dress, dropped it, and headed to the shower.

HOT WATER STREAMED down her body. She'd washed her body, one part of her tender after a long period of inactivity. She now stood with water streaming over her head, letting the hurt, anger at herself for feeling hurt, and exhaustion filter out of her body.

Her eyes flew open, and adrenaline spiked in her body when the glass shower door opened.

"Fucking raspberries get me every time," Harlan said, shutting the door, a grin on his face, one part of his body obviously happy to see her.

One arm covered her breasts, the other hand shielding between her legs. "What are you doing here?"

He smiled at her attempt at modesty, stepped forward, and ran his tongue from her neck to her ear.

Her body shivered in response.

"Did a calculation." His hand skimmed the side of her breast, his fingers leaving a trail of fire before branding her hip.

"And?" She stepped toward him, running her hands up his spine, his muscles quivering under her fingertips.

He lowered his head and pulled her begging nipple into his mouth.

She moaned, his tongue hot and demanding. He then paid attention to the other breast. She melted into him, his arm propping her up. He smiled against her skin.

"In Easter Island it's one a.m."

"Where's that?" she murmured, electricity spiking her nerve endings.

"Don't care." His mouth blazed a trail of tender but sharp nips down her neck until she moaned. He grabbed her hand, releasing her hold on him, then spun her around. Her hands braced on the glass.

His fingers found the hot flesh between her legs. She distantly heard a wrapper before his hand was back working its magic. One arm around her waist, keeping her upright.

"We've still got all night." He tilted her hips and powered into her, knowing the angle that made her pant his name.

And pant his name she did.

The air left her in a rush. The sensation of his hand between her legs and the length of him filling her—exquisite. Higher and higher he thrust; his hand pushing hard circles on her clit sent liquid fire burning through her veins. Standing on her toes, straining, every muscle in her body wound tight. He stopped, pulled out and, ignoring her protest, lifted her. She gripped his slippery shoulders. His hands cupping her butt, she crossed her ankles behind his hips.

His eyes locked on hers, feral and possessive, his hungry mouth taking hers. Devouring her. And she gave it back, hungrier for him by the second. Drowning in him, drowning in the sensations invading her body and mind like Vikings. Their tongues clashed, their breathing labored. He growled when he thrust into her. The tension of release howled inside her. She gripped his shoulder with one hand, the other slammed against the glass of the cubicle. She screamed as her body pulsed around his. His tempo increased until, after a long shudder, he stilled.

The water abruptly stopped.

He eased himself out of her. Pushing the glass door open, he grabbed a towel from the rack and wrapped it around her shoulders. "I'm stopping the clock in Easter Island. It's one a.m. We still have twenty-three hours."

He picked her up as if she weighed nothing and walked into her room. Throwing back the fluffy quilt, he deposited her on the bed.

Exhausted and unable to form a word, she shivered when cool air smacked her body. He slid behind her, one arm around her waist, pulling her into his warmth, as her eyes drifted closed. His lips brushed the back of her neck.

"I want this," he murmured. Sophie's eyes flew open.

———

THAT AFTERNOON, Sophie set another cup of coffee on her desk and pulled open Beth's case file, desperate to find an answer for Beth and in need of a major distraction.

Earlier, she'd woken in a tangle of limbs. When she slept she'd moved away from Harlan, but as soon as she was out of "Harlan" radar, he became agitated, hauled her against him, and his body then relaxed.

She'd slipped out of bed to find Harlan's smoky gaze on her, his face unreadable.

Wired, in need of caffeine and time away, she'd headed to the kitchen.

She turned when Harlan entered the room. He leaned against the doorframe, hair wet from a shower. Her mouth watered at the denim plastered to his thighs, the tight black T-shirt stretched across his chest. With an effort, she turned her head back to the computer screen and felt his stare searing her skin.

He pushed off the wall and came to stand in front of her, his arms crossed against his impressive chest.

Feeling nervous and unsure, a hesitant smile played at her lips.

"How'd you ditch the security?"

Pain sliced low and hard in her heart. She fought the need to press her fingers to her chest to put pressure on the internal wound.

Wow.

Just wow.

She took a long gulp of coffee, holding it in her mouth, preferring the pain of the scalding liquid over the steady thump of hurt in her chest, buying time. She swallowed and set the cup on the counter, pleased it didn't rattle. "I wanted a girls' night out," she said, meeting his gaze, "without you or any of your people trailing me."

His gorgeous blue eyes flashed and, before she could react, his mouth landed on hers, and he kissed her hard.

She tensed and resisted.

He pulled on her ponytail until she had no choice but to angle her head back.

She shook her head.

Her back arched, her hands moved to the artery in his neck, and her fingers kneaded.

He flinched but pulled back.

Tension thickened the air until it hurt to breathe.

"Tell me, Sophie," he ground out.

Her spine straightened. "No."

He stared down at her, his face unreadable. "You infuriate the crap out of me."

Her head snapped back. Well, wasn't that what every girl wanted to hear after she'd had the best sex of her life and then been held like precious cargo?

"Then go," she said, hearing the scrap of hurt in her voice and hating it.

"Sophie," he said with a growl.

She stared him down until he shook his head and rubbed his hand across his creased forehead. "There's double detail on you today." She stilled.

Wait.

Something wasn't right. Nothing had changed since yesterday.

Unless.

Unless *he* wasn't telling *her* something.

"Anything changed from yesterday?" She scanned him and could read nothing.

Without hesitation, he shook his head. "Nothing."

"Then drop the double detail. Drop all the details."

"No." He leaned forward and kissed her forehead, his face hard. "Please don't ditch anyone, Sophie. I need to know you're safe." Something unfamiliar flashed in his eyes. Something that made her breath hitch and her heart pound.

After he walked out of the room, she heard the front door close with a soft click.

She stood and made another pot of coffee, her hands shaking.

At the rate she was downing coffee, she'd soon resemble an extra on a zombie show.

She wandered her living room, not bothering to crack the blinds to see who was parked across the street or in her driveway.

There were far too many things on a collision course in her head, starting with Harlan's whispered words.

She sat next to her dog on the couch, threw an arm around his warm body, and let herself analyze. She came up with three scenarios.

Scenario one could mean he wanted this. *This* being her body that had been tucked against his. That made sense.

I can run with that.

Scenario two could mean he wanted one particular part of her body that he'd been occupying exquisitely a few moments earlier. She could *definitely* run with that.

What made little sense was if he was referring to him and her. As in a couple. Together. That made no sense. He'd been clear from the beginning he wasn't a relationship guy. She didn't even know if *she* wanted a relationship. They spent half their time fighting, which was exhausting and exhilarating.

Physically, she wanted him as much as he wanted her.

She let her mind sift.

If they were ever at a place where she felt safe enough to tell him the truth, about her father, about everything, with that soft part of her she kept hidden, exposed...

If they ever got to the place where they had something, *yeah*, she'd run with it because she wanted *it*, too.

A Pongo special pulled her back into the room. She coughed and patted her dog's head.

"Good boy, Pong, you're like an alarm clock."

She concentrated on the computer screen and the case notes in front of her. The mystery of finding Beth's missing mother was turning out to be harder than she'd expected.

She pulled up a spreadsheet on her computer, scrolled down to the end. She'd phoned, emailed, or spoken to pretty much every person in Colorado who'd known Suzie when she'd been here. She'd contacted the casino she used to work at to see if she'd returned there, but the woman in the department aptly named "Talent Scouts" wouldn't give out any information. She'd found a telephone number written on the back of a receipt. With nothing else to go on, she punched in the cell number. The previous calls had gone to voicemail.

A woman answered with her name and before Sophie could tell her she wasn't selling anything, wanting her to convert to her religion, or had any connections to Nigerian princes, she hit dead air.

She took another gulp of coffee.

Change of attack.

Danielle Winters hadn't been pleased when Sophie phoned back and started talking before she could hang up. Sophie told her she was searching for Suzie West on behalf of her daughter. After a lengthy silence, the woman said she'd talk but not over the phone.

Danielle had turned into her one and only lead.

The answer lay in Vegas, which wasn't in her budget or Beth's. If Sophie ate only generic-brand peanut butter out of the jar for a week and maybe pulled an extra couple of shifts at Pipe's, she could hop a plane to the city of sin and be back the next day or the day after. Plus, if she stayed in a hotel way off the strip, she could keep expenses down.

She picked up her phone and spoke to Beth, then called Danielle back and asked if she could see her tomorrow. Danielle agreed, but could only meet with her in the morning.

Half an hour later, a confirmation from Southwest sat in her inbox. She'd catch their first flight out at six twenty-five tomorrow morning. She'd leave for the airport straight after her shift tonight. Southwest would return her to Denver around ten p.m. the day after, which gave her an extra twenty-four hours to track down the elusive Suzie if she was still in Vegas. A car had been booked at Rent-a-

Bomb. She'd found what looked like a cheerful hotel which, according to the internet, was so far off the strip the famous lights weren't visible. Her email pinged. A photo of Beth and her baby daughter, Hannah, landed in her inbox.

Now, all she had to do was pack a small bag, jam her computer into a carry-on, and ask Titus if he could feed Pongo—oh, and she'd be telling Mr. Double Detail that she'd be ditching all details and heading to Vegas.

Later that night, Sophie walked into her living room and dropped her overnight bag on the floor. Her heart did a little squelch. Harlan had come back twenty minutes earlier and was wrestling Pongo on the couch. She tightened the belt of her trench coat.

Harlan's eyes cut to the carry-on bag at her feet and he frowned.

"After my shift I'm heading to the airport. I have an early morning flight to Vegas."

Pongo's tongue lolled out the corner of his mouth. He stared up at Harlan, love written all over his face. "Titus will feed Pongo and make sure he doesn't starve to death, although with the amount of calories in him I think that would take a hundred years plus an ice age."

"Vegas?" Harlan asked, his voice deathly quiet.

"Yeah. A case I'm working. The only lead I have is there, and I'm going out to meet her." They locked eyes. "This is work, Harlan, and I'm not stopping work because I've been followed a couple of times and two men *once* had eyes on me at a strip joint."

Two days in Vegas would also give her time, distance from him, and perspective. Three things she needed. Oh, and to over-analyze his three murmured words while chowing down on salt and vinegar potato chips while watching Genoa City's latest dramas.

Hard eyes held her gaze. "That's because I have eyes on you twenty-four-seven. They won't come near you because I'm here."

She shrugged a shoulder. "I'm going to Vegas and I'm leaving now or I'll be late for my shift."

He rubbed the back of his neck. "Fuck, Sophie."

"We've gone through this. This is work." She couldn't keep the tiredness out of her voice. She picked up her bag, walked to her dog, and kissed his head. "Be a good boy for Uncle Titus, okay?"

"I'll take you."

She opened her mouth, but he cut her off.

"Are we going to fight about this, too?"

"Yes." Her hands went to her hips. "I have a driver's license and a car."

Twenty minutes later, Harlan pulled into the parking lot at Pipe's. Embarrassingly, her car had thrown a tantrum and wouldn't start. She opened the passenger door, hitched her overnight bag on her shoulder, and twisted back to face Harlan. "See you."

"Yep." He stared straight ahead.

The sound of the SUV roaring out of the parking lot rang in her ears when she shut the door of the back entrance to Pipe's.

She removed her coat in the changing room, stowed her bag in her locker, and joined Gemma and Cope behind the bar. Gemma squeezed her hand. "MMA championship fight on ESPN tonight. It'll be a little crazy."

A little crazy didn't cover it. She'd spun on a man who slipped his hand up her thigh. She'd grabbed his wrist and yanked it back until he yelped. "Never touch women without permission. Ever."

Annie had arrived, looking stunning in skinny jeans, sneakers minus laces, and a plain white T-shirt. She sat on a barstool in front of Cope and popped peanuts into her mouth. Her eyes darted around the room. "This place is better than *Days of our Lives*."

"How are the Brady's and the DiMera's?" Sophie shouted over the noise, slapping her empty tray on the bar and relaying her next drink order to Cope.

"Are you a fan?" Annie stared.

"The Newman's and Abbott's send their regards."

Annie grinned. "Oh girl, we have to talk."

Heavy metal music from the pool table area sounded almost soothing compared to the grunts, and the overexcited commentator talking up a cage fight. Sophie shook her head at the bloody men on the screen and turned back to the men leaning against the bar and sitting at tables glued to the action.

"I could lay there and offer free shots served on my boobs, and I doubt they'd move," Gemma said.

Cope spluttered. "Jesus, Gemma, don't say shit like that." His face red, he turned away, adjusting the front of his jeans.

Sophie grinned and rolled her shoulders, grimacing at the shooting pain between her shoulder blades. Her triceps had issued a strike notice and her biceps were about to hold a stop-work meeting.

"At this rate I'll have shoulders like the Incredible Hulk." She loaded drinks on the tray. "I'm glad I'm in Vegas for two days."

"You're going to Vegas and you didn't tell me?" Annie spun on her stool and glared at her.

She froze.

"Who's going to Vegas?" Gemma's glossy brown hair bounced on her shoulders from the high ponytail.

Heat belted Sophie's face.

"Is this related to the bounty hunter from Hostage?" Gemma asked. "Which you haven't given us a detailed account of, I may add."

"You were at Hostage?" Cope turned to Gemma, his mouth a thin line, eyes flashing.

"Yeah," Gemma said, her eyes wide. "Did you know they have these colored wristbands—?"

Sophie waved a hand in front of her face. "I'm going to Vegas on a case. A daughter hoping to find her missing mother. I didn't think to tell you," she said honestly.

"Text me when you get back. We have to have another girls' night." Gemma squeezed her shoulder. "I like the way you stopped Wandering Hands over there. You know you can get Cope to step in."

Cope had finished glaring at Gemma and turned to glare at her. "Soph, if anyone even hints at touching you, let me know."

Sophie loaded shots of Wild Turkey onto her tray. "I prefer to fight my own battles. If I go running to you every time someone tries for a grope, they're more likely to corner me when you're not around. If I deal with them straight up, they'll be less likely to cop a drunk feel when I'm alone."

"I don't like any of them touching you, but I get where you're coming from," Cope said. "Hold up your hand and I'll kick their ass outside, just like Mick."

"Thanks."

She'd mentioned to Cope in passing that Mick had delivered a snow globe to her house. She ran a random question past Gemma about who'd have access to personnel files. Gemma had assured her all the files were locked in the office at Pipe's. Gemma had tried to question her further, but Sophie had blown her off. Sophie figured Mick was still banned or didn't want to come back. Either way, she didn't care.

Sophie weaved through tables in her section and deposited the shots in front of a group of men, their eyes trained on the TV screens.

"Hey, Soph. You want to catch a bite to eat after this?" Dug loomed in front of her. She startled. "Hey, Dug."

His ability to materialize out of thin air always made her jump.

In black jeans and a long-sleeved, navy T-shirt that stretched across wide shoulders and hugged chiseled abs, he stood with a hip leaning against the table.

A group of drooling women stared at him.

"I can't, but thanks. No fraternizing with the staff." His hazy green eyes ran the length of her frame, then landed back on her face.

"Pipe won't know if you don't tell him." His easy grin made her blush.

She shook her head.

"I *will* wear you down." He leaned in, his breath tickling her ear. His lips barely touched her neck.

She jolted. Before she could speak, he grinned and melted into the crowd.

She made her way to the next table, took an order for more whiskey, then headed back to the bar.

"Girlfriend, your man who hauled you through Hostage is standing by the back door. He has one eye on you and the other on Dug, and it looks like he wants to commit a felony." Annie took a sip of her drink. "This is *way* better than the Brady's and the DiMera's."

Sophie turned and searched the bar. At the back, Harlan sat at a table for one. He didn't acknowledge her, his eyes trained on Dug, who stared back at him. Sophie didn't need an antenna to pick up a weird vibe bouncing between them.

Sophie pushed thoughts of Harlan to one side, but felt his eyes burning through her uniform. She hauled her butt between her section and the bar, calculating tips as she went. Pongo would now have his teeth cleaned, Lori from Tequesta, FL, sister's Pat and Sherry from Tuscaloosa, Alabama, and Andrea from Roma, Texas would all be receiving refunds and a card from Josiah O'Connor.

She turned to where Harlan had been sitting to find the table empty. Strangely disappointed, she pushed on.

She smiled and stopped by a table filled with regulars. She'd enjoyed getting to know Maggie and asked about her daughter—a sophomore at Arizona State. When she spotted Sybil coming through the door, Sophie made sure she had a fresh drink and a ready supply of bar nuts. Two hours away from her twin toddler boys, once a week, cured Sybil's woes.

Eventually, Cope called last drinks, and the bar emptied. Forty minutes later, she changed into black jeans, a black T-shirt, and slipped a jacket around her shoulders. She pulled out her phone after it vibrated and read a text.

FRANCO: *Staff entrance. Waiting.*

The man doesn't pen sonnets in his spare time, I'm guessing.

She said good night to her friends, got a quick hug from Gemma, and hit the back door to find Harlan guarding it.

White bulbs that spelled out Pipe's sputtered out. A stray cat streaked across the parking lot, eyes flashing in the milky moonlight.

An icy breeze pushed trash across the lot. After the heat of the bar, the fresh air cleansed her lungs.

"Why were you here earlier, and where'd you go?" she asked.

He threw the strap of her bag onto his shoulder, held her hand, which she had to admit felt kind of nice, and guided her to his Range Rover. He pulled her closer to his side, his heat soaking into her tired bones and loosening weary muscles.

Tonight, she was too tired to fight being hauled against him. Red tail lights flashed ahead of them.

"A blast from the past," he said cryptically.

He opened the car door and waited until she got in, then walked to his side and got in.

They drove in silence to the airport.

"I'm flying Southwest." She pulled up the app on her phone.

"I know."

Of course he did.

Dawn streaked across the sky with splashes of purple and tangerine. Morning birds were up and announcing to the world it was time to fly. A bus packed with tourists stopped ahead of them. Excited people exited the bus, sporting fanny packs.

He pulled alongside a line of weary travelers. A family chanted "Disneyland" over and over while a grinning father pushing a mountain of luggage on a dolly trailed them. A business executive in a crisp suit pulled a battered orange Samsonite and overtook the California-bound family.

Sophie swung her bag onto her shoulder, pasted on a radiant smile, and opened the door. "Um, thanks for the ride. I'll see you in a couple of days." Harlan stared straight ahead.

Alrighty then.

The man was sending more mixed signals than a DiMera and Brady family, is-he-a-serial killer-or-my-third-cousin-with-amnesia, cliffhanger. She shut the door and entered the terminal.

Twenty minutes later Sophie sat at the gate nursing a beverage that, according to the chirpy attendant, was coffee. The attendant's definition of coffee was under debate.

A slow line of people trickled past, none stopping at her gate. Seemed that heading to Vegas at six in the morning wasn't a popular commuter flight. She abandoned the cup to a nearby trash can. Her body cried out for her to find a comfy spot somewhere so she could curl into a ball and sleep.

Two older women plunked their butts down beside her. According to their conversation, they were leaving their menfolk behind to see *Thunder From Down Under* and live it up a little. They'd saved their bingo money and, apparently, *Thunder From Down Under* was in for a treat.

"Delores. Check out that honey walking toward us. I hope he's in the show's lineup. There'll be some five-dollar bills in his Calvin Klein's."

"Lordy be, Phyllis. That's a fine-looking man. Now, if I were ten years younger."

"Twenty, Delores."

A barrage of cackles followed.

"Morning ladies." A deep, throaty, and familiar voice replied.

Sophie's heart missed a painful beat. "What are you doing here?"

Harlan nodded to a man leaning against a column, a newspaper tucked under his arm, who nodded then walked away. "Going to have some fun in Vegas. There're hours left on the clock." He trailed his knuckle down her cheek.

Her spine snapped straight. She stood, hands on her hips, her throat tight. "No you're not."

THIRTEEN

"Yeah. I. Am." Harlan grinned down at a pissed-off Sophie with flashing dark eyes, her kissable mouth in a thin line, color on her cheeks. He inhaled her raspberry scent and relaxed slightly.

After a tense conversation with Holden Abbot working under-cover as a man named Dug—who wouldn't tell him anything about why he was all over Sophie—Harlan's anxiety had ratcheted up. He had to hand it to his boarding school bud. He was an excellent opera-tive who could turn into a priest, a cut-throat entrepreneur and now a biker. The man was part chameleon who had more than a passing interest in Sophie. Harlan had let him know Sophie was very much his.

Her dark eyes narrowed. "No, you're *not*."

"Yeah, I am." He sat beside her and pulled her close, her soft curves molding against him, then tucked her hair behind her ears. "I'm not leaving you unprotected."

"Well, ain't she the lucky one," one of the older women sitting next to Sophie said. "If I was her, I'd be heading to Victoria's Secret."

Her companion elbowed her in the ribs. "Delores, I wouldn't be packing any of Victoria's Secrets."

Harlan grinned at the older women then bent his head toward Sophie. "*We* could go shopping. Seeing you in your Pipe's uniform, gotta say, I'm glad we're hitting the City of Sin." He ran his finger along her jaw. His voice still soft, he said, "Don't wear underwear tomorrow."

Her head snapped back, her face red. "I am *so* wearing underwear."

He nuzzled her ear. "When I walk up behind you, I'll flick up your short, short skirt and in one thrust be inside you."

She shivered under his touch.

"I didn't bring a skirt, so that isn't happening, *and* I've got a spare set of underwear," she said from the corner of her mouth, her ears an adorable pink.

"Did you bring your uniform?" He kissed her collarbone, dragging his lips up her satiny neck.

She stilled at his touch, but he could feel her pulse quickening through his lips.

"Stop it. We're in public," she whispered, her head whipping left, then right, as if she'd been caught stealing from a collection plate. "And yes," she said in a quiet voice, shooting him a look from under her inky lashes, then looking away. Her bottom lip snagged between her teeth.

"Yes, what?"

So caught up in the image of removing the thong from her body, he'd lost the thread of the conversation.

"Yes, I have my uniform." The image of Sophie walking next to him in Vegas had his cock appreciating the picture.

Wait.

Sophie in that skirt in Vegas.

He hadn't thought this through.

Sophie walking around Vegas in sheer black stockings with her long legs on display and silver studs across her breasts spelling out "Pipe's" would have more men wanting Sophie than he could handle.

"I've changed my mind. Don't wear it. I don't want to be dropping fuckers who want their dick in you."

"That's funny." She swatted his shoulder. "Men don't notice me, and they don't want their dick in me."

He stilled. "What?"

Here was the paradox he couldn't get his head around.

Sophie was stunning, and she had no freaking clue.

"Yeah, Sophie, they do."

"No, they don't," she said, sounding like his words hurt.

He turned his head. Her face was tight.

"Sophie, why don't you think you're beautiful?" he asked quietly.

"Because I'm not. My father told me all my life that it was better to go through life 'natural' like me than to get unwanted attention, so don't say things like that, because they hurt." Pain leaked from her voice.

Another reason to hate Josiah O'Connor.

She had no idea of the number of men and women who turned when she walked past. He'd watched the clientele at Pipe's tonight drool over her, and it wasn't just her stunning looks. She talked and joked with men and women, asking about their day, if they needed a refill of bar nuts, how their kid was doing in college. She had a natural warmth when she wasn't hiding it.

"Sophie, you are beautiful." He kissed the hinge of her rigid jaw.

She turned her head, but not before he caught a tremble in her mouth. He gripped her hand tighter, giving her the time he sensed she needed. Right there, he'd gained another inch. Getting closer to the real Sophie.

Petrov's face surfaced in his brain. Yeah, this was about the assignment, but it was also about a desire to know her. See the real Sophie. Peel away the layers and find the softness that she hid.

Her warmth pressed against the length of him, making him totally aware of every inch of her long, firm thigh against his.

She turned to him, her face serious. "So while we're in Vegas, you won't interfere with my case?"

His hand tightened in hers. "No, I won't interfere with your case. Take one of my jumpers again and I'll make you pay. Do your party trick on anyone other than me. You'll pay a *lot*."

She grinned, making her eyes all sparkly.

Damn.

"Oh, I'm never giving up my party trick. I could have put a collar on Lopez, and he'd have followed me out like a puppy."

His fingers flexed around hers. He didn't like the stab of jealousy straight to his heart, picturing Sophie performing her party trick on another man. "Yeah, we've got to have a chat about your party trick." He leaned in closer. "I'm hoping you brought the Silver Bullet."

She sucked in a breath. "Stop it," she whispered, averting her red face, but not before desire flashed in her eyes.

Yeah, he intended to have fun in Vegas. A lot of fun.

Finally, he could relax. The assignment with Diaz had been completed by Zeb, who'd collected the chip smoothly. The man and his family were on a plane over the Pacific. Zeb, Israel and Arabella were monitoring their other cases.

Since he and Sophie had checked in online earlier, they were boarding group A and were soon buckled in. When the plane moved, she'd clutched his hand like she was going to meet her maker. During takeoff she'd all but climbed onto his lap.

"I'm not a frequent flier," she said a short time later when the seatbelt sign flicked off.

"I guessed that." He chuckled.

"First time on a plane," she confessed.

He banked the information.

Did he always have to be on a case? Couldn't it just be him and his girl hanging?

But Sophie was more than a girl—she was a paid assignment. It was getting harder and harder to remind himself of the fact.

She went to pull away her hand, but he held on, liking the feel of her hand in his.

"Been to the City of Sin?" he asked.

"No."

That surprised him. He'd have thought with its jackpot of sinners the man could fleece, O'Connor would have been all over it.

She leaned in and whispered, "Do you think they sell silver bullets there?"

He blinked slowly. Again, when he thought she couldn't surprise him, she did. He kissed her slow and long until she melted into him and they were in danger of dissolving the seats. "We'll find one."

If they weren't circling the airport, they'd be making an entry into the mile-high club.

The plane landed without fanfare in Vegas.

He grabbed their bags from the overhead locker, held her hand, and exited the plane, scanning the area ahead as he went.

"Wow. Are we in a casino already?" Sophie asked.

Harlan breathed in stale tobacco and warm beer and looked down at her, not understanding. "We're in the airport."

Her hand landed on his arm. "How many slot machines are there?" She turned a circle, her eyes wide. "They're everywhere, and people are playing them at eight in the morning?"

He shrugged. "Last minute roll of the dice hoping lady luck will smile down on them."

He turned a professional eye on the crowd. Men in the uniform of Texas—jeans, boots, and Stetsons planted on their heads—sat beside California surfers, all plying machines. A group of business executives sat at a bar knocking back Bud before rejoining their lives, their Vegas vacation now consigned to poker nights, the odd elbow in the rib, and a secret smile at a Fourth of July barbecue. A group of women all wearing name tags and dressed in pink scuttled past, the leader, Robin from Boise, Idaho, proclaiming that this weekend would be the best meeting of minds and cosmetics on the planet.

"If we keep this up, we'll never get out of the airport," Harlan said twenty minutes later, blowing out an exasperated breath.

Every few steps, Sophie had to stop and stare at *everything*.

He loved it when her cheeks got all pink. "This place is mesmerizing." She pulled a map from her bag with one hand. "Right. We've got to get moving. I've got to get a cab to the rental company, then we can swing by the hotel, drop our bags, and meet with Danielle at eleven." A cloud drifted across her face. "I hope this isn't a bust, and she turns up."

Harlan didn't answer, knowing her meet would be a fifty-fifty call. In their line of work, the chance of someone turning up to offer information without a cash incentive was fairly low, unless emotions came into play.

They made it to the line of cabs. She gave the driver the address, and they headed north. Waves of heat rose from the desert in a shimmer. Dark clouds stewed on the horizon. "I wish I'd worn different clothes." Sophie fanned herself with a tourist book she'd grabbed from a rack in the back of the cab.

Even in the comfort of the air-conditioned cab at nine in the morning, the mercury climbed on its inevitable journey of hitting triple digits by noon.

Harlan had been surprised when they headed away from the strip.

Twenty minutes later, he knew why.

Sophie stood in front of a peeling Rent a Bomb sign, her hands on her hips, sunglasses protecting her eyes.

"I'm not arguing with you. This is my case, and we're on a budget. This car is perfectly capable of getting me where I need to go." She unlocked the door of a dying mustard-colored Corolla. A scented pine tree with curling cardboard edges hung from the rearview mirror. The vinyl seats spilled foam. She threw her bag on the backseat and waved to the attendant who'd helped her sign the paperwork. "Besides, everyone knows that Corollas are safe, reliable, and fuel efficient."

At fifteen dollars a day, you got what you paid for.

They both went to climb into the driver's seat.

He cocked an eyebrow. "Do you know your way around Vegas?"

She returned the favor. "No, but I have my phone and Google

maps. I've got an hour before I meet with Danielle. I'll drop my bag at the hotel, then I'll find my way there in plenty of time."

He kept his voice low and even. "It'll be easier if I drive. I know the area, and I can get us around faster."

Sweat prickled the back of his neck. It was already boiling and would only get hotter. The sooner they were in air-conditioned comfort, the better.

She jumped into the passenger seat after he stabbed the remote four times.

Bent forward, she played with the nonexistent air conditioning. Her shirt rode up, giving him a taste of creamy skin and a sneak peek at a cotton waistband. He'd always been a Victoria's Secret man until Sophie. Now, plain cotton made him hard. Painfully hard.

She tried the window button, which didn't work, then gave up and turned to him, reciting the address which he punched into his phone. "Have you worked in Vegas a lot?"

"I've worked a few big security jobs here." He scanned the address. "Are you sure this is right?"

She beamed at him. "Yeah, why? It's cheap and cheerful, according to the internet, so a win-win all round."

"It's not a part of Vegas I'd hang around in."

She turned and her eyes sparkled. "Let's find out."

He pulled into minimal traffic. At nine in the morning, most of Vegas would be stacking z's. Surprisingly, the car hummed along at a respectable speed.

Sophie found a radio station and sung about being locked out of heaven and sex that would take her to paradise. Yeah, he had an opinion on that.

He stopped outside the address, leaving the car running.

Nestled between Bubba's Bail Bonds and Cash for your Stash pawnshop, the neon sign trying to spell out Rita's Hotel but only managing "TA's" sat between them. A group of men stood in front of the doorway to the pawnshop. The grate on the cast-iron door slid, the door opened, and after a brief discussion, one person walked in.

Two tired working girls perked up when he stopped the car, but went back to chatting when he shook his head. Too young to be hooking, too old and jaded to be high-end escorts, they took what they could get.

Cheap bourbon, cheaper scent, and crushed dreams wafted from the pavement.

Sophie craned forward, tipping the sunglasses on top of her head. "Maybe it's better inside," she said, indecision washing across her face.

"We're not staying here."

"I think we should go view the room." Sophie worried her bottom lip.

He turned in his seat, his hands tightening on the wheel. "It's a pay-by-the-hour hotel."

"It's by the outlet mall," she said, as if trying to sell him on the point that getting a bargain at Gap and Old Navy would solve everything.

"It ain't happenin'." He pulled his phone out of his pocket and started hunting through his contacts.

"I can't afford somewhere on the strip. I'm working with a strict budget, and this place is the only one I could find in my client's price range." She waved her hand, her voice rising. "I'm sure it will be fine for one night."

He lifted sunglasses to the top of his head and turned to face her. He reached forward and tucked that insubordinate curl of hair that wouldn't be tamed behind her ear. He shouldn't, but he somehow loved that curl.

"I'm not lying awake all night wondering when a strung-out junkie will break down the door looking for a buck so he can get his next fix. Nor do I want to hear a girl in the next room, getting paid by the hour, pretending she's getting off on the twenty-dollar hand job she's delivering." At her wide eyes he continued. "I'd rather be in a safe room, fucking you on the bed, in the shower, and on the couch after having watched you get off with a vibrator. I'll be able to fall asleep with you in my arms knowing you're safe."

Her eyes went wider, and she sucked air through her teeth.

"So, the room's on me. We'll both come out winners."

She flicked her glasses down but gave a sharp nod. He punched in the address of Sophie's contact.

"SHE LOOKS LIKE HER MOM." Danielle Winters looked down at the photo of Beth with her daughter, Hannah, cradled in her arms.

Danielle placed two cups of iced tea on a faded Formica table and sat across from Sophie.

Calendar shots of summery places with the month written across the bottom dotted the walls. Old furniture gleamed with polish. A bunch of plastic flowers sat in a glass vase on the table. A daytime game show set to mute flickered on the TV in the corner.

"Thanks for the tea." The cool fluid washed away the desert dust coating her throat.

"Are you sure you don't want some?" Danielle asked Harlan, who stood in the corner with his head bowed, his fingers tapping on his phone. He shook his head and smiled.

Sophie twisted her head and caught the tail end of his smile and, for the brief time it lit his face, her heart stilled.

Sophie had explained to a surprised Danielle that Harlan had accompanied her from Colorado. She didn't give an exact reason, and Danielle didn't push.

"Suzie and I worked together for a couple of years. Suzie liked to have fun, but time catches up. Tips were dropping off, and it started to worry her. She liked to be taken to the best bars and showered with gifts. She loved her nickname—'Slow Screw Suzie'." Danielle took a sip from her glass.

Sophie smiled encouragement.

"Anyway, Suzie figured it was time to get attached to a man who could keep her how she wanted to be kept. A big accountant conference stayed at our hotel, and Suzie spied Jim West. Originally from Oklahoma, he'd done well for himself, real well, and Suzie decided he was her catch of the day. Poor Jim, I don't think he stood a chance. When Suzie set her mind and her sights on a man... well, her record stood for itself." Danielle shook her head. "They were married three days later by a fake Barry Manilow. He was good, too. Had the white jumpsuit on and sang, 'Can't Smile Without You.' I witnessed the marriage. Jim was head over heels." Danielle rubbed her throat. "Jim was a quiet man. A good man. I thought seeing how much Jim had fallen for Suzie, she'd settle down." Danielle had a misty look in her eyes.

"Did you hear from her again after that?" Sophie gently pried.

"She left for her new life in Denver. We kept in touch. At first, Suzie loved 'playing house' as she called it. She fell pregnant straight-away. Unfortunately, she didn't fit in with the neighbors' wives or make any friends. People either loved or didn't love Suzie, mostly the latter."

Sophie looked across at Harlan who stared down at his phone. His gaze flicked to hers, then back to his phone.

"After Bethie was born, I went up for a visit." Danielle took another sip of tea, then cleared her throat. "Huge disaster. Suzie didn't enjoy being a mother. Jim didn't understand why Suzie didn't want to spend time with their daughter or him. As soon as I arrived, she told us she had to get away for a while."

Danielle stared at a place only she could see. "That baby missed her mama. Her eyes would get wide, and if it wasn't Suzie walking to pick her up, that little face would screw up, and she'd howl."

Sophie wondered what motherhood would be like if it wasn't like the happy, dishwashing moms in commercials. "Suzie would beg me to visit and send a plane ticket. This went on for about six months." A sad smile touched her mouth. "I loved caring for Bethie. She calmed down and Lordy, that baby was the sweetest thing." A melancholy look flittered across her face. "I left it too late to find Mr. Right. By the time I got around to it, all the good ones were gone." She blinked. "Anyway, the last time I went there, Suzie never came back. She left a note saying motherhood and marriage weren't for her. I knew she wasn't coming back. Jim went to the police, but they said she'd left of her own accord and it wasn't a police matter."

"Do you know where she is now?" Sophie held her breath.

"I saw her six months back, in the CVS on Paradise Road. She startled when she saw me, then pretended I didn't exist." Her face hardened. "Jim moved not long after Suzie left. I lost contact, but I always said if I could ever do anything for little Bethie, I would." She paused. "Suzie's working as a cocktail waitress at a certain kind of bar, which means you wait tables, double as a dancer, and do whatever you're willing to do to pull tips."

"How can you be sure it was her and where she works?" Sophie asked, hopeful but pragmatic. A lot of time had passed—Danielle could be mistaken.

"Oh, it was her all right. She looked horrified to see me. Plus, I know the uniform. It's a no-questions-asked bar. Suzie had a jacket on, but I saw what she was wearing." Danielle grabbed the pen and pad out of Sophie's hand and printed the name and address of the bar, then tore off the sheet and handed it to Sophie, who handed Danielle a photo of Beth and her baby.

"Keep it. I think Beth would love for you to have it." She pressed her lips together when Danielle blinked away tears. "Why don't you give me your email address so if Beth wants to contact you, she can?"

"I'd like that. I understand if she doesn't want to, but that would be real nice." The older woman wrote her info on the pad, her hand shaking.

"Thank you." Sophie stood and held out her hand.

Danielle surprised Sophie when she pulled her into an awkward hug.

"Would you give something to Bethie for me?"

"Sure."

Danielle went to her purse and took out a small photo of her holding a baby; a beautiful smile lit her face. "It's the only photo I've got of me and Beth, but I want her to know she was loved." Danielle paused. "I hope Bethie finds the answer she's looking for."

Sophie squeezed Danielle's hand, Beth's happy ending vaporizing before her eyes.

A short time later, the Corolla hummed along the concrete highway. Sophie stared out the window lost in thought. The parched brown landscape reminded her of crisscrossing the countryside with her father. All she needed was the smell of extra-strong peppermints and a religious channel pumping out odes to Jesus to complete the picture.

The meeting with Danielle had left her sad and strangely emotional, like it was her time of the month and her hormones were all over the place.

She rubbed her hands across her face and kneaded her temples.

Harlan's hand gently tugged hers and transferred her hand to his thigh.

She stared at a line of identical, small, detached terracotta-colored dwellings that housed the workers of Vegas, away from the bright lights and showgirl smiles.

"How did your mother die?" Harlan asked.

She shrugged. "I don't know. It upset my father when I asked about her, so I quit asking." An ache bloomed in her chest when she thought of a mom she couldn't remember.

She stared harder out the window.

I'm sure not going to ask about his mom.

They drove in relative silence. The wheeze of the dying air conditioning taking its last gasp of breath and the thwack of insects hitting the windshield were the only sounds apart from the top hits playing.

To her right, a blue glass building emerged, rising toward the sun like an offering. Bronze glass shimmered to her left. Puffy white clouds waltzed with gray clouds swirling with attitude.

"The buildings are all so huge." She leaned forward, straining the seatbelt. "Wait. Is that the Eiffel Tower?" She blushed. "I mean not

the real one, obviously. I didn't know they had a fake Eiffel Tower."
She spun sideways. "Is that Hooters?" Her finger pressed against the
window. "Okay, so I don't want to go to Hooters, but every girl
dreams of going to Paris."

She turned to Harlan, knowing she sounded like an excited
fangirl catching a Harry Styles concert and not caring.

"There's too much to take in. Can we go around again?"

"Sure." Harlan lifted his glasses, his gorgeous blue eyes sparkling,
a warm smile directed at her.

She blinked, unable to breathe at his beauty.

They stopped at another set of lights. Sophie punched the button
on the door that supposedly controlled the window and, by some
miracle, it lowered. She breathed in warm air scented with tacos, the
sweet smell of sugar and, strangely, chlorine. A couple walked past,
hands entwined.

"We're in Vegas, baby. Let's have some fun," the woman said.

She didn't hear her partner's reply, but the words stamped on her
heart. One night in Vegas with Harlan.

She smiled. *Oh yeah.*

Time for some fun.

FOURTEEN

"Why are we stopping?" Sophie asked, craning her neck to take in the shimmering building, apprehension in her voice.

Harlan understood that she didn't have money. He got that this hotel was out of her league, but he wanted this night to be special. And knowing she'd be curled into him tonight, her head on his shoulder, her hair tumbling over him... He wanted that.

Strike it.

Needed that.

"We're at the hotel." The car sputtered to a stop beside a red-and-gold-suited valet. Harlan exited the car, grabbed their bags, then handed the valet the keys and a sizable tip.

He opened the passenger door.

Sophie didn't move.

"We can't stay here." Her arms were folded across her chest.

"We *are* staying here." He held out his hand, gearing up for yet another fight.

Dark flashing eyes met his. "I can't afford this, nor can Beth, so we're not."

"I'm paying." He forced a deep breath.

"No, you're not. I'm working." She tightened her ponytail. "I get what you said about Rita's Hotel, but there has to be a compromise between rent-a-room and where Willian and Kate stay."

She was working, and he respected that, but keeping her safe was *his* job.

"Sophie, I've got this."

Her chocolate eyes swung to his, then looked away.

"Your head on my shoulder tonight, unable to move after I've fucked you senseless. You safe. That's what I want."

She looked up at him, indecision and desire written across her face. She bit her lip and his cock fired into life at the "I want to be fucked senseless" look on her face.

"I'll pay you back," she said firmly.

He chuckled and grabbed her hand.

Yeah, you will, but no currency will change hands.

He went to VIP check-in, gave his name, handed over his card to a perfectly made-up woman who smiled a perfectly made-up smile who had nothing on Sophie. Seconds later, along with two keycards, he was directed to a private set of elevators. He grabbed Sophie's hand, figuring this way they'd at least make it to the elevators before Christmas, her soft hand fitting his perfectly.

On the way to the elevator, he stopped at the concierge's desk and had a discreet word. The man nodded without blinking. Harlan waved his card against a keypad, and the elevator opened. He swiped his key card against a glass panel, and they were whisked upward.

He pulled his phone from his pocket, noting that Sophie followed suit.

A couple of texts from Zeb, nothing urgent. One from Jason that made him smile. He'd speak with him later. He'd received the info on one Asia Brown and her sister Jamaica.

Another of his Range Rover SUV's was parked outside Sophie's house, giving the impression they were holed up, which they were. His dick roared to life. Christ, any more boners without a happy ending, namely being inside Sophie and he'd be claiming disability.

The doors of the elevator opened. Sophie stepped forward, then shot back into the elevator, grasping the handrail like she'd been stabbed. "We've got the wrong room," she gasped.

Harlan chuckled, threaded his fingers with hers, and pulled her into the room. "This is ours."

"This isn't in the budget." She pulled on his hand, her eyes wide, her face pale. "This isn't in Beyonce and Jay-Z's budget."

He explained the situation. "This room is safe. If I have to go out, I can, knowing you're protected. The elevator is by keycard only, and we have the only two cards. All the doors have double security. Unless Spiderman is coming to pay a visit, no one can get in." He paused, steeling himself for the inevitable reaction. "Before you go all riled up, I know you don't have a dress, and I want to take you out tonight, so a woman is going to arrive in about an hour, with a selection of dresses and shoes." She opened her mouth, eyes sparking. He held up his phone, cutting her off. "Important call, babe. I've got to take this." He turned his back and grinned.

"Jason, I heard you're so dumb that when you heard it was chilly outside you ran and got a bowl and spoon," Harlan said.

"Fuck me, Harlan, if you were any slower I'd have to water you once a week," the irritated voice returned.

"Heard you're so dumb that you thought a quarterback was a refund."

A bark of laughter shot out of his cell.

"Take it you've read my encrypted email?"

"That's all you've got on Asia?" Jason's tone turned serious.

Harlan shrugged. "Yeah, there isn't a lot on her."

Jason read. "Asia Brown attended Thomas Riley High School in Compton and graduated with a GPA of 4.8. Her grandmother's name is Alice, who died six months ago from complications related to Alzheimer's. Her mother's name is Celeste, and she abandoned her and Jamaica on Asia's third birthday. Father unknown. Clean DMV record, no outstanding debt. Has an online shop where she sells dresses she designs. Has lived in the same apartment since her mother dropped her off, and she has eighty dollars and twenty-four cents in her checking account." Jason huffed out a breath.

"What's going on with you and this woman?"

As far as Harlan was aware, Jason had never run a personal background check on a woman. As a serial dater, Jason didn't do commitment and was fully upfront about it.

"Nothing." Another breath blew out.

Harlan eyed Sophie taking photos of the room on her phone. "I've got different feelers out on her sister and her junkie boyfriend. I'll be in touch."

"Appreciate it." The call ended.

Harlan stared down at the phone. He'd heard a saying about Jason at boarding school. 'Still waters run deep.' That fitted the man perfectly. A moody genius with a darkness that girls loved. He wore a 'fuck off world' scowl, but the man cared more than he let on. Hurt someone who even hinted at harming those he held close and he'd remove their bowel with a spoon and force feed them their entrails, but it didn't take a genius to see the man lived in a world of pain. Harlan and the boarding school brothers knew why, and it fucking killed them.

"Can we see the Bellagio fountains? They're free and they dance to music. How cool is that?" Sophie sat on a leather sofa, bare feet tucked underneath her, flicking through a guidebook.

"Got something to do first." He bent, tilted her head, and kissed her, his tongue waltzing with hers. A tremor moved from her body and traveled the length of him. He pulled her to standing. Her fingers traced across his ribs, his stomach, her touch undoing him. He groaned in her mouth.

He undid the button on her jeans, and lowered the zip. His palm flattened across her stomach He then went down the front of her jeans, over the waistband of her underwear, her skin soft, firm, and trembling under his touch. She widened her stance. The perfect combination. "I've been thinking about being here since last night."

He rubbed her clit through the cotton of her underwear, then pushed aside the fabric before sinking into her tight, wet warmth.

She melted into him and moaned.

She bucked her hips, arching her back, driving him deeper.

"You like that?" He kissed her neck.

Her head dropped back. "Yeah."

His fingers were coated in her. "Missed how you taste." Hazy chocolate eyes widened, and her lips parted.

He withdrew his fingers, and she sighed when his thumb glided over her swollen clit. He transferred his fingers to his mouth and licked down to his knuckle. Her salted caramel taste made his mouth water.

Her hand brushed her breasts, then dropped back to her side. She ducked her head, but not before he caught the tinge to her cheeks.

He cupped her chin with his hand. "There's no shame in listening to what your body wants." He dropped a finger into her mouth, which she licked, the shyness clearly leaving her in a surge of desire.

"I want you so bad it hurts," she murmured.

Desire, want, and an overwhelming need to stamp his DNA in her raged through his body. "Get your jeans off, baby."

She wiggled out of her jeans, kicking them away, her chest heaving.

"Get yours off," she panted.

He growled, but his jeans went the way of hers.

"Get naked." He stalked the tiny distance between them.

She dragged her T-shirt from her body, unhooked her bra, and hesitantly dragged her thumb across tight nipples.

Jesus, if he wasn't careful he'd blow watching her hands on her breasts.

He ripped his clothes from his body, dropped to the carpet, and grabbed her ankles, his body wound tight. "Sit on my face. I'm going to lick you until you come, and you're going to do the same to me."

Her gaze went to his throbbing dick twitching in anticipation.

She licked her lips and dropped to her knees, her eyes glazed, the sweet scent of her muskiness unbolting him. His hands clasped her soft butt while his tongue teased her opening.

If he died now, he'd be good to meet his maker with Sophie on his tongue and her moaning his name.

He sank two fingers into her, stroking high. Scorching heat poured from her.

She leaned forward. His fingers clutched her thighs when her mouth found his twitching cock, her tongue working him before she took him deep.

Christ.

His body bucked upward. If she kept her mouth on him much longer, he'd be coming in her throat, and he had every intention of coming in her sweet body. She moaned against his cock, the vibration going straight to his balls.

He bit her ass, and she gasped, her mouth never leaving his cock. She ground herself into his face. He felt her build. Felt the tension grip her muscles. She caressed his cock taking him deeper until he was a heartbeat from coming. With his hand he eased her mouth from him, ignoring her protest, instead concentrating on her. He alternated between sucking her clit, circling it with his tongue, and thrusting with his fingers until her body stiffened and she cried out, convulsing around him, her inner muscles contracting around his fingers like a vise.

Her moisture ran down his face, soaking his hair.

"Beautiful," he murmured.

He moved her limp body, so she nestled in his lap. Her head slumped, sweat dripped down her cleavage. He leaned forward, licking the salt from her skin.

A dreamy smile hit her face.

He reached into the back pocket of his jeans on the ground, grabbed a condom, then shifted her back slightly and in record time sheathed himself.

With one thrust, he entered her.

She moaned, her eyes opened, and she stared at him. Her bottom lip snagged against her teeth. Her breasts mashed against his chest. She tilted her hips to meet his thrusts.

Her nipples were dark and swollen against the snowy flesh of her breasts.

"I love hearing your little gasp when I do this." His hips pushed higher. On cue, a throaty moan slipped from her lips.

"Tell me what you want," he said between thrusts.

"I want you," she said without hesitation.

He thrust harder and deeper, taking ownership of her, telling her with his body she was his.

She moaned his name, and he couldn't control it any longer and thrust his release.

He eased out of her, laid her spent body on the floor, and gazed down at the most beautiful woman in the world.

Sophie without her guard up.

Mesmerizing.

"I thought you'd be covered in ink, but you've only got this word. *Praesidio.*" She traced her finger over his ink. "What does it mean?"

"Protect." He spoke gruffly, forcing that terrible night long ago out of his brain. He didn't need the black mood that accompanied it.

"Who do you protect?" Her touch made his dick twitch and something weird constricted in his chest.

"Whoever needs protecting." He wound her hair around his finger, pulling her to him. "Something happened a long time ago at boarding school. A group of us didn't look out for a vulnerable kid who paid a terrible price, so we have it inked on us to never forget." He grazed her forehead with his lips.

"You went to boarding school?" she breathed. "How wonderful."

He chuckled. "It was pretty shit until I found Zeb, Holden, Jason, Gabriel and the Gillard brothers. There's a group of us who are tight." He sifted her soft hair through his fingers.

"Where did you go to school?" he asked, drinking in her amazing raspberry scent that scattered his thoughts.

"Homeschooled. My father was religious and didn't believe in traditional school." Her fingers now played with his. "I would have liked to have gone to a school with the same people every day, same teachers. My dad wasn't a good teacher. I either Googled stuff when I could or tried to figure it out." Her forehead creased. "Still can't do division," she confessed.

"I can't draw for shit," he chuckled, surprised that had slipped out.

Fuck me, she's truth serum.

A comfortable silence stretched between them. He could stare down at her body all day and never get bored.

She stretched. "I'm going to head for the shower. I need a power nap before dinner and the fountains."

He stilled, his eyes feasting on her round butt, and drifted to the top of her left thigh.

"Interesting birthmark." Her head half-turned.

"It's a heart."

"It is. I look forward to tracing it with my tongue." She blushed even harder.

He stood and moved toward the kitchen and the trash can. "Have your shower, and I'll call the bar where Suzie works to see if she's there."

She stood, her mouth open in protest, but he cut her off. "Whoever answers the phone is more likely to tell a guy wanting some Suzie action if one of their staff is working tonight."

Her nose wrinkled. "As wrong as that sounds, thanks." Her hands shielded her breasts. "Um... can you turn around or something so I can run to the bathroom?"

"Sophie, you have curves. Beautiful, soft curves." He walked to where she stood, trying to cover herself. He leaned in and kissed her shoulder. "I'm going to watch your sweet butt and get hard doing it."

"Stop it." She ducked her head. "And stop looking at me."

"It's the best view in the world." He chuckled when she sprinted to the bathroom. He should send an update to Petrov, but not after just thoroughly fucking the asset he was supposed to be guarding. He'd email later when his dick wasn't hard.

Petrov might have to wait awhile.

Later that evening, Harlan threw the remote on the sofa, one eye on the time, the other on the game.

It had taken him two point five minutes to throw on black dress jeans, a dark blue long-sleeved shirt, and boots.

"Jesus, Sophie. We're late, would you—"

Harlan froze when Sophie walked into the room adjusting an earring. A bronze-colored silk dress clung to her curves, hitting mid-thigh. Gladiator-type sandals with laces crisscrossed up her long legs. The dress dipped to a V, showing a swell of breast. Her hair in a braid lay on her back. Bronze gloss stained her lips. Her skin shimmered. The soft scent of raspberries filled the room.

"You're fucking gorgeous," he growled, meaning every word.

"I'm *not* gorgeous." She frowned. "It isn't something I'd ever wear." She rubbed her index finger down her cleavage. "And I'm really worried the tape will unstick, and I'll flash the world my B's."

The thought of another man's eyes on her made him want to punch the fucker for even daring to look.

And it shouldn't.

But it did.

The thought ripped through him.

He'd do anything to kick something hard because he shouldn't be having any feelings for Sophie.

I don't do relationships or fucking feelings.

He should be totally focused.

Sophie's hand landed in his and squeezed.

"Are you okay? You look pissed, annoyed, and, if I didn't know you better, a little sad."

He looked at her hesitant face.

But fuck me, it's hard to stay focused when the most beautiful woman on the planet is at my side.

He scrubbed his hand across his face. "Yeah, babe, all good."

But it wasn't. It wasn't good at all.

He kissed her hard, only stopping because his stomach sent a loud complaint that it needed food. Stat.

Sophie giggled and burrowed into his side. "My man needs feeding."

He froze along with her.

"It's a figure of speech," she said, moving away from him, pink staining her cheeks.

"We're going to dinner, then we're seeing the fountains." His hand grasped hers.

Her man.

TEN MINUTES LATER, they stood outside a pair of opulent gold doors. A menu promised New Zealand Bluff Oysters from virgin waters, pink venison, and Wagyu beef.

"Through those doors; we've got reservations."

She stood with one hand on her hip, eyes flashing. "Buffet is in my budget and there's one here in this hotel."

She smiled slowly. And he had good reason to think he was fucked.

"So, let's compromise. You chow down on hand-reared lamb while I dig into all-you-can-eat meatballs, breadsticks, and cream puffs. We'll meet back here in ninety minutes. Ready?"

If he had his blood pressure taken it would have cardiologists dismayed. "Seriously? You want mass-produced salad, bread rolls, and vats of meat sauce?"

"Yep, I do. It isn't just a buffet. According to the guidebook, it's a *Vegas* buffet." She rolled the word "Vegas" as if it were spun sugar on her tongue.

"What does that mean?" He ran his hands through his hair.

"No idea, but all you can eat for forty bucks is a winner."

His mouth touched her ear. "If it's about the money, I'm paying."

She stood tall and proud. "*I'm* paying."

Like her, he'd grown up without much, and he got that she didn't like taking handouts. He admired her tenacity and her skills as a PI, but tonight he was taking Sophie out, and when he took women out, he paid.

The smile on her face slipped. "Besides, I've got to pay you back for Beyonce and Jay-Z's room."

She leaned in to him, her soft breast pressing against his arm, which he tried hard to ignore. But when she was this close, his body pulsed *everywhere*.

"You can pay me back, but not in currency." His hand rested on her hip.

She looked confused before her face flushed. "Oh."

With his hand splayed across the bottom of her spine, he guided her toward where he wanted to go, but she stopped and dug in her heels.

"I don't mind meeting you back at the hotel, but this is probably the only time I'll come to Vegas, and I really want to try one of their buffets."

He swore at the determination scrawled on her face. He didn't want to draw attention by having a stand-up fight. He gave her a nod and was rewarded by a smile that made relenting worth it.

Almost.

They stood in a line for what seemed like forever, Sophie entertaining herself by people-watching. She grabbed his arm, pointing to someone who'd won a jackpot. Did he see the old man with the girl who seemed young enough to be his granddaughter, but the girl sure wasn't acting like a granddaughter?

He smiled, not minding how her hand slipped into his, or how she got close to whisper something in his ear, her breast mashed against his arm, her fresh, fruity scent killing the high-end scent behind them.

To Sophie, Vegas with all its glitz was one big, new, and exciting toy. He'd seen the real Vegas behind the sparkly lights, and it wasn't pretty. Sophie's face had grown solemn at the people hooked up to oxygen, sucking on cigarettes and feeding slot machines, forever hopeful Lady Luck would shine down on them. Since broke casinos didn't exist, the odds weren't stacked in the gamblers' favor.

Finally, they were shown to a table after having another fight about who would pay. Her hand had landed on her hips, her eyes flashing. She'd insisted on paying for herself since she'd be billing her client, then confessed she'd only bill Beth half because she had a baby to feed.

Strong, tenacious and proud, and he'd bet she'd never invoice Beth for the job. Sophie tried to hide her soft center, but it burst on through. The more he got to know her, the more he saw her vulnerable side. Kind of reminded him of a teacher he'd had in elementary school—Mrs. Bickerstaff, who'd come across tough as balls, which in hindsight he figured she had to be, because if kids sensed weakness they went for blood. She'd always bring extra food for the kids who hadn't had breakfast and books for kids who didn't have any, and when he didn't have the money for a class trip, he found out she'd paid for him. It was her who'd sent his application to Stamford Brook School for Boys. He mentally thanked her every day. She thought she'd won a first-class cruise around the world with her husband, Fred. It was the least he could do.

"If I eat another cream puff, I swear I'm going to explode." Sophie rubbed her stomach and drained the last of her glass of wine.

He chuckled. They'd relaxed in each other's company. With no threat of danger on the horizon, he'd sat back and surprised the crap out of himself by enjoying himself; enjoying her. Sophie darting between serving bowls and piling her plate high had been the night's entertainment. He'd have to do a serious round of pushups to work off the butter-and-wine-soaked chicken.

Twenty minutes later, they were walking down the strip. Vegas threw on her sparkly party dress and came to life at night. The air, still hot, dried his eyeballs. Taxi cabs honked at jaywalking tourists, their necks craned, taking in the lights. A woman flicking business cards tried to push one into Harlan's hand so he could be loved a long time. He shook his head and kept moving.

When he had Sophie by his side, nothing compared.

"That is so pretty," Sophie breathed.

They stood in front of the Bellagio fountains. The crowd swelled around them, waiting for the magic to start. Jets rose from the water, music filled the street, and the fountains swayed in time to the collective ooh's and ah's of the crowd. He stood behind Sophie, his hands on her shoulders. He'd scanned for potential threats but with a crowd this size the only thing he could do was keep her close.

She leaned back in to him, and his arm circled her waist. Her body molded against his perfectly.

"Nightcap?" she said after insisting they stay and watch the fountains a million more times until she'd had her fill.

"Sure."

He could do a scotch before they headed upstairs. In Vegas terms, the night hadn't begun. He had a bag of tricks he wanted to try, one in particular.

He threaded his hand in hers, liking the way she squeezed his fingers. He steered them inside the bar. Sophie shuffled her feet, hemming and hawing about where they'd sit.

A woman sang on a small stage, lost in the song, her Billie Holiday voice blending with a man scat singing beside her in the dim light.

He pulled Sophie toward a free table that had opened up.

"No." She frowned, then pointed to a spot at the back of the bar, and her frown cleared. "There."

He slid into the booth, leaned back on the leather, pulled her close until she was flush against him. His arm around her shoulders, he sucked back a mouthful of Johnnie Walker Blue. Sophie set down her margarita, glanced at him, blushed, then glanced away.

"What's up?"

She turned and whispered, her lips sweeping his ear.

"You know how you said not to wear underwear?"

He turned and stared.

"Yeah."

"I've been waiting for you to flick up my dress."

Red crept up her face, and she worried her bottom lip.

All night? He was seriously off his game.

His fingers inched up her silky thigh, dragging her dress along for the ride. Right where cotton should meet her hip, his fingers met nothing but smooth skin.

His lips swept along her collarbone. "Open your legs."

Why she'd chosen this table became clear. At the back of the room, with minimal staff walking past, it offered privacy. With a hanging tablecloth, the part he wanted access to wasn't on display.

She opened her legs a fraction. Her back straight, she stared at the wall, looking all high school principal, but the hitch in her breath gave her away.

His thumb found her clit.

Already soaked for him.

She took a sip of her drink, her hands shaking. She opened her legs wider.

"I'm so hard I could fuck you right here," he growled in her ear.

She didn't answer, but her breathing became labored.

One finger dipped inside her wet heat. When she tilted her hips, his finger drew slow circles on her thigh, then back to her clit.

He glanced around the club. People either had their heads turned toward the stage or were talking amongst themselves. Their night hadn't kicked into gear, but his had, courtesy of the bewitching, gorgeous woman beside him.

He murmured in her ear, loving her shiver. "You like that people might see?"

She nodded, still staring straight ahead, panting.

He picked up his drink and took a sip, every muscle in his body wound tight. He stroked his fingers higher and smiled at her moan, his finger never moving from a slow circle on her clit.

"Oh, God." She sucked in a breath, her body arching before she came with a long tremble, her body pulsing around his fingers, sweat slick on her skin.

He pulled down her dress, lifted his fingers to his mouth, and licked her from him. He then bent his mouth to her ear. "If we don't leave now, I'm going to fuck you here, which I'm totally up for. I can lift you on my lap and you can ride me, or we can take it upstairs, as long as I'm inside you. Your call."

She slid out of the booth, and he followed.

"WHAT'S THAT?" Sophie said, fairly certain she knew exactly what he held in his hand.

"I've been dreaming of you using this on yourself." His voice purred like he was a big, hungry tiger and had a startled gazelle in his sights.

Her eyes widened.

In front of another person?

She shook her head.

Like I did tonight.

Tonight she didn't know if she'd go through with telling Harlan she was sans underwear, but a part of her was aroused by the knowledge and power that she could literally bring him to his knees. She'd been so turned on in the bar with Harlan's hand between her legs, knowing exactly what she needed, when they were in full view.

For the first time, she could be herself. It was empowering, and she wasn't afraid to tell Harlan who made her life so brazen, so intense, so *liberating*.

He ran his knuckle down her face, his touch leaving a trail of sparks.

Her nipples tightened into peaks, ready for his tongue. "I know you're struggling with how I like sex, Sophie, but I'm struggling letting you have as much control as you do."

Something hit deep and low in her belly. And it wasn't just desire that rolled across her body in waves, nor the hunger burning in his eyes, but also how he compromised for her.

She took the vibrator from his hand. She turned the base, and it hummed into life. She dropped on the couch, her legs unsteady, her heart pounding.

"Lift your dress," he ordered. He stood across from her, his arms crossed, his face flushed. Her thighs widened at his roughly spoken words. She wriggled the dress up her thighs.

"Higher, above your hips."

She swallowed and complied, shimmying the fabric to her waist.

"Lean back and open your legs," he said, his voice rough with need.

Her muscles clenched in a tight spasm when the smooth metal touched her clit.

"Wider."

A tremor vibrated deep in her belly. Moisture slicked her thighs.

Oh God, this is so wrong, but so... right.

She complied again.

Her eyes locked on Harlan whose gaze was fixed between her legs.

"Oh, this is good," she murmured, pushing the vibrator inside her, opening her legs wider until her inner thigh muscles shook.

His eyes blazed. Sweat beaded his forehead.

She stared at him. For the first time she held this man in her hand like putty. The power swept through her, the confidence making her bolder.

Her hand dropped between her legs. She rubbed her clit. "This is amazing," she murmured. The sleek but impersonal metal was definitely doing its job, though she missed his unique heat and *their* connection. "But you're better." She dropped the vibrator.

He prowled to her, his hand on the sizeable bulge in his pants. He then dropped to his knees. When his tongue rolled across her clit, she arched off the couch, unable to breathe, her body a slave to him.

Her brain short-circuited when he pushed his slickened thumb against her butt, stopping when she stilled.

"Trust me," he said, barely getting the words out, concentrating on her and listening to her body.

He pressed his thumb into her.

She'd do anything and everything he wanted.

His expert tongue circled and flicked her clit, then played at her opening. Just when an orgasm grazed her core, he pulled back and started the whole dance again.

"Please," she begged, her hands digging into his soft hair, holding him prisoner, grinding against him, desperate.

"What do you want, Sophie? Tell me." He looked up at her, his face glistening, his gaze hungry.

"You," she gasped, pulling the dress from her body.

Anything. She'd do anything.

"Tell me." He pushed her legs wider.

"You, Harlan, I want you."

And she did. Wanted him with a hunger that scared her.

Harlan reached into his back pocket and pulled out a foil square. He ripped the clothes from his body and sheathed himself. With his eyes burning through her, he picked her up by her hips and backed them until her spine was pressed against the floor-to-ceiling glass wall.

She arched, taking him fully inside her, stretching her limits until every exquisite inch of him filled her.

"Oh..." she breathed.

Her ankles locked around his hips, her fingers digging into bunched, slick shoulders. Hard muscle quivered under heated skin when she kissed the underside of his jaw. She breathed in his musky scent, and her body sighed.

She gripped his sweat-slicked shoulders, her body strained and arched, digging for release, her stomach muscles twisted into a hot mess. Harlan thrust harder into her, pushing her to the brink, then stopped.

"Don't stop. *Please* don't stop," she begged in a frustrated growl.

"Or what?" A tiny smile touched his lips, but his ragged voice gave him away.

She milked the length of him with her internal muscles.

He growled and thrust into her harder.

The hot bubble of need burst. She cried out as the power of the orgasm ripped through her, shredding her, her body pulsing around him as he shuddered his release. If he hadn't been holding her, she'd have slipped to the ground in a puddle.

He carried her to the giant bed, pulled back the covers, and deposited her on thick cotton sheets, brushing damp hair from her face with unexpected tenderness, then walked into the bathroom.

Happy tears threatened to fall and dangerous emotions like belonging danced tantalizingly within her reach.

If they were having this much fun in Vegas, would it be the same when they got back home? Would they both be at each other's throats, going after the same jumpers? Would she catch him at Javier's gym working out? Maybe he'd even step into the ring with her. She stretched, then frowned.

No, Harlan wouldn't like it if she got in the boxing ring again.

Then reality, that cold hard bitch slapped her, hard.

Harlan wouldn't like it.

She avoided his gaze when he walked back to the bed, staring out at the Vegas skyline. A dark and nasty stone pulled her stomach downward. She concentrated on the red flickering helicopters that streaked across the neon sky.

Midnight blue eyes scanned her. "What's up?"

"Nothing."

His finger trailed down her cheek leaving a trail of warmth. "Something's troubling you."

Tonight she'd done things she'd never, ever done before, would never have done before. Had she done those things because she wanted to, or because deep down she'd turned into what he wanted her to be? If he'd asked her, she would have handed him herself on a party platter.

And it scared the shit out of her.

She didn't have time to go somewhere in her head and analyze it. She gripped the sheet tighter to her body.

Would she again disappear and turn into the woman he wanted? Miss Compliant who'd do every barked command without a thought or an opinion?

She bit her lip.

She turned her head to find him staring at her, his face unreadable.

"Would you ever be in a relationship where you gave up control?" she asked in a quiet voice.

Have you ever let someone in? Have you ever been too afraid to confess your biggest fear without judgment? Have you ever lost yourself to another person—become who they wanted you to be, because, at some base level, you didn't want them to see the real you?

He paused before answering, his sincere blue eyes boring into her. "I don't do that level of commitment."

She clutched at the tattered threads of self-control, turned her head, sucked back a breath, and held it deep in her aching chest, pushing her finger against a hard knot on her breastbone. Alone, later, she would analyze what had happened tonight.

Alone.

The word whispered across her soul.

Harlan slipped into bed and pulled her back to his front, his arm around her waist, anchoring her to him.

She slid out of his embrace and out of bed. Harlan moved with her.

"Prayers," she whispered in a shaky voice.

He nodded.

She murmured a long line of thanks for all she had. After she finished, she stayed in the prayer position, gathering her thoughts around her like a coat that didn't fit as comfortably as it used to, until her body shivered in the air-conditioned cold.

When she slid under the covers, hoping Harlan had fallen asleep, he pulled her tight in to his body.

She twisted in his arms and stared at the neon lights until the first rays of dawn yawned into life, Harlan's deep and even breathing behind her.

Tears tumbled down her face unchecked.

FIFTEEN

Harlan closed the door of the car and blinked at the heat that dried his eyes. Sandwiched between a small liquor store and a twenty-four-hour laundromat, behind saloon-style doors was the bar Danielle had directed them to, the name Hooders spelled out in white peeling paint.

The place had "desperate" written all over it. He'd caught bail jumpers in places like this. Fraught gamblers wearing shiny suits purchased at Goodwill. They'd sit nursing a beer, convincing themselves that tomorrow would be their day.

Everyone wanted cheap beer and a place to forget for a while, including girls who'd come to Vegas with hopes and dreams of landing in a show and hitting it big time, but who found out there were a lot of girls searching for the same dream. Now they worked in bars like this, trying to pay rent and earn their ticket out.

"Let's get this done."

He turned at the brittle nerves in Sophie's voice.

She caught him staring and flicked her glasses from her head to cover her face.

When she asked if he'd ever give up control with a quiver in her voice, he'd answered honestly. He wouldn't lie to her. Raw emotion had twisted her face for a second before she'd rolled out of bed to recite the longest prayer known to man.

She'd slid back into bed, and he'd kept her close all night, waking once when he thought he'd heard a shuddering sigh, but she hadn't moved when he whispered her name. He tucked that one lock of hair behind her ear, felt her flinch.

Something had changed, and it turned his stomach sour.

"Not every story comes with a happy ending. Most don't."

"I know," she said in a quiet, cryptic voice and walked into the bar.

He followed Sophie's ponytail bouncing on her shoulders, wearing her uniform of black jeans, polo shirt and black flat boots. Forever stunning. He chose a table at the back of the club.

Bored-looking girls rode poles onstage. Occasionally Miss "Love Me Tender," according to the handwritten sign propped next to her, would remember where she was and tweak her breast or gyrate against the pole before zoning out again.

Men sat in a couple of groups, but mostly they sat alone, nursing cheap warm beers, their hopeful eyes trained on the stage. Ten feet to Harlan's left, a woman gave a lap dance. A tired twenty sat on the table. Stale beer and cheap perfume mixed with warm air trickling from a busted air conditioner.

The real Vegas.

He hadn't missed the waitress who had perked up when Harlan walked in, then frowned when she'd caught sight of Sophie. Her interest had been rekindled once Sophie had walked away. The waitress now sidled up to Harlan, twisting her blond hair and pushing out her artificial Ds.

He shrugged and held up his hands. The waitress's head swung between him and Sophie, an "I'm not getting it" look on her face.

Yeah, she wouldn't. Even wearing jeans, boots, and a polo shirt, Sophie outshone anyone in a room.

The waitress leaned forward and whispered in his ear that she'd be off in a few hours and could give him a Vegas experience that he'd still remember when he bounced his grandbabies on his knee.

Under the heavy makeup, she looked younger than he'd first thought.

He turned her down, frowned at her name tag, "Margarita," and asked what brought her to Vegas. Turns out Margaret had graduated foster care at eighteen. She'd hung with a dangerous crowd, made mistakes, and ended up in Vegas to earn money to go to community college. She wanted to form a nonprofit to provide low-cost childcare by the hour so moms could get to job interviews, attend classes, and not have to pay for all-day childcare that they couldn't afford.

He handed her his card and told her he had a couple of contacts who could help her with enrolling in college and applications for her nonprofit if she found herself in Denver. He knew people who were always on the lookout for good wait staff. The pay wouldn't set her up on a tropical island, but it was clean money without having to sit on an old man's lap and wait for Viagra to kick in.

The hairs on the back of his neck rippled. Sophie sat alone nursing a diet soda, staring at him, her face a mask.

Margaret slipped his card into the pocket of her apron and told him with misty eyes that he'd be hearing from her, sooner rather than later. She planted a soft kiss on his cheek. The hairs on his neck flamed when he caught Sophie's eye. She swung her head away.

A woman pulled out a chair and sat across from Sophie. Both were in his peripheral vision. The woman toyed with a dark ponytail. What once had been a kick-ass body had softened to middle-age spread. Since she and Soph were deep in conversation, he headed to the bathroom.

He walked back into the bar to find an empty table, a chair on the floor, and no sign of either woman.

Fuck.

A steel band tightened around his chest, pulling across his lungs, making it hard to breathe. He jogged to the bartender who paled and pointed toward the door.

He sprinted outside, breathing in heat, his heart about to burst out of his chest. Sophie sat in the passenger side of the car, staring out the side window.

"What the fuck?" he said, jumping into the driver's seat. His heart felt bruised from smashing into his ribcage. "You can't up and leave like that." He pulled his hand through his hair. "Jesus."

Her lips sucked in. She turned, her face unnaturally pale. "Yeah, actually I can. I'm not at your command. I'm here working on a case. Case is done. I'm going home."

He stared at her. "For the fifteenth fucking time," he said in a low voice, flexing his fingers. "There is a threat to your life. Until that—"

She punched a button on the radio.

He killed Celine before she hit a high note.

Sophie glared at him, then fiddled with the buttons on the car radio.

Something had gone down. Something he couldn't get a handle on.

"What happened in there?" he said, changing tack.

What happened last night?

Celine sang about her heart going on.

Sophie turned to him, eyes vacant. "I'm going home. You can be on the same flight as me or not. Your call."

His gut screwed into a tight ball and threatened an escape plan.

Some dude started singing about going to Rio, my-o meo.

"Fuck no." He punched the off button.

"Either you start the car, or I'll call an Uber. I don't have a preference."

He started the car, threw it into gear, and pulled into traffic, gripping the steering wheel.

His phone pinged at the same time as Sophie's. He'd have to pick it up when they got to the rental car center.

"Oh no."

He swiveled his head. Sophie held her phone in one hand, her eyes huge in her pale face.

"What?" he barked.

"It's from Gemma. Someone attacked Annie last night outside Pipe's. The man had her against her car, a hand at her throat, demanding 'where is she?'"

Fuck.

Fuck.

"Is Annie okay?"

"The guy disappeared when Dug pulled him off. Dug stayed with Annie, who refused to call the police." Nerves rattled Sophie's voice.

He had to think the name Dug instead of Holden. The man was undercover but wouldn't give him a hint of his case and if it pertained to Sophie. Thank fuck he'd been there.

Harlan pulled the car over and relayed the conversation to a very-agitated Zeb.

"Jesus," he said to Zeb. "Let me know when you get any details." Zeb agreed and told him he was heading out to Annie's.

There was a lot of shit happening back in Denver. He needed to be there now.

He pulled the Corolla into traffic, pushing the car to its limits.

"Could it have been Mick who attacked Annie?" Sophie asked.

"No," he barked, harsher than he intended.

She swiveled to face him. "How can you be so sure?"

"He's dead."

She sucked in a breath. "What? When? Why didn't you tell me?"

"It was on a need-to-know basis." He gripped the wheel tighter.

"And you think I didn't need to know?" Her voice rose with every word.

The temperature in the car dropped to Arctic conditions. Sophie kept her head turned on the drive to the airport.

SOPHIE HAD EMOTIONALLY AVOIDED Harlan since last night, and even more so when she'd met with Suzie at that bar. She'd hated the blinding fury that had slashed through her insides when the gorgeous waitress had leaned forward and kissed him. For one heart-wrenching second she'd wanted to go to him, sink down to the ground, and be who he wanted her to be—lose herself, something she'd sworn she would never do again.

It hadn't been hard to distance herself when Harlan had found out about Annie and the guy who attacked her. He'd kept close to her physically at the airport, but emotionally he'd been distant and on his phone constantly.

Her heart had stilled when Harlan had said she didn't need to know about Mick. It shriveled when she realized he'd never let her know what was going on.

Harlan had grabbed her hand before takeoff and didn't let it go. She was too tired and wound up to argue and, if she had to play the truth game, his hand on hers calmed her.

Finally, they made it to her house. Sophie dropped her bag, sank to her knees, and hugged Pongo, surprised that Titus hadn't greeted her.

"Hey, baby boy. Were you good for Uncle Titus?" She pulled his soft ears and smiled when five farts filled the air.

Sophie pulled her cell from her pocket.

No update from Gemma.

Nothing from Annie.

She glanced around her house. A dying fly spun on its back on a windowsill. The scent of overripe oranges tinted the air. Titus usually opened a window for her. Strange, Pongo's bowl was empty. Something Titus would never let happen. He loved her dog and showed it by feeding Pongo treats.

"I'll check on Titus." She moved to the door, her heart starting to hammer.

As always, Harlan followed.

After knocking on Titus's door and getting no reply, Sophie

turned, her heart now trying to escape from her throat. Nerves clutched her stomach and wouldn't let go.

"What if something's happened to Sally?" Desperate, she pulled out her cell and tried Titus's number again. It still went to his cheery voice, asking to leave a number, and he'd call you back.

She left another message.

Out of the corner of her eye, a man approached.

Harlan pushed in front of her, legs wide, hand to the gun in the waistband of his jeans, one hand on her.

"Sophie?"

She peeked around Harlan to find Steve, her neighbor and Titus's assistant with the neighborhood watch. Trepidation on his face mixed with a bit of fear when he glanced at Harlan, then at her.

"Hey, Steve." She tried to move, but Harlan held her in place.

"If you're looking for Titus, he's in the hospital."

She swayed. Harlan pulled her tighter into his body.

"What? What happened?"

"Far as I can tell, he came out here to collect a package, and someone got him in a headlock from behind."

"Where's the package?" Harlan asked Steve, who shrugged.

She fought, but Harlan's arm kept her locked in place.

"Stop it," she said, trying to pry his fingers off her arm.

"We're visible. Out in the open. You're a target," he clipped.

"We're going to the hospital. Now." She twisted out of his grip and ran toward his car. Her stomach was in knots and her throat burning.

If anything happened to Titus or Sally...

This is all my fault. If I hadn't been in Vegas, sampling buffets and Harlan, I'd have been here, and Titus and Annie wouldn't be hurt.

"Hurry," she said to Harlan, barely able to get the twisted cry out of her throat.

NO SOONER HAD the car come to a halt at the hospital than her shoes hit the concrete. She told the kind-looking woman at the desk that she was Titus Carroll's family and stumbled into his room.

Titus sat propped on pillows, a bandage on his head, hooked up to a drip, arguing with a no-nonsense doctor. Sally lay curled in a chair beside him, her eyes never leaving her husband's.

"Right. Good. You're here. Someone with a bit of sense," Titus said, his eyes cutting to her and Harlan standing behind her.

Titus with a bandaged head filled her body with a cold, shattering fear.

This is because of me.

"Tell these people I have to go home," Titus said, sounding like he was still in the army and had been promoted to general.

Sophie walked to his bed and gathered his frail hand. Before she could say anything, the doctor cut in.

"Family. Good. Titus has had a significant blow to the head."

Acid clawed at Sophie's throat, but she pushed it down.

"Significant my ass. I've had worse run-ins at Costco when they give away fried chicken samples."

The doctor looked between her and Harlan. "He's had a scan which is all clear, but we'd like to keep him here for observation overnight, possibly longer."

She opened her mouth to agree when she caught Titus's pleading, desperate appeal.

"Sally can't stay. This is too much for her," he said in an urgent whisper.

Sophie faced the doctor. "I don't have hospital training, but I can stay with him and run checks every hour."

"It has to be a trained professional who can pick up on minor changes."

"Tell me what's required and I'll take care of it," Harlan said. "If he needs a nurse at his house around the clock, it'll happen."

Sophie let out a breath.

The doctor nodded. "I'd feel a lot more comfortable releasing him under those conditions."

Harlan moved to speak to the doctor. Sophie made it to Titus's bed and sagged onto it, the adrenaline that got her here starting to bleed from her muscles.

"I'm sorry." She reached out and placed her hand over Sally's, who held Titus's hand. "Are you okay?" she said to Sally, gently squeezing her hand. Sally didn't squeeze back.

Titus's sharp eyes focused on her. "Nothing to be sorry for. I was collecting a box addressed to you, and a man came up behind me demanding to know where you were. I tried to turn around, but he had me in a headlock by that stage, I'm afraid." His eyes hardened. "I swear, if I were ten years younger he'd be hog-tied on your front lawn waiting for the men in blue." He shook his head. "But he shoved me, and I fell."

"I'll look after him," Sally said in a creaky voice.

Harlan came to crouch in front of Sally. "I know you will. A nurse is going to come and stay with you in case he gets dizzy."

"Pat," Sally said, her voice rising. "Why didn't you bring Wednesday?"

"She couldn't make it this time," Harlan said, smiling at her.

Sophie hauled in a splintered breath at the tenderness on Harlan's face.

Titus intervened, totally focused on Harlan. "You'll look after my girls?"

Sophie fought a massive lip wobble and failed.

"Always," Harlan said, gently squeezing his shoulder. "When you're ready to leave, call me and I'll arrange for Arabella to pick you up."

Titus nodded once, his eyes misty.

Sophie stood and kissed Titus's forehead. "Get some rest. I'll see you later."

"No visitors for twenty-four hours. Complete rest and no excitement," the doctor said.

Sophie said nothing when Harlan pulled her in to his side and walked to the car. The trip back to her place was choked with heavy silence. The car purred into her driveway and came to a halt. Harlan turned in his seat.

"What happened in Vegas—"

Sophie turned. She'd been caught up in worrying about Titus and Annie. "What?"

"Vegas, Soph, what happened in Vegas?"

Oh, hell no.

No way were they going near that now, or maybe never. "Nothing."

Life kept throwing curve balls. One more curve ball to the head and she'd collapse, and she couldn't afford that.

She made it to her living room and the familiar scent of her candles, the gentle hum of the fridge, her dog.

She rubbed her chilled arms.

God, I can't do this.

She maneuvered around the coffee table and held up her hand when Harlan walked toward her, a determined look on his face. "Please don't."

"Don't what?" She made it to the snow globes and stopped, having run out of room.

"Get too close."

Damn. Even she heard the catch in her voice. She turned her head away.

His warm hand cupped her chin. For a moment she melted in to his hand, loving his strength, his warmth, his everything.

"We've been closer than this all weekend. What happened? What changed?" His voice slid down her spine.

She clamped her mouth shut.

It didn't appear he'd be taking no for an answer and, because for once Karma stood in her corner, her phone pinged. She swiped her finger across the cool glass.

ANNIE: *Can you come over? I need to see you.*

Sophie tapped out that she was leaving now.

She turned to Harlan. "I'm going to see Annie."

She picked up her bag, and with legs that felt like they were melting with every step, she grabbed the car keys off the rack.

Harlan's hand curled around her shoulder, bringing her to a halt.

"I'll follow you to Annie's. Israel will take over. Zeb and I will sit down and work out a plan to end why people close to you are getting hurt." She stilled.

Wait. Your plan?

I don't think so.

She took a breath, turned, and faced him. "You want to fill me in on your plan?" He glanced at his watch, looking impatient.

"It's on a need-to-know basis."

Wow.

Wow.

"And you're saying I don't need to know?" Her voice rose. "Again?"

His eyes flashed, and his mouth tightened. "When the time is right we'll talk."

"Sure we will." She turned away.

This was her mess to clean up. Not Harlan or any of his crew. Hers and hers alone.

SHE MADE it to Annie's house without remembering the drive. She should have pulled herself over and written herself a ticket, but she wanted away from the vehicle— and the man inside—following her.

One look at the welts on Annie's neck and Sophie's knees buckled.

"I brought enough margarita mix to free the world of its woes," Gemma said, walking through Annie's front door, dragging a cooler behind her. "I've also got Pringles for Soph, and ice cream and crackers for Annie, which is the most disgusting snack on the planet."

Annie stopped loading wine into the fridge. "Did you get the Cheez-Its?"

"Yesssss."

Sophie had collapsed on Annie's sofa, her hand running over the fur of an ancient cat that claimed her lap the moment she sat down.

Old-style jazz played on a turntable in the background.

"There're two reasons we're here. One is the utter devastation on Sophie's face when she got out of her car and looked at, I'm guessing, Harlan Franco," Annie said, sitting across from Sophie.

Sophie blinked.

"Two is finding out who this creep is looking for, because Zeb doesn't want to play, which makes him tailing me about as much fun as having a public colonoscopy without anesthetic. The man thinks I'm a postage stamp, and he's an envelope, except there's no licking involved."

"But that's good, isn't it?" Gemma stared at Annie, frowning. "Wait, no it's not."

"If any man approaches me, Zeb growls and they turn away mid-stride." Annie looked confused and hurt. "The man has made it perfectly clear he isn't interested in me, at all, but no other man on the planet can approach. He's driving me insane."

Sophie took a sip of margarita, forcing it down her throat.

"We need to figure this out, so Zeb Carmichael will be gone from my life and I can walk this earth a free woman."

"Why didn't you call the police?" Sophie asked.

Annie looked at Sophie. "Where I'm from, you *never* call the police. You take care of your own business, which is why you're here."

"There's something I haven't told you." Gemma twisted the hem of her shirt.

"What?" Annie and Sophie said in unison.

"I received a phone call. A guy barked, 'Where is she?' I was so shocked I didn't answer. The guy said if I wanted easy money, to ring or text back with the information, and an envelope of money would turn up in my car. They phoned back each time more agitated. The last time, I let the number go to voicemail. They asked if I knew where *you* were. Sophie."

Now Sophie could add Gemma to the list of people hurt or about to be hurt because of her. Sophie caught the flash of pain and desperation on Annie's face. This situation had to end, and only she could end it.

"I..." she trailed off, not sure if she wanted to do this or, if she did, how to have the conversation.

"We're your friends," Gemma said, her eyes serious. "You can tell us anything."

Annie turned to her. "Do you want to tell us what's going on?"

She didn't. She so didn't, but people she cared about were getting hurt. Good people. People like Annie and Titus and, somehow, it all linked back to her father and his cons.

Friends... I never thought I'd have friends, but Gemma's right.

She took a deep, shuddering breath that hurt her lungs.

These *were* her friends; they'd wormed into her heart, and she wanted them to stay. Wanted it so much she ached.

Trusting one another was something friends would do.

Unexpected tears blurred Sophie's eyes.

Annie gripped her hand. "We don't judge, Soph. You can tell us, and it will go to our graves." One of Annie's hands moved to the welts on her neck.

Watching Annie's fingers drift along the bruises and seeing bright, strong Titus with a bandage on his head, small and vulnerable in the hospital bed, caused something inside Sophie to splinter.

In stuttering sentences, she told them about her life with her father, finding out he'd been nothing but a con man who fleeced the needy. The fear that somehow her own daddy had used her, played her. The paying back to all the people her father had stolen from. The fear of losing Titus, Annie being hurt, and how it all looped back to her father.

"Oh, Sophie." Gemma pulled her into a hug, tears sliding down her face.

After letting the warmth of Gemma seep into her, their tears mixing, she pulled back. "Another thing. Now I've made you cry." She sniffed.

"Don't worry about her, she cries at Super Bowl commercials." Annie waved her hand, her eyes glossy. "I'm sorry, Soph. You've had some shit thrown at you. You're one of the strongest woman I've ever known, and where I come from women are born with a set of balls."

"You're going to pay everyone back?" Gemma said, finally releasing her hand.

"Every single one," she whispered.

"How are you going to stop whoever is doing this?" Annie asked.

An idea had germinated in her head.

"Gemma, the person who phoned you, do you have the number?"

Gemma dug through her handbag for her phone. With her face screwed up in concentration, she eventually handed the phone to Sophie. "This is the number."

Sophie took the phone, punched in the number on her phone, and sat back, her body tense.

"You've got a look on your face, Soph. A look I don't like." Annie leaned forward. "What are you going to do?"

"I don't know," she lied, knowing exactly what she was going to do.

"Have you talked to Harlan about what's happening?" Gemma asked, looking worried.

Sophie shook her head. "He won't talk to me. Besides, I've got my own game plan, and it doesn't involve anyone else getting hurt." Sophie squeezed Gemma's hand.

"If you need us for anything, call. I mean *anything*," Gemma said.

Emotion rippled up Sophie's throat. She nodded, unable to speak.

"Girl, we've got your back." Annie dipped her cracker into a bowl, scooped out vanilla ice cream, and popped it into her mouth.

"I think you should talk to Harlan. I have a good feeling in my bones." Gemma nibbled salt from her margarita glass.

Annie widened her eyes. "She should absolutely *not* talk to him."

A smile drifted across Gemma's face. "Let yourself fall for him, Soph. Love is beautiful and, if you let it, it will fill you with joy."

Annie turned in her seat, a brow arched. "Says the woman who's never been in love."

"Says the woman who loves with her soul," Gemma countered. "I don't think you should give up on him, Soph. He's searching for a connection, he just doesn't know it." Gemma popped Pringles into her mouth.

"It's too much of an emotional risk." Annie leaned back in her seat.

She had to side with Annie. It was way too much of an emotional risk, with a bleak outlook. She couldn't tell them, couldn't tell anyone, about the humiliation of losing herself to three previous lovers and almost losing herself to Harlan in Vegas.

"Oh, I have news..." Gemma raised her eyebrows repeatedly. "Dug has been asking after you. A lot."

"Go for it, girl. I approve of that one. Dug materialized out of nowhere and tore that man off me like a Band-Aid." Annie scraped the bottom of the bowl of ice cream with crackers.

Sophie caught the tremble in Annie's hand. The woman was tough, but this had rattled her.

"We need a distraction, and I've got the solution." Annie played with the TV remote. "What we need is to critique terrible porn, and that's an order."

An out-of-focus logo filled the television screen.

The warmth of friendship and feeling mentally and physically exhausted stole over Sophie like a gentle, summer rain. The last thing she remembered was Gemma laughing at Megatron's not so mega tron.

SOPHIE WOKE to Annie shaking her.

"Honey, your phone's going off every couple of minutes."

"What?" Sophie struggled to a sitting position.

"You fell asleep an hour ago and now your phone is ringing constantly."

Adrenaline pushed the margarita haze aside. She grabbed her phone as it started ringing, Pongo's face on the screen. Only one person would call every few minutes. Sure enough, his name appeared on the bottom of the screen in big, ominous letters.

"Hello," she rasped.

Harlan's clipped tone filled her ear. "I'm standing outside to take you back to your place." He paused. "And tomorrow, Sophie, you're going to talk to me."

Her hand tightened around her phone. "No, Harlan, tomorrow *you're* going to talk to me."

———

"SO WE'RE GOING to talk, right?" Sophie spooned oatmeal into her mouth the next morning. She'd checked in with the nurse looking after Titus, who was fine, but Sally hadn't slept well, and the nurse wanted them both to have a quiet day.

Today was the day they talked about *her* plan.

"I can't, Sophie. I have to go."

Harlan stood across from her, not looking happy, stuffing his phone back into his jeans. Lines hugged the corners of his eyes, which were underscored by faint bruising. He hadn't slept well; nor had she. The second she moved away from him, he hauled her back. She'd gone to the bathroom during the night to find him waiting by the bathroom door. He'd said nothing when he followed her back to bed. Something was up, but he wouldn't share it with her.

"Really..." Sophie said with a long breath.

"I have to make this meeting."

She counted to five before replying. "Of course you do."

He leaned in and kissed her jaw. She kept her face neutral, while her heart played pinball on her ribcage. "I'll be back in one hour, then we'll talk about Vegas."

"Vegas?" The word shot out of her mouth.

"Yeah, Vegas."

She put the bowl on the countertop instead of throwing it at him. "Not about who hurt Titus and Annie?"

"No." His answer was swift and brutal.

She pushed up on the balls of her feet, her body tense. "It's me they're after. It's my life we're talking about. People are getting hurt because of me." Yet again, another stare off.

"One hour," Harlan said.

She let out her breath. "You're such an ass." He laughed and headed out the door.

Nothing had changed. Nothing *would* change.

He'd spoon-feed her what he wanted her to know.

Enough.

She waited two and a half hours, then changed into jeans and her lucky Kansas City Chiefs shirt.

I'm done waiting for Harlan. Time for me to take control.

She pulled on a gray sweatshirt and tucked her hair into a baseball cap. She sent Gemma's mystery caller a text that said to meet her in one hour at the Starbucks at Cherry Creek Mall and Titus a text she'd see him later.

She grabbed a can of dog food on the way out the door.

I hope Fang's hungry.

An hour later, she paid the cabbie. Nerves executing dive rolls in her stomach, she forced her feet forward toward the suburban shopping mall.

She walked into the Starbucks on high alert. She'd negotiate the terms of a settlement for what her father had stolen, and then no one else would get hurt.

After a few minutes, her name was called as a hand cupped her elbow.

"Come with me."

A man guided her toward the exit.

She turned and scanned the man.

Middle-aged. Brown hair, forgettable.

He led her to a black Jeep, buckled her in, and then walked to his side of the car. A man sat in the backseat on his cell phone. Sophie turned in her seat to look at him. He was younger than the driver, with a scar that cut a diagonal red slash across his face. His cold, brown eyes held hers, and the hairs on the back of her neck rose in unison.

"You don't look like the usual prayer-for-cash con my father ran, so I'm guessing something different?" she said casually as they pulled into traffic.

If this man came with the two Jeeps that had previously tailed her, her father must have played in a bigger con job than she'd expected. She kept count of the number of turns the SUV executed.

The driver smiled, his eyes on the road. "My boss, he's looking forward to meeting you. He has *plans...*"

The way he said the last word slithered down her spine and landed in her bowels.

"Yes, payment plans." Her mouth dried. "We need to negotiate terms of the debt my father owed and work out a payment plan."

"You're prettier than I thought. Maybe if things don't work out with my boss, you and I..." His gaze lingered on her breasts.

The man in the back chuckled.

Stay strong, Buttercup.

Right now she did not need her father in her head, especially since he was the reason she sat here.

She pressed her knees together.

Harlan would walk into her place, carefully hanging his keys on the hooks screwed into her kitchen wall while calling her name. He'd throw Pongo a treat, then gently pull on her dog's ears until Pongo would splay on the floor, his tongue hanging out.

Damn.

She turned to the driver. "Let's get this done so we can both get on with our lives and no one else will get hurt." A flash of metal caught her eye. A sharp pain in her neck.

Shit.

Her fingers probed the raising welt.

Shit. Shit. Shit.

She fought the wave pushing her down. She fought the fear paralyzing her that she'd made the biggest mistake of her life. One she may not survive.

She struggled against the tranquilizer, but it became a losing battle.

The driver said something. Before she slipped into unconsciousness, her brain processed that they'd picked up the wrong person.

Oh, she'd totally screwed up.

It wasn't Sophie Callaghan they wanted, but some chick named Sarah Something.

SIXTEEN

Harlan pressed his foot on the accelerator, and the Range Rover responded instantly. The meet with Babic would hopefully give him an answer. The unease that curled his gut wasn't abating. Babic's insistence he hand over the case files wasn't sitting right. Babic had sent repeated texts, which Harlan ignored. Yesterday, one of his men turned up at the office with an order from Babic that his man wasn't leaving without them. Zeb hadn't taken too kindly when given the message. The man had left empty-handed.

The package sent to Titus turned out to be another snow globe, but Mick hadn't delivered it. Mick had been found by chance by a guy changing his tire on a disused track hundreds of miles away from Denver. The man's dog had wandered and found the shallow grave. Wildlife had taken their shot before the dog found him. The coroner had little to go on, but there was just enough of him left for a positive ID from his sister, along with the wallet in his jeans.

Harlan had driven to his office to meet with Zeb who'd also had no sleep and looked like shit. Keeping an eye on Annie, who did not want to be watched, Zeb was running on fumes. He and Zeb had analyzed the possibilities. Who knew about the snow globes? The name that kept coming up was Babic.

Petrov had been in contact minutes after Harlan had sent him abbreviated file notes on a secure line, including Sophie's birthmark, and that someone had been sending her snow globes, but the person they had thought responsible had been found dead. Petrov had surprised him by asking if she collected snow globes. He replied that O'Connor had apparently given her the first one, Dorothy, from the Wizard of Oz. After a stretch of silence, Petrov said in a rough voice that he wanted to meet with her as soon as he was back in the country, but dismissed the idea that Babic had any ill intentions toward Sophie. Harlan wasn't convinced, so he'd lured Babic to a meet this morning with the promise of turning over the files.

Harlan watched from the carpark when Babic drove in two hours later than the agreed time. Harlan slammed the door of the Rover and stalked into Babic's office without knocking, a manila folder tucked under his arm with sheets of bare facts on Sophie. Height, weight, age. Nothing that tied her to Petrov.

"You're late," Harlan growled. He wanted nothing more than to have his hand around the man's throat and have him against the wall.

Babic spun in his chair, snapped the cover of his laptop closed, and stood, a soulless smile on his face.

"Finally, you have acknowledged my level of authority." Babic held out his hand. "Case files."

Harlan smiled through the cramp in his jaw and kept his body loose.

"Why are you sending Sophie snow globes?" he asked quietly.

Nothing moved on Babic's face.

Babic crossed his arms. "I have no idea what you're talking about. What is a snow globe?"

The strong, nauseating scent of Babic's cologne filled the office. He stared at Harlan, the lines on his forehead deepening. A tic pulsed in his jaw.

Harlan advanced.

Babic's gaze landed on the folder. He licked his lips.

"Titus? Not nice beating up an old man." Harlan kept his voice deliberately low and smooth.

Again, nothing moved on Babic's face, expect the slight flare of his nostrils.

Babic held out his hand. "I know nothing of a Titus." His fists curled. "That you think I'd beat up an old man means you know nothing about me." A bitter grin curled his lips. "I shall make it known to Petrov what you have accused me of." A look of cold fury spread across his face. "The case files," he said in a voice that would scare the crap out of most men.

Harlan studied him for a beat longer. Had he got it wrong? Nothing in Babic's answers indicated that he knew anything about snow globes. Nothing in his body language gave him away when he'd mentioned Titus. Even so, something held him back.

Babic's cell cut through the tense silence. He stalked to his desk, his eyes never leaving Harlan. He slid his finger across the glass and answered with a terse "yes." His eyes widened before he turned his back.

Harlan strained to hear any of the conversation, but could hear nothing. Babic stayed silent.

The hairs on the back of Harlan's neck flamed into life.

Babic turned, a triumphant smile on his face.

A smile that twisted Harlan's bowel.

Babic picked up his computer and tucked it under his arm.

Harlan went to block him, holding out the folder, but Babic brushed past him, surprising Harlan with his speed and strength.

"I no longer need your notes." Babic wrenched open the door and walked with determination toward the parking lot, not once looking back.

Something was wrong. Something was very wrong.

Harlan jogged out of Babic's office toward his car, his phone at his ear. Zeb confirmed everything was as it should be.

Whatever had gone down with Babic's phone call had changed the man's demeanor. He'd gone from pissed and surly to victorious.

He had something on Sophie.

He skidded out of the parking lot toward Sophie's place, his blood running cold. An hour later than he'd meant to be.

Zeb had checked in with the entire team of covert operatives guarding Sophie's house. A gardening crew was across the street. A meter reader walked around the block. A man whose car had broken down looked bored while on his phone waiting for AAA. Harlan had driven away, leaving Sophie safe.

He'd put five men on the first street behind her house. He put another five men on the second cross street. Sophie was covered. No one had anything to report. But the meet with Babic didn't add up. They had to have missed something.

Harlan hooked his keys on the rack in the kitchen, noting a mug in the sink.

If he had to relive an image of Titus in the hospital—a bandage on the old man's head, Sally curled into a ball in a chair, her eyes locked on her husband's, her face deathly pale—one more time, he'd explode.

No one else would be hurt.

"Soph," he called.

Nothing.

A sixth sense told him she wasn't there.

Please make this an administration fuckup, and she's sitting with one of my staff.

He dropped into work mode and did a thorough recon of the house, his intestines trying to bail out his ass. He pulled out his phone and called Zeb, who barked that no one had her, and he'd be there in ten.

No sign of Sophie.

He jogged to Titus's, hoping like hell she sat across from Sally having a cup of tea. The fresh-faced nurse told him Titus and Sally were resting and no, she hadn't seen Sophie.

Zeb's car rolled to a halt behind Israel's. Zeb exited the car, already in conversation.

"Annie doesn't know where she is. She's going to check with Gemma and Pipe and get back to me." Harlan closed his eyes, assessing the information.

Sophie had vanished.

Under his watch.

And it was his fucking fault. He'd been an hour longer than he said he'd be, and he'd paid the price.

How the fuck had she disappeared?

His heart beat so hard it hurt his head, but it was nothing like the pain driving adrenaline around his body.

They had nothing.

Not a single fucking thing.

Zeb's hand landed on his shoulder. "Let me run this."

"No," he barked, the words grating out of his raw throat.

"You're too close, man. Let me run this." Zeb's hand gripped deep into his shoulder.

Harlan closed his eyes, pulling himself together. Every thought had to be laser-focused on finding Sophie and bringing her back to him. If he let her lovely face into his head, he'd be screwed and so would she. He couldn't think about her attitude and how she made him fight for a glimpse of Sophie the woman. He wanted Sophie the woman—all of her.

The world was closing in. One wrong move and he could jeopardize her, which meant for once stepping back and putting Zeb in charge.

He stared at Zeb and nodded. He was giving up the one thing he never gave up.

Control.

Zeb's hand squeezed his shoulder. "I've got this." Harlan turned at the slap of the door opening.

Annie and Gemma ran into the room, breathless and pale.

"Have you found her?" Annie asked, her eyes wide, mismatched flip-flops on her feet.

Zeb moved directly to her side, looking pissed. "I told you to stay where you were, and I'd keep you updated."

Annie glared at him.

Zeb's eyes narrowed.

"Please," Gemma pleaded, nervously rocking back and forth on the balls of her feet, rubbing her biceps.

"Let's run what we have." Zeb planted his legs wide, his arms crossed.

Pacing the room, Harlan gave them a quick rundown on the meet with Babic. He had to keep moving. If he stopped... "I checked with county, and the jumper Sophie took down at a local gym is still locked up."

"Have you spoken to Petrov?" Zeb asked.

Harlan shook his head. He wouldn't call until he had confirmation, either way.

"I know how Sophie got out," Gemma said in a quiet voice. "The night we went to Hostage for a girls' night out, I picked her up in a local park. She talked about running the maze, a demon dog named Fang, and going through fifteen backyards."

"We'll work that angle. Call cab companies. Was there a pickup from the park today?" Zeb spoke to Arabella who'd just walked into the room. She nodded, then opened her laptop.

"Got it." Ten minutes later, Arabella looked up from her computer. "The cab took her to a large suburban shopping mall, twenty-five minutes away from the park."

"We need people on Sophie's circle. But if *we* didn't know where she was, how could *they*?" Harlan asked, still pacing, not letting any of the images of Sophie being someone's fuck-toy into his head because, if he did, he'd lose it.

Zeb moved closer to Annie, who took a giant step away, her gaze narrow. "I will stab you if you come near me."

Israel moved directly to Gemma, who looked up at him, startled. "No, I'm good, but thanks, Thor," she whispered.

Israel didn't move.

"No seriously, I'm good." Gemma's voice rose, and she backed away.

"Sophie said she had a plan," Annie said, her eyes flashing. "Said you wouldn't talk to her, so she was running her own thing."

Gemma held out her phone as if it would bite her. "I received text and phone messages asking if I knew where Sophie was, and if I did to let the guy know and I'd receive an envelope of cash."

"Fuck." The words sunk into Harlan like acid searing through his flesh.

"She took down the number." Gemma's eyes filled with tears.

Annie reached out and grabbed her friend's hand. Arabella took the phone and held it to her ear. Her brow creased.

"No answer," she said. "I can ping the cell tower the last call came from. It'll take time. These guys are professionals but I'm on it."

Harlan's blood turned to ice. He'd kept Sophie out of the loop and controlled the situation, so she'd taken matters into her own hands. He should have talked to her this morning. He should have been *here*.

Pongo pushed his nose into Harlan's hand. Three swift pops filled the air. Anguished brown eyes stared up at him.

Harlan picked up a chair and threw it against the wall. Zeb nodded to Arabella. "Let us know, yeah?" Harlan dialed Babic.

No signal.

The man was never out of range.

Cold sweat crawled across his body.

"Arabella, can you run this number for me?" He barked out Babic's number.

After what felt like four hours, but had been only twenty minutes, Arabella closed her laptop and stood.

"I've hacked the CCTV of the area. Sophie walked into a Starbucks and willingly walked out five minutes later with a man. The image is grainy and I can't get a detailed look at him. They left in a black Jeep. I could only get a partial on the plates, which were obscured intentionally." She paused. "I cross-referenced roads in a twenty-mile radius, but with only two digits from the plate to run, the variables are too great." Her face turned pained. "I've pinged the number you gave me. It's switched off. The last signal came this morning."

Harlan stopped pacing and said the words that speared straight into his barely beating heart.

"We've got nothing."

SOPHIE ADJUSTED HER FEET, then her hands.

No cuffs.

That's a good sign.

A pillow cradled her head. She tugged on the blanket that covered her.

Another good sign.

At least she wasn't naked, shackled to a concrete wall in a rotting cell with a cellmate called Bubba.

"Sophie?"

A vaguely familiar voice infiltrated her haze.

"Sophie, you're safe."

The friendly voice didn't hold a threat.

She opened one eye and shuffled backward.

"You."

Dug looked down at her, his face deeply unhappy.

Her stomach rolled, and her hand covered her mouth. "I need to go to the bathroom." Her body was now awash with unpleasant, urgent sensations.

She stood, fighting a wave of nausea and the wobbles. Dug walked ahead of her, opened a door, and flicked on the light. With her hand over her mouth, she pushed past him and rushed into the bathroom, slamming the door behind her.

After her body was empty, she gulped a mouthful of water out of the faucet. She touched the red mark on her neck and winced.

She checked out the room. One window, too small to climb out of, no doors that led to other rooms. Her hand hit her back pocket.

Damn.

Her phone hadn't made the journey with her.

She quietly opened the bathroom cabinet, looking for something she could use as a weapon.

Don't think I can fashion a bar of soap into a killer weapon.

"Sophie, are you okay?"

Her eyes flicked to the door.

No lock.

"Have you got my Taser?" she asked, leaning against the door, gripping the door handle. She was no match for Dug, but she'd go down fighting.

"No."

She leaned her full weight in to the door. "Who *are* you, and why did you have me kidnapped?" Her teeth chattered.

She ignored the bats swooping in her stomach.

"I didn't kidnap you." His anger was palpable.

A memory floated through her brain. Just before the man stabbed her with a hypodermic needle, he'd said another woman's name.

The doorknob turned. She pushed back.

"Who are you?" she said, trying to resist the twist of the metal.

"Come out, we need to talk."

Dug had never scared her, but she didn't know him. Her internal radar hadn't picked up any threat from him, and he *had* saved Annie.

She gnawed the inside of her cheek.

"I'd never hurt you."

With nowhere to go, she released the handle, and the door opened with a smack.

Dug dragged his hand through his hair, exactly the way Harlan did, and Sophie's world tilted dangerously. Dug grabbed her icy hand

and walked her into what would have been a living room, but a small, round table and two plain wooden chairs filled the space. An Allen wrench sat on the table.

She looked for her bag.

Nothing.

The room didn't offer much info on its occupant. Two pillows and a blanket lay on a thin mattress. No TV, no sofa, no pictures. She craned her neck to see into the small kitchen. No toaster, no kettle, no plates. Seemed Dug went for minimalistic decor. Thick curtains hung from every window.

"Do you have my bag? I need to phone Harlan, Titus, and my friends." Her heart hitched. People must be going out of their minds wondering what had happened to her.

"I don't have your bag or your phone. It was fucking luck that I got *you*."

She jolted at his tone.

"Sit, we need to talk." It wasn't an invitation, but a command.

"I need to phone my friends." A slight note of hysteria crept into her voice.

She sifted through her head trying to remember any actual phone numbers, cursing herself and her useless, sluggish brain.

"Sophie. I'll take you back to your place. I've been waiting for you to wake up."

Wait.

She gripped the back of the chair.

"I was in a Jeep. How did I end up here?"

"I followed you from the mall and waited for a quiet intersection. It took longer than I expected."

Her fingers dug in to the wood. "Why didn't you take me to a hospital or call the police?"

He stared at her. She could read nothing on his face. She rounded the chair and perched on the edge.

"What were you doing at the mall alone?" Dug sat across from her, seemingly relaxed, but his sharp eyes rested on her. "Why did Franco send you to the mall *alone*?"

She opened her mouth, then snapped it closed.

"We can sit here all night." Dug leaned back in his chair and crossed his ankle over his knee, arms across his chest.

"All night?" She shot out of her chair, pulled back a curtain, and stared into the darkness. "How long have I been here? Wait. Where am I exactly?"

Dug's hand tugged the curtain back into place. "You've been out for hours. The safest place is here, and where this is, is on a need-to-know basis." Her head snapped back.

Oh no. Oh, hell no.

"Do *not* tell me, I don't need to know," she said, unable to stop the anger creeping into her tone.

"You don't need to know." Dug's unwavering gaze never left her.

Her blood steamed.

Why was it that nobody kept her in the loop?

"What's Franco running?"

She sat but pressed her lips together.

The neutral mask Dug always wore slipped, and she sucked in her breath at the fear that rolled across his face.

"You could have been killed or used as a fuck toy."

"He isn't running anything. I was there to make a deal so none of the people I care about get hurt," she said, unable to catch the tremor in her voice. She took a deep breath. "I'm sick of people not telling me why people I care about are getting hurt. My life. My play."

Dug listened intently, his total focus seemingly on her.

She met his gaze. "It's all a misunderstanding. Before I was punched with a hypodermic, the man said another woman's name. It isn't me he wanted, which I don't get. Why are people I know getting hurt when it's another woman they want?"

"You need to talk to Franco." Dug's mouth dropped to a thin line.

"No, I don't. This is my mess, care of good old Dad, which I have to clean up." Hysteria had raised her voice, but she didn't care. "I can do this on my own."

Dug leaned forward suddenly, catching one of her hands. "If I hadn't been low on groceries and seen you the moment you stepped from the cab, I'm thinking this would have had a whole different ending." Dug squeezed her now-trembling hand. "Talk to Harlan, trust him." His words seeped into her brain.

Trust him.

Maybe she'd been a fool thinking she could do this on her own. Maybe she couldn't. If Dug spoke the truth, and it had been only luck that he'd spotted her, she could have been far, far away with the man from the Jeep using her as his toy.

The words *too stupid to live* flittered across her brain.

She swallowed.

"Why didn't you take me back to my place?"

"Because if Franco had left you out in the open and exposed, you wouldn't be going anywhere near him." Dug gentled his voice. "You're going to have to decide if you trust Franco enough to talk to him. You two are playing a dangerous cat-and-mouse game. Next time, you won't be so lucky."

She sucked in a tortured breath through her teeth.

This meant standing in front of the man, emotionally naked, and exposing the part of her heart she'd kept guarded all her life.

"What if I can't?" she whispered, raw emotion scraping her throat and tears spilling down her face.

He wiped a tear with his thumb. "Then I'll make sure you're safe."

"Who are you?"

Dug swiped his thumb again across her face, regret soaking his words, a wistful look on his face. "Someone you'll never know."

She stared at him until her eyes burned.

"Soph, it's time to make your choice."

SEVENTEEN

Harlan had gone back to the control room to check in, which he could have done via a text, but he wanted to make sure his team was doing okay. They all felt the loss of Sophie on a personal level. After the check-in, he'd be heading back to her place, where he figured she'd turn up.

If she turned up.

Fuck.

He could not run that scenario.

"Twelve hours since she disappeared, and we have nothing." Zeb dropped into a chair and swore. "Fuck, I feel like *that night* all those years ago at school." Zeb's mouth was a tight line. "We didn't protect her," he said on a raw gush.

Harlan felt those words like sandpaper to his gut, rubbing him raw. His eyes flicked to Israel who paled at Zeb's words.

"Different ending." Israel shook his head. "Different ending."

Edgy tension gripped the room. Arabella had taken up residence, refusing to leave. Coffee was delivered from the café on the corner every hour. Israel and his other comms man, Quade, hadn't moved from their chairs since Sophie had disappeared. Every CCTV camera in Denver continued to be hacked in the search for the Jeep.

The walls started pushing in.

His phone pinged. Another text from Annie.

Gemma and Annie had promised to stay at Annie's, and he'd give them hourly updates. Zeb and Israel checked in with them every twenty minutes. Harlan had put outside security on them as well as Titus and Sally.

"I'm out. You know where I'll be."

Chairs swiveled in his direction. He got slight nods from all.

Half an hour later, he threw his keys on Sophie's kitchen counter, inhaled the scent of raspberries, and froze. Each passing hour reminded him with a slash to the heart that there was a reason he didn't get close to anyone. Emotions fucked with your decisions, made you weak.

Made you vulnerable.

He hated the feeling eating his gut, making him hyperaware, when he shouldn't be feeling *anything*. Especially now, when he needed to be focused, but images of Sophie assaulted his brain at completely random and unpredictable moments.

Sophie in Vegas watching the fountains—the wonder and joy on her face, as she'd leaned back into him. At the jazz bar, owning what she wanted, and she'd wanted him. The hurt and pissed-off look on her face when he hadn't trusted her with what was happening in her life—he said he'd be an hour and he'd been three—cut him deep. It was his fault Sophie wasn't sitting on her couch with Pongo watching her shit TV.

The terrible, cold pressure in his body that he'd never see her again tore through his skull. He'd take the pulsing ache in his head over the empty blackness in his heart.

He hadn't felt like this since he'd been a kid and he'd watched cancer eating his mother alive. Hadn't felt like this since that black day at boarding school where they'd nearly lost one of their own. The vulnerability, the fear, the helplessness, all came crowding back. He'd vowed that he'd never let those out-of-control feelings bombard him again. He'd gone through life shut down, which had worked brilliantly until Sophie had inched her way under his skin.

His phone rang. "Have you found her?" Annie asked.

Harlan closed his eyes, willing patience. "Not yet."

"What about if we do a missing persons on TV?"

"We'll find her."

"Promise?" Her voice broke.

He rubbed the back of his neck. "I'll get her back."

"She's in deep with you," she whispered.

He flinched at the stab of pain, unable to deflect it, then stuffed his phone into his pocket.

The front door opened at the same moment his phone signaled an incoming text.

His hand automatically reached for the gun tucked into the back of his jeans, his heart exploding out of his chest.

Sophie took two steps inside, saw him, and jerked to a halt.

He stalked across the room and pulled her against his body, her rapid heartbeat barely keeping up with his. He inhaled her sweet raspberry scent, and the tension bled from his body.

"Harlan, I can't breathe," she said, and only then did he hold her by her shoulders, not letting her go.

Never letting her go.

She stared at him, her face terrifyingly blank. Her dog threw himself off the sofa and lumbered over to her. She spun out of his hold, sank to the ground, and buried her face in her dog's neck.

He planted his legs wide and folded his arms across his chest. He sucked in an audible breath. "Did anyone hurt you?" he ground out.

"What?" She kept her face buried in her dog's neck.

"Did anyone *hurt* you?" Tension banded across his skull. He cupped the back of his neck.

"No." She stood, and her fingers went to the angry welt on her neck.

He glanced at the welt, then back to her, rage building in his body. "Somebody did hurt you."

Punching walls wouldn't help right now; instead he pulled the tie from her hair, buried his face in her neck, breathed deeply, and touched his lips to her skin, inhaling her. His eyes were unfocused, feeling only... her.

"Fuck, Sophie. I lost you. I had no angle to run. Nothing. You put yourself out there, made yourself vulnerable, then you were gone." He dragged his hand through his hair, acid in his mouth. He tucked her stiff body under his chin. "Gone."

Her body loosened, her head nestled into his neck.

He closed his eyes.

Fear, relief, anger, and frustration wrapped together in a complicated ball and squeezed inside his skull.

"I need to phone Titus, Annie, and Gemma." She moved out of his arms, and he missed her heat. Fuck, he missed her.

"Titus doesn't know. Too much stress after the fall. I'll call Annie. I've been giving her and Gemma updates." The text had come from Israel. An unmarked car with no plates had dropped her at the end of the driveway, then sped off.

Sophie walked toward her bedroom while he phoned Annie.

"Tell me you have her," Annie breathed.

"She's home."

"Tell her we'll be around with margaritas, girly snacks, and we'll critique bad porn," Annie said in a wobbly voice. "You can stay, Harlan, and Thor if he's around."

"Not tonight, babe. She's going to be plastered to my side. As for the other stuff, I don't drink margaritas, I don't know what girly snacks are but I'm thinking 'no,' and life is too short for bad porn. Israel I'm guessing is of the same opinion. Soph will phone you."

He turned to find Sophie staring at him. Sweatshirt hanging from her body, wearing black leggings, biting her lip, but her gaze was strong.

She took his hand and led him to the sofa. Sophie sat, and Harlan sat beside her. She pulled her hand from his and folded both her hands in her lap. Icy fingers gripped his heart at the determination on her pale face.

"I need to talk to you," she said, her voice strong.

Harlan looked down into her heartbreakingly beautiful face and braced. He didn't know where they were headed, but he'd deal with it, and they'd move on.

Pongo lay on his bed, one eye on her. Sophie's eyes rested briefly on her snow globe collection. She swallowed repeatedly, then faced him.

"I loved my daddy. Loved him so much I thought my heart would burst. I was his little girl." Pain rippled across her face. "I thought we were doing the world a service. Helping people when they needed a prayer the most, but it turns out he wasn't who I thought he was." She paused, vulnerability spilling from her. "When he died, I found a journal with the names of the people who'd paid him to bring rains, cure the sick, and find love." Her voice dropped to whisper quiet. "And I never knew. The charismatic preacher with the plain daughter."

He closed his eyes briefly.

If he could dig up O'Connor, he'd do it so he could kill the fucker all over again.

"Your dad wasn't the preacher who ripped off my mom." Relief briefly washed over her face.

"That's why we had to leave in the middle of the night." Her teeth indented her lip. "I can't believe I didn't see it when I was younger, but I didn't." She pressed her hands to her cheeks. "I've been paying back the people he stole from. Each name gets an envelope with the amount he swindled and a card signed by one Josiah O'Connor."

Christ.

She paused. He went to grab her hand, but she shook her head. It took everything in his power to keep still.

"He also had a detailed journal on Alexander Petrov. Newspaper articles, dates and times of where he'd gone. It goes back years. That's why I went to the mall, alone, so no one else would get hurt. I thought my father had pulled a massive con against Petrov. The plan was to fix my father's mess, negotiate the terms of the payback, and work out a solution."

O'Connor had been a total fuckup, but her determination at righting her dad's wrongs moved him deeply. He leaned in and rested his forehead against hers. "You're a kind woman."

He'd do anything to take away her pain, absorb it into his body. She needed to know that this wasn't about some con her father had pulled, but the truth would only hurt her more.

Her forehead still rested on his. "I can't do this on my own. It's too big, and I realized today this is about more than just me. The man in the Jeep said another woman's name. Sarah. Dug told me to talk to you," she said in a quiet voice.

Harlan's head snapped back, breaking the connection. "Dug?"

As in Dug, who is really Holden Abbot who I've known since boarding school. The same man who has Praesidio inked on his body. The government agent who's protecting what's mine.

"He saw me being followed, rescued me, and took me back to his place until the tranquilizer wore off."

His fingers flexed.

She stood and paced, her hands on her hips, her voice strong. "I don't understand what's happening or why, and I have no idea who this Sarah is."

His heart pounded, and a thin layer of cold sweat coated his body, but he stayed silent.

She stared out the window, wringing her hands. The only sound in the room was the hum of the fridge and the thump of his heart beating out the words 'tell her.'

"I've had three lovers." Her voice was strong.

He rubbed at the permanent ache on the back of his neck. "Jesus, Sophie, I don't care how—"

"Please," she whispered.

He gave a sharp nod. If she started going into detail, he'd have to walk away.

Her eyes flickered closed. "You asked what went wrong in Vegas."

"Yeah." He drew a quick breath. She'd gone from being totally into him to refusing to look at him. Her body language had screamed, "stay away."

"The night we had. I would have done anything you'd asked me. *Anything,* and that scared me. A lot. Was I doing it because at a subconscious level I wanted to please you, or was I doing it because I loved it?" She turned her head away. "When the waitress kissed your cheek in the bar, jealousy shot through me. I wanted to walk over and sink to the ground and be your submissive. Be who you wanted me to be."

Harlan blinked and froze.

"God, it's so embarrassing." She pressed her hands to her cheeks. "It's what I do. A desperate woman wanting a connection so badly that I lose myself. I won't do that again, get so caught up in a man, I no longer know what I want or who I am."

He stared at her tortured face.

A brittle laugh escaped her. "Pathetic, right?"

He wanted everything about her, all she had to give, but not if she wasn't true to herself.

"The only woman I want is the woman standing in front of me now."

Her breath hitched.

He walked to where she stood, vulnerable and breathtakingly beautiful. He wrapped her hand in his. "*You* held the power in Vegas. Until then, I thought I had the power in our relationship, but you did." Her fingers spasmed around his. "You wanting me instead of a vibrator made this personal. Made *us* personal, which makes us equal." He twisted a piece of her hair, bringing her closer until he tasted her sweet breath. Her dark eyes were hesitant and glassy.

He smiled. "Yeah, baby, hurts me to give it up, but it's the truth."

He leaned in and, brushing his mouth against hers, he felt her shiver. He smiled against her lips. "FYI, I love this Sophie without her guard up, but don't change, Soph, for me or anyone. Don't get me wrong, I'd love you doing what I tell you to do, soft and compliant, but we're going into this without bullshit. Besides..." He brushed the hair from her forehead. "I like you fighting me at every turn." He paused and stared her straight in the eye, meaning every word. "I'd skin myself rather than hurt you." He'd do anything to keep her safe.

Anything but tell her the truth.

A small stab to the gut.

He angled his head down and kissed her, tasting her sweet lips, her tongue dueling with his, her arms wrapping around his neck.

He broke the kiss. "And I think you liked what we did in Vegas. Your scent filling the room, your skin on fire, so wet I nearly exploded looking at you."

He kissed her like he'd never be full of her.

That unanswered, unstoppable thread—stronger than steel—bound them, pulled them closer.

If he could, he'd gift-wrap the moon and hand it to her with a bow.

He stilled.

The moon with a bow?

If he asked himself if he'd ever think those words, he'd have taken out his gun and shot himself. But this was Sophie, who moved him in ways he couldn't define and didn't know if he wanted to.

He nuzzled her neck, the adrenaline leaking from his exhausted body. He needed sleep and Sophie next to him. He dug his hand through his hair. A lot had come out tonight. A lot he had to process, but one thing he knew, Sophie wouldn't be going anywhere without him for a long time.

She made him *feel.*

He smiled against her neck.

And it felt fucking awesome.

"We're going to bed. I can sleep now that you're here with me."

"Don't you want to debrief?"

He stood, took her hand, and walked toward the bedroom. "There are some answers that aren't mine to give, but I promise that tomorrow you'll have them. Tonight, can you promise me you'll stay with me?" He pulled out his phone and sent a group text that Sophie was home, and they were out for the night.

Sophie nodded before stripping to her plain underwear and crawling into bed. He joined her and pulled her into his arms, waiting until her breath evened out. He then walked into her family room, leaving her bedroom door open so he could see her.

He checked his email. Petrov was back in the country. He sent an update, including the fact that O'Connor had kept detailed information about Petrov's movements and that Sophie believed it was Petrov trying to hurt her. He hadn't come clean about her abduction for the moment. She was safe, and he'd deliver the news in person.

Meanwhile, the Jeep had been found abandoned in an alley. Only Sophie's fingerprints were on the dashboard, where she'd clutched the hard plastic. He sucked in a barbed breath, aware how close he'd come to losing her. He'd called in favors and had close to fifty people looking for her, and he hadn't been able to find her.

But Holden/Dug had, and he had no idea what the endgame was, but his gut screamed at him that it wasn't good.

He pulled out his phone and placed a call to the man in question but got voicemail.

Harlan crawled back into bed behind Sophie and held her tight. During the night, he woke when Sophie left the bed.

He was halfway out of the bed when she walked back in from the bathroom, the scent of mint trailing her, wearing the T-shirt he'd worn last night.

"I didn't mean to wake you." She slid in next to him.

"Nightmare?" He reached for her, pulling her into his arms and kissing her forehead.

She shook her head. "Had to say my prayers."

He woke again when weak sunlight streaked down his face. Sophie curled into his body.

"You want to talk about anything?" He traced over the fading bruise with his finger.

She turned in his arms.

"I don't know where this is going, but it's going." He touched his lips to her forehead.

She looked up at him, her face unguarded. "No more secrets."

He blinked, opened his mouth, then shut it. Something clutched at his insides.

Tell her.

He *should* tell her. Tell her everything. She'd been kidnapped, and he could have lost her completely.

Fuck.

He closed his eyes.

Soon, it would all be over, and they'd talk about their future, but he had an obligation to his client. Petrov needed to meet her without his interference.

"Are we good?" Sophie asked.

He opened his eyes and stared at the ceiling. "Yeah, we're good."

"I want this," she said, sliding her arms around his neck, kissing along his jaw. She started moving south, her mouth leaving a trail of fire. His cock went from asleep to throbbing. She continued working her way down his body. He lifted his hips when she pulled down his boxers. His body twitched, and he groaned when her lips wrapped around his cock. Her tongue flicked the underside of him, and his balls twitched. He looked down to see his fantasy come to life. Sophie with her hair a wild mess across his stomach, her lips wrapped around his cock, and her hand between her legs.

"Jesus," he ground out. His balls pinched deeper. He pulled her up his body, ignoring her protest. They were going to revisit her getting herself off with her hand while he watched, but he had other plans.

She yanked his T-shirt over her head, revealing her perfect naked body.

"I want this," she whispered, her eyes drilling into his.

She positioned her body so her clit lined up directly with his cock.

"You've got this," he whispered.

Without having the words to say what he didn't know how to say, what he'd never said to another person on the planet, he told her with his body, making love to her, long, slow, and sweet. She gripped him until he came undone inside her.

He'd never had a connection this deep to a woman who undid him completely.

It could have been one minute, ten, or twenty; he didn't know. Time had suspended.

Her soft lips brushed his. She sat back and in the half-light, scanned him as if committing his face to memory, then rested her cheek on his chest, her arms around him, her hair a soft, dark blanket across his chest.

Her head shot up. Her jaw slackened, and her face bleached of color.

"We didn't use a condom."

He blinked, reality kicking him in the balls.

Fuck.

Fuck.

Every six months when he had a physical he got tested. Even though he'd never once had sex without a condom, he got tested anyway as an added precaution.

Around Sophie, he didn't make smart choices.

"I'm on the pill. Irregular. Before you, I haven't had... um... sex in years. I'm, um, clean." She fanned her face with one hand. So cute he couldn't help but grin.

His hand trailed from her breast to her hip. He smiled at her shiver. "Years?"

"Yeah." She bit her lip. "Have you, um, always used a condom?"

He drank her in. Her hair wild, her lip snagged, sexy and inno-cent in one giant scoop.

"Always. You're the first woman I've been bare with."

"Bare?" Her puzzled gaze moved over his body.

"No condom."

He couldn't describe how amazing she felt, skin on skin.

He tucked her hair behind her ear.

"I want something." Her voice was shy but strong.

"Okay," he said slowly, not able to get a handle on where this was going.

"I want more of what we did in Vegas."

He stilled, not getting her meaning. Then he did, and his heart all but beat out of his chest.

Owning Sophie. All of Sophie. Yeah, he wanted it, but he had to make sure this was what she wanted and not what she thought he wanted. "If you're doing this because you know I want it, then no."

She stopped him by cupping his face and kissing him, her lips soft but firm. She owned the kiss. She owned him.

He groaned when she pressed her breasts into his side, then gently cupped his balls. His hands in her thick, glossy hair, anchored her to him.

She broke the kiss and looked at him. "I'm doing this because *I* want this. I want to feel all of you. I liked the intensity of you filling me. I want to feel more."

Her dark eyes hooked him and dragged him in. "Hard to argue when you've got me completely by the balls. Literally and figuratively."

She smiled and let go of his boys. "I know what I'm saying." Her smile struck him deep in his heart, which pulsed for the first time in a long fucking time.

He growled at the thought of owning her.

All of her.

He shook his head with regret. "Can't do it. I won't hurt you. We're not going into this unprepared."

"I, ah, um, got stuff. Lube at Spanky's." Her hand flicked toward the bedside drawer. "It's there."

He scanned her face. Her eyes, dark, wanting, sincere, and full of need.

"We can stop anytime." He opened her bedside table and picked up the tube.

"I know, and I trust you."

"Flip over," he ground out.

Without hesitation, she flipped and raised her butt.

He closed his eyes. He'd dreamed of this image for a long time.

Reality was way better.

His thumb rubbed between her legs and worked her clit until her head slumped and her body pooled around him. He snapped off the cap, squirted thick gel into his fingers. He kissed her neck, branding her with his tongue. She moaned, bucking her hips, tilting them higher. His thumb circled her clit. No lube needed. Always wet and ready for him.

He angled her hips and pushed fingers into her pussy, stroking high at the spot that made her purr. She groaned when he worked a slickened finger into her butt. He stilled when his knuckle met resistance.

He stopped all movement.

"Don't stop," she moaned, her head dropping forward. "It's so intense." She pushed back.

His thumb pressured her clit. Her spine softened, and she tilted her butt higher, her moans driving him to the brink.

He worked another finger into her butt, slowing when she stilled, getting used to the sensation. His cock twitched.

He removed his fingers and coated himself and her in lube.

He worked himself into her, slowly, stopping when she stilled. He growled, looking down at his cock entering her. "Don't stop. Please don't stop. It's everything..."

"Tell me if it's too much." Sweat ran down his face. He inched in deeper, not wanting to hurt her. Tight, hot, everything about her overwhelming, overpowering.

He'd spent his life waiting for this woman.

His woman.

Her body stiffened in climax, her muscles clenching him. He filled her completely. He stilled, letting her body adjust.

She angled herself backward.

She rocked her hips, her body building, again.

"You have no idea what you do to me," he grated out.

His body strung, holding himself back. Her hips flared, her body tightened then collapsed, and she shuddered around him on a low moan. He gave in to the sensation, ground into her, and came seconds later.

He cradled her hips and slowly withdrew from her body. She collapsed on the bed. He reached over her and kissed her neck for a long minute, tasting her, scenting her, owning her. He then walked to the bathroom, grabbed a towel, and gently cleaned her, kissing a trail across her thighs.

He turned her over to find her dark eyes on his.

"I'm okay." A smile tugged at the corners of her mouth. "More than okay. I loved it."

He curled into her body, one arm around her waist. She snuggled back, gripping his arm. His thigh imprisoned hers. He kissed the back of her neck, then moved his mouth to the side and sucked the skin. He nipped at the spot.

"What are you doing?" Her fingers flew to where a welt was rapidly appearing.

"Been wanting to do that for a while. Mark you. Make you mine."

She sat up in bed, her eyes flashing, her mouth open.

Pongo landed on the bed followed by a string of farts that would wake the dead.

"Good timing, Pong." He dropped a kiss on Sophie's head. "Got a call to make." After he got out of bed and pulled on his jeans, he grabbed his phone from his back pocket and checked in. Babic was still in the wind. His phone had never reactivated.

During breakfast, Sophie caught up on one of her television shows. She turned to him, her mouth open. "Can you believe what Jack said to Sharon?"

"No idea who you're talking about." When she started to explain, he leaned forward and kissed her. "And I'll never want to know. But for the record, that was a dick move on Jack's part."

Her arm curled around his neck, pressing him closer.

"So you do listen to me." Her face melted into a smile that outdid the sun.

"Always hear you, babe, even when you're rabbiting on about your shit TV shows."

She surprised him by kissing his neck, hard.

He pulled away, his fingers trailing the spot.

"Marked you and made you mine," she said, eyes sparkling.

"Yeah, you did." He couldn't help the grin stretching across his face. Being marked by Sophie felt right.

If he died right now, he'd die a happy man.

He pulled his phone from his pocket when it pinged a text. He froze, then called Petrov, his eyes never leaving Sophie.

"We'll be there." He swiped his finger across the screen.

Sophie's head shot up. "Where will we be?"

"There's someone who wants to meet you."

EIGHTEEN

Sophie tensed when Harlan's Range Rover came to a halt on a circular gravel driveway. After the mysterious phone call, they'd driven for hours. Harlan had given short, evasive answers to her questions until she'd given up. Harlan the Bounty Hunter now sat beside her. Only hours ago she'd been a ball of goo. His smile had melted her heart, his hand possessively in hers. The way he'd let her lead this morning had dissolved any last thoughts of them not being a couple.

Until now.

She hadn't had time to finish her coffee. He'd grabbed her jacket, and all but dragged her out the door, leaving the cup on the counter.

She shivered, wrapping her jacket around her as if it could shield her from what she didn't know, but the world she'd woken to this morning had changed.

She tried again. "Harlan, where are we—"

"We'll talk later."

She pressed her lips together to anchor the scream of frustration.

She turned her head. She was deep into Harlan and yet, again, the man from this morning had morphed into a total jerk. Her heart dropped in a painful thud, and she wiped her sleeve across her eyes.

She opened the car door, stepped out, and crossed her arms, anger hiding the hurt.

"I am not going another step until you tell me what's going on."

He stopped, his face blank, but his eyes flashed. "Do you trust me?" he asked in a quiet voice.

She looked at the man who only this morning had held her like treasure and the man who stood in front of her now. He pissed her off, infuriated her, and made her feel more than she'd ever thought she'd feel for a man. Bottom line, she trusted him. She worried her lip. Deep inside in the locked box in which she kept her heart, she knew she loved him.

"Sophie?"

"Yes," she said in a whoosh, "but we've got to talk about your Jekyll and Hyde personality. Get you some help."

Harlan's hand on the bottom of her spine pushed her toward an enormous mansion that sat nestled in a backdrop of towering trees. Wind whipped the branches, which bowed to their master. Gunmetal gray clouds muscled white ones out of the way.

His fingers flexed on her spine when a solid, wooden door opened before her foot hit the front step. Harlan's hand disappeared, close but not touching.

She shot him a quizzical look, but his face was a rigid mask.

They walked into a massive living area. Thick rugs were scattered over a gold-and-brown-flecked marble floor. A massive nude painting stretched from the ceiling to the floor. Rich leather chairs in different colors were dotted around the room, each pointing toward a huge hearth fireplace that ran the length of the room. A Kansas City Chiefs flag draped across the back of a ratty chair, completely out of place in the opulent room.

She stared, transfixed, at the red and white. A feeling of security stole over her. She jolted at a memory that rose to the surface, then sank.

"My name is Alexander Petrov."

Sophie spun, blood roaring through her veins.

An elegantly dressed middle-aged man stood across from her, his hands tucked into the pockets of expensive jeans. A light-blue collared shirt flared against a dark-blue cashmere sweater, tan casual leather shoes on his feet.

The man to whom she owed every last cent.

And Harlan had brought her *here*?

Why?

Sticky breath caught in her lungs.

"Come. Sit." Petrov indicated a sofa where she sank onto the soft tan leather, her body trembling.

She craned her neck. Harlan nodded once, his intense stare never leaving her. The hairs on the back of her neck rose like soldiers. She tried to swallow but couldn't.

Petrov sat across from her, poured two glasses of wine, and placed a glass in front of her.

"I have a daughter." Petrov leaned forward, hands between his knees, his intense, dark gaze on her.

He *had* a daughter. She knew as much as Google gave up about the man, but the disappearance of his daughter and the death of his wife years later from grief were well documented.

"The last time I saw her she was two, nearly three." She nodded.

"My wife was religious, very religious." Petrov took a sip of wine. "My line of work became a constant problem in our marriage. Because of an inherited condition, I couldn't have children, so we adopted a little girl. The love of my life." Petrov's face softened.

Sophie twisted her fingers in her lap.

"Ekaterina took our daughter to a religious revival in Malibu close to our home, hoping for strength to stay in our marriage or the strength to leave. She slipped out without her bodyguard." Petrov's hand shook slightly when he placed the glass on the table. "I blame myself. I didn't see how unhappy she was." He cleared his throat before continuing. "Ekaterina met a preacher, and she told him about me, about my business dealings. The preacher told her he'd pray for her, and everything would work out for the best. A short time later, in the crowd, our daughter was ripped away from Ekaterina's grasp."

"Oh no." Sophie's hand went to her throat, for the loss of his daughter and the fear holding her spine rigid at the mention of a preacher.

"A missing person report was filed. I have been searching for my daughter ever since. My wife blamed me, my business dealings. Though I set about becoming an honest business owner, she never forgave me." He looked lost in thought. "She killed herself two years later. She couldn't live without our daughter."

"I'm so sorry," Sophie whispered, not knowing what to say when there were no words. The pain pouring out of the man painted the air.

"I've had a likeness drawn of my daughter every year. One of my men saw you and reported back. The likeness is startling."

Wait.

Sophie shook her head, trying to clear her thoughts.

"The day before she was taken from us, I'd given my daughter a snow globe. Dorothy and her ruby slippers. We'd watched the Wizard of Oz the week before. We loved that movie. She loved the snow globe so much, she wouldn't let it go. She held it in the bath and when I tried to pry her fingers from it when she went to bed, she stared at me fiercely and said 'no.'" He shook his head.

What?

Sophie blinked slowly.

"It was one of her birthday presents, but I couldn't wait and gave it to her the day before."

Petrov stared at her, like he could reach into her head and read her tumbling frantic thoughts.

"May seventh."

"I have a snow globe which has the seventh of May engraved on the bottom," Sophie said slowly, "but my birthday is September twenty-ninth."

The intensity burning in Petrov's dark eyes pinned her.

A bad feeling started kicking around Sophie's intestines.

"S. You are my night and day." Petrov paused. "The S is for Seraphina... my Sarah."

Wait.

"The man who took me thought I was Sarah. My Dorothy snow globe has that inscription." She leaned forward, gripping the table. "What's going on?" Her voice rose with each word.

Petrov stared at Harlan, his face stony. "We'll discuss that later."

Sophie stood and paced, pulling on her ponytail, her stomach in a twisted, massive knot. "Will somebody tell me what's going on?"

Petrov pushed a phone across the table.

Sophie stopped pacing and stared at the picture on the screen. A family photo. A younger Petrov held hands with a little girl with dark, unruly hair. A striking woman held the little girl's other hand—a happy, smiling woman who looked at her daughter with love.

With trembling fingers, Sophie swiped her finger across the screen.

The next picture showed a toddler sitting on Petrov's lap in a chair that resembled the old chair in the room. Petrov and the girl wore matching Kansas City Chiefs T-shirts. One of Petrov's arms held the girl close, the other raised in victory. A bowl of purple dip and crackers were on the table. The girl in the picture was laughing and staring up at Petrov.

Sophie closed her eyes. A memory swam to the surface. The smell of beets, an arm around her waist, laughter, red and white letters.

The next picture showed a girl with dark ringlet hair in a red dress and black leather shoes clutching a snow globe in one hand. The girl held Petrov's hand. Love radiated out of the picture.

Sophie zoomed in on the snow globe.

Dorothy and her ruby red slippers.

At the fourth swipe, Sophie dug her nails in to her palms.

Petrov lying on a sofa; sprawled on his chest lay a baby in a diaper.

"I don't understand," she whispered.

Petrov smiled at her, a tender look on his face. "You used to get bad colic. Nothing would calm you except being walked. Ekaterina came looking for us and took this photo. You were six weeks old." He paused. "I know, Seraphina, that you are my daughter right down to the heart-shaped birthmark on the top of your left thigh."

Sophie's body jerked.

"What?" she whispered.

Petrov's dark eyes drilled into hers. "You have a heart-shaped birthmark on the back of your left thigh."

"How... how do you know that?"

Petrov indicated the screen. "If you zoom in, the birthmark is visible."

Her head spun to Harlan, who stared at her. None of the intensity left his face.

Oh God, no.

She closed her eyes and clenched her fists to stop from collapsing. If she pressed her hand to her chest, her heart would be visibly punching against her skin.

"Franco Security has been guarding and gathering information on you until I was sure. I'm sure, Seraphina."

Sophie kept her eyes closed, too many thoughts and emotions suffocating her brain, but one actual answer to a question steamed ahead of the other thoughts and landed front and center with a soul-jarring thud.

She'd been nothing but an assignment. A *paid* assignment. A mark in the ledger. Her body convulsed at the pain slicing through her heart.

"Oh God," she whispered, rubbing her chilled arms, opening her eyes.

"Sophie, we'll talk later." Harlan's words were like fingernails down a blackboard.

"No, we won't."

"Sophie, we will." At Harlan's barked words, she turned.

"No we won't, because we never do," she screeched, hating that she screeched, but unable to stop the pain and misery pouring out of her.

She turned her head at the sting of humiliation. And she'd trusted him. Completely.

Only this morning she thought they'd made love. Not just had sex, but made love. She'd given him all she had to give—body and soul—and it meant nothing to him. He'd faked *everything*.

She dug deep. Harlan would not see pain circling her body like sharks, taking painful chunks out of her heart.

She wrapped her arms around herself to stop her teeth chattering, held her head high, and looked him straight in the eye. She'd give him what he'd never given her.

The truth.

"I let you in. You worked your angle until I stood in front of you emotionally naked," she whispered. "I gave you *me*. I loved you." Her hand pushed against her chest, dragging out the now hot, ugly words. "And you took, knowing what it meant. You took it anyway, knowing we had no future, knowing I was only a paid assignment to you." A thick, suffocating bubble of emotion slid up her throat. "You said you'd rather skin yourself than hurt me." Her voice cracked. "You lied."

Something flared in his heartache-blue eyes before he seemed to process it and shut down. "Sophie. We'll. Talk. Later."

Useless tears pounded her sinuses, but she sucked them back. She needed out, and only one man could help her.

Sophie turned to Petrov. "Can we talk, the two of us?"

He nodded once to Harlan, who stalked to her side.

Close, but not touching. On the job.

"I'll be outside, then we'll talk," Harlan said, his voice strong, confident.

No more bullshit.

No more being used.

She wrung the raw last words she'd ever say to Harlan Franco.

"We're done."

SOPHIE DROPPED onto the seat in the car and threw her bag on the passenger seat, then carefully placed the folder Petrov had given her on top. She looked up at Petrov, her words thick. "I need to get away. This is a lot for me to process, and I don't know what to do." Her voice crumpled. "May I borrow the car? I'll pay you back."

"Take the car for as long as you need. One of my men will escort you until you reach your destination." Petrov passed her a phone. "Contact me using this phone when you're ready." He reached in and squeezed her shoulder. "I have no doubt of who you are." Tears blurred his dark eyes. "It's time for you to come home."

She nodded, unable to speak, then gunned the car into life. Following Petrov's instructions, she left the property via a concealed exit. Soon she hit asphalt, and the Audi started eating up the miles. She concentrated on hugging the white line.

One thing at a time.

She swatted at the tears on her face. All the men in her life who'd meant everything to her had used her. Her preacher father and now Harlan. Used her to their own advantage.

God, I am so stupid.

Her bruised heart kicked against her ribs. She'd fallen in love with Harlan. A man she thought would protect her, cherish her, love her.

Rain lashed the car in silver sheets. She let the tears fall.

She let anger take control of her heart, because if she didn't she'd pull the car over and dissolve.

No, I won't.

Getting over Harlan wouldn't be easy and would take time, but she would, because she had to. She drove, not thinking, only doing. Compartmentalizing one thing at a time. She needed to get home, get safe.

Turning into her street hours later, she spied a black SUV parked in front of her house.

Damn.

Harlan had positioned one of his men outside her house for reasons she didn't know and didn't care. It had been tough to lose Petrov's tail, but she'd eventually ditched him thanks to the Audi, some well-timed, illegal turns, and Karma playing on her side for once.

She uncurled her numb fingers from the steering wheel, her throbbing knuckles protesting.

I need time away.

Only one place came to mind, and it was a long shot. But she didn't have many shots to take. Staying with Annie or Gemma wasn't an option with Zeb and Thor constantly around. Titus needed peace and quiet.

Twenty minutes later, she pulled into a crowded parking lot and found a space in the back. She entered through the back door, and without knocking, walked into Pipe's office.

Glasses were perched on his nose, a stack of papers in front of him.

The adrenaline filtered from her body as she slid into the chair in front of his desk.

"Stay as long as you need. There's an apartment above. If you need someone or something dealt with, let me know."

"Can I borrow a phone? I need to let a couple of people know I'm safe." She pulled in a fractured breath. "Then I'm going away for a few weeks."

She didn't know or trust Petrov enough at this stage to use his phone. It would stay untouched and turned off until she wanted to make contact.

Pipe pulled a string of keys from his pocket, selected one, unlocked a drawer on his desk, selected a phone, and passed it to her.

"Burner," he said by way of explanation.

Not long ago he'd made it clear he didn't want her working there.

Tears threatened at his kindness. "I don't understand. You don't like—"

"You put up with my shit and didn't walk." He leaned back in his chair. "I didn't think you had it in you. Didn't think you'd fit in. I'm not wrong often. Glad I listened to my niece." He shuffled papers. "Now get your head cleared and your ass back here. I need you back at work." He pushed a pen and piece of paper across the desk, shrewd blue eyes tracking her. "Anyone you don't want bothering you?"

She wrote a list of names starting with Harlan, Zeb, and Dug. Thor sat in the middle, Babic and Petrov rounded out the list. She then pushed the paper across the desk.

He read it and nodded.

She sent him a wobbly smile, then stood and tucked the folder Petrov had given her under her arm.

Pipe pushed keys toward her. "Triple lock the door at the end of the hall, which takes you directly to the apartment." His eyes bored into hers. "There's food in the pantry. If you want something, call me and I'll organize it."

"Can I bring my dog here? I promise to keep him away from the bar, but I need him, along with Annie and Gemma."

Pipe nodded, paused, and squeezed her shoulder before walking out the door.

First up, she had to get in contact with Titus and make sure he was okay. She had to organize a meal to arrive on Thursday and subsequent Thursdays. She had to get her toothbrush and toothpaste. Get Pongo and hit the road, while not processing what had happened with Harlan.

Tomorrow she'd be far, far away.

HARLAN PACED OUTSIDE the closed door, mentally berating himself for not telling her everything. A cramp had hold of Harlan's stomach and wouldn't let go. He'd fucked up. Badly.

Sophie's words, each one heavier than the last, cut him deep. No more secrets.

Every breath wound in ice, chilled his body. *This* is why he didn't do relationships. This is why he had an endless stream of women who wanted the same as him. This is why he hated the emotion, the vulnerability, the indecision of not being in control tearing through him in a never-ending cycle.

He'd take all the fucked-up feelings as long as he could get his woman back.

This ended now with him taking back control.

Harlan turned the handle of the door. He'd given them time. Now he needed to talk to his woman.

Alone.

Harlan pushed against the door. Locked. He thumped the hard wood.

The door opened. Harlan peered around Petrov looking for a riot of dark hair.

"She's gone," Petrov said, his stance wide, his arms across his chest.

Icy fear lassoed Harlan's heart. Harlan pulled car keys from his pocket.

Fuck.

"She left unguarded?"

"One of my men is on her until she gets where she needs to go," Petrov replied.

Harlan turned on his heel and headed for the door.

"Franco."

Harlan turned and stilled at the coldness in the man's eyes—a glimpse into what he had once been.

"Fuck with my daughter and you fuck with me."

His head whipped around. "Then we're going to have a cluster-fuck of a problem, because I'm not staying away from her."

. . .

HOURS LATER, Harlan threw his phone on Sophie's counter where it landed with a thud next to his keys.

"Sophie," he called.

No fat, fart-dropping dog met him.

He stalked to her bedroom. Clothes were still in drawers. Nothing missing, except Sophie.

He walked back into the family room, the pressure in his head pounding. He tried to block the scent of raspberries, but it filled his head.

You said you'd rather skin yourself than hurt me.

Judging by the devastation on her face, he'd ripped open her chest, pulled out her heart, and tossed it to the ground. He felt open and exposed, and he hated it.

Sophie's phone went straight to voicemail. He called Annie, whose phone did the same. Israel had informed him that Gemma had stopped by with a coworker named Cope and had taken Pongo for a walk. Harlan had thought little of it what with his world sliding into the gutter. Sophie had called Titus. She'd told him she was safe, had her dog, she'd left town, and no, he didn't know where she'd gone.

Harlan closed his eyes, and his brain pictured Sophie staring at him like he was the only man on the planet.

His phone pinged, bringing him back to reality. Pulling it from his pocket, he jogged out her front door. He would find her and bring her home.

To him.

SOPHIE PUSHED OPEN the back door of Pipe's. Drizzle hung in a soft mist of gray, the sun a small blob against a whitewashed sky. She jogged to the Audi and drove to her destination.

With her mouth dry and her legs not taking instruction from her brain, Sophie walked up to the front door and knocked. Beth opened the door, her daughter on her hip.

"Sophie, how lovely to see you, but I thought you were going to courier your notes over." Beth stood sideways, letting Sophie into the room.

She pulled the envelope from her jacket, thankful that Gemma had found her case notes and her computer. "I wanted to do this in person."

Hannah gurgled on her mother's hip.

"If now isn't a good time, I can come back. I've got a few things to do..." She let the words trail.

"Come in." Beth smiled, then closed the front door.

Beth led the way into the dining room and placed Hannah on a fluffy pink rug with smiling plastic turtles scattered across a backdrop of waltzing bunnies and penguins.

Sophie smoothed her hands down her jeans and told Beth about her mom, her dad, and Danielle. She then told her the news no daughter wanted to hear. She carefully pulled out the photo of a smiling Danielle holding a baby, love written all over her face.

Beth reached out and took the photo, her fingers trembling.

"Danielle wanted you to know you were loved." The words scraped out of Sophie's raw throat.

Beth nodded, tears in her eyes.

"I'm sorry your mom doesn't want to see you."

Beth looked at her daughter. "I knew in the back of my brain that if she had wanted to find me, she would have, but I hoped. It would have been nice to have the connection, you know?" Beth's voice trembled.

Sophie reached out and grabbed her hand. "I think it's the people in your life who make a family. The people who'll stick by you no matter what." Titus and Sally's faces swam into view. Annie and Gemma, now grumpy Pipe. "Danielle left me her contact details. She was thrilled to hear you've got a family of your own—"

"I'd love to contact her." Beth looked up from studying the photo, her eyes misty. "I appreciate you seeing me in person. I know you're busy. It means a lot having you tell me, instead of reading case notes."

She paused. "Thanks." A waver trembled her voice. "Will you stay for lunch? I've got tacos."

Sophie returned the smile. "The cilantro queen didn't bring any cilantro."

Beth pulled her into a hug.

Sophie stiffened, then relaxed into the woman's embrace, inhaling the scent of baby lotion, milk, and Nivea she'd forever associate with Beth.

Beth pulled back. "Don't be a stranger and send me the bill."

Sophie nodded, knowing this account wasn't going on the books. "Sisters without mothers." She smiled. "Let's stay in touch."

A beautiful answering smile lit Beth's face. "I'd like that."

A short time later, Sophie walked into the back entrance of Pipe's, past Barney and his smiling dinosaur friends. She walked up the stairs to the apartment, her hand gripping the smooth, worn banister. She pulled keys from her bag, but stopped dead at the opened door.

"Did that dog fart?"

Annie's horrified voice and Gemma's giggle loosened Sophie's muscles.

She pushed open the door to find Annie pressed against the wall, her hand over her mouth.

Pongo turned his head, dropped a shotgun of farts, and lumbered over to her.

Sophie sank to her knees, ignoring the stench, and hugged her dog tight.

Gemma let out a whoop, grabbed Sophie by the armpits and pulled her into a hug. Annie joined them before she pulled back and scanned her. "What is it? What's wrong?"

Twenty minutes later, Sophie had emptied her heart and left it flapping in the wind.

"Which is why I have to get away." Sophie pulled her hand across her eyes. "I stood there in front of him stripped bare and vulnerable, and he'd played me the whole time." She sucked in her cold lips.

"Betrayed and conned by the biggest con man of them all. And I didn't see it." She turned her head. "It's *humiliating*." The cramp that had started in her stomach at the beginning of the conversation burrowed tighter.

"You're right to walk away." Annie's blue eyes flashed.

"Maybe you should hear what he has to say," Gemma said, biting her lip.

Sophie shook her head. "No. I'm done. Even if I wanted to hear what he said, he'll do the usual, 'We'll talk tomorrow. Give me an hour Soph, then we'll talk,' but we never did. Now I know why." She dug her hands into her pockets. "I thought we were building something. Turns out I'd only ever been an entry in his accounts ledger." She hitched a breath. "And I didn't see it. That's the embarrassing part. I didn't see the con right under my nose, and if anyone should be able to spot a con, it's me."

"Oh, Soph." Gemma hugged her, pulling her tightly in to her body. "You deserve the best there is out there."

"Yeah, girlfriend, you do." Annie joined the huddle, her hand brushing hair from Sophie's face.

"I don't know what to do with this. It's too much. I don't want to see Harlan. I don't know what to think about Petrov being my dad and my father ripping me away from a family who loved their little girl. I have to get away and process." Sophie rubbed her temples.

Annie stepped back, panic flashing in her eyes. "But you'll come back, right? You'll text us?"

"I'll be back. We may not be bound by blood, but we're family," Sophie said, not bothering to hide the quiver in her voice. "I'll text you when I get where I'm going."

"Damn straight we're family. When you're back, we're having margarita night. We've got to critique terrible porn and make voodoo dolls of Harlan Franco. I know where my pins are going." Annie stilled, then slowly blinked. "Wait. That means that lick of chocolate will no longer be on my tail." She looked skyward. "Thank you, baby Jesus."

"Or Cope and Thor," Gemma said. "It's getting harder to pretend around them."

"Pretend what?" Sophie and Annie said in unison.

Gemma turned pink. "Nothing."

Annie pulled her vibrating phone out of her back pocket.

"Harlan," Annie said, her eyes narrow.

Sophie blinked, the cramp in her stomach now through to her intestines.

"Time for me to go." Sophie hugged her friends.

NOTHING, *I have nothing.*

After a debrief with Zeb, Israel and Arabella, Harlan had come to the bone-crunching answer that they had three-eighths of fuck-all when it came to finding Sophie. He closed his eyes and took a breath that did nothing to quiet the shallow beat of his heart. Petrov insisted that their contract was finished, and that he would protect Sophie. Dug/Holden was smoke and hadn't returned his many calls or text messages. He had no idea of the car Sophie drove. Petrov wasn't giving him an inch on that front, either, only to say she'd sent him a text and would be in contact. Sophie was now vapor.

Regret crawled through his gut. He should have talked to her, told her why he'd been staying close to her. But he'd done what he always did and tried to control the situation *his* way.

If anything happened to her, he'd never forgive himself. He punched in Annie's number. Still not picking up. An incoming text from Zeb alerted him that both Annie's and Gemma's cars were in the lot at Pipe's.

He grabbed his keys and stalked out the door. On a drive he didn't remember, he pulled into Pipe's parking lot, the tires crunching on the gravel. Rain streamed down the windshield.

He ducked his head at the icy rain slicing down his back and entered the crowded bar.

Annie sat on a stool at the bar, Gemma by her side. Gemma stiffened and turned, looking straight at him. She hunched closer to Annie, whose blond hair whipped, her narrowed frosty eyes focusing on Harlan.

Pipe walked toward him. He stopped inches away, arms crossed.

"Where's my woman, Pipe?"

Pipe's eyebrows rose. "She's gone, and since you were on top of the list she wrote of people she didn't want to see, you may want to check your relationship status." Harlan's hands curled into fists.

Annie walked toward him, her face fierce.

"Where is she?"

"You think I'd tell you? Think again." She poked him in the chest. "When she gets back, I'm going to make it my *mission* to find her a man. A *fine* man who won't use her *and* won't *con* her."

"She has a man," Harlan growled.

Annie's eyebrows shot up. "She thought she did."

His spine straightened, but he said nothing. Instead, he turned to Gemma, who shook her head. His world got very small and very dark.

"Bringing you home, Soph," he said to the room in a quiet but determined voice.

For a split second he thought Gemma said "yay" before he turned and jogged out the door.

NINETEEN

Three weeks later

Sophie breathed warm California air. She sat at a picnic table at El Matador Beach in Malibu and stared in the direction of Australia. The sun, a giant licked lollipop, dropped into the sleepy ocean. Pongo sat by her side stared out to sea.

She'd left Denver and, with no idea where to go, she'd driven to her presumed birthplace of California. Petrov had mentioned Malibu so here she was. With Pongo clipped into the backseat, she'd driven west, brought prepaid debit cards and stayed at cheap motels until the need to keep moving faded.

It didn't escape her that she was doing exactly what her father had done—when it got too hot, he ran—but she'd be heading back to face what life had to throw at her.

The pain of Harlan's betrayal had ebbed, and she'd begun to heal.

It had taken a lot of Pringles, a lot of hanging with the good folk of Genoa City, but mostly her time had been spent with her butt plonked on this bench, watching the sun rise, then set. She'd started reading her correct Taurus horoscope, which was just as ambiguous as her old Libra one.

Tonight would be her last night in California. Her heart now felt like a fresh bruise instead of the slash of a razor when she thought of Harlan. She'd drip-fed him out of her head, processing what they'd had, then burying it with a clutch of flowers on a grave, until her mind was dotted with graves and colorful flowers.

She'd read the contents of Petrov's folder twice, crying at the life and lives lost. The mother she'd never known. A life changed—her father going legitimate the only redemption in the story. She'd run her fingers over the sketches he'd had drawn every year. It had been strange to watch herself evolve, the likeness uncanny.

She understood Petrov's angle for the info gathering and guarding her; he was worth a fortune and his interests had been pure —a man searching for his lost child.

So many questions would catapult into her brain at random intervals. Why O'Connor had taken her from her family, she'd never know, and it hurt. Questions had stormed her brain until both hemispheres were fried. Did he take her for a ransom, then couldn't give her up? Was it a random act—a spur-of-the-moment idea to take a little girl and use her in his cons? Did he genuinely think she'd be better off with him and away from a father who wasn't exactly leading the life of a saint? Had every happy memory of them been a manufactured lie?

After the second night, she'd called Petrov, asking questions and verifying data, dropping into PI mode. He never called her, instead letting her take the lead on the relationship, which she appreciated. At first it had been stilted and uncomfortable, but she'd relaxed and listen to the stories of when she was little. Watching the Kansas City Chiefs games, eating her dad's favorite game day food, borscht soup— the weird smell of beets solved.

Somewhere along the way in her head, Petrov had become her dad.

It turned out her mother had read about a newborn baby surrendered at a fire station. Petrov had pulled strings, and the light of his life had come through his door.

She asked why he'd been sending snow globes, but he hadn't been the one to send them. Something for her to work out.

Not Harlan. Not anyone from his team.

Her.

Earlier, she'd phoned Titus on Pipe's burner phone for her daily update. Both he and Sally were fine. Titus appreciated that Annie loved cooking for them but could she please stop, because the woman couldn't open a bag of chips without it being some sort of disaster. Sophie had laughed when Titus filled her in on Annie's attempt at a pot roast. Neither the pot nor the roast had survived, but they'd had tasty Thai takeout.

Annie had sent her daily text updates. Harlan had turned up at Pipe's with what Annie called a "determined look" on his face, but what Gemma had texted was "heartache." Zeb, much to Annie's exasperation, still took to turning up at random, unwanted moments.

Going home would mean possibly running into Harlan, who'd likely have a newly minted blond sub attached to his arm.

She turned her head, dismissing him and his sub. When and if she saw Harlan, she'd be polite and professional.

She ruffled her dog's head and pulled out her phone. She punched in a number and laughed when a terse voice barked in her ear.

"ARE YOU SURE YOU'RE READY?" Gemma looked up from coating her lashes in mascara.

Sophie pulled on her skirt and frowned. "Did you shrink this? I swear it's shorter."

Gemma grinned. "No, I didn't shrink it." She paused. "What if Harlan turns up?"

She shrugged. "If he does, I'm fine. I'm moving on with my life, and I expect he's on another assignment."

Sophie pulled on the tank top trying to cover her breasts. A wave of weariness swept through her. The drive from Malibu had taken her longer than expected. She'd stopped on the outskirts of Vegas and hung with Pongo on a balcony watching the night lights. She'd then hauled straight through to Grand Junction, stopping for the night before she'd driven straight to Pipe's to start her shift. Pongo was asleep in the apartment above with Pipe checking on him more than necessary. Seemed the man had a soft side for farting dogs.

After a conversation with Petrov this afternoon where she insisted she'd used his car long enough, her battered car sat beside Gemma's Prius at the back of the parking lot.

"Girlfriend, let's slay this room." Gemma pulled on her hand.

Sophie ran her hands down her sheer-black-stocking-clad legs and adjusted her boots. "Yeah. Today, Christyn Baray from Pennsylvania and Pat from Birmingham, Alabama will get a crisp hundred-dollar bill from Josiah O'Connor."

Gemma stilled. "You're still on a mission to pay them back? Couldn't you ask Petrov for help?"

"This is my debt." Sophie pulled on her ponytail and gave herself a once-over in the dusty mirror. Nothing earth-shattering, but she'd do. "A debt is a debt until it isn't."

"That's something Annie would say." Gemma rolled her eyes.

Half an hour into her shift, Sophie was in full swing. Annie had arrived, hugged her, and positioned herself at the bar. Cope had hugged her until she couldn't breathe. The bar was packed, thanks to a TV cage fight and girls in bikinis wrestling in Jell-O. A few locals had welcomed her back with warm smiles. Sybil had given her a running commentary on her twin toddler boys. Thanks to the bar being full, she'd be making good tips tonight. Maybe even Pongo could get that sparkly collar she'd had her eye on at Petco.

Pipe entered the bar from his office and walked straight to Sophie, who stilled.

"If you don't bring in your car to get fixed, you're fired."

"I missed you, too." She leaned in and kissed the older man's bristly cheek. "Thanks."

Gemma arrived breathless, plonking down her empty tray. The smile slipped off her face, and she stiffened.

"Oh no," she breathed, her face paling.

Annie spun her head, her eyes narrowing. "Damn it."

Sophie ignored the hairs rising on her neck and started counting shot glasses of whiskey on her tray. The table were good tippers who didn't like to be kept waiting. "I'll be back in three."

She turned and froze.

At the back of the bar, Zeb and Thor leaned against the wood, unhappy looks on their faces. Zeb pushed off the wall and stalked to her, dropping a kiss on her forehead.

"Never disappear like that again."

Thor followed Zeb. "I'll take you shopping for appendages if you promise never to vanish again." He grinned, then his gaze flew straight to Gemma.

The red and white of a shirt coming her way caught her eye.

Go Chiefs.

She blinked.

Wait.

I know that chest.

Harlan stopped in front of her. One second she stood staring up at him, the next the tray was back on the bar and she was plastered against his chest, his arms locked around her, his hands flexing on the back of her head.

Her hands wedged between them. She pushed against solid muscle, which made him pull her in to him until breathing became a challenge.

"Let me go." She pushed harder, emotion tightening her throat.

"No." He tugged the tie from her hair, which cascaded around her. He leaned in and breathed deeply. "Fucking raspberries. Thank God."

"Let me go." Desperation leaked into her voice.

"I can't."

She pushed out the truth. "I don't want this."

His fingers flexed against the back of her neck. "You want this." His voice was a hoarse whisper.

"I don't." The words spun from her heart. "Stop telling me what I want instead of *listening* to what *I* want."

"Don't do this, Sophie," he growled.

"It's done." Regret tinged her words. "I need a man who'll guard my heart no matter what the cost to his bottom line."

He released her, and she moved back a foot.

"What are you wearing?" Sophie asked before she could stop herself.

"It's blistering me as we speak."

Deeper lines had curved around his dull blue eyes. Dark stubble peppered his pale and haggard face. For just a moment, she thought maybe he regretted what he'd lost.

"We need to talk." He gripped her elbow.

And just like that, same old Harlan, right on cue.

"You had your chance to talk, many, many times." She pulled out of his grip.

"Fuck, Sophie, these last weeks without you were the darkest of my life." He pulled her close, and before she could react, he leaned in and scented her neck.

Her body did a full shiver. The unmistakable current that ran between them hadn't dimmed.

"The connection between us runs deep," he growled.

She nodded. "And it always will, but I need more than a physical connection."

He dug his hands through his hair. "I fucked up. I didn't let you in. I'm sorry. You started out as an assignment, but we became more, and you know it."

She crossed her arms. "After I shared *everything* you still didn't trust me, wouldn't talk to me." Her voice shook, but she pressed forward. "Most of my life I've been inadvertently involved in a con. I just never picked you as the biggest con man of all."

"Sophie." Pipe arrived at her side.

"It's okay, Pipe. Harlan and I are done, but thanks." She moved out of Harlan's reach.

"We're not fucking done." Harlan glared at her.

"Yes, we are. For once, *you* need to listen to *me*. Done. Done. Done." With shaking hands Sophie picked up the tray of whiskey shots and delivered them to the table to find all eyes were glued on her. Heat raced up her chest and stained her cheeks.

She ignored the pissed vibe from behind her and carried on working the bar.

"Proud of you," Annie whispered when Sophie walked past. Gemma squeezed her shoulder, and Pipe gave her a sharp nod.

Sophie didn't need to turn to know that Harlan had left the building, her internal radar letting her know the instant he walked out the door.

"They've gone." Gemma's eyes swung between the door and Sophie.

"We have to have a girls' night because Zeb needs to stay gone. He's not getting the message." Annie downed the last of her water, her long nails drumming the bar.

Gemma shot a look at Cope. Sophie noticed her anxious expression and the way she kept touching her ear.

"Tomorrow night. My place. We'll hash out plans over margaritas," Annie said, a determined look on her face.

At the end of her shift, Sophie stacked the last of the glasses in the dishwasher, then finished wiping down the tables. Gemma and Cope were restocking the bar. After weeks away and having nixed any form of exercise apart from walking Pongo, who walked slower than a sloth, the muscles in her arms, shoulders, and chest were dripping off her bones.

Pipe arrived at her side with Pongo, the latter delirious with excitement, popping sounds filling the air.

"I'll walk you to your car." Pipe kept hold of her dog's leash.

She nodded. Too tired, mentally and physically, all she wanted was to crawl into her bed and sleep for a week.

The unexpected encounter with Harlan tonight had shaken her more than she'd admit. Still, it was done. He was gone from her life.

Pipe clipped Pongo into his seatbelt. Miraculously, her car only needed five turnovers to start.

"Tomorrow, bring in your car. I mean it," Pipe barked.

"I can't pay you."

"I don't care. Bring it in."

Sophie nodded and gave him a wave. Tomorrow she'd turn up early at her job, but she would pay Pipe.

Without remembering how she got there, she pulled into her driveway. A chill wind whipped her hair when she stepped from her car. She flicked her finger across her phone, and the flashlight beam activated. She spun in a slow circle, checking out the area. All the good folk of the neighborhood were tucked in bed.

"Good to be home, Pong." Her dog danced on his leash.

"Okay, okay, you'll be in bed before you know it." She ruffled his head and waited while he did his business in record-breaking time, for once not having to sniff every blade of grass four hundred times before selecting the *one*.

Her fingers skimmed over the alarm code.

She opened the door and pulled her dog inside, threw the locks, then flicked the lights for the living room.

Nothing.

Weird. Bulb must be out.

She pulled her phone from her pocket and flicked on the flashlight function again, then headed toward the kitchen.

Pongo whined at her feet. An explosive string of farts erupted.

"Jeez, Pong, what's with you?"

Pongo yanked on his leash, a deep, raw growl rooting Sophie to the spot.

"Seraphina."

The lamp on her desk flicked on.

Sophie tried to swallow but couldn't.

Standing beside her desk, holding a damaged snow globe with a knife through the middle, stood Babic, his chilled eyes locked on her, impeccably dressed in a dark silver suit, a white rose in his lapel. A smile that a demented clown wouldn't wear twisted his face, a white dress draped over his arm.

"I've been waiting a long time." His voice sent a spasm up her spine.

Pongo sat at her feet, still growling, farting every time Babic spoke.

"I've been groomed to take over Petrov's empire. When my parents died, Petrov took me in and trained me to be him. That night I saw you at Hostage..."

"What do you want?" She tried to lick her lips, but couldn't.

"You, Seraphina. I want you. I thought you'd taken my dream away from me, but I realized *we* can have it all." He held up the dress. "Tonight, you will be my bride. With you by my side as my wife. Petrov dead, going back to the way the company used to be run before Petrov lost his balls."

With lightning reflexes, Babic moved across the room toward her. Pongo lunged at him. Babic kicked out hard, sending Pongo flying before landing with a whimpered thump in the corner.

When she went to move, Babic's hand landed on her shoulder, his fingers digging deep. She cried out in pain, desperate to get to her dog.

Babic's eyes flicked to where Pongo lay. "It is only a dog. Who cares?" His soulless eyes flicked back to Sophie. Babic ran his knuckle down her face, and she fought the shudder of revulsion.

"I should have taken you the first night I saw you. Made you mine. I nearly had you at the strip club; my men were close until Franco moved in. He had no right to touch you." He yanked hard on her hair, snapping her head backward until she cried in pain. "He will never touch you again."

"Have you hurt him?" she croaked. Her throat closed, and her heart twisted painfully that Harlan was bleeding out in a gutter. Or worse.

"Not yet." He smiled, showing white veneers. His hot sour breath sent bile clawing up her throat.

"Mick won't be hurting you again. I had a man at Pipe's who saw him try to hurt you." He smiled, and Sophie's heart plunged. "Nobody hurts what is mine."

"You're mad," she whispered.

"Not mad. Only taking what's rightfully mine." He pulled harder on her hair, and she swallowed a whimper. "Tonight I come for my trophy."

He walked her into the kitchen. "Perhaps we shall drink a toast. What would be better than to have Petrov's daughter as my queen? Did you like the snow globes? They are all the places we will see together."

He leaned down and pressed his mouth against hers in a quick, cold, wet kiss. She pressed her lips together and tried to turn away. With her head pulled back and her scalp on fire, she couldn't see anything that could be a weapon. She did a quick mental image of the room.

Her hand gripped the counter, then flew over the surface, coming to rest on a coffee mug. For once, Harlan hadn't been the sitcom mom and had left it for later. In one quick motion, she swung the mug toward Babic's head and connected hard. He grunted once, then let her go.

With her heart beating out of her throat, Sophie skirted sideways to the knife block and hoped like hell that Harlan had patiently stacked the knives in the block instead of throwing them in a drawer like she did. Her hand wrapped around a handle. A scream in her chest died when two hands gripped her throat, hard. The knife clattered to the ground.

"Maybe I should take what is mine now." One hand moved to the front of her jeans and yanked down her fly.

Oh God, no.

Huge black spots appeared in front of her eyes. Struggling to breathe, she kicked backward, her heavy boot connecting with bone. The fingers on her throat loosened.

"Sophie. Get down!"

Sophie dropped to the ground in a crouch, blood roaring through her veins the only sound as she gasped for breath.

There was a thud, then Babic collapsed to the floor.

She pulled cable ties from where she kept four that lined her bra, stumbled to Babic and restrained him, grunting when she pulled the last tie into place. She looked down at the object lying by his head and blinked in surprise.

Harlan walked to her side, staring down at Babic, and grinned. "Watching you hog-tie a man gets me hard." His face darkened when he looked at her neck. "Should have killed the fucker."

Harlan's unmistakable scent threatened to undo her, but she regrouped. She hauled Babic into a sitting position, who opened one eye and snarled at her. She pulled the cable tie tighter until Babic hissed.

Sophie bent and picked up the snow globe. Antarctic penguins lay abandoned on silvery tinsel. The door of the cabinet that held the globes was thrown open.

Harlan glanced down at the snow globe. "Sorry about that." Harlan scratched his head. "Not a bad idea, though, collecting these things from the places we visit together."

She stilled.

He walked toward her, his eyes never leaving her face.

"Us in Kona, you in a bikini, me rubbing oil *everywhere*." Her nipples tightened.

"A log cabin in the Rockies in winter. Snow. A roaring fire. You naked."

"You'd walk into a shop that sells snow globes and not expire?" she asked. Her mouth and her brain needed a sit down to clarify that the topic of Harlan Franco was banned.

He held up his hands. "Can't promise anything. Could lose my man card, though." He frowned. "I've got to get this shit off. It's a wonder I haven't combusted on the spot." He ripped the Chiefs shirt from his body. "Thank Christ." She stared at a line of cursive lettering under his heart.

Oh my God.

Her hand flew to her throat. At her expression, he touched the new line of ink under *Praesidio*.

Her name in cursive script.

"I only put ink on my body that's significant." He paused. "I'll protect you until the day I die."

Sophie stared at her name, her face slack.

Harlan enveloped her in a hug. "I love you," he murmured against her ear. "Love you more than I thought I could love another person." He paused. "I'm committed to us, which is why your name is inked on my heart forever."

She laid her head against his chest, choked with a mixture of longing and confusion, falling deeper into this complicated man.

"I thought you didn't do that level of commitment." Her voice wobbled.

He cupped her chin with one hand and angled her face toward his, dark sapphire eyes boring into her. "For you, I do."

Pongo waddled over, sat beside Babic, and let out a string of nerve-agent farts.

"Good boy," she whispered as Harlan shuffled them out of the way.

"You promise to let me take charge of every situation?" Harlan said.

She went to pull back, but his fingers flexed against her head. "No."

"Good."

He rested his forehead against hers.

"I'll probably fuck up. I've never had this, never wanted this, but I need you. Need us."

Sophie stood on a precipice. She could walk away and lead the safe life she'd always craved with a man who'd guard her heart and who'd she come to cherish. Or, she could go toe-to-toe with this exhausting man every day. A man who made her feel more than she ever thought she'd feel.

"Sophie?"

She looked into Harlan's tortured face and opened her mouth.

EPILOGUE

Six weeks later

Gemma poured margarita into Sophie's glass, Annie beside her. They sat outside in Sophie's backyard, at one of the two newly varnished hardwood tables. Hurricane lamps sat in even rows. Fairy lights strung through trees created silvery shadows across the ground.

Thursday night at Titus's now included Gemma, Annie, and most of Harlan's crew. Pipe had made a fifteen-minute appearance, eaten a sausage, then left. Much to Sophie's delight, Beth and her husband, Robert, walked through the front door, Danielle beside them, cradling Hannah.

"I'll be back." Sophie put down her glass.

Danielle walked straight to Sophie and hugged her. "Thank you." Hannah gurgled on her shoulder.

"Nice to see you." She squeezed Danielle's hand, her vision blurry.

"Look at us crying like we're watching a Nicholas Sparks movie." Beth joined in the hug.

Titus, along with Petrov and Clarence, manned the brand-spanking-new barbecue. DeMilo and his mother and sister played with

Pongo. The scent of chicken, burgers, and crisp salad filled the warm air.

Sophie eyed a shy, pretty girl who made a beeline for Harlan whose face lit up when he hugged her. He introduced Margaret to Sophie who marveled at the transformation of the waitress at Hooders who had arrived in Colorado that day and was taking Harlan up on his offer to help her start a non-profit to provide low-cost childcare by the hour so moms could get to job interviews, attend classes and go grocery shopping. Sophie hugged the girl and told her she'd help anyway she could.

Dug made a five-minute appearance. She'd had no idea who the unfamiliar man was. She did a double take like an employee on *Secret Millionaire*. His hair was blond, his eyes now hazel, not green. He wore a beautifully cut dark blue suit. He had a brief conversation with Harlan, Zeb and Israel, then they group man-hugged. He trained a warm smile in her direction, then left.

Petrov turned and grinned, holding a sausage in a tong.

Sophie smiled back.

Her dad was always the first to arrive and the last to leave. Sophie didn't think a backyard barbecue would be up his alley, but he loved "Backyard Thursday."

He came around for dinner at least once a week as they got to know each other. Sophie had made it clear from the beginning that she didn't want his wealth, just wanted a father and daughter relationship. She'd been firm that Harlan was in her life, and he'd smiled at her and said "good," because he wanted nothing to do with a clusterfuck.

Life had turned out better than she'd ever imagined. Babic was facing a long list of charges including murder, attempted abduction, breaking and entering, and cruelty to animals. In jail he'd had a psychiatric breakdown. Somewhere in Babic's mind he believed that Petrov had killed his parents and by taking Sophie, he'd take what meant the most to Petrov. Petrov had been stunned, unaware of the hate that had been bubbling in Babic for years. He'd only ever taken pity on an orphan. The doctor had some name for it. Sophie just wanted him in prison for a long time.

Harlan materialized at her side.

"Found the journal yet?" She grinned up at him.

He shot her a tight smile. "No, but I will."

"Sure you will." She leaned up and kissed his jaw.

They'd argued about O'Connor's debt. Harlan had insisted that *he'd* be paying them back. Sophie had compromised and made a bet —if he could find her father's journal using only old-fashioned detective work, then maybe they could pay them back together.

To date, the journal remained hidden.

"Love you, Soph." His lips grazed hers.

She never tired of hearing him say it. The words slid across her soul like a purr.

"Love you, too."

She never tired of saying the words she meant with her heart and watching his face go all soft, like he'd inhaled them and swished them around his body before letting the words settle in his heart.

"Are you margarita'd?" His lips grazed the back of her neck.

"Getting there, why?" She leaned her head back, knowing he'd scent her neck, which she understood was his way of saying she belonged to him. His tongue on her skin scorched her blood.

"I love fucking you when you're half margarita'd. You're soft and pliable and let me run with what I want, and tonight I want. A lot."

She chuckled. "I let you *think* I'm soft and pliable. All the while I'm getting you to do what I want you to do."

His hand brushed against her heart, and she winced.

"Still hurt?"

"Yeah, but it's getting better." She grinned up at him. "I'd do it all again tomorrow."

He pulled her to him and crushed his mouth to hers.

His name inked in cursive under her heart matched her name on his. When she'd taken off the bandage, he'd stared at his name inked on her body, stalked to her, picked her up, and barely made it to the bed before he expertly removed her clothes and made love to her.

"Guess this means we're stuck together for life."

"On that note." He pulled a box from his pocket. His face was apprehensive.

Sophie stared open-mouthed. Gemma squealed behind her. She vaguely heard Zeb chuckle, and it sounded like Titus clapping his hands and telling Sally something. Her focus was on Harlan.

"Sophie Seraphina Callaghan Petrov, will you marry me?"

Sophie held her breath as Harlan slipped an emerald ring—her birthstone—onto her finger. It twinkled in the afternoon sun.

"Thought we'd honeymoon in Paris. Not the hotel in Vegas, but the one in France. Maybe get a snow globe." Sophie stared at the ring, tears filling her eyes.

"Sophie?" Harlan's strangled voice pulled her out of her head. "I thought asking you in front of our family and friends would be the way to go, but if this is too much, or you don't want to marry me..."

She looked into his tortured face. Silence had captured the crowd. She looked around at her family. Annie clutched Zeb's bicep. Gemma, with tears streaming down her face, gripped Thor's and Cope's hands. Her dad looked ready to scoop her up and take her away. Titus, with his glistening eyes, held Sally's hand, which he also patted.

"Yes," she whispered.

"Yes, this is too much, or yes..." Harlan's voice trailed.

"Yes, to everything."

"Thank fuck." Harlan pulled her into his body and kissed the top of her head.

"I love you, Harlan." She smiled into his chest.

"Love you more."

"Girl, we've got some planning to do." Annie arrived at her side, wiping her eyes. "We've got some serious dress shopping and cake tasting afternoons ahead." She smiled, and Sophie knew she was doomed. "Shoes, Sophie, we've got to go shoe shopping."

"Flowers," Gemma said, hugging Sophie. "Cute things for the tables."

Sophie paused. "Will you be my bridesmaids?"

"Try to keep us away. We're family." Annie squeezed in and the three of them hugged. "Besides, we're going to throw you a kick-ass bachelorette party in Vegas. I've got the *Thunder from Down Under* on speed dial."

Sophie laughed when Harlan growled beside her.

Her father gave her a quick, nervous hug. "You've got terrible taste in men."

Harlan clapped him on the shoulder, laughing. "Love you, too, Pops."

She clasped her dad's hand. "Would you walk me down the aisle?"

"I'd be honored," he said gruffly, wiping his eyes. He thumped Harlan on the back, then moved away.

Sophie smiled at her friends who were now her and Harlan's family.

Harlan's lips grazed hers. "Felt that shiver." He touched his lip to her earlobe. "You're bound to me," he whispered.

"Bound to the bounty hunter." She smiled up at him.

"For life."

Turn the page for the next in the Bound to the Brotherhood series

BOUND TO HER FAKE FIANCÉE BOSS

"I need a fiancée." My boss, Jason Johnson, glowers at his computer screen. "By Saturday." More scowls. "And today is Thursday, or I don't get the house," he mutters.

I, Asia Brown, personal assistant to commitment billionaire phobic Jason Johnson, CEO, the evil mastermind behind Johnson Incorporated, a smile inwardly. No, I snort, then gulp air like I've swallowed something awful, maybe a toad.

Good luck.

I place a triple-shot espresso on his desk—no caramel frappalatte for Jason Johnson.

He asked me to arrive before him so I could have his coffee ready, but I flat out refused. If he wants a coffee, he can haul his well-muscled ass out to the machine in the break room and learn how to make it himself. Or visit Starbucks like regular folk. He'd shuddered.

I'm not getting in at five am. Six is barely tolerable. Catching the metro is impossible in Los Angeles.

I put on my blank face and place the coffee on his desk. "Mr. Johnson, I've moved your four to four-thirty. The presentation folders for the Galbraith acquisition are complete."

By me at eleven-thirty last night.

"Lunch will be in the boardroom at midday. Here's a personal list of facts for the key players in the meeting." I hand Jason the paper I've spent long nights researching and phoning around the secret phone tree of personal assistants I joined two days into the job.

I slip the folders onto the polished table. "Jack Galbraith plays golf every Wednesday, followed by a massage which comes with a happy ending that his wife Jacqueline turns a blind eye to." I flick through the next sheet of paper in my mind. "Jack Chase, the CFO, has a controlling interest in two offshore properties which violate his non-compete and is therefore in breach of contract." I pause and give him a pointed look. "Emma Galbraith has a political history degree, is ruthless in the courtroom, and detests you."

Emma lasted four weeks with Jason and thought an announcement was on the horizon, but Jason did what he always did and gave her the, 'it's not you, it's me' speech, leaving me to order a tennis bracelet from Tiffany's, flowers, and be the shoulder to vent and or on.

"You were overseas for two weeks, but she saw it as a sign she was the one who'd finally captured your dark heart," I say. "She was picking out 'save the date' cards and a dress."

Jason swears.

I cock my head. "I know, right? How dare she think she'd meant something to you."

"I don't know why I hired you." He squeezes the back of his neck.

Yeah, well, we both know.

Twelve months ago, when I'd interviewed for the job, I'd sat next to California girls with glossy manes, size D boobs, killer shoes, and clothes I could only dream would end up at Goodwill where they'd be altered into my apparently signature 'hot school ma'am' look, according to my bestie Darlene. The Callie girls ignored me and spoke in hushed private school vowels. There I was, the poor cousin from Hicksville in the brown but awesome ankle-grabbing skirt I'd sewn, and a white shirt I'd snagged from the sale rack at Target. I'd clutched my resume to my chest, worrying my inner cheek with my teeth, after having chewed my way through rolls of antacids.

I'd been planning my next interview—a data entry job in Torrance, Los Angeles. I mean, being a personal assistant and the money it paid would be a dream job, but I was realistic about my chances.

"You."

I'd ignored the deep, rumbling voice that could strip panties from bodies on a growl, knowing it would be targeted toward one of the Barbies in the room.

I'd been working out the Metro system on my phone when an all-male spicy scent rippled over me. I stared up at six foot plus of tight sculptured muscle. A black business shirt rolled to his elbows showed golden skin. Tussled, thick dark brown hair that you itched to run your hands through. Cheekbones that were sharp, sculptured, and could possibly cut paper and diamonds. A forehead that looked permanently creased like he'd never smiled in his life. Puffy lips that should look feminine highlighted his face. And his eyes? Jesus, his eyes. A deep, stormy brown.

"You've got the job."

When I'd asked later why he'd hired little old me, feeling quite proud of my resume, his words struck like a slug to the chest.

"I figured you're here for work and not my assets."

While I'd stood there like a moron, he'd waved an impatient hand. "You wouldn't want to bang me on the boardroom table."

I blinked, then what he meant took hold, and boy did it take hold.

Translation. *I* don't want to bang *you* on the boardroom table because you're ugly and short.

What every girl wants to hear.

A look of dismay had crossed his face before I scuttled away with my face on fire. Admittedly, it looked like he'd started an apology, but there was only so much humiliation a girl could take in one day. I was not going to stand around and listen to him stumble and dig a deeper hole.

When I first started, I'd thought there must be more to the man. No one could be so cold, so detached, so unfeeling, as in totally devoid of human emotion. I'd spent way too much time hitting up Doctor Google, punching in his personality type, only getting returns on Jeffrey Dahmer, the Son of Sam, and a guy in India who likes to pickle human feet.

How do you find discarded human feet anyway?

Not that I thought Jason would ever harm anyone or pickle random body parts. The only time I've seen any capacity for emotion is if he loses a deal, which is rare. He takes to hurling things against walls when that happens.

I'm itching to crank open his head and see if circuit boards and wires are powering him. I made him a birthday cake last year with his name—minus the N, as I'd run out of room. I'd found the cake in the trash, not a slice eaten. That hurt like little knife nicks to the heart. I'd stayed up all night making it, thinking maybe my world-famous (in my head) chocolate butterball cake could thaw his soul.

Nope.

The man didn't have a soul—his words. I've seen moguls white-faced and wiping their eyes after leaving his boardroom.

Jason turns a pen over in his fingers; something glitters and works behind his dark coal-wrapped-in-thunder, dipped-in-molasses, then flung-into-outer space eyes.

"I've shifted the seating so Emma Galbraith will be away from you in case she's brought knives or sharpened pencils—HB's can inflict damage. If she's into voodoo, I can't help you. I don't have enough time to study up on the dark arts."

Jason says nothing. He stares at me until all the little hairs on my neck stand to attention.

He's got his weird eyes on. Something's up.

I know this look. He gets it when he's going in for a major negotiation, but since the Galbraith meeting is a done deal—to give him his due, Jason is a master negotiator—I don't know what else there is to negotiate.

"Take a seat," he says in his rich, bedroom, and ultimately bored voice.

"Why?"

"I want to negotiate something with you." The Montblanc pen he's been twiddling like a conductor's baton now lies still in his fingers.

"Be my fake fiancée for ten days."

"No." The word whooshes out of me on a shout of laughter as I rocket to my feet.

Sure, I enjoy needling him with a fake horoscope and song of the day, but we're not besties. Hell, we aren't even friends. We have a barely functioning boss/employee relationship. All I know about him comes from the internet (serial dater, wickedly handsome, richer than God, and born without a heart—his words). He's never asked a single thing about me in the year I've worked for him.

He rakes a hand through his thick, messy hair and stares out the window. "I've lied to my grandmother about having a fiancée. She hates my lifestyle, and in a hasty move, I told her I'd met someone and asked her to marry me."

My eyebrows reach for my hairline. "You lied to your Grandmother?"

Wow, he's reached a new low.

His perfect features pucker into a scowl. "I lied because I adore her, and I don't want her worrying about me. She's got high blood pressure, and apparently, I'm part of the cause, so, yes, I lied to her."

I'd give anything to have my grandmother back from the grave. I get the devastated look that flashes across his face. I adore the woman who'd raised me too, but the choice of living my own life and making my own decisions, right or wrong, is a freedom I'll never give up.

"Asia?" His voice lands me back in the room.

I stare straight into his stormy eyes. "Why me? Surely there must be some woman in the known universe you haven't pissed off, shunned, or ghosted?"

Something flashes across his face, and I fight the flinch.

Not one I'd bang on the boardroom table.

A girl has some pride. *This* girl has a lot of pride. "Sorry, I'm washing my hair."

"For ten days?"

"It takes a long time."

It does, it really does. No product can tame the mess. Well, none CVS stocks.

He begins to pace around his office, his long legs eating up space. "Asia Brown, I'm stuck. You're my employee, so, you know, HR and rules."

"I'll check, but I don't think there's a section in the HR manual entitled 'taking your assistant to be your fake fiancée for ten days and the rules and regulations that entails'."

He looms over me, his scent reminding me of a forest after a summer shower, all woodsy with a hint of spice and him. If I breathe deep, I'll get lost for a second.

"Asia, please. It's perfect. You're my employee, which is a line I never cross. Think of it as a vacation. A country vacation. You don't want to see my Grandmother die, do you?"

"Cheap shot from the balcony seats, Mr. Johnson. I'm not the cause of your grandmother's blood pressure, nor am I going to spend ten days with you outside of work, so the answer is a definite no." I stand. "Your horoscope for today is: Words that seem harmless will come back to bite you. Act at once. Song of the day is 'Gamble everything for Love'."

I smile at his growl and start planning ten sweet days without my boss.

"Are you sure this is the right address?" I crane my head. Not where I expected my assistant to live. Actually, I don't know much about her apart from she doesn't take my crap, works hard, has a smart mouth which irritates and occasionally makes me smile, and dresses like a sexy librarian. I recheck Google Maps and the address from the file I pulled from HR this afternoon. Compton isn't a part of LA I frequent, but then again, I hate all parts of LA, from where I live in Santa Monica to my office in the downtown district. Give me the smell of grease, lubricant, put a wrench in my hand, and I'll die a happy man. Car engines are my crack.

But I'm a man on a mission. My grandmother's email stipulated that her house, the house I grew up in (that I need, but she thinks is the root of all my problems) will be gifted to some ridiculous charity unless I show her I am settling down and, in fact, have a fiancée and my past doesn't haunt me. Ok, so maybe I'd rather sing the national anthem decked out in Buffalo Bills gear on the Patriots side in Orchard Park than admit I have skeletons in my closet—two to be exact.

Besides, Cynthia has issued a summons that I must attend her soirée. She doesn't issue direct orders very often, so when she issues this one, I have no choice but to show up with a sparkling fiancée on my arm and looking like a well-rounded human being.

"This is it," Gabriel Pederson, my driver and Stamford Brook brother confirms. His driving skills are legendary. He's part of a tightknit brotherhood who attended the same boarding school on scholarship. Our ties go deep, our loyalty deeper, and our love deeper still. We will drop whatever we are doing for a brother in need.

Gabriel is taking a career break after a stint in the marines figuring out his path. He needed a job. I needed a driver. A perfect match. I'll miss him like shit, but know that he'll eventually move on. Driving a billionaire asshole (his words and I agree) is not a career path for him.

I glance at the building. Not what I expected. I pay well, so why is Asia living here?

"Do you know Asia?" I ask Gabe, trying to get some sort of inside scoop on her.

"Yeah, everyone knows Asia." He swivels his head. The man is grinning like a fool.

"Have you got a thing for my assistant?" My eyebrows shoot up.

"Everyone has a thing for your assistant." He shakes his head. "She's smart, funny, gorgeous, and kind."

I ignore his comments. "Quick, give me the scoop."

He pats my arm like a child. "You're on your own on this one, brother. You'll have to get to know her."

"I don't want to get to know her. I just need her to do something that will be mutually beneficial." Like get my hands on the deed to the house, a house that I hate and love. It's not like I haven't wanted to visit. I've felt the pull over the years, but remorse and regret, my two best friends, hang out in my heart playing tug-o-war.

Another quick shake of his shaggy head. "I'll circle. Call me when you're ready." Gabriel brings the car to a stop.

Good call. Probably be missing a few car parts—like wheels—if he stops, parks, and comes with.

I step from the Bentley and make my way toward a nondescript apartment block with a group of teens hanging around looking shifty and bored. All turn and stare as I approach. A warm, California winter wind whips my hair, the clouds dark above us, and a rumble of thunder teases the sky.

"You're in the wrong neighborhood." A teen pushes off the wall.

"Possibly," I say, striding up to him. "Do you know if Asia Brown lives here?" Dark, glittering eyes regard me. "She's about four-foot, dark hair, smart mouth, wears a lot of brown, as in her last name, ironically."

He's right in my face. Any regular guy would move away from a group of now pissed-off teens on approach, but I'm not normal, and I'm not going to smack a sixteen-year-old kid or a group of them.

"What you want with Asia?"

"Ah, she does live here." I bound up the stairs. The main door to the building is open, which pisses me off. There should be some sort of security door.

I make it to the fourth level, barely breaking a sweat, and meet a woman flicking through her mail. She's standing across from apartment four zero eight—my destination.

Our eyes meet. Her eyes sweep over my suit (handmade), my shoes (same), and she sniffs at my cologne (again, handmade). I take in her five-foot slim frame in denim jeans, green T-shirt. Long, dark hair curls down her back.

"I'm looking for Asia," I say.

Without breaking eye contact, she takes a step and bangs on Asia's door.

"Girl, there's an expensive smelling dude at your door. You want me to toss him?"

I fight a growl and lose.

I don't have time for this shit.

Dark brows pull in.

"He growled at me. Like I'm a cat."

"Tell him the answer is no," Asia replies.

This utterly infuriating woman. If I had anyone else to ask, I would.

"Off you go." Her eyes are back to sorting her mail, but her body is tense. She positions herself in front of Asia's door.

"Asia," I speak to the paint peeling blue door. "I have to talk to you. It's important."

"Say it," her singsong voice calls from the other side of the thin door.

"What?" I ask perplexed.

"That one little word." I know she's smiling.

Oh, for fuck's sake.

"What are we, twelve?" I mumble.

Her neighbor cocks her head. "Manners will get you a long way in life, my momma always said."

Yeah, well, I haven't had a momma for twenty-three years.

"*Please,*" I say.

A ping from my pocket has me reaching for my phone, and my

typically sixty heart beats a minute climbs. Maybe Gabe has been jacked.

"Wasn't so hard, was it?" Asia leans a shoulder against the doorframe.

I look up from my phone and do a double-take.

Holy shit.

This is not the woman who makes sure my presentations are perfection, who is best friends with all the assistants in the building and possibly the universe. The same woman I hired because I'm not going to be sued, or who'd want to bang me on the boardroom table. Five had already tried.

Her hair, which I've never seen out of a tight bun (which gives her face a slightly pinched look like it hurts), is now a mass of dark brown curls around her face and cascading down her back. My gaze drops to a tiny pair of denim cut-off shorts she must've stolen from Barbie. They barely cover her firm thighs.

Jesus.

My eyes linger on her pink toenails for a second, then rake up her tiny frame to a pink camisole that molds across her chest. Such a contrast to the high-necked clothes that hide her body.

I dig my hand through my hair.

She's fucking gorgeous, and my assistant, so end of conversation.

Her head swings to something behind her, then back to me. "Oh shit. Catch."

My hands automatically catch a bundle of tabby fur.

"Hey, buddy." The cat proceeds to climb from my arms and perch on my shoulder like I'm some sort of pirate.

"I'm sorry. Blossom, come here." Adorable pink slashes Asia's cheeks. "She launches herself at people like a missile."

"Blossom?" I reach up and pet the cat's head, noting stumps where her ears used to be.

Poor baby.

"Yeah, I figured she needed a pretty name. Blossom has been in a few battles, hence the no ears, half a tail, and missing teeth."

A smile that could melt Antarctica transforms my assistant. Her hazel eyes sparkle, her pillowy pink lips tilt upwards, and, I swear, her whole body gets in on the deal.

I'm mute, like a fifteen-year-old who has hacked his dad's premium porn account with my figurative dick hanging out of my pants.

I've never seen her smile like that, and never at me.

"Thanks, Darlene." She squeezes the mail flicker's shoulder, and I follow Asia into her apartment.

"You've got terrible taste in music."

Her eyes widen. "You cannot *not* like 'Midnight Train to Georgia', that's like illegal in all fifty-two states and territories."

I bite back a smile. It's an awesome song, admittedly, but not on my playlist, being more of a podcast person. My boarding school dean's words float into my head. *Never stop learning. The minute you do, someone will be there to take your place.*

That someone is my twin brother who should be standing here. His and my mom's lives aren't celebrated, no flowers laid where their ashes are scattered. Forgotten by everyone but me.

I push back the black dog who snarls on its chain in my mind. The fucker always lurks. There's not a day that's gone past since I was seven that I don't see my brother's smile, hear his laughter, then freeze when he screams.

As if my father can sense my mood, I swipe open my phone at an incoming text. My mood sours to outer space dark when I read it.

BEFAF or Biological excuse for a father: Running a bit low on cash. Investment didn't pan out. I will pay you back.

I shove the phone back in my pocket. He hasn't paid me back the half a mill I've already lent him and never will. I used to think he wanted to reach out to his only living child. That died a long, drawn out, painful death. I should block his number, but a useless part of me holds out hope he'll send a text asking to grab a coffee. Yeah, I know, I need an exorcism.

I walk around Asia's apartment, my hand on the back of the cat in case she falls. At six-two, it's a drop.

A queen-sized bed is covered in a ridiculous number of colorful cushions. I pass a sewing machine; fabric is heaped over every available surface, including a TV in the corner on an old wooden box. Nothing matches, everything's old, but it works—a small kitchen with a stove, a fridge, and a tiny table with two chairs. I frown at the half-eaten instant noodles on the counter. Framed prints of Vogue magazine covers on the walls. I want nothing more than to sink on her worn yellow couch for five minutes. It looks way more inviting than my top of the line sofa that an interior decorator said matched the gray and black monochrome. It could be hot pink for all I care. I spend as little time at my apartment as I can.

"Mr. Johnson, I assume you're here to discuss your pressing problem and not my excellent taste in music. The answer is no. I'm not going to pretend to be your fake fiancée so you can get off the hook with your grandmother. Why don't you fess up and admit to her you'll never settle down?"

I ignore the Mr. Johnson comment because it pisses me off and turns me on when she says it in a low, throaty voice, like now. I turn from checking out a weird collection of tiny plastic toys. I pick up a helicopter and spin the rotor.

"Kinder Egg toys." At my apparent blank face, she continues. "You know, Kinder Egg, right?"

"No."

"My sister and I used to collect them when we were kids." Her hazel eyes mist. "It's a nice childhood memory."

"Being a child is only a necessity to become an adult." I don't dwell on my childhood, ever.

She shakes her head. "There you are, Mr. Cyborg."

The cat is getting restless, judging by the claws massaging my shoulders. I gently lift her to the ground.

I get to the point of the visit, already bored and itching to hit my private gym. If I work out hard enough, maybe I'll get a few hours of sleep tonight. "I'll pay you fifty K for the ten days."

Her mouth drops open, and it's all I can do to run my gaze over her curves. God, I want to bury my face in her hair and sleep there for a week. It's a riot of curls, and I itch to run my fingers through it and see if it is as soft as I imagine. She always wears it up in a tight bun, which makes her look older than twenty-five.

I read her face. Shock, surprise, then her eyebrows pull in.

I jolt.

God, if she thinks I'm doing this to sleep with her, she's wrong. She's the best assistant I've ever had. She puts up with me, makes me occasionally smile with her stupid horoscopes and even stupider song titles about lonely people.

As if.

It's not like I can ask any of the women I date. They'd either hang up on me, send a sniper, or think we were getting back together. I like women, enjoy their company, but I have no plans *ever* of settling down behind a white picket fence. The dog and kids make my stomach roll. Work is my thing, and I'm good at making money. One day, maybe one day, if I make enough money, I'll look in the mirror and like what I see.

"One hundred thousand," she says with her hands behind her back, her chin tilted, and her hazel eyes piercing mine. "With conditions."

Now it's my turn to look surprised. "What do you need a hundred K for?" I ask. Curious. I look around. "Got it. You want out of here."

Most of my money goes to charity, which I keep on the down low. Being a ruthless, cut-throat bastard keeps competitors edgier when they walk into negotiating a deal with me. Suits me fine.

"We should keep things impersonal."

"You're right," I reply, and truth be told, I wouldn't have it any other way. I'm not into relationships. Outside of my boarding school friends who group text, I like my own company, which is why her daily comment about me being lonely pisses me off. I'm not lonely. I love being alone.

"Good, so we have a tentative deal." I stuff my hands into my pockets, holding in the grin. The easiest deal I've ever made. "We'll keep it simple, set some rules, then have a quiet breakup soon after we get back."

She sits down on her couch and pulls a notebook toward her; it's white cover is adorned with sketches of dresses.

I glance around the room again, taking in a mannequin in a green dress I'd missed in the corner. I move a bunch of pins stuck in a sponge from the sofa and sit myself next to her. I'd sit across from her if she had another chair. It's far easier to negotiate when my head is not lost in a fog of coconut and vanilla. Is it oozing from her pores like nectar or wafting from the mass of hair?

"Are these your designs?" I ask, distractedly looking at the open notebook. Her sofa is tiny, and my leg presses against her warm, firm thigh. It's distracting.

"Impersonal, remember?" She shifts in her seat, causing the ribbon thing on her top to slip down her arm. My traitorous eyes shoot to the gift of her chest and the perfect handful of breasts pressing against purple lace.

Jesus.

"Yep," I reply, gruffer than I intended. My mind may agree, but my dick doesn't and salutes like the soldier he is.

She flicks the notebook until she gets to a blank page.

"Public displays of affection only when vital." I snatch the note-book and write it down. "Nothing makes me want to vomit more than displays of affection, especially in public."

She grabs the notebook back. "Agreed. Though I love seeing a couple really in love swept up in the moment, or a man holding my hand just because."

I make a gagging sound.

She shoots me a withering look, and I swear the temperature in the room drops. "No kissing." She writes in her proper script.

I look at her kissable lips. "I agree in principle, but to be convincing, there may be times when we have to kiss. We *are* supposed to be engaged."

The cat weaves between my legs. I scratch her head, tracing over the bumps and hollows on her head. She arches her back and leans into me. At least one female in the room likes me.

I snatch the notebook back and scrawl, *no tongue with kissing or anything else.*

The thought of dominating her mouth makes me smile.

"You've got your weird eyes on. Stop it." She snatches the notepad back. "No going off for trysts, however discreet you may be."

"For both of us." I give her a pointed look to which she rolls her eyes.

I snatch the notebook back. "No sex."

Her face pinks. "Well, of course, no sex. That's a given." She nibbles on her bottom lip. "But by yourself is ok, right? Or with a discreet battery boyfriend."

Now it's my turn for my mouth to hang open. I Imagine this curvy bundle of woman getting herself off with her hand or vibrator.

My suit's uncomfortably small and hot. Really hot. I clutch the back of my neck and look down, fighting the image forming in my head.

She shoulder-bumps me. "Kidding," she laughs.

I expel a big breath from my now tight chest.

"The look on your face just now? Damn, I wish I had my phone camera ready."

That comment sends icy water down my spine. "No pictures without consent," I note and underline it twice. "If you don't stay for the whole ten days, the deal is off."

I want to get out of this room and far, far away, like the Arctic Circle where I can chill off.

"Fair enough." Her lips are thin. Her flat eyes catch mine.

She'd rather cozy up with Satan himself than spend ten days playing my loved-up fiancée.

"This arrangement is to stay in this room. No one at work needs to know. I don't shit where I work."

"Agreed. The look of horror on my friends' faces that I'd made a pact with the devil. I'd rather go on *Naked and Afraid*."

I have no idea what she means, but a large part of my brain would love to see her naked; the other part hates that she'd ever feel afraid. "Sign here. I'll have a proper contract drawn up tomorrow."

She takes the notebook, adds a few lines here and there, then signs her name. "This is fine. I won't break my word." She tilts her stubborn chin. "Will you break your word, Mr. Johnson?"

"No, I fucking won't." I stride toward the door. "I expect you to be a *very* convincing fiancée, Ms. Brown."

"I'll be all over you like a rash."

Jesus, it's going to be a long ten days.

"Tomorrow, we're going to Montana."

Get your copy here: Bound to her Fake Fiancé Boss

Want more in the Bound series?

Holden and Arabella's story – Bound to the Bodyguard:

Bound to the Bodyguard

ALL THE SCOOPS

I'd love for you to join my newsletter and get to know you. I promise not to be spammy. I send the occasional newsletter about upcoming releases, my completely boring life, and living with the Fake Gordon Ramsay. Join here

I'd adore you forever if you'd pop on over and left a review.
Click here:

I'd adore you forever if you'd like to get advanced copies of my wee books with the option of posting an honest review:

Click here, my lovelies. Join here

ALSO BY HAYSON MANNING

Bound to her Fake Fiancé Boss

Bound to the Bodyguard

Ten Days with the Highlander

ACKNOWLEDGMENTS

To my bestie and author friend Barbara DeLeo for taking this self-publishing journey with me. Your friendship and smarts mean the world. I couldn't do this without you. You mean the world to me.

Samanthe Beck who read and reread and showed me what an outstanding author, and the best friend a girl would wish for. Love you!

To my team. Helen S - you make my world. Tesh - so glad we're doing this thing together. Andrea - my favorite Italian. Ona - love you girl. Lori - couldn't do this without you and a cuppa. Maggie - your kind words soothe the soul. Deborah - you make me a better me. Deb. Kirsten my friend for life. When no one else wanted to proof death certificates at BDM you got me through. Anna, Sally, Jason - who always inspires. Thank you to all of you. You make my world a better place.

Maddee from Xuni who designed the website of my dreams.

For the people in my past who've made me a better writer, to the people in my future who make me want to write more.

Sherry Willingham and Pat Anderson for their proof-reading smarts, input and friendship. You've been with me since Wife in Name Only. You are treasure that I adore.

Regina Wamba for your amazing cover art. You're amazing, patient and kind.

Amy Heart for her proofreading and changing my Kiwi speak. Thank you. A HUGE shout out to Jen Katemi proofreading who made this book. Your insights were golden! Thank you

To the Fake Gordon Ramsay for keeping me overfed.
To you, the reader, you make me want to keep writing.

Printed in Great Britain
by Amazon